ALSO BY MELISSA GOOD

Dar and Kerry Series
Tropical Storm
Hurricane Watch
Eye of the Storm
Red Sky At Morning
Thicker Than Water
Terrors of the High Seas
Tropical Convergence
Storm Surge: Book One
Storm Surge: Book Two
Stormy Waters

Science Fiction
Partners: Book One

Moving Target

Melissa Good

Yellow Rose Books

Texas

ISBN 978-1-61929-150-8

First Printing 2013

9 8 7 6 5 4 3 2 1

Cover design by Acorn Graphics

Published by:

Regal Crest Enterprises, LLC
P. O. Box 1321
Nederland, TX 77627

Find us on the World Wide Web at
http://www.regalcrest.biz

Printed in the United States of America

Chapter One

DAR ENTERED HER office and closed the door behind her. The windows that surrounded the room showed the pearlescent light of dawn as she dropped into her chair and nudged the power switch on her desktop computer.

Nothing could happen on board the ship until after lunch. So she decided to come in to the office and get caught up on things before she joined Kerry out at the pier.

While she waited for her PC to boot, she pulled her inbox over and began sorting through its contents. Security reports were on top, and she set those aside for reading. A two page single spaced incident report followed, and this she studied, resting her head on one hand as she read.

Their security department had been thorough. The Army ringer hadn't stolen a uniform at all, and now Dar wished she'd shown the woman to their services manager. She'd worked for him after all, applying for a job the day after Dar had gotten back from Orlando, and passed their mandatory background check.

Of course, she'd gotten herself assigned to the swing shift, starting at noon, and working until eight. Who would notice if she stayed a little later? How many nights did she prowl the hallways, looking for tidbits?

And for that matter, Dar wondered, why search her office? She looked around the big room. There was nothing, absolutely nothing in the office worth searching for. She kept her desk locked, but only when she was doing evaluations. Otherwise, the most scintillating item in her desk drawer was a handful of Hershey's kisses deposited regularly by Kerry.

Dar hated paper. She never printed anything out if she could help it. Everything she did was kept locked up tight in her system shares on the network. The Army brat could have riffled through her office for hours and not found anything more interesting than the half done sketch of Kerry on her notepad, laying face up in the hollow drawer at the desk's center.

So, what was she looking for?

Dar reviewed the report again, and couldn't find anything in it to fault—outside of requiring the cleaning company to do the same government level security scan they did on their own new hires.

Well, with a faint shake of her head, Dar turned and opened her mail program. If that's what they had to do, then that's what they had to do. She typed up a request to security and copied the cleaning vendor's president.

Then she went back to looking at the reports. Eleanor had turned in a terse, one page missive, reluctantly admitting to the identity of the marketing admin who'd logged into the spare PC. It was an older woman, Mary Hingtanton, who had been with ILS for fifteen years, and was close to retirement.

Why had she been logged on there? According to Eleanor it had been stupidly simple. She'd been ordering lunch for the senior managers, and forgotten the order. She'd logged onto the network to get it from her mailbox, and then forgot to log off.

True?

It was very plausible. Dar knew Mary, who was a fluffy, elderly woman with a heart of gold. She didn't really suspect Mary of being the Army's accomplice, but it all seemed just so...pat. Dar grumbled under her breath and swallowed a gulp of her café con leche.

Could it have just been opportunistic, as Mouser had said? Dar didn't want to believe it. The coincidence was just too strong for her to buy into the notion that the little runt had just gotten lucky.

With a sigh, she turned back to her mail, and composed a note to Eleanor.

Eleanor –
   I'm sure Mary didn't do any of this on purpose. Try to find out if she saw anyone else in the break room while she was on the computer. I just don't buy it all happening by happy accident.
   We're still looking for someone who logged in by your area on Saturday. Anyone in your group griping?
Dar

"She's gonna love that," Dar murmured. Then she turned back to the reports and scanned the next one from Duks. Again, she shook her head. Coincidence that someone had gotten to one of his people with an offer they couldn't refuse at this very moment?

It all seemed just so unlikely. Dar wanted to find the pattern behind it, the one thread that would link it all together and make it make sense, because right now, it wasn't.

The Army people, the auditors, the mystery person in marketing, cellular devices...hackers...Dar briefly covered her eyes, the chaos making her head spin. Then she rubbed her eyes and settled down to answer her mail, deciding to do something about something she did understand.

IT WASN'T OFTEN that Kerry could watch the sun rise on a weekday through the sliding glass doors to the townhouse. She was sprawled on the couch, the newspaper open in her hands and a steaming cup of hot tea nearby as the warm, golden light spread across the room.

The crew wouldn't be at the pier until nine, so that had given her a while to relax after Dar left. They'd decided to skip the gym, since Dar's foot was really bothering her. Kerry hadn't felt like going alone, so here she was browsing the front page with plenty of time before she had to leave.

It felt sort of good not to be rushing around. She didn't mind their usual schedule, but after all the malarkey going on around the pier and the office it was nice to simply relax for one morning. She scanned the headlines, taking a moment to read about a prehistoric site discovered during a construction dig then switching over to a story covering some new additions to the airport.

She'd really been wondering if she was going to show up in the business section, but nothing was there from their friend the reporter. In fact, no mention was made about the pier at all, which surprised her a lot. She'd expected to see it splashed everywhere. After all, it was summer and there weren't any hurricanes brewing. Why wasn't the story being covered?

"Hm." Kerry made a note to give their reporter friend a call. Maybe she could mend a fence from last night, and get a little information at the same time. In the mean time, she lifted her cup and sipped the contents, enjoying the blackberry tea and the rich taste of the honey she'd sweetened it with.

Chino was curled up on the end of the couch just past her feet, very happy with the fact that Kerry was keeping her company. Kerry patted her on the leg with her bare toes, as she turned to the important part of the paper — the comics.

What would it be like, she wondered suddenly, if she could do this every day? Not read the paper, but relax at home and not have to go to work? Kerry pondered Dogbert's image while she considered the thought. "Hm." She poked her lower lip out a little. "It would be fun, for about two days, Chi."

"Growf?"

"Yeah, about two days, then I'd go postal." Kerry shook her head and went back to the cartoons. Dar had once said to her that she didn't care if Kerry wanted to stay home and — what was it? Sell seashell futures? Or write poetry, or whatever.

But she knew aside from how she would feel having Dar support her, that living an isolated life out here just wasn't in the cards. She was a social creature, and she liked the interaction with her co-workers and friends on a daily basis.

In fact, she wondered if even Dar would now choose a less interactive lifestyle, though Dar was far more a loner than she was. She suspected Dar had gotten used to having people around her and that she'd miss it if she made a change.

Wouldn't she? Kerry let the paper fold down onto her chest and gazed past it at the sunlight catching dust motes in the air. Or had Dar sacrificed her natural comfort in isolation as a trade off for their relationship, deferring to Kerry's more social wishes?

Hm. Kerry now wondered if she should worry about that. Would it all get to be too much for Dar one of these days? Or would she just consider it a worthwhile price? "Well, I could ask her," she murmured. "Or would she freak out if I asked her?"

No, she decided after a moment, Dar would not freak out to be asked, and she resolved to do so in the very near future. With a slight nod, she picked up the paper and went back to her reading.

She put the paper down as her cell phone rang. With a tolerant look, she picked it up and answered it, without glancing at the caller ID. "Kerry Stuart."

"Mm. Formal." Dar rumbled softly. "I like it."

Kerry wiggled her toes. "Hey." She wondered, as she had before, if Dar was in some weird way psychic, since she always seemed to call when Kerry was thinking the hardest about her. "What's up?"

"Nothing."

"Nothing?" Kerry repeated. "So..."

"Just wanted to call you," Dar said. "Maria called in sick, and it's too quiet here."

Kerry looked around. "It's pretty quiet here too," she said. "Chi's sleeping on the couch, and I'm reading the funnies. Did you get your stuff done?"

"Pretty much. I'm going to go over and talk to Duks in a few minutes, and find out what happened with his auditor. Mark's meeting with the guys who invented that cellular thing today."

"Yeah?" Kerry stretched her legs out, arching her back a little. "You want to stay there and talk with them? That was a pretty wild gizmo."

After a moment's silence, Dar grunted. "No. Mark knows what to ask," she said. "I wish we could tie any part of this together. I can't figure out how any of it is connected."

"You mean all the stuff that's happened the last two weeks?"

"Yeah."

Kerry considered. "What if it isn't?" She suggested.

"You mean we have twelve different security issues in two weeks and none of them have anything to do with each other?" Dar's voice rose at the end of the statement, gaining a touch of incredulity.

"Well?" Kerry smiled. "Hon, if you can't see a connection, maybe it's not there."

Dar sighed audibly.

"Did that Army guy contact you?" Kerry asked.

"Left a message yesterday," Dar said. "I was going to call him just before I left — give me a reason not to talk long."

"Good plan," Kerry said. "Hey, look at it this way. He obviously is interested in the new stuff you're working on. Why not sell it to him?"

Dar grunted. "It's not ready."

"So tell him that."

"I don't want to sell it to him," Dar replied. "He broke into our office. Why should I give him what he wants?" She asked plaintively.

Kerry sighed. "Because he's willing to pay for it, and if this ship thing goes down the tubes like you and I both expect it to, we need something to fill the gap, Dar."

"Hmph."

"Think about it."

"The ship thing will work out." Dar argued. "It's just going to be a bitch."

Kerry stared pensively at the ceiling. "We'll get it working, Dar, but I looked at the numbers yesterday, and given what our costs are, there's no way we're going to put in the lowest bid."

"We could fudge that."

"And do the same thing Telegenics does?" Kerry replied somewhat sharply. "No thanks, Dar. If we win, I want it to be a legit win, not a low ball."

Dar was silent for a brief moment, then chuckled. "Okay, I'll talk to the dogface," she said. "We'll work something out. Need anything from here?"

"You."

"Besides that."

Kerry considered. "My projects portfolio, matter of fact. It's in my top desk drawer."

"You got it. See you in a bit, Ker."

"See you." Kerry folded the phone closed and laid it on her stomach. She let the paper drop to the coffee table and closed her eyes, allowing her thoughts to drift pensively, focusing on what Dar had said, and what she hadn't.

DAR LIMPED DOWN the hallway that connected her office to Kerry's and popped the door open to her partner's office. It was quiet inside, as she'd expected, and she went directly to the desk and sat down behind it.

Unlike her own, Kerry's desk had a judicious amount of personal items on it. Where she just had her fighting fish and her inbox, Kerry had several small ceramic animals, some trinkets she'd picked up on their vacations, and pictures.

The largest one was a completely non-business related shot of Dar, and she gave it a brief glance as she rolled back to open the drawer. A second picture was of the two of them together on the back of the Dixie, and the third was of them and her parents on the pier.

The pictures were positioned so Kerry could glance up from her monitor and look at them and Dar had often seen her do just that—as though she were giving her mind a time out and focusing on the things she felt were most important in her life.

Dar did that too, but she kept the photos on the screens of her PC and laptop rather than out on her desk.

Why? Dar retrieved the slim, leather portfolio from the drawer and paused, leaning her forearms on the desk blotter as she regarded the pictures. Did Kerry think she was embarrassed and didn't want to be that public about their relationship?

With a slight frown, Dar started to push herself to her feet, pausing when the outer door opened and Mayte entered. "Ah." She watched the young woman's body jerk in surprise. "Sorry. Morning."

"Oh! Ms. Dar!" Mayte blurted. "I did not expect you to be in here!"

Dar held up the portfolio. "Just getting something for Kerry. How's your mom feeling?"

Mayte approached, viewing Dar with a touch of trepidation. "It is the flu, I think," she said mournfully. "Which of course means my papa and I will probably also get it. Poor mama!"

Flu. Ick. "She need anything?" Dar asked. "If she does, or if you need to go get stuff for her, take off. That's an order."

Mayte smiled shyly. "I think she is fine for now, thank you," she replied. "But I will tell her you said that. It will make her very happy to hear. She felt bad about staying home today."

"Why?" Dar started to limp around the desk. "We have sick time for a reason. Tell her to take off any time she needs. No one needs to be in here when they're feeling crappy."

Mayte looked at her injured foot, and then looked at Dar's face, blinking innocently. "*Si*, I will tell her that."

"I don't count." Dar muttered, heading for the door.

"Ms. Dar, did you for really save Kerry from a shark?"

Dar stopped in mid motion, turning with one hand on the door latch. "Huh?"

"They were talking in the break room just now." Mayte blushed. "About that you saved Kerry from a shark, and that is how you got your foot hurt."

A shark? Dar looked down at her foot in reflex. "Um..."

"That is a very brave thing," Mayte said. "Was it a very big shark?"

Well. Dar looked at the respectful, almost worshipful expression on Mayte's face. Theoretically it could have been a shark, I guess. "Happened too fast." She temporized. "I couldn't really see that well how big it was."

"Wow." Mayte smiled.

Dar opened the door. "If you need us, we'll be at the pier." She decided a change of subject was needed. "Okay?"

"Okay." Mayte nodded. "I hope you have good luck there today."

"Me too." Dar edged through the doorway and waved the portfolio in goodbye as she closed the door behind her.

Shark. She shook her head as she headed back to her office. Well, at least it was positive for a change, but she couldn't help but wonder how the story had gotten so out of whack.

Maybe Kerry would know.

KERRY BECAME AWARE of her cell phone ringing again, and she opened her eyes, her mind struggling to reconcile the change in the light outside as she flipped the phone open. "Hello?" She cleared her throat of its huskiness, a sense of disorientation coming over her.

"Hey. Where are you?" Dar asked. "Here somewhere?"

Kerry half rolled over and spotted the clock on the entertainment center. "Oh, shit." It read 9:30.

"I'll take that as a no." Dar chuckled. "Thought I didn't see your car in the lot."

"Jesus. I fell back asleep on the couch." Kerry got up, swinging her legs down to the ground. "Give me ten minutes and I'll be on my way over." She scrubbed her hand over her face, trying to get some alertness back. "I can't believe I did that. Holy Moses."

"Ker, relax."

"Teach you to leave me here alone." Kerry stood and headed for the bathroom. "I've got to splash some cold water on my face. Hang on."

"Kerrison!"

Kerry paused. "Yes?"

"Would you chill, please? Take your time. There isn't jack squat going on here yet." Dar laughed. "If you fell asleep, you probably needed it. Stop freaking out."

"I'm not freaking out." Kerry trudged into the bathroom and glared at her rumpled reflection. "I just hate being a dumb ass!"

"You're not a dumb ass."

Kerry sighed. "Okay. Let me get my act together and get out of here. I'll see you in a little while." She hung up and turned, tossing the cell phone onto the water bed before she filled the sink with water and cupped her hands in it, splashing a large quantity onto her face. "Jesus." She pulled a soft, fluffy blue towel from the bar and patted herself dry.

She felt a little dazed, and she realized she'd been in a deep sleep when Dar had called. At the edges of her memory, she thought she detected hints of a bizarre dream, but nothing concrete popped into her mind.

Okay. She ran her fingers through her hair that was slightly damp from the water. Dar said nothing was going on, so she had time to get down a cup of coffee, and maybe not feel like such a space case. Accordingly, she headed for the kitchen, pausing to let Chino out as she went to the coffee maker.

While she waited for the water to drip, she pulled down the flat screen and keyed up her mailbox, reviewing the new items in silence as the kitchen filled with the scent of freshly brewed coffee. Dar liked to listen to her mail read by the device, but Kerry preferred to review it visually, even though the small keyboard was awkward to use.

She just didn't like ordering around a machine. It felt weird.

She opened the first mail, stifling a yawn with the back of her hand, then cursed as she heard her cell phone go off again. "Son of a biscuit." She bolted for the bedroom, racing around the couch and diving into the waterbed as she scrambled to grab the phone. "Hello?"

"Hey, sis," Said her sister Angie.

"Hey." Kerry rolled over onto her side. "What's up? You okay?"

"Not really. Me and Andrew are outta here." Angie told her. "Got anything you think we could move into fast down there? I thought about Virginia, with those college friends of mine, but it's just too weird."

Kerry scratched her ear, thinking hard. "I talked to my old apartment complex. They've got a two bedroom. Is Brian coming too?'

Silence. "I don't know," Angie answered unhappily.

Jesus. "Okay, well, it's a nice complex, and the manager said he's got two units he can rent on short notice. You could use that until you guys...until you figure out what you want to do," Kerry said. "I can set it all up for you if you want me to."

"Is it a nice place?"

Kerry pondered. "I lived there," she said. "Yeah, it's upscale, a lot of professionals live there. It's gated, and there are a lot of child development places around." She wondered, suddenly, if Angie expected her to invite them to live with her and Dar.

God. She hoped not, for a number of very selfish reasons.

"That sounds okay." Angie responded, after a long sigh. "I don't know if I can do this."

"I did." Kerry reminded her.

"You're you." Her sister shot back. "And you don't have a baby."

Kerry caught the omission. "Is he keeping Susie?"

"Yes." Angie said. "He... well, Andrew isn't his son, you know?"

"Bastard."

"Well, yeah." A faint attempt at wan humor came across. "That's the problem," she said. "And maybe I'm being gloomy or... Bri may surprise me and come too. He didn't say no, just that he had to work some stuff out."

"Jesus."

"Yeah." Angie murmured. "Sorry, didn't mean to land this on you, Ker. I know you must be busy."

Kerry smoothed her hand over the rumpled bed linen. "Actually, I'm at home at the moment. I...well, anyway, whatever I can do to help, Ang. Just let me know, and I'll make arrangements. You driving down?"

"I don't know yet," she said. "I'd hate to make that drive with the baby. I'm going to wait a day or two and see what's up with Brian. Maybe we'll fly down and get a car somewhere when we're there. Are you sick or something?"

"No...I just had...um...something to take care of. I'm leaving for work in a little while, but listen, keep me in the loop, okay?"

"I will." Angie sounded relieved. "It's a good feeling to know we've got a place to go to when we get there. Do you think Brian will have a problem getting a job? He's doing really well with the law firm. I figure I can find something to do part time."

Brian had made junior partner, and Kerry felt pretty sure he'd be all right, if he decided to join Angie, of course. She found it hard to believe he'd just abandon her. It wasn't the Brian she remembered from her years growing up with him.

He'd lived in his older brother's shadow, but he'd retained a core of decency that she didn't think, or didn't want to think, had disappeared. "I think you'll be fine." She reassured her sister. "Don't worry, sis. It'll work out."

Angie sighed again. "My other choice is moving home."

Absolutely a zero choice. "Hm." Kerry murmured. "Well, it's a big house, Ang, and it's just mom in it now."

"I know." Angie said quietly. "She wants me to go live there, but Ker I can't. I can't take those oh, so Christian pitying eyes on me twenty four seven."

"Yeah." Kerry nodded. "I hear you."

"I knew you would understand."

Kerry did with an internal sympathy that hit right in her guts. "I do. So relax, talk to Bri, and make the best decision you can, Ang. We'll work things out if and when you get here."

"Thanks, Kerry." Angie replied warmly. "I love you."

"Love you too, sis. Talk to you later." Kerry hung up, then quickly rolled off the waterbed just in case her body got any ideas of repeating its earlier trick. She juggled the cell phone in her hand as she went back to the kitchen, deep in thought.

Sometimes, she reflected soberly, it took someone else's misfortune to jog you to the reality of your own lack of it.

KERRY SHOULDERED HER briefcase and picked up the bag from Atlanta Bread Factory as she hopped out of her car. The sky had gotten cloudy overhead, and there was a bit of a rumble far off, but the breeze had picked up and its coolness was welcome.

She felt a bit conspicuous, to be honest, crossing the parking lot at nearly eleven instead of nine. However, the men working around the front of the terminal merely looked up at her, then went back to what they were doing, and the light stream of people coming down the steps from the terminal didn't give her a second glance.

Okay, so it was conspicuous mostly in her mind. After all, even her own staff would probably assume she'd come from the office and no one would question her anyway.

Definitely not with Dar there. She remembered once in a staff meeting when someone—had it been Jose? Yeah. Jose had questioned her being ten minutes late and Dar had turned to him and said... Well, it hadn't been nice, and it had been typical Dar, and Jose had gotten mad. But he'd never asked her about being late ever again. She'd felt a little awkward about it then, and she told Dar that.

Dar had told her to get over it. So she had, but she was still aware of how people felt.

Kerry pushed her sunglasses up on the bridge of her nose and mounted the two steps up to the entranceway, slowing a little as the door opened and the security guard stood back to allow her inside. "Morning." She murmured.

"Morning, ma'am," the guard replied. "Ms. Roberts asked me to tell you when you came in that she was in the back," he informed her promptly. "And that she's looking for you."

"Thanks." Kerry removed her glasses and stuck them into the pocket of the light cotton blouse she was wearing unbuttoned over a plain, green t-shirt. Inside most of the techs were waiting around, relaxing and sitting on top of the switches they had yet to install. "Hey guys."

Several of the techs turned, and waved. "Morning, ma'am!" One called out. "Just got here in time, beat the rain, huh?"

"Looks like it." Kerry kept moving, crossing the front part of the terminal and heading for the office.

Near one wall stacks of new boxes were being opened, revealing servers and rack mount kits that would be their next task once the infrastructure was in place. Kerry was, frankly, more worried about that than the network gear since they would be installing new systems almost everywhere on the ship.

"Hey," Mark intercepted her. "We're still on track for after lunch. They figure at 1:00 p.m. they'll let us start going back on board. I was going to have my guys take in the gear, then Randy's team was gonna haul up the new boxes. Do you know if they got the racks put in?"

Kerry paused. "Hang on, let me get my file." She led him to the back office. Inside, several of their administrative people were busy at work, and at the back spare desk, Dar was huddled over her laptop pecking away furiously. "Hey boss."

Dar looked up. "Hey." She leaned back and waited for Kerry to come over. "Good morning." Her eyes twinkled, as Kerry stuck her tongue out. "Raining outside yet?"

"Not yet." Kerry sat on the edge of the desk and put her lunch bag down. "Did you bring my folio? I need to check something for Mark."

Dar produced the folio and handed it over. "What's this?" She tapped the bag with one finger, sniffing delicately at the brown surface and waggling her eyebrows.

"Lunch." Kerry opened her folder and checked the schedule, running her finger along one line on the topmost document. "According to this, Mark, we got the server racks in Monday." She announced. "So we're set to go."

"Great." Mark nodded. "You know what the worst part is going to be?"

"Which one?" Dar and Kerry answered at the same time. They exchanged glances and grins.

"Getting the user stuff out." Mark proceeded on gamely. "I don't think most of those places are ready for it; the offices and the bars and stuff."

Kerry sighed. "Probably not. We'd better stage everything in here, like we're doing with the infrastructure, and wait for each space to be finished."

"Man." Mark shook his head.

"I know." Kerry acknowledged the impossibility of it all. "We have three days. Assuming we get the network in today and the servers mounted that only leaves two days to get all the end units in, programmed and running."

Dar whistled softly under her breath as she typed.

"Do you know something we don't?" Kerry closed her folio and eyed her partner. "Or are you being cheerful for some other reason?"

"Hm." Dar stopped whistling. "Maybe I just like a challenge?" She looked up.

"Dar, this isn't a challenge, it's a nightmare." Kerry chuckled. "C'mon now."

Dar leaned back, lacing her fingers behind her head. "Depends on how you look at it." She disagreed. "Sure, there's a lot of work involved, and sure, we have a ridiculous amount of time to do it in." She shrugged. "That's all we have, so we just have to turn it around and look at it in a positive light."

Kerry blinked at her. "Huh?"

"If we do this, no matter if we get the bid or not, we win." Dar told her. "Because we'll have done something everyone here thinks can't be done."

Mark nodded. "Yeah. But on the other hand, boss, everyone expects the impossible because you're here, and you always get whatever it is we need to do done."

Kerry crossed her arms and also nodded. "He's right."

Dar looked from one to the other. "He is?"

"Of course," Kerry said. "There's not one person in this building who thinks you're not going to make this happen, Dar."

"Okay." Dar rocked back a little. "So why are the two of you so gloomy then?"

Kerry and Mark exchanged looks. "Did we just talk ourselves into a corner?" Kerry asked, with a slightly incredulous tone.

"Um yeah." Mark agreed sheepishly. "I think we did."

Dar spread her arms out to either side. "Pick one, folks. Either you believe this non-existent mojo I have to create miracles, or you don't."

Mark started backpedaling out of the office. "I'd never dis Dar's mojo," he said, just before disappearing out the door. "Never!"

Dar looked at Kerry, one eyebrow lifting.

"Honey, I'd never dis your mojo either, but that has nothing to do with this project." Kerry smiled charmingly at her, her grin broadening as she watched the visible blush rise up Dar's neck. "Anyway, I guess we'll just go like heck, and let the chips fall where they may. I'm a little more concerned about all that gear in the open with no one to watch it."

"They've got security." Dar commented. "Once that stuff's down, they'll be responsible for it."

"Doesn't help us if it gets stolen and we don't have it to demo."

"Hm. Good point."

"We'll think of something." Kerry opened her portfolio again and studied the contents.

"Mm." Dar turned her attention to the paper bag, now that the other people in the office had stopped peeking at her and grinning. She removed the contents, flattening the bag and setting the wrapped sandwiches on top of it.

"Okay, I'll be back." Kerry hopped off the desk and headed for the door. "Watch my sandwich for me, will you?" She vanished into the hallway, bouncing a little to the music trickling in from the setup area.

"Sure." Dar sat back and observed the wrapped item. "Does it do tricks?" She called after her partner, ignoring the muffled snickers from the other workers in the room.

After a second, Kerry's head popped back around the doorframe. "I've got a trick I'd love to show you. It involves a water balloon and an underwear waistband. Want to see it?"

Dar scratched her nose, and made a face.

"Didn't think so." Kerry disappeared again.

Dar chuckled and went back to her laptop, nudging aside the lunch bag for the time being. She lifted her head as she heard muffled giggles, and gave them all a droll look. "Something wrong?"

"No, ma'am." The closest of the workers shook her head. "Not a darn thing."

"Good." Dar leaned back and propped her knee up against the desk edge, pulling the laptop onto her lap.

"Ms. Roberts?"

Dar looked up. "Yes, Edith?"

"I heard yesterday that you wrestled a shark in the ocean, and saved Kerry from being eaten by it." Edith turned around in her chair.

"Is that true?"

Dar found herself the center of attention. "Um..."

"And that's how you hurt your foot, right?" One of the other women chimed in. "I heard you kicked it right in the teeth!"

Dar looked at her foot and then back up at the room. "Well, um..."

"Man that must have been scary." Edith shook her head. "Now I know why I don't go in the ocean!" She turned back to her desk.

"You can say that again." The woman next to her tsked.

"Well, now, hold on." Dar rallied to the defense of her favorite environment. "The ocean's a wonderful place to go. I've been diving in it since I was four, and I hardly ever get as much as a nick."

Everyone looked at her foot, then up at her face.

"This was at the shore!" Dar protested. "We were twenty feet from the beach! Last time I saw a shark when I was underwater was, um..." She considered. "Last month."

"Brr!" Edith went back to her PC. "All I can say is, Kerry's one lucky woman."

Dar focused her attention back on her screen, the last few words ringing in her ears. They made her smile.

"OKAY." KERRY CROUCHED down in front of the row of boxes. Balanced on the tops of them were six large rack mount servers, their LED's flickering promisingly. "So, we've got the two main servers up, the accounting system and the point of sale system. Right?"

"Right." Randy Escobar squatted down next to her. "I hooked 'em up on that switch there, and tried them out, but I think some of them need to be on different networks."

Kerry got up and looked behind the servers. "You plugged in all the network cards?"

"Yeah. Wanted to make sure all of them worked."

"Okay." Kerry nodded. "We can deal with the nitty details later. Long as the hardware is up—are those thirty six gig drives?"

"Raid five, yeah." Randy agreed. "And the backup device will hook up to this server here." He patted the first large machine. "Decent system."

Kerry examined the back of the machines, then walked around and examined the front of them. "Okay, so here's the plan," she said. "Mark's group is going to get the backbone in, then patch everything."

"What a mess."

"Yeah, a lot of cable." Kerry agreed. "While they're patching, I want you to get these mounted and plugged into everything."

"Do they have AC in there?" Barry asked. "Cause if they don't, Kerry, you know these suckers will be up for about ten minutes and then they'll shut down."

Oh, crap. Kerry rested her arm on the server. "You know, I didn't know." She had to admit. "Let me think about this a minute." She consulted her schedule. The air conditioning was in process along with their cabling and the electricity. Did the ducting get finished before they all got kicked off? "Well, plan on installing them at any rate. Let me find out what's going on with the AC vendor."

"Sorry, Kerry." Barry looked apologetic.

"Not your fault. I should have remembered that." Kerry got up and headed toward the backdoor. She could see several vendor crew chiefs assembled outside, and she headed toward them. Halfway there, she stopped and stood, as another idea occurred to her. "I bet the air conditioning is the last thing we're gonna get." She mused. "So..."

"Hey, Ker?" Mark came up behind her with a sheaf of paperwork.

"Mark, how many spare portable AC units do we have?" Kerry turned and faced him.

"Huh?"

"Portable AC units. I know we got them for the communications center as Dar bought them after the last AC outage in the building."

Mark thought a moment. "Um...six, I think."

"Great." Kerry nodded. "Send someone with a truck to the office. Get all six, and have them back here asap." She directed. "Make sure they remember the drain hoses. I remember us having to use that one in accounting and it costing me a replacement carpet in Duks' office."

"Um...okay." Mark handed her the sheaf of papers. "Here are all the packing slips. I guess the bean counters need them." He trotted off, leaving Kerry in relative solitude.

She looked down at the papers. "Yeah." She tucked them carefully into her folio. "They will, when I get done with them." With a sigh, she walked over to the windows and peered out at the ship, noting the heavy clouds gathering over it.

"KERRY?"

"YEAH?" KERRY turned from where she was seated on a box, watching the rain come down.

Mark took the box next to her. "Crappy weather."

Kerry kicked her heels lightly against the cardboard. "You came all the way across the room to say that?" She gave him a curious look.

"No. I was gonna say, I've still got those tarps we used over at Bellsouth. You think we could put them up between here and that ramp and not get soaked?"

Kerry observed the downpour, which suddenly seemed to be driving sideways instead of up and down. "Nope." She pulled one knee up and circled it with both arms. "I think we're going to get soaked no matter what. Got a change of clothes?"

"Everyone does." Mark replied succinctly. "After yesterday."

Kerry chuckled softly. "Yeah, I sure was glad I did." She admitted.

"That was about the yuckiest situation I've ever been in."

Mark was quiet for a few moments, his eyes following the rain. "Those guys you were with yesterday are really rocking high on you."

Kerry rested her chin on her knee. "That's a good thing, right?"

"Yeah." Mark agreed. "I mean, like...I tell all kinds of BS stories about the old days, and DR and all that, you know? But these guys, most of the young ones, they just don't get it."

One of Kerry's eyebrows hiked up. "Hm. So us ancient types have to teach them?" She guessed. "Oo...I can hear my joints creaking now."

Mark laughed. "No, that's not what I meant."

Kerry rested her cheek on her knee, watching him and waiting for the explanation.

"It's—I can tell people until I'm green in the face how cool you guys are and all that, but they don't really get it until they get like, ah." Mark paused.

"Up close and personal?" Kerry suggested.

"Something like that, yeah."

Kerry reflected on her experience the prior day. She hadn't intended on providing a quality work moment for her staff, but she wasn't stupid enough to disregard a good result when it happened. "I didn't do that much," she commented.

"Not what I heard," Mark said. "Carlos told me you climbed up inside that rack and hauled the switch and all that."

"Hm."

"And everybody cracked the hell up when you yelled at DR through that door," Mark said.

"Well!" Kerry got up, and checked her watch, seeing it was near to 1:00 p.m. "The woman has open cuts in her foot! She scared the bejesus out of me!"

Mark also got up, joining her at the window. "I know...it's just like...well, like Carlos came back and you know what he said? He said you sounded just like his brother and sister in law. Or just like me and Barbara."

"We are." Kerry glanced at him.

"Well, yeah, I know that. But he didn't." Mark explained carefully. "That guy was really not into gay people, you know? He wasn't really a 'phobe or whatever, but his family's really conservative."

"So's mine." But Kerry smiled at him. "Thanks. I'm glad to hear that. Usually what I've discovered is when folks realize gay people are just as stupid and goofy as straight people, they chill out." She leaned against the glass. "Just about time for us to get moving."

Mark turned and put his fingers between his teeth letting out a shrill, piercing whistle. "All right, people! Let's get ready to move out!" He waved a hand. "Two guys to every box and somebody get over here with an umbrella for the boss!"

Kerry turned. "Hey!"

A crowd of techs moved toward them, but behind them Kerry caught sight of Cruickshank and her filming team. Just as she was about to cut through the stream of people and intercept them, she saw Dar neatly slip in from the side corridor and stop them cold.

Satisfied, she turned and pushed the doors open, allowing the thundering roar of the storm to enter the building along with a huge gust of warm, wet air. She could see the guards drawing aside on the gangway, and already some of the workers were starting to trickle warily back on board. Chief among them, she noted, was Andrew.

"You guys ready?" Kerry called back over her shoulder. "If we run fast enough, we'll get there before the damn rain soaks through those cardboard boxes."

Techs were hoisting the heavy switch cartons between them and gathering at the door behind her. An air of excitement seemed to be building, as the techs not carrying boxes slung tool belts on their shoulders and others carried smaller boxes of patch cables.

Carlos came up behind Kerry, holding a handful of plastic. "Hey, um..." He held it out. "I don't have an umbrella, but I got an extra one of these, if you want it."

Kerry took the bright red rain slicker. "Thanks, Carlos." She gave him a warm smile in return. "You'd think after living here a few years I'd know to carry one of these in the summer."

"How's your hand doing?" He glanced behind him, as though to judge how close they were to moving out of the building. "I did that once, cut my hand on that crossbeam. Hurt like crazy."

Kerry held up her hand, neatly wrapped in a symmetrically perfect crisscross of gauze bandage, taped into place by two evenly spaced strips of bright orange tape. "It stung a lot yesterday, but as you can see, I can't move it a lot today so it's been fine." She curled her hand into a fist and punched the air. "I feel like a boxer."

Carlos grinned, and held up his own hands. "You box?" he asked, making a few passes. "Someone said you did."

"Kickbox." Kerry said.

"Me too."

Hm. Kerry judged they were about ready to go. She pondered asking Carlos what his views were on gorgeous brunettes with blue eyes, just to see if they had that in common too, then decided the freak out factor was about six points too high for the occasion. "Hey, we can compare technique later," she said instead. "Okay, everyone ready?"

"Ready." Mark said. "You want to put that jacket on?"

"Yeah, in a..." Kerry blinked as the jacket was taken from her hands and shaken open, then held for her to climb into. "Um..."

"Um?" Dar's voice sounded amused. "Put it on, or you can't go out to play, Kerrison."

"Wench." Kerry muttered, getting into the jacket. "Did you—ah."

She spotted the reporters right behind Dar. "Are we the sound bite today?"

Cruikshank poked her head forward. "Matter of fact, you are." She agreed cheerfully. "We're gonna stick with you guys today, since you're the ones behind the gun. Mind?"

Kerry accepted the unobtrusive pat on the butt from her partner as she fastened the rain slicker. "Nope." She turned to the door. "Okay, let's go, guys!" She headed out into the rain, followed by a veritable cavalcade of nerds, lugging nearly a thousand pounds of gear out into the deluge.

Dar held the door for them waving Cruickshank and her crew out after them with a flourish. "G'wan. That's where all the action is."

"Oh, you bet." The reporter pulled her rain hood up and trotted outside happily. "You know, Ms. Roberts, this is turning out to be just a humdinger of a tale, isn't it?" She smiled back at Dar. "You coming too?"

Dar cocked her head to one side. "Wouldn't miss it for anything," she said, watching as the reporters turned and hurried after her crew, who were running as fast as they could toward the gangway. There were a few other contractors straggling that way, but a big group of them were under the overhang on the building side, unwilling to get wet.

"Hey!" Dar yelled at them. "What's the matter with you? You a bunch of girls or something?"'

The contractors whirled to stare at her.

"Get your ass over there and start working!" Dar barked. "Move it!"

"Hey! Fuck you!" One of the men yelled back.

"You don't have anything I'd even want to take a picture of, much less touch," Dar retorted. "C'mon, you pansy ass–move it!"

The man started in her direction, but someone, apparently his supervisor, hauled him back and shoved him toward the ship instead. "I'm gonna kick your ass for that, bitch!" The man threatened.

Dar recognized his voice as one of the men she'd passed in the stairwell the previous day, threatening the same thing only with someone else. She just laughed. "Bet you don't." She remarked. "Cause either my dad or my girlfriend will knock you silly."

She waited for the crowd at the gangway to clear—the last of their group gaining entrance and the contractors following—before she let the door shut and strolled out into the rain, tilting her head up and enjoying the warm blast of water. She opened her mouth and caught some on her tongue, convinced she could almost taste the clouds on it.

"Paladar!"

Whoops. "Yeah, Dad?" Dar shook her head, now completely drenched with rain.

"What in the hell are you doing?" Her father was standing inside the ship with his hands on his hips.

Dar held her arms out as she approached the gangway and started up it. "Enjoying the sunshine?"

"Lord, you have lost your mind." Her father pulled her inside. "Did them drugs Steve gave you make your head turn over?"

Dar just chuckled, and shook her head. She gave her father a pat on the back and headed for the steps, shaking her body like a dog to scatter the raindrops everywhere as she followed the sound of many stomping feet ahead of her.

Chapter Two

IT STILL SMELLED. Kerry strolled conspicuously closer to the big open doors on the main deck, braving the rain splatter to clear her lungs. It wasn't nearly as bad as it had been the previous day, though, and she could see carpet cleaners working very hard on the central staircase to remove the lingering stench.

She stayed near the door anyway. It gave her the best perspective of the activity going on around the main part of the ship, and she could direct the various teams of her technicians as they crisscrossed the hallways. "Mark, did you check the server room?"

Mark paused in mid step. "Was it doing tricks, boss?"

"I meant for AC and power." Kerry gave him a droll look.

"Oh. Right." Mark reversed his course. "Hang on."

Kerry intercepted him. "Nah, go on. I'll check it." She regretfully gave up her spot near the door and crossed the round atrium, going to the far side of the steps and trotting up them to the next landing. She turned into the hallway and glanced at the cabin numbers as she walked, then stopped in front of the inside cabin she'd taken over for their new systems.

The door was open. She unlatched it and pushed it inward, reaching in and flipping on the lights inside. What had once been a small, inside stateroom had been stripped out entirely to its bare walls and rebuilt as a miniature, but functional, IT space.

One side was lined with floor to ceiling racks that were bolted to the deck. In the first one, a switch was mounted, already spilling brightly colored cables from its front to several jacks. Opposite the racks were two long worktables with chairs that sported rubber leg bumpers instead of wheels. Awkward to move around, Kerry had learned, but necessary so that they didn't roll and crash into things when the ship was in rough waters.

She had experience with that on the Dixie. There, everything inside could be locked down, or tied up so nothing went flying during those infrequent times they were out in bad weather. Even the bed had — what she'd joked to Dar — seatbelts.

In here, there were no seat belts. But corners were padded, and the racks all had locking sides and doors, and felt quite sturdy as she tugged on them.

However, there was no AC in the room. The overhead lights were on, but that was it. Kerry felt sweat starting to run under her shirt after being inside for a few minutes, and she knew the servers would survive for a shorter time than she would in the heat.

Well, muskrats. Kerry put her hands on her hips. She really didn't want to have to haul the big portable units in, but it was looking like she wasn't going to have much of a choice.

"Oh, hello there Ms. Stuart."

Kerry turned to find their reporter friend behind her. "Hi."

The Herald reporter slipped inside and stood next to her. "Is this profound?" She queried. "The way you're looking at it makes me think so."

Kerry took a step back and leaned on the worktable. "No. Well, I mean...it's where our system servers are going to be, so I guess it's profound in that sense. But actually it's just giving me a hive at the moment because the AC's not on in here."

The reporter looked around. "That's true," she agreed. "Does that matter?"

"Sure," Kerry said. "We can't run the servers like this. They'll overheat."

"Ahhh," the woman murmured. "The other ships are pretty far ahead of you," she told Kerry. "They've mostly got the, whatever those are, up and running."

"Ah well." Kerry produced a mild grin. "We'll get there."

"Without AC?"

"We'll bring in our own." Kerry unclipped a walkie-talkie from her belt. "Dar? You there?"

"Yeeees." Dar's voice came back after a brief pause.

"Can you send the ice boxes up to the server room? It's hotter than melted cheese whiz up here." Kerry spoke into the device crisply." The switch is mounted, so I'm going to tell Barry to get moving."

"On the way." Dar signed off with a click.

"Barry?" Kerry switched channels on the radio. "This is Kerry, you on?"

"Right here, Kerry," Barry replied. "You ready for us?'

Kerry sighed, looking around. "Well, you can mount them in here, anyway. I'm having the portable air units brought up."

"Okay, be right there."

Kerry clicked off, and returned the radio to her belt. Between the radio, her cell, and her PDA, she'd briefly contemplated finding a tool belt to wear, but one look at the devilish expression on Dar's face when she suggested it put visions of bright pink leather in her mind. So she dropped the idea. "Okay."

The reporter leaned back against the worktable. "So, you bring in your own air conditioning units. I take it these aren't the window things you see on old houses in these parts, right?"

Kerry nodded. "They're rolling portable units that vent the hot air back up into the plenum." She tapped the ceiling, pushing up a panel. "And, since we used to have a bathroom in here, we can stick the drain hose...let me see..." She investigated a capped pipe in the corner, removing a pair of pliers from her back pocket and wrestling it off.

"Yep. There."

"Hm."

Kerry turned. "We do have an advantage being local," she said. "We have all the resources of our office here to work with, and of course, we know the area."

"And the weather." The reporter chuckled.

"And the weather," Kerry agreed. She went behind the racks, squeezing between them and the wall, inspecting the railings that connected them.

"Not much space back there."

"No." Kerry agreed. "I compromised between needing air circulation space and needing to be able to extend the servers out on their rails. It's pretty tight in here."

"Let me ask you something, Ms. Stuart," the reporter said. "What exactly are the ramifications for you if you don't succeed here?"

Kerry leaned on the back rails, peering through the smoky gray door at her. "Me personally?"

The reporter walked over and peered through the door back leaning a hand on either side of the opening. "You personally," she said. "The rest of these companies, they've got technical people here, or people with a vested interest in this prospective contract. You could have sent someone else in here. Why didn't you?"

Everyone seemed to be asking that. Kerry wondered if she and Dar shouldn't have been asking that a little more strongly themselves.

"Is it that you didn't feel like you could trust anyone to do it?" The reporter persisted.

"No." Kerry answered. "That's not it at all. I send teams all over the country to do this."

"Exactly." The woman nodded.

What could she say, really? That they'd promised Alastair they'd do it? That would just make him look bad. That they wanted to beat Michelle and Shari? That would just make them look bad. Having no really coherent response, Kerry fell back on nerdiness instead. "You know, the fact of the matter is that both Dar and I happen to buy into to a certain theory of management that sort of requires both of us to keep our hands in and really know the nuts and bolts of what we do."

"Really?"

"Really." Kerry smiled. "It's not like I really do enjoy kneeling here on questionably clean floors getting iron filing dust up my nose. Honest."

"Interesting." The reporter smiled back. "I think that might explain a lot about the things I've heard from many of your clients."

Kerry finished her inspection, and squeezed back around the edge of the rack, dusting her hands off on her jeans. "Maybe that's why we've been as successful as we have." She suggested. "When you get to the management level of Dar and me, you tend to lose touch with the day to day. It's a real tough thing to not let that happen. Because we're so busy it's hard to put aside the time to read the tech journals, and preview the new gear, and think outside the box. But we do."

The reporter clapped. "Beautiful quote." She complimented Kerry. "Ever think of going into politics?"

Kerry was saved from having to answer by the arrival of Barry, walking backwards and bumping the doorframe with his shoulders. "Hang on a second, let me prop that open." She got to the door and pushed it as far as it would go, then pressed her back against the wall. "C'mon in."

"Thanks." Barry backed cautiously inside, wincing as he scraped the backs of his hands on the doorway. "Whoa. They don't do wide loads in here, huh?"

Kerry sucked in a breath as the server skimmed by her right at button fly level. Very different from a desktop PC, the server was all stainless steel and weighed a ton.

"Put 'em on that desk." Barry grunted. "We gotta install the rails."

A second pair of techs followed them in, with a second server, and there was a third set who waited patiently outside the door. Kerry stood back and merely watched, unable to do much to either help or hinder the process at the moment.

Beside her, the reporter leaned over and studied the server now resting on the table. "Big."

"Commercial grade." Kerry agreed. "Quad processors, four gig of main memory and five 36 gig drives in a RAID 5 array."

The reporter looked at her. "I should have guessed you were bilingual." She remarked pleasantly.

"Ugh." The second group of carriers carefully edged out of the room, making space for the third to come in. "Man, it's hot in here."

"Man, it's small in here." The third set worked their way in, and took up the remaining space on the table with their load. "Is every place on this thing so cramped?"

"Pretty much," Kerry said. "Space is definitely at a premium. This used to be a passenger cabin."

"I'm surprised they let you take it," the reporter said. "It's lost revenue for them."

"They had no choice," Kerry said. "I told them either I took a passenger cabin, or they gave me their crew lounge. Guess which they picked?"

The techs chuckled. The reporter crossed her arms, but she smiled. "Well, that's been a problem on all four ships, really. I think..." She looked around. "Yeah, I think definitely you got the most space out of them. The ship behind you has this stuff squeezed into something I suspect might have been a washroom."

"I think the satellite people are here," Barry said, over his shoulder. "They're, uh..." His eyes flicked to the reporter. "Having a discussion with Ms. Roberts."

Uh oh. "Problems?"

"Well," Barry opened the box of rails and pulled one out, checking it to see if it was right or left handed. "Uh...I don't really know." He chickened out. "It's all that WAN stuff."

"Uh huh." Kerry removed herself from being a doorstop. "I'll go see if I can clarify the WAN stuff." She sighed. "The AC units are on their way up. Please remind the guys to put the drain line in. I don't really want to have to swim upstream later to get back here."

"Will do." Barry agreed cheerfully. "Be glad to see them." He wiped his forehead with his sleeve.

Kerry started out, glancing to one side as the reporter joined her. "Don't you want to see them mount the server?" She asked politely.

"Oh sure." The reporter agreed. "That's my leadoff tagline. 'mounting servers in a sweaty ex-bedroom. No. I'll go with you."

Figures. Kerry sighed. Just figures.

THE TOP DECK of the ship was accessed at the top of the stairwells through a set of wooden doors with round glass portholes. The surrounding walls were metal with rust markings on them and evidence of many rounds of steel plate patching.

It creaked up here. Dar could also feel the slight motion of the ship as it rocked in its berth, the wind from the storm shoving against the sides of the relatively narrow vessel. At sea, she could only imagine what it would be like, and was personally determined not to find out.

She peered out the porthole and spotted the techs outside standing in the rain and surrounding a huge pile of gear.

Dar reasoned that Cruickshank and her boys wouldn't follow them out into the rain, and as she looked behind her she was pleased to note her reasoning was correct. Already wet, she didn't mind the warm rain in the slightest as she headed across the open top deck toward the stanchions they were trying to mount the communications gear on.

She hadn't been up top before. The small swimming pool, drained for resurfacing, appeared sad and full of cracks; its concrete very discolored and crumbling. Around it, an old turf surface was unraveling, part of it taken up and in the process of being replaced.

On one side was a bar with worn wooden stools bolted to the deck, and on the other a tiny bandstand with two, low, cracked steps leading up to it.

Shabby. Like the rest of the ship. However, Dar could see there was a stack of new teak wood under tarps nearby, and the cracked pieces were being replaced. Eventually, she supposed, it would be presentable.

Not now.

They stopped under the metal structure, and looked up. "See?" The man nearest Dar pointed. "That's all we got to connect it to. I'm telling ya, it's gonna blow overboard first time they crank this tub up."

Dar hopped up onto part of the structure and examined the beam in question. It was rustier than a sixty eight Chevy, and even she could see the popped rivets and crumbling slivers of steel coming off the beam. "How much does that thing weigh?"

"'Bout a hundred fifty, sixty pounds," the man advised her.

Dar reached up and curled her hands around the beam, then pulled herself up onto it, grabbing hold of the supports reaching up from it and bouncing up and down on the beam. "Any shavings?"

The satellite techs scurried out of the way watching her with wide eyes. "What in the hell are you doing?" the tall man asked.

"I weigh as much as that damn satellite. You see anything moving?" Dar swung back and forth on the side supports, throwing her body to either side with as much violence as she could muster.

"Hey! Be careful, lady! It's slippery up there! You're gonna kill yourself!"

"Nah." Dar, however, was mindful of how unstable her sandals were. "I've been running around on spars since I was in short pants." She hopped up and down again. "I say you put it up here." She grabbed hold of the edge of the beam and slipped off, dangling by her hands for a second before she dropped lightly to the deck.

"I don't know." The man shook his head. "That thing's going to cut loose if there's any stress."

Dar walked to the side of the beam. "So put strapping in, and make sure your contracts specify that they pay for new equipment every time it falls over. Guarantee the metal gets replaced in a week." She patted the steel.

The satellite contractors gazed unhappily at the metal, shading their eyes from the falling rain. "I don't know," the supervisor finally said. "I guess we could mount it then see what happens. Did they even run the cabling?"

One of the other techs wrestled a rusted cover off a box mounted on the side of the beam. "Yeah." He peered inside. "Looks like it...yeah, there's the co-ax."

Dar came around behind him and looked as well. "My contractor did that. Let me know if it doesn't work. He's still here."

The supervisor gave her a friendlier look. "You a gymnast?"

"No." Dar became aware of the camera crew, focusing on her from the safety of the overhang. "How long is this gonna take you?"

"Couple hours."

Dar glanced up. "Hope it stops raining"

The tech shrugged. "Stuff's waterproof." He indicated their surroundings. "Kinda has to be."

"We're not."

"Huh. Yeah." The satellite technician scratched his head, and glanced over his shoulder. "What's with the camera?"

"Don't ask." Dar deliberately turned her back on it. "Your guys putting in the control gear for this thing in the communications room?" The rain had now drenched her through, and her shirt was sticking to her body. On the other hand, at least she wasn't sweating.

"The geek guys are doing that," the tech told her. "We don't touch that crap."

Figures. "Okay." Dar pushed away from the steel support. "I'll leave you to it then."

The man looked up. "You sure you want us to do this?" He queried. "Lady, I'm not kidding. I think it's gonna come down."

Possibly. But Dar needed the satellite up so she could start the applications they'd been contracted for. "Tell you what," she said. "I'll go tell the engineer they need to put metal stabilizers on this thing if you get your part of it started. Deal? They can solder the angle irons on here, and not touch your gear." She tapped the side of the metal beam.

The tech studied the area, then nodded. "Okay." He agreed. "Deal. But you sure you can talk for those guys? I don't want no trouble."

Dar grinned at him, her eyes twinkling in the rain. "I'm sure," she said. "See you inside." She turned and headed back toward the doorway leading inside, seeing not only the camera crew, but a tousled blonde head peeking out at her.

She could almost see the exasperated look in her partner's eyes as she strolled toward her with unhurried strides. As she got to the door and opened it, she shook herself vigorously, scattering rain drops everywhere, including onto the cameramen who scrambled back away from her with puppy sounding yelps. "Don't you folks have something better to do than stand here blocking the door?" She asked sternly.

"Can I ask, Ms. Roberts, what you were doing out there?" Cruickshank asked, almost breathlessly. "I can't tell you what that looked like."

Dar cocked her head to one side. "What did it look like?" she inquired. "I was just discussing the mounting points for our satellite system." She gave Kerry a sideways glance, then she brushed by the reporters. "Excuse me. I've got other things to attend to."

"Hi." Kerry greeted her. "Everything all right out there?"

"Peachy." Dar steered Kerry toward the stairwell, ignoring the gaggle of press around them. "They're going to get the dish up, but it's going to take a while. How are the servers going?"

"They're going," Kerry answered.

They hit the top of the stairs and started down, taking the steps two at a time and leaving the press momentarily behind. As they got to the eleventh deck, Dar abruptly turned left and scooted down a hallway with Kerry at her heels.

They paused and listened. The sound of thundering footsteps continuing down the steps made them both smile. "Okay." Dar ran her fingers through her wet hair, pushing it back off her forehead. "Problem was the stanchion they're mounting it to is as rotten as a six week old apple."

"Ah." Kerry nodded. "And that explains you climbing all over it like a monkey."

"Eh." Dar shrugged. "Made good film, I bet."

Kerry cleared her throat. "Actually sweetheart, your shirt's transparent." She delicately plucked the wet fabric off her partner's skin. "That made even better film. I almost stabbed the camera guy when his tongue came out of his mouth."

Dar looked down at herself, then up at Kerry. "Really?"

"Really." Kerry examined the pale green, very light cotton fabric that was still, indeed, very see through and left nothing to anyone's imagination in regards to Dar's physique. "I think you need to change."

Dar looked both ways down the corridor, then simply removed her shirt, standing there in the hallway in her bra as she wrung the garment out onto the plastic protecting the new carpet on the floor. "Huh. Maybe that's why those guys warmed up to me out there."

"Dar." Kerry looked nervously in the direction of some voices.

"Hm?"

"If that camera crew comes round that corner, I'm going to go insane and we'll never hear the end of this."

"Oh, relax." Dar started to walk the other way toward the communications office. "It's just a bra. I saw a billboard with some chick wearing one coming off Brickell this morning." She continued to wring the shirt out, her shoulders bunching and flexing as she squeezed as much water out as possible.

Kerry decided to simply enjoy the show, and she only just kept herself from walking backwards to watch. "Is that beam going to cause us a problem?"

"Maybe." Dar finished twisting the shirt to within an inch of its textile life. "I told them to put some extra strapping up. That whole top superstructure is a piece of crap. I figure the entire damn smokestack will fall over before the dish will."

"Oh. That's not good." Kerry paused with her hand on the door latch to the communications room, waiting for Dar to put her damp shirt back on. "How long do you really think it's going to last?"

"Past this week, I don't really care." Dar tugged the clammy fabric on. "Still see through?"

Kerry studied her. "Not...no, it's okay," she said. "But you're dripping all over the floor from those jeans."

"They'll cope. It's a ship. They should be used to water." Dar jerked her jaw at the door. "Open." She hesitated, giving Kerry a look. "I know that's not a good long term answer. But between you and me, I don't honestly think this is a long term ship."

"You think there's a scam in here somewhere." It was not really a question.

Dar nodded. "I think there's something. Too many things just don't make sense." She flicked her fingers through her bangs once more, then focused on the entrance.

Kerry opened the door, nodding slightly in confirmation. She followed Dar inside the communications office in somber, yet attentive silence.

"HEY, KERRY? YOU on?"

Kerry unclipped her radio and answered it. "Yup. What's going on, Mark?'

"My guys say we're ready to light up the network. You okay with that?"

Kerry frowned. "Of course I am," she replied. "Since when does someone need my approval to push the on switch around here?"

The radio crackled. "Ahem...ah, just trying to be PC, boss, that's all," Mark replied meekly.

"PC my gopher's eyeball," Kerry told him. "Turn the suckers on." She clicked off and went to the base of the ladder, peering up. "Jesus."

Dar, up on the ladder with the satellite techs, her head poked halfway up into the plenum, looked down at her. "Problem?"

"People being weird," Kerry said. "They're going to turn the switches on."

"Cool." Dar resumed her inspection, edging a step higher and flashing her light into the space. "Did you find the problem?" She directed her words to the SAT tech up inside the ceiling, sweating and cursing under his breath.

"Not yet," the man replied. "Fucking cable is so tight in here I can't see it."

Obligingly, Dar went up one more step, this time onto the top of the ladder, and extended her arm to direct her powerful flash over to where the guy was working. She could feel the ladder moving a little uncertainly under her and she gripped the ceiling supports with one hand. "Ker?"

"On it," Kerry replied.

The ladder moved a bit more then stabilized. Dar felt a hand curl around her ankle, and she relaxed. "Thanks."

"Son of a bitch," the tech muttered.

Dar craned her neck to see if she could see what the problem was. "Ah hah." She immediately saw the junction box installed on top of the cable access point.

"Stupid electricians. What a bunch of freaking morons." The tech sighed, wiping droplets of sweat out of his eyes. "Now what are we gonna do? There's not even clearance to plug in."

Dar leaned forward and examined the box, acutely aware of Kerry's thumb gently rubbing against her skin. It was a very warm feeling, despite the heat in the room, and she took a moment to take a breath before she peeked around the electrical piping that was blocking the way.

It was infuriating. The contractor had, to her eyes, almost deliberately ran his conduit and junction box right up against where the co-ax terminated, making their connection pretty damn near unusable. "Crap."

"Yeah." The SAT tech snorted. "So now what?"

"Now we have to get those bastards back in here to redo it," Dar said.

The tech laughed. "You don't really think they're gonna do that."

"Not willingly." Dar carefully backed off the top step. "But let me see what I can do." She emerged from the ceiling, moving down another step and receiving a pat on her calf as Kerry got out of her way. She got down to ground level, and rested her elbow on one of the steps of the ladder. "We've got a problem."

"So I gathered," Kerry said. "What can I do?"

Dar eyed her thoughtfully. "I think this is my gig."

"Your gig?"

"I have to go find the electrical contractor and scream at him until he moves some conduit," Dar said. "I will probably have to threaten legal action, and I might need to go find whoever owns the company and shake him by the neck until he piddles on the floor."

Kerry studied her quietly, then sniffed. "Your gig." She agreed. "I'm going to go down to the server room and see how they're doing in there."

Dar looked around. The communications room was a bit of a shambles with wires hanging out everywhere. A crew technician was sitting in a chair near the back of the room just watching them, arms crossed over his jump suited chest. The only neat looking space was their rack full of routers and gear.

What a mess. Dar steered Kerry out the door and into the hallway, walking with her toward the central staircase that would take them down. It was hot, and they both wiped their foreheads at the same time, causing them to chuckle a little.

"Dar. I have to ask you something." Kerry plucked the sweat dampened cotton of her shirt away from her skin. "Because everyone is asking me this. Your mother asked, the reporters asked...so I'm going to ask you."

"Mm? Is this like the last personal question you asked me? " Dar inquired. "If it is, I want to know why my mother was involved."

Kerry bumped her, shoulder to shoulder. "You're such a brat sometimes. Have I ever told you that?"

"Once or twice." Dar allowed.

"No. What I was going to ask—that everyone is asking is—why in the hell you and I are here."

"Ah." Dar sighed. "Yeah, while I had my head stuck up in that ceiling I thought about that, too. You know..." She stared pensively at the wall. "I wish I had a decent answer for that right now, Ker. All I know is that I just have a bad feeling that if we weren't, a lot of this stuff wouldn't get done, and we'd end up having to explain why."

Kerry considered that, as they turned the corner and started down the steps. "So, we don't trust our staff to get it done."

"No." Dar agreed. "We don't. But that's not their fault. This is out of their scope."

With a tiny shake of her head, Kerry let her hand run down the center banister. "I've been insisting to everyone that's not the deal."

"Hm."

"So now you tell me it is."

"Well, it is for me, Ker. It doesn't have to be for you." Dar protested mildly, as they walked down the steps in perfect sync. "You could be here...to um..."

"Take care of you." Kerry smiled a little. "Make sure you keep dry, keep out of sewage, and bring you your lunch."

"Tell me when my shirt's see-through." Dar spotted John on the next level. "Hey, John!"

The wiring contractor whirled, spotted her, and trotted over. "Been looking for you two," he said. "Listen, I got my guys together last night, and found the fella who bumped into Ms. Stuart, here."

"Yeah?" Dar was faintly surprised that someone had actually admitted to it.

"Yeah, it was Steve." John nodded. "Good old boy, but lazier than a dog. He was taking a nap inside that closet when you all came up there."

Kerry put her hands on her hips. "He told you that?"

John shrugged. "I don't hire Rhodes scholars," he said. "Anyway, he said he didn't put no balls of cable anywhere, but what he did see was some guy walking around picking up scraps outside near where he was."'

"Really." Dar folded her arms.

"Yeah, and he said the guy didn't look like a contractor. He had long sleeves on," John said. "Now, gotta tell you, Dar, he could be talking out his ass, but seems to me it'd be easier for him to just keep his trap shut than come up with some wild ass tale like that."

"Unless he was trying to put the blame on someone else," Kerry said.

The contractor shrugged. "Yeah, could be, but he ain't a storyteller. He'd have just said one of my other guys, or an electrician or a ship guy did it. Not make up some fella in long sleeves."

"Long sleeves." Dar mused. "Yeah, that would be unusual. Well, anyway, thanks John. Listen, do you know the name of the electrical sub?"

John snorted. "Johnson. Those sons of bitches."

Sons of bitches. Yeah, Dar recalled using them for something at the office once that had denigrated into a lawsuit. "Figures Quest picked them. Lousiest jerks in the business."

"You know it." John agreed. "You need something from them?"

"You go look in the comm room," Dar said. "Let me go see what I can get out of them." With a sigh, she collected Kerry with a tug on her sleeve and started down the steps again. "Damn, damn, damn. That's not good news."

Kerry just put her hand on Dar's back, and scratched it lightly with her fingertips. A flash of motion coming at them from below made her pull up and grab the back of Dar's shirt, slowing her partner just in time to keep them both from plowing into Peter Quest hurrying in the other direction.

"Ah." Quest paused, spotting them. "I was looking for you." He folded his arms. "So. How are things going?"

"Fine." Kerry answered. "We're making a lot of progress."

"You are?" Quest seemed a little astonished. "I mean, I'm sure you are. But with everything and all the hold ups, I'm sure you're far behind the other ships. Is there any point to going on?"

If Dar and Kerry had been dogs, both their ears and their hackles would have lifted and made quite a spectacle there in the middle of the stairwell. "I dunno," Dar finally answered. "I'll let you know on Friday."

"We may surprise you." Kerry added, with a gentle smile.

"Everything has to work." Quest warned. "My people have already started reviewing the systems on the other ships. They know what they're doing."

"So do we," Dar replied calmly.

Quest looked at them, then he went around them and continued up the steps, shaking his head.

Dar and Kerry stood quietly for a moment, then turned and looked at each other. "You know what I'm thinking, Kerrison?" Dar asked. "Aside from the fact that our lunch is sitting on the desk in that office, and I'm going to need to rethink my approach on the electricians?"

"Mmhm." Kerry took her arm, and they continued downward. "I think you're thinking about long sleeves."

Dar glanced behind them. "Yeah."

"Well, so am I." Kerry felt herself getting angry. "So am I."

THE STORM KEPT on keeping on, drumming against the windows with boring repetition. A low rumble of thunder now joined it, and the light had dimmed so much outside it felt close to evening.

Dar leaned back in her borrowed desk chair, her forearm over her eyes as she put her cell phone down on her chest. "Jesus."

Kerry looked up from the desk where she was sitting, licking a croissant crumb off her lip before she spoke. "No luck?"

"No luck." Dar confirmed. "I'm getting nowhere with that bastard." She sighed. "He told me to go talk to our lawyer."

"Ew."

"Which I can do, but it's not going to get that conduit moved and he knows it."

Kerry got up and carried Dar's sandwich over with her. She sat down on the desk her partner had taken, and unwrapped her lunch, offering her a neatly cut half. "Here."

Dar stuck out her lower lip in a pout. "I'm mad."

Kerry broke off a corner of her sandwich and presented it to the lip. "Have some lunch."

Dar accepted the tidbit and munched a little on Kerry's fingertips in the bargain. "So now what do we do?" She swallowed. "I'm gonna end up having to pay a goddamned electrician to come in here and move that thing, aren't I?"

More expenses. "Well, do we have a choice?"

"Sure." Dar leaned to one side and put her head down on Kerry's leg, despite the wide open door. "We can blow this joint and go out on a sunset cruise. How about it?"

Kerry produced a sound somewhere between a groan and a sigh. "Honey, don't tease me like that." She smoothed one of Dar's dark brows with her index finger. "Should I call the guy we use at the office? The electrician, I mean?"

Dar reluctantly lifted her head and reached over for the rest of her sandwich. "I guess." She took a bite. "He's pretty good, and maybe he'll do us a favor this one time." She glanced up at Kerry. "Especially if you ask him. He likes you."'

Kerry's brow twitched. "Oh, I don't think he especially likes me."

"Yes, he does."

"Dar."

"He does." Dar insisted, with a slight grin. "He asked Maria, way back when, if you were available."

Kerry blushed, scrunching her face up and covering it with one hand as she turned a bright reddish pink color. "Don't tell me that."

Dar chuckled. "Why? He's not bad looking."

"I know. But now I have to go ask him to do a favor, and I'm going to feel so weird." Kerry explained. "What, ah, what did Maria tell him?"

"Hm, let me think." Dar chewed on her sandwich, apparently pondering the question. "How detailed—hm."

Kerry closed her eyes. "God."

"I think she just said no." Dar relented, nudging Kerry's knee with her elbow. "C'mon, this is Maria. Do you really think she'd chatter away about us in front of some scrungy guy in carpenter's pants?"

"I didn't think she'd dump chili on someone." Kerry looked

mollified, however, and she continued eating her sandwich, swinging her legs a little. She glanced at Dar after a quiet moment. "How's your foot feeling?"

Dar studied her injured foot, encased in a pair of light sneakers as a grudging compromise between her preferred sandals and the boots Kerry had really wanted her to put on for protection. "It," she wiggled her toes, "it's okay."

"Hm."

"How's your hand?" Dar tried some misdirection.

Kerry wiggled her fingers. "It's okay." She mimicked, raising an eyebrow. "Tell you what. How about you take those wet sneakers off for a while and I'll see what I can do to get my electrician friend over here to solve your problem. How's that?"

Dar put her head back down on Kerry's leg and exhaled, warming her skin even through the thick denim. "I love you." She announced with casual honesty. "Whatever you want to do sounds great to me."

Caught a little off guard Kerry put her sandwich down and took a moment to catch her breath. She gazed down into Dar's eyes and found herself lost in them. She reached out and gently cupped Dar's cheek, the intensity broken only when the sound of a few staff members approaching made them straighten up and sent Dar back into her slouched position in the chair.

Dar took a bite of her sandwich, chewing it in silence.

"Oh, there you are." Edith came in, spotting Dar in the chair. "The catering company wants to know what time we want dinner brought in."

"What are they bringing?" Dar asked casually. "Please don't tell me pizza again."

"Oriental smorgasbord."

The mixed cultural metaphor almost made Kerry do a mental double take. But her brain was really too busy dealing with hormones, and the sweet flush of emotion brought on by Dar's unexpected romanticism. She knew she was still blushing, and so she was glad she had her back to the staff.

Did she care? She suspected strongly that Dar didn't. One glance at the devilish little grin on her partner's face told her that. What about the staff? Kerry collected herself and half turned, peeking at the two women who had just entered.

Neither appeared to notice anything out of the ordinary.

Hm. "How about six and nine." Kerry suggested. "You know how it is with Chinese."

Edith chuckled. "That's not a bad idea." She took the suggestion seriously. "Especially if you all are going to be working on this stuff all night. What if we had them refresh it every couple hours?"

"Sure." Dar finished up her half sandwich. "Make sure they bring in more cases of water, too. It's hot as hell in there." She settled back in her seat and cocked her head at Kerry. "Right?"

"Right." Kerry nearly had to sit on her hands. "Do we know where all those reporters are, by the way? I know Cruickshank is with Mark, but I haven't seen our friend from the Herald."

"She went over to the other ship," Edith said. "I heard her talking to one of the security guards on her way out. She seems pretty nice."

"Hm." Kerry had her doubts.

"I'll message Mark and find out what they're up to," Dar told her. "Any word from the server bunch?"

Kerry got up and went back to the other desk. She sat down and picked up her radio, keying it and pausing briefly to compose her thoughts before she spoke. Her eyes wandered a little, meeting a pair of blue ones across the office, and after a second, she un-keyed the radio and let it drop to her lap, completely distracted.

Jesus.

Dar stuck her tongue out a little, just the tip of it. Then she pulled her laptop over and focused her attention on it, leaving Kerry to communicate in peace. As it happened, she had an email from the Army bastard, so it gave her a good excuse to stick her nose into her screen and read it.

"Ah, Mark. You there?"

She could hear the slight huskiness in Kerry's voice, and it made her smile, and that was a good thing, because the email certainly wasn't making her do anything of the sort. Damn Army bastard. "No, I won't be available for a meeting tomorrow. Or the next day. Or next week." She grumbled under her breath.

"Right here, boss." Mark replied. "What's up?"

"How's it going upstairs?" Kerry watched Dar scowl, her eyes narrowing as she started to rattle out a response to whatever she was reading.

"Great!"

Kerry turned her eyes to the radio, shaking it a little. "What?"

"Great." Mark repeated. "We made some really cool friends!"

Huh? "Want to, ah, explain that?" Cool friends? Last time she'd been inside the ship it had been filled with hot, somewhat ill-smelling workers who were mostly cursing and giving them dark looks. What the hell had Mark done, have a crate of rum craned on to the pool deck?

"Sure." He sounded very cheerful. "We only needed one of those AC units in the server space, so we loaned the other one out to the bridge on the ship. They're like, loving us to death right now."

"Oh really."

"No kidding," Mark said. "Man, I thought those guys up there never smiled. I was way wrong. I think the big guy with all the stripes just invited me to become a part of his family."

Ahhhh. "I see." Kerry had to smile, and she heard a soft, reluctant chuckle from Dar's direction. "How are the servers doing? Barry get them up yet?"

"Eh." Mark made a verbal shrug. "He was muttering something about active directory when I was up there a minute ago. Least we lost our shutterbugs."

Uh oh. "We did?"

"Yeah, they filmed the boxes coming up, then took off."

Well, that could be a good thing, or a bad thing. With the luck they'd been having so far, Kerry wasn't betting on a good thing. "Okay." She sighed. "Let me know if anything else happens. I've got to go see a man about a pipe."

Silence. "Uh..."

"Literally."

"Right, later, boss."

Kerry put the radio down, and switched to her PDA. She opened it and scanned through her phone book listings, selecting one and then dialing it on her cell phone. "Dar?"

"Uh?"

"Please invent a gizmo that gets mail, lets me talk, and keeps track of my addresses at the same time." Kerry cleared her throat. "Hello, Pete? Hi. It's Kerry Stuart, from ILS?"

"Before or after I change the nature of Internet hacking for you?" Dar inquired, one brow hiking up.

Kerry gave her a sweet, loving look and a wink.

Dar snorted, and shook her head, going back to her mail but not before catching Edith peeking at her with an almost amazed expression. "Problem?" she asked, raising both eyebrows.

"No, ma'am." Edith turned around and went back to whatever it was she was doing.

Dar suspected she was well and truly blowing her image. Ah well. She suspected she might grow to like the new image better anyway. It seemed more fun. She opened her next mail, and, with a sigh, started to answer it.

Chapter Three

KERRY FOUND A spot near the window and amused herself by watching a bird trying very hard to fly against the rain. It was a seagull, and she reckoned it really should have known better, yet there it was flapping and flapping and going absolutely nowhere against the stiff wind.

She felt a certain kinship with it. Her cell phone rang and she answered it, hoping it was decent news. "Kerry Stuart."

"Well, hi there, Kerry, it's Pete."

Ah. Fifty-fifty chance. "Hi, Pete." Kerry responded. "Am I going to get lucky today?'

The man laughed. "Oh, ain't that a loaded question. Ah, yeah, listen, I got one of my guys, Guillermo, and he's gonna come over there and help you out. Be about a half hour, he's just finishing up some stuff in your building right now."

Well, what do you know? "Great." Kerry responded. "I don't think it'll take him long. Pete. It's just a junction box. In fact, if he just moves it, and runs an extension line down, and puts it right back, that's fine too."

"Whatever you need him to do, Kerry, you go ahead and ask him. I told him to just do whatever you say." Pete told her. "Okay?"

"More than okay. You definitely came through for us, Pete. I owe you one." Kerry winced a little as she said it, wishing her partner had kept Pete's romantic inquiries to herself. "These guys here are completely unprofessional."

"Johnson? Yeah." Pete made a clucking sound of professional censure. "I've had to come in and clean up a lot of their jobs. I think they got in some legal trouble with the city, surprised they're out there."

"Trust Quest to hire the very best." Kerry muttered. "Well, anyway..."

"Hey, listen," Pete said, suddenly. "You don't owe me anything, Kerry. Your boss stood up for me plenty when some of them others wanted to bring in their relatives and whatever to work your place. Consider it a payback."

Kerry smiled at her reflection in the window. Then she glanced up to find Dar's slouched form in the same reflection. "Well, you know, she stands by people who stand by her."

"You got that right." Pete agreed. "Anyway, I'll try to drop by in a little bit, make sure everything's okay. See you later."

"See you later." She turned and got up, walking over to where Dar was sitting and dropping a hand to her partner's shoulder. "We're all set."

Bright blue eyes flicked up to study her. "Yeah?"

"He's sending a guy over." Kerry confirmed, with a smile.

"All right. Good job." Dar complimented her. "So what's next?" She set her laptop aside and gave Kerry her full attention. "Network is in, right?"

"Right." Kerry said.

"Servers in?"

"Eh." Kerry waggled her hand. "I hear there are some integration issues."

"When isn't there?" Dar asked rhetorically. "I swear, even when they pre-load those damn things, just looking at them the wrong way while booting up blows a driver."

"Mm." Servers were something she was, in fact, more familiar with than her partner. Since the company she'd come from had been primarily an applications developer, Kerry had spent a lot of time working with the intricacies of the devices, and their related operating systems. "Well, I'll go take a look at them and see what the deal is."

"And then," Dar glanced at the rain, "can we start moving all the rest of this mess in?"

"I don't know. From what I saw on my last walk through there, I don't..."

Dar got up from her seat. "C'mon. Let's go take inventory of where we are." She started off toward the door, latching on to Kerry's sleeve and pulling her along. "If we can't install today, I want to get everyone back in here, and just line all that stuff up."

"Okay." Kerry amiably allowed herself to be towed across the carpet. "Are we going to stop for an umbrella, or are you going to thrill and shock the staff when we get there?"

Dar stopped. "Hm." She glanced down at her now dry t-shirt, and then looked at Kerry.

"Nope. Can't borrow my shirt." Kerry shook her head solemnly.

"Hah. You always take mine." Dar protested.

"Dar." Kerry stood back, indicated herself, then looking pointedly at Dar. "How silly do you want to look with my shirt on, honey?"

"Hm." Dar looked speculatively at her, as though considering the question in due seriousness. "It'd just look like a crop top." She held her hand just below her rib cage. "Aren't those trendy now?"

"Oh, that'll help." Kerry started laughing. "I can see explaining it to Mari now, you fashion slave, you."

"Well, it's better than my wet see through act." Dar sighed, and looked around. "Damn it, I forgot to bring my bag in from outside, too. I had a change in there." She gave the room an annoyed glare. "Remind me to have them bring over a couple cases of those tacky t-shirts Jose ordered for the trade show."

"We should make our own departmental ones." Kerry said. "With Gopher Dar on them."

Dar looked at her, brow arching sharply.

"Well." Kerry turned around and surveyed the big room. Instead of stacks of network gear, now the techs were pulling computers and the touch screen point of sale systems out of their boxes. Bits of shredded Styrofoam were drifting around on the carpet, and the scent of new hardware was very sharp in the air. "How about we help unpack things, until the rain slows down."

Dar's expressive face scrunched into an engaging scowl.

"Okay. Want to maybe work on budgets?" Kerry tried a different route. "Or, hey... you can help me put together the pricing for those guys in New York."

Dar put her hands on her hips, exhaling noisily.

"Want to run away and join the circus?" Kerry mimed carrying a backpack. "We could train elephants."

Finally, Dar started chuckling. "Sorry." She sighed. "I don't know what's wrong with me today. I've been antsy as a turkey in November." She leaned back against the glass and stuck her hands into her pockets. "I just want this whole damn thing to be over with. I'm tired of it. I'm tired of this stinking building, and that rust bucket outside, and this damn rain."

Kerry chose a spot next to her and claimed it, leaning back also and hooking her thumbs into her belt loops. "Want to go back to the office? I'm sure you could get stuff done there."

"Trying to get rid of me?"

"No, hon. I'm just trying to make you a little happier." Kerry pressed her shoulder against Dar's. "Since you won't run away to the circus with me." She turned her head and looked outside. "Or, to hell with it. Let's just get wet. I like you in a see through shirt. Hell with the rest of the staff."

Dar's shoulders relaxed and she chuckled again but this time with a far more casual tone. "Nah," she said. "Give me a minute, and we can go cut up some cardboard. My damn jeans are still damp and I don't really want that to get any worse."

Kerry patted one of her partner's thighs, and grunted. "Yeah, they sure are," she said. "I hope you don't catch cold in the air conditioning in this place."

Dar grimaced. "Me, too," she said. "That would suck."

"Mm. But I'd get to make you chicken soup." Kerry found a typically silvered lining in the thought. "And you'd get a chance to stay home and work on your new model."

The both reflected on the rain drumming at their backs against the glass. Finally, Dar straightened up and removed her hands from her pockets. "Okay."

"Over it?"

"Yeah." Dar headed for the stack of PC boxes with a determined, if limping, stride.

Kerry jogged to catch up, as a crack of thunder rattled the air behind her

THE RAIN FINALLY stopped near sunset. Dar and Kerry went out onto the dock, and met a group of the techs including Barry and Mark as they came off the ship. They stood in the middle of the open space with the still damp air moving over them.

"How's it going?" Kerry asked.

"Okay." Barry shrugged. "I mean, the boxes are coming up, but we knew they would."

Dar's eyebrows lifted skeptically

"We can't really do much until we get the end units in, though." Mark added. "And start testing all that interfacing crap." He hefted his backpack. "I wanted to keep going, but they've got some kind of special stuff going on tonight. They chased us off."

Kerry put her hands on her hips. "Wait, that wasn't supposed to happen."

"No." Barry pointed down the dock. "But they're all doing it. I heard them talking."

They turned and looked where he was pointing, seeing streams of workers coming off the next ship down. Loud, yet indistinguishable voices rang out as the men poured through the gates, some shooting rude hand gestures at the ships.

"Damn." Kerry exhaled. "That sucks. If we could just keep going, we'd just about catch up from yesterday."

Barry nodded. "I don't want to hang out in there, but you're right, Kerry. Things went really good today." He glanced at Mark. "Right?"

"Yeah."

"Did the electrician take care of that connection?" Kerry asked Mark. "I saw him pass the back doors."

"Yep." Mark appeared pleased. "Not just that, but he did a bunch of other stuff for us. Good guy. He's from the office, isn't he?"

"Yeah." Dar murmured her brow furrowed in thought. "What did they say this special thing was?"

The techs were quiet. "I don't think they really exactly said." Barry admitted. "Some nautical thing or something?"

Dar headed for the gangway. "I'm going to go talk to the captain. See what I can find out about the nautical thing." She called back over her shoulder. "Stay here. Don't let anyone leave yet."

They all watched her head up the ramp before Mark shook his head. "That captain guy was okay with us, but man, he was not messing with wanting us all out of there. Hope he doesn't chew her head off. He looked like he could be a bastard."

"Not if he knows what's good for him." Kerry excused herself and started after Dar. "Besides, Dar's a nautical sort of person too maybe they'll hit it off."

Barry shook his head. The other techs remained prudently silent. "Didn't DR say for everyone to stay here?" The server manager asked.

Everyone, with the exception of the now missing Kerry, rolled their eyes and headed for the terminal building.

"She did, I heard her." Barry protested, following them. "Won't she get mad?"

"Man." Mark held the door for the group. "You deserve to be an MCSE."

"What?"

DESPITE THE LINGERING stench, and the clutter of tools and materials everywhere, Dar found the ship much more appealing with most of the workers off of it. Now that twilight was in the offing the oppressive heat had dissipated. As she strode through the central atrium she could see signs that all the work was having some kind of effect at least.

The floors had been mostly redone, and bright rounds of carpet were inlaid between circles of newly polished marble. The railings had been resurfaced with a new coating of brass and the curved reception desks sported handsome teak inlays.

Dar started up the center steps feeling just a touch better about the project. Their systems were in, and the staff was working well. All she needed was to keep the momentum going. She looked around as she climbed upward, seeing only one or two of the workmen heading quietly in the other direction.

By the time she reached the deck where the ship's bridge was, she was quite alone. All the hammering and noise of construction had stopped and as she walked along the plastic covered carpet. Dar could see a slow veneer of modernism creeping over the aged surfaces.

It was like an eighty year old woman getting a radical facelift.

That threw Dar's mind onto a different track, and she pondered over it as she walked down the long corridor that would eventually take her to the front of the ship, and the bridge. Eleanor had revealed to them all at their last meeting that she was taking a few weeks off to go get herself 'done.'

Everyone had accepted this, and congratulated her, except for Dar. Dar had been a bit puzzled as to why the woman would want to spend ten or fifteen thousand dollars to have invasive surgery just to look like someone had stretched saran wrap over her face.

She just didn't get it. So then, Eleanor had, with some justified exasperated snarkiness, reminded her that as the youngest person in the room, to please shut up until it was her turn to be ancient.

So that brought her to thinking about what she'd do when she did become ancient. Would she take Eleanor's route and get 'done'? Outside her immediate laughter at the thought, she'd found a touch of insecurity in wondering if Kerry would want her to...would want them to try to hang on to youth with tenacious claws right up until they qualified for Medicare.

Logically, she didn't think so. Dar continued down the corridor, glancing ahead to where the walls started to narrow as she approached the front of the ship. But you never knew, really, how people would change over the years. Maybe Kerry's thoughts would change. Maybe hers would.

Dar's nose wrinkled in displeasure.

She didn't really think hers would. Just the thought of her parent's reaction to her getting a facelift was enough to make her run in the other direction hollering like a banshee. But, she decided, as she got to the end of the hall and faced the door to the bridge, if Kerry decided she wanted to do something like that, and it was important to her...

Well, then, she'd at least think about it.

Dar tested the door latch and found it locked. She knocked on it lightly.

Hopefully, neither of them would turn into vain harridans as they got older. Dar sighed, and knocked again. Hopefully they'd just enjoy a long life together and take life's changes as they came.

The door opened, and she was faced with a man in a starched white uniform and a very unfortunate toupee. "Yes?" He asked gruffly.

"I'd like to speak with the captain, please." Dar decided to mind her manners, at least for now.

The man glared briefly at her, then, surprisingly, backed up and opened the door all the way. "Come in."

Dar stepped inside. The bridge was relatively small, but probably twenty degrees cooler than the hallway and there were several men inside enjoying it. They turned and looked at her as she entered, watching her curiously.

Dar returned the attention, picked out the oldest guy with the most stuff on his sleeves and walked over to him. "Captain?"

He was, perhaps, sixty years old with silver gray hair and shrewd eyes. "Yes?" He responded politely. "What can I do for you Madame?"

Madame? "I'd like to discuss your plans for this evening," Dar said.

Several of the other men chuckled as the captain raised his eyebrows at her. "I am sorry, Madame, do I know you?" he inquired. "I do not believe we have met."

"We haven't." Dar turned and pointed at the air conditioning unit. "But I own that."

The smiles disappeared from the officers' faces replaced by looks of apprehension.

"So, can we talk?" Dar turned again to the captain, easing her words with a smile. "I solved a problem for you; maybe you can do the same for me."

The captain looked doubtful, but he stood and gestured toward a small office at the rear of the bridge. "By all means." He waited for her to precede him. "But it will have to be done quickly, as we are preparing to remove the gangways and you must be off the ship."

The door to the bridge opened as they got to the office, and the staff captain entered. He took one look at Dar and his eyes started to emit sparks, but she stepped past him, and the captain closed the door to the office before he could speak.

Probably a good thing. Dar found herself inside a closet smaller than the head in the Dixie. The captain seated himself behind his desk, and she took the rickety chair in front of it, turning it around and sitting on it with her arms resting on the back.

They looked at each other in silence for a moment. The captain steepled his fingers. "Madame, I don't know what it is you think I can do for you, but please, be quick in asking," he said. "We have little time."

Dar glanced around. "We're the ones with little time, Captain. You've got plenty of it, since you're not going anywhere."

A faint smile crossed his face. "But you are wrong. We are going somewhere. We are leaving, casting the lines, and removing ourselves from this port."

Dar blinked. "Now?"

"Exactly now." The man nodded. "So as you can see, we really cannot help you. I would..." he cleared his throat, "like to thank you with all my heart for the loan of your piece of machinery. It has made it so comfortable for us today."

"I thought you weren't leaving until Friday." Dar tapped her thumbs on the chair. "So this is over? The renovations?"

The captain lifted his hand. "Not exactly. We are leaving, yes," he admitted, "but we will be coming back. It is just that the government people, the..." he cleared his throat again, "they insist we move away so they can examine the water damage, or so they say."

"Ah."

"Is that all?" the captain asked. "I do really have many things to do."

Damn, damn, damn. Dar thought fast. "What would it take to get you to let us go with you?" she asked. "My crew."

The man blinked at her. "It is impossible."

"Why?"

"You are not authorized to sail on the vessel." The captain spluttered. "I cannot be responsible for all of you to be on the ship. It's insanity."

Dar leaned forward a trifle, her eyes narrowing a bit and the more feral part of her personality flexing its paws and extending sharp claws just the tiniest amount. "What would it take, Captain?" She held his gaze with hers. "Name your price."

For a moment, he merely looked at her. "You insult me, Madame." He responded stiffly, then hesitated just enough. "I do not even know who you are."

Dar removed her wallet, opened it, and retrieved one of her business cards. She tossed it on his desk. "That's who I am." She fished in the wallet and removed something else. "And I'm not a stranger to the water." She tossed over a small square of well laminated cardboard, her captain's license with its surprisingly old issue date.

The man picked up both and examined them.

"Look," Dar said. "That blowout yesterday put us behind. I just need the time to catch up. My people need to get things onto this ship, put them in places, and make sure they work. It's better for us to do it without the rest of the circus onboard, and I'm willing to pay for the privilege."

The captain tapped both cards on his desk. "All right," he said. "I will accept your offer, but here is what I want." He slapped his hand on the desktop. "You cannot buy me, woman. I am not for sale."

Dar waited.

"But my crew on this ship, they have been screwed by these people. We have had nothing but canned garbage since we have gotten here." He stood. "You bring on to this ship a meal, some good drinks, some comforts for my crew, you can stay."

It was absurd. Dar almost felt like crying. It was like finding a clean spot in the middle of a garbage heap. "No problem." She managed to say. "Give me an hour."

"An hour?"

"An hour." Dar stood also and extended her hand. "Deal?"

The captain reached over and took her hand, squeezing it powerfully. "We have a deal," he said. "You have how many people?"

"Thirty—one." Dar mentally counted. "You?"

"Two hundred."

"Done deal." Dar released his hand. "See you in an hour." She turned and opened the door, drawing it back and gracefully gesturing him to go first. Then she followed him outside and headed for the door, not forgetting to give the staff captain a smile as she passed.

"WE'RE GOING TO what?" Kerry stared at Dar's back, as she trotted past her on the stairwell. "Dar!" She turned and bolted after her partner, catching up to her and grabbing the back of her jeans. "Whoa!"

Dar halted and turned around. "Yeees?" Her eyes twinkled mischievously. "C'mon, Ker. You wanted to ride on the thing, didn'cha?"

"Are you serious?" Kerry asked. "The ship's really leaving?"

Dar nodded. "EPA's asking them to move so they can review the water." She explained. "So they're taking off, that's why they kicked everyone out." Tugging Kerry's belt loop, she started to move down the steps again. "I got the captain to agree to let us stay on, but we've got a ton of prep to do and only an hour left to do it in."

"So, we're going."

Dar gave her a sideways glance. "We're going."

"On the ship."

Dar stopped. "Ker, you need a cup of espresso or something?" She asked curiously. "You're not usually this slow."

Kerry gave her a poke. "*You* are the woman who chased me down on this thing the first day and wanted to carry me off over your shoulder because you were afraid it would sink. Now you want to sail on it?"

Had she done that? Dar frowned, and then her brows lifted. She had. "Well, they've had time to stuff silly putty in the holes." She temporized. "Anyway, they're not going that far."

They both started down the steps together. "All the staff?" Kerry asked.

"Yeah." Dar nodded again. "But the price was that I've got to get the catering guys in here and feed the crew." She pulled out her cell. "Hope they're up for it."

"The crew?"

"The caterers." Dar punched a number in. "Get our guys ready to start moving everything in sight onto the ship. Just dump it in the hold and we'll hump it upstairs later."

"Hm." Kerry skipped a few steps to keep up with Dar's powerful strides. "Think your dad wants to come along? I think he can carry a few PC's in each hand."

"He might have left already."

They got to the bottom of the steps and entered the shipping hold, stopping as they spotted Andrew seated on a crate, kicking his heels against it. "Guess not," Dar said. "Hi, Dad."

"Howdy, Dardar." Andrew greeted her amiably. "Whatcha up to?"

"Hey Dad." Kerry went right up to him and put her hands on his knees. "Guess what?"

"Wall." Andy considered. "I guess that this here boat's fixing to leave," He said. "Heard them kicking over those mules back there." He thrust his thumb over his shoulder. "Thought they were staying till Friday."

"They're making them leave to check the oil leak," Dar explained.

"Ah." Her father nodded. "Figured."

"Was that mom's idea too?"

Andrew scratched his jaw, and gave his daughter a mildly sheepish look. "Ah do not believe she had anything to do with that this time," he said. "So y'all going home?"

"Nope." Kerry smiled. "We're going on the ship."

Andrew stared at her, then looked past her to where Dar was lounging against the wall. "Ya'll are joshin' me."

Dar shook her head. "No. We're behind the rest of them. This was the only way we could catch up. All of us are going." She watched her father's face. "Wanna come with us?"

"Hell yes." Andrew snorted. "If you think I'm letting you kids out on this here crate by yourselfs you have lost your minds."

Kerry leaned over and kissed him on the cheek. "You're so sweet." She grinned, then headed for the gangway. "I'll get the guys going, Dar. I'm glad they all brought a change today."

Dar's cell phone rang, and she answered it. "Steven?" She listened. "Yeah, it's Dar Roberts. Listen, I've got a very big job for you, I'll pay premium for it, but it's got to happen in less than an hour." She listened again. "I am nuts, but I want it anyway."

Andrew pulled out his own phone and studied it, then selected a sequence of numbers with studied precision.

"Okay, here's what it is," Dar said. "I need a class A dinner, the works, with alcohol, for two hundred and fifty people, delivered to the pier."

"Cec?" Andy spoke into the phone. "You ain't gonna believe this."

"Steven, don't give me bullshit. Either you can do it, or I'll find someone who can." Dar was perfectly well aware of the fact that she couldn't find a caterer in under an hour and she knew their regular guy knew that as well. "Hell, I'll get Hooters to cater it if you can't. They're close, and I bet their serving staff's cuter than yours."

"Yeap, ah surely am." Andrew half listened to Dar. "Ain't no way...huh?"

"Okay." Dar felt relieved. "Don't skimp, Steve. Some of these guys have been living on Spam for three weeks. They deserve it."

"Cec..."

"Tell me about it. I've been kicking a time clock in the ass all week." Dar argued. "Look..."

"Now, you just hold on there a minute, ma'am!" Andrew sounded slightly exasperated. "Ah don't—"

"Full bar, not that jug wine crap you brought to the office."

"Ceci, you cannot just walk in this here place."

"Mine? I don't, wait, yeah, make sure you have Corona, and a case of limes. We set?"

"Yes, ma'am, ah will be here." Andrew sighed, and closed his cell phone.

"Thanks." Dar folded her phone, at the same time as her father did. They looked at each other. "This is gonna be a circus. We're going to end up with Kentucky Fried Chicken and a keg of Budweiser."

"Your mama's headed this way," Andrew said. "So ah do hope that there chicken comes with them little cartons of coleslaw or she's gonna starve to death."

Dar chuckled wearily, limping over to the crate and taking a seat next to her father. "Wonder when the dancing bear shows up." Kerry could more than handle getting the troops together, she reasoned. No sense in both of them stirring up trouble.

Andrew chuckled softly. "You figure t'get this all squared away tonight?"

Dar exhaled. "Well, we'll get further than we would if we didn't try it," she admitted. "There's still so much construction going on it's hard to say how far we'll get, but...hey. Gotta try."

"Damn straight." Her father agreed.

"Speak for yourself." Dar answered dryly.

Andrew looked at her, then chuckled again. "How's that foot?" He nudged Dar's calf.

"Eh." Dar regarded her foot. "I think it's getting better. Hurts less."She glanced out the open gangway door where she could already see a cluster of people and boxes starting to head their way at a double march. "You wouldn't believe the crazy ass stories those people came up with as to how it happened, though."

"Yeah?"

"Mm." Dar shook her head. "I tell one person I got bit by a fish running after a Frisbee at the cabin, and the last I heard I'd gotten it saving Kerry from a shark."

Andrew laughed. "Jungle talking. Always does it."

"Jesus."

Kerry jogged up the gangway and into the hold. "Okay, everyone's with the program." She announced. "And would you believe it, Dar? They're all excited as kids." She came over to where they were sitting. "I told them they had to work all night and go out on this tub and it was like I'd announced the quarter bonuses." She rested her hand on Dar's thigh. "Just weird."

"For them it's an adventure." Dar smiled.

"For us it's an adventure too." Kerry retorted. "Dar, do you know how much work we have to do tonight?"

Dar nodded. "I know." She circled Kerry's waist with her left arm.

"Ah can help." Andrew offered. "I got me some books on all these things you brought in here."

"On our stuff?" Kerry asked.

"Yeap."

"And you read them?" Dar looked at her father. "Jesus, Dad...six pages and I'm snoozing with those damn things."

Andrew waggled his hand and managed a lopsided grin.

"Well, that's probably more experience than some people we've hired." Kerry headed for the gangway as the first load of gear started up. "C'mon guys...we don't want the ship to sail without us, right?"

"Right." The chorus of voices answered her.

Dar sat back and watched as the line of people and boxes started to stream onto the ship. Eyes moved in her direction, and she saw the hesitant grins appear before the techs went to drop their boxes off near the far wall and head back for the next load. "You guys ready for this?" she asked.

"You bet, ma'am." Carlos replied, with a bright smile. "This is gonna be cool."

Oh yeah. Dar found herself smiling back, almost unconsciously. Cool. It was going to be a mess. It was going to be annoying, and aggravating, and frustrating.

"Ah do believe that feller might be correct." Her father commented. "Ah do like this sorta mess to get fixed up."

And very possibly her angle to success. "You got it." Dar got up off the crate and gathered up her energy. "Let's do this thing." She walked to the edge of the gangway and looked out, craning her head around and peering down at the ship Telegenics was outfitting.

She spotted Michelle and Shari on the dock talking with Quest. Shari was moving her arms a lot, and even from where she was, Dar could sense the heated nature of the discussion.

Would they notice the steady stream of equipment heading to her ship? Dar started down the gangway. "Be right back." She called over her shoulder.

"Where are you going?" Kerry yelled after her.

"To make some trouble." Dar replied, hopping off the end of the ramp and heading down the dock. "Keep my crate warm!"

"Uh oh." Kerry drummed her fingers against the rusted steel plate. Torn, she half turned as one of the techs called out to her, asking a question. She stared at him, then held up one finger. "Hold that thought."

"Ma'am?" The tech queried, watching as his boss disappeared down the ramp at a high rate of scamper. "Hey, where's she going?"

"T'where she belongs." Andrew got up and went over to him. "Here, put that thing there, and that other box sideways, son. Ain't no way that's gonna fit otherwise."

"Uh..."

Andrew cocked an eyebrow at him. "Y'all ain't gonna make me mad, are you?"

"No, sir." The tech scurried to do as he'd been told.

"Damn straight." Andrew leaned against the wall, with a satisfied expression.

"DAR!" KERRY SCRAMBLED off the gangway just as another group of techs reached it. She pointed up, and then went after Dar, catching up to her in a few strides. "Hey."

"Hey." Dar replied. "Thought I told you to keep my crate warm."

"You seriously thought I was going to stay there?"

"Not really, no." Dar admitted.

"Well, okay then." Kerry settled down at her side and they walked along the pier toward their erstwhile enemies. She'd started putting Quest into that category lately, and based on the glare he gave them as they walked up she suspected she was dead on right. "Evening." She greeted them cordially.

"Ms. Stuart." Quest responded, in a brief tone.

Dar strolled around them and stopped to their east, forcing them to turn to keep her in view. "Another challenge you tossed us, Mr. Quest?" she asked. "At this rate, I figure the bomb squad to show up next."

Surprisingly, Michelle chimed right in. "Just exactly what I was saying. You can't expect to keep changing the rules, and have us pay for it."

"Right," Shari said.

"They aren't my rules!" Quest lifted his hands. "I can't do anything about these damn government people! I told you that."

"So what are we supposed to do?" Shari asked, her hand indicating Dar and Kerry as well as herself and Michelle. "You get in government trouble, and we have to pay for it? Hell no."

Dar and Kerry exchanged somewhat bemused glances.

Behind them all, the techs had started toting in cartloads of monitors, terminals, and boxes of the various accoutrements computers require.

"Ah, that's right." Kerry spoke up. "Mr. Quest, we really can't be expected to be penalized because of all these external factors. It's not fair."

"Right." Michelle agreed.

Having nothing else to add to the conversation, Dar decided to just fold her arms across her chest and listen.

"Well, I can't be held responsible either!" Quest argued. "A deal is a deal. You want the contract? Then fulfill your part of the deal."

He turned and stalked off, heading for the gate in the fence that would take him outside of the pier area. Outside the wire, three men were waiting, and as Dar looked at them, one turned away and almost triggered a sense of familiarity in her.

"Well." Michelle exhaled. "So much for that." She eyed Dar and Kerry. "Not that it would have helped you much anyway. Bad luck, huh?"

Dar shrugged one shoulder. "Happens."

Shari looked at her. "What drugs are you on today?"

Kerry felt herself bristle, and wondered if it was a visible reaction. Did her hair fluff out like a cat's, maybe? Certainly, Michelle edged away from her, so something must have shown.

"Drugs?" Dar asked. "Tetracycline, why?" She unfolded her arms and stuck her hands in her pockets instead. Curiously, Shari's taunting didn't even bother her in the slightest.

"Because for someone who's going to lose big, you're too damn relaxed," Shari said bluntly. "Give up already? Going through the motions, Dar?"

From the corner of her eye, Dar watched as Mark led a group of six other techs out the door to the terminal, steering a huge flatbed covered in gear. "Yeah, maybe." She drawled. "Can't fight fate all the time, can ya?"

Kerry patted her arm comfortingly.

"Well." Michelle ran a hand through her hair. "Not like we can say much at the moment either. I can't believe they made us stop work. It's just not fair."

Shari snorted. "At least we know no one's getting an advantage." She looked at Dar pointedly.

Dar produced one of her best, most innocent smiles, as the last of the gear trundled past behind their backs and went up the gangway. "Nope."

"Doesn't that bug you?" Shari persisted. "Not having an angle?"

Michelle took Shari by the arm and simply turned and started walking. "Come on. I'm not listening to this crap again." She sounded angry. "I've had enough already."

"Hey!" Shari protested, pulling on her hand.

"Either come with me, or stay here and act like a jackass, again." Michelle turned and spat at her. "Make up your mind." She released Shari's arm and started marching for the gate again.

Shari looked at her, then turned and looked at Dar and Kerry.

Never one not to take an advantage when she saw it, Dar draped an arm over Kerry's shoulders and gave her a kiss on the head. She winked at Shari, and smiled.

Without a further word, Shari turned and followed Michelle.

"Mm." Kerry grunted contentedly. "Nice."

"Yeah." Dar turned them both around and pointed. "Nice timing. I don't think they even noticed us taking half the domestic inventory of Computers R Us on board."

"Couldn't care less about that part." Kerry put her arms around Dar and hugged her tightly.

Puzzled, but not unhappy, Dar returned the hug. "You want to grab our bags?" She asked. "Might as well get on there and make sure it's all getting to the right places."

"Sure." Kerry released her, and patted her side. "I'll have the security guys clear the front doors for the caterers, too. I bet they'll come in here on screaming tires."

"Bet you're right." Dar lifted her hand and waved as Kerry made tracks for the terminal. She fondly watched her partner's determined little swagger, then she retreated back to the ship's gangway and climbed up it, noting the angle had increased a little as the tide came in.

The sun had come out too, and it was preparing to grace them with a decently photogenic sunset. Dar gazed benevolently at it, as she ducked inside the hold and found her father organizing the troops. Around them, the ship's crew went about their tasks, giving the techs skeptical looks, but staying out of their way as they dogged down hatches and prepared the ship for sea.

Dar knew those sounds. She'd gotten to sail one or two times on Andy's ships, illicit adventures where the crew would hide her when they went out for a day cruise, or when the ship was repositioning from one pier to the other. The scent of diesel was the same, and the sounds of metal doors being rolled closed and locked was the same.

She wondered if her father found it as nostalgic.

"Hey. You there." Andrew suddenly raised his voice. "Get that box out from that doorway, son. Doors gonna close there and make that a pancake."

"Yes, sir." The tech in question started tugging the box out of the way. "Sorry, I thought this was open space."

"Ain't no open space on a ship," Andy said. "Every little inch's got someone's claim on it."

Dar walked over and joined him, watching the boxes line up against the back wall. "Lot of stuff."

"Ain't that the truth." Her father agreed. "Y'know I can remember when the most techno thing we had on one of these here things was a water fountain." He reminisced. "And wasn't that a six day wonder when they put that in."

"I remember that." Dar recalled, with some surprise. "I brought you a bag of shirts from mom that day. I remember wondering why everyone was staring at that damn fountain like it was a television set."

Andrew chuckled. "Cause sucking that there stuff from the commode sink was not a whole lot of fun, Dardar." He reminded her. "Not everybody liked getting a drink from the hose, neither, like you did."

Dar licked her lips in memory, and produced a grin. "I ever tell you about the first time Kerry took a drink of hose water?"

"Heh." Andrew glanced around at the cramped ship hold. "You know what, Dar?"

"What?"

"It's a hell of a lot better to be the skipper of the damn boat," he said. "I would not go back to doing this if they paid me all the dollar bills in the Navy."

"Hm." Dar remembered those stolid seamen who suffered the cramped spaces and shared their hoarded candy bars with the scruffy child she'd been. "I'm damn glad you'll never have to."

Andrew looked at her, then chuckled. "Darn good thing you went after them computer things, ain't it? Or we'd all be having crackers and peanut butter stew down there in Stiltsville." He clapped her on the shoulder. "Got all the stuff you all need?"

Dar nodded.

"Got a pair of jammies?"

"We don't wear them." Dar replied absently, then shot her father a look as the silence lengthened. "Hey, you asked."

Andrew pointed at the techs. "Got some pills for them fellers?"

Dar peered at them. "Dad, we're just going offshore."

Andrew lifted his grizzled eyebrows.

"I'll go get some." Dar sighed, and headed for the gangway. "No sense in wasting good roast beef."

Chapter Four

KERRY HAD TO admit she felt a little excited. She was standing outside the terminal, checking her watch as she bounced from foot to foot waiting for the caterers. It was close to the time they were supposed to depart, and she didn't want to either miss the ship or miss the dinner. "C'mon, c'mon."

From where she was standing, she could see the bridge that connected the port to the rest of Miami. At this time of night, in this time of the year, it was probably the only major roadway in the vicinity bare of traffic. But that helped Kerry's mental state because she knew she'd see the big catering truck before it got anywhere near the terminal.

If she looked behind her, she could see lights beginning to come on aboard the ship. Dar had their bags inside, and she'd heard rumors that they were being assigned cabins. From the few she'd stuck her head into over the past weeks, Kerry was pretty sure she'd rather sleep on the deck. The musty smell and the grungy interior hadn't seemed appealing in the least, but she did appreciate the ship's attempt at hospitality.

Ah. Her eyes caught a white panel truck cresting the rise and heading in her direction. Unfortunately her peripheral vision also caught Michelle Graver approaching obviously intent on talking to her. "Pig farts." She composed her expression, and half turned, giving the oncoming woman an inquiring look. "Hello again."

"Hi." Michelle mounted the two low steps to the foundation Kerry was standing on and approached her. "Listen, can we talk?"

Kerry watched the truck out of the corner of her eye. "Uh, yeah, sure. We're about to tie things up here but," she drew in a breath, "I've got a minute."

Michelle faced her. "Look, you're screwed."

The truck parked right across from where they were standing and the doors flew open, allowing two sweating men to jump out and run for the back. "What do you mean?" Kerry asked, edging over a little so Michelle was forced to turn her back completely to the truck in order to talk to her.

"C'mon, Kerry. You're not stupid. You were behind a day, and now with this—there's no guarantee when they'll let the ships back into port," Michelle said.

Kerry watched what appeared to be an entire football team worth of men pour out of the back of the truck dragging carts and a whole lot of other things out after them. "And?" She cocked her head slightly. "Forgive me, Michelle, but shouldn't you be kicking back a beer at that? Why talk to me about it."

Michelle sighed. "Look." She ran her fingers through her hair. "None of the other bidders are friends of yours."

"Ah, you are?" Both of Kerry's very blonde eyebrows lifted.

"No. But they aren't either. You don't get anything out of them getting the contract." Michelle said. "On the other hand, if we get it, and you help us get it, maybe you will get something."

The wind was fortunately blowing from behind them. It carried away the noise of the catering men setting up, and almost left them in a sound vacuum. Probably a good thing considering Kerry felt like her sense of moral outrage was caterwauling at the top of its imaginary lungs.

"What exactly are you offering here?" Kerry asked warily.

"This doesn't have to be a losing situation for you," Michelle said. "You know you can't win the bid, hell, I bet you can't even get all your systems working by Friday. It's not your fault."

"Michelle, please cut to the chase." Kerry spotted a line of perspiring caterers heading her way, pushing laden carts. "What exactly do you want from me?"

"Join with us," Michelle said. "You and Dar, and your team. Help us win the bid, and we'll cut a deal with you. There's enough business on this account for both of us."

Kerry looked over at the ships, then at Michelle. "From this guy? C'mon, Michelle. We both know there's something sourer than lemons about this whole thing."

"Not from him." Michelle moved a step closer. "From the rest of the industry. We both know who's watching."

Ah. Kerry backed up a few paces and took hold of the door handle pulling it open as the first of the caterers carts clattered up the cement incline. She half turned to look back at Michelle. "You're serious?"

Encouraged, Michelle moved closer to her, giving the carts a brief look. "Serious as a heart attack. You've proven yourselves. You're a tough adversary, everyone knows it, hell they have it on film. And for the record, I did check that shipment and it did get delivered here by a clueless trucker. So thank you."

"Careful." Kerry cautioned a rushing caterer. "Back there, that's right. Out that door." She indicated the back of the terminal.

"What do you say, Kerry?" Michelle asked.

"Whoops." Kerry put a hand out and steadied one of the women, who gave her a brief nod of thanks. "Let me talk to Dar." She finally responded to Michelle. "I'll tell her what you said, and see what she thinks."

"Can't make up your own mind?" Michelle almost laughed. "Funny, I didn't have you pegged as a bottom."

Kerry's brow creased momentarily. "Dar's my boss," she said. "It's her decision, Michelle. You do realize a Chief Information Officer does outrank a VP, right?"

Michelle just shook her head.

"Anyway, I've got things to do, so I'll have to bid you a good night." Kerry prepared to follow the cavalcade of catering. "Enjoy your night off."

Michelle reached for the door. "What's with all the food?" She asked, since Kerry seemed to be genially ignoring her jibes.

"Dar's hungry." Kerry shrugged and smiled. "Gotta go." She pulled the door shut and locked it, then waggled her fingers at Michelle before she turned and headed for the back door.

Well, she would talk to Dar, and she would tell her what Michelle said. And then, probably, they both would get a good laugh out of it and maybe share a beer.

Okay, maybe not share one. Kerry liked her beer, and if she wasn't mistaken, the last big cart they'd taken through had a distinctive tinkle of bottles in it. She quickly checked their office and found it empty. She locked the door and went to the back where she could now see dock workers preparing to let the ship loose from its moorings. "Uh oh, not without me you don't."

She shoved the back door open and headed for the gangway. At the top of it she saw the last of the catering carts vanishing, and behind them, she spotted Andrew directing traffic.

Just as she was scooting across the pier, she heard a rattle of the fence behind her. Turning, she spotted Ceci on the other side of the locked gate. "Hey!"

"Let me in there!" her mother in law yelled.

Kerry veered, and got to the gate as she spotted two big security men heading their way. She quickly threw the latch and opened it, letting Ceci in as the men started to yell. "Oh oh."

"Oh, please. I've seen more dangerous things than those guards swimming by the boat in the morning." Ceci replied with a touch of testiness. "What is this crazy nonsense about all of you going out on that thing?"'

Kerry took her arm and headed toward the ship. "Can we argue about this onboard? I don't want to tangle with those guys no matter how not dangerous they look."

"Hey! You there! Stop!" The guards broke into a run. "Hold it!"

Kerry broke into a run too, with Ceci right behind her. It was a fairly long stretch of pavement, but they had a shorter distance than the guards and a better angle to the ship.

"Just how I wanted my evening to start." Ceci yelled.

Kerry sucked in a lungful of humid air and just ran faster. She could hear the pounding steps of the guards closing in on them, and she pulled Ceci up by the arm and pushed her ahead toward the ship. "Go go!"

They reached the gangway and bolted up it as Andrew stepped to the edge of the opening and peered out. "What's all that there noise?"

"Us." Kerry scrambled past him, hauling Ceci with her. "The damn punky fake police are after us."

"Hey!" The guard nearest the ship yelled. "Stop!" He pointed at them. "That's an illegal intruder! Stop!" He skidded to a halt as Andrew unclipped the gangway and it swayed. "Hey! Put that back! Hold it! I'm warning you!"

"S'all right, relax!" Andrew uncoiled a rope tied off to the gangway and hooked it securely to a crane hoist dangling nearby. He put his fingers between his teeth and let out a sharp whistle, and after that no one could hear anything because the crane started up and began to hoist the gangway off and away from the ship's side.

"Hey!" The guard mimed, waving his arms. "Stop! Stop! I'll call the police!!"

Andrew waved amiably back at him, then stepped back and cleared the opening. "All right, young fellers. G'wan and close this here." He indicated the hatch.

Ceci backed up against the wall, and Kerry joined her, to stay out of the way. "You know something?"

"What?" Kerry asked, wiping the sweat off her forehead. Her heart was racing, and she felt a little shaky from the unexpected chase, even though she didn't really think the guards were any physical danger to them.

"I've never seen this from this side."

The crewmen unsurprisingly obeyed Andrew, working the various wheels and levers as a counterbalanced steel door slowly moved down and slammed into place with a grinding shudder.

Kerry felt her ears pop, just a little. Now that the outside was closed off, she could smell the scent of diesel and oil much more strongly, and as she watched the crewman mutter something into an aged phone set, she felt the rumble of the engines as they engaged. "So, what do you think?"

"Hate it." Ceci went over to Andrew and put a hand on his arm. "Hey sailor boy."

Kerry's nose wrinkled and she wiped off her forehead again. "Yeah, me too." She sighed. "I'm going to go find Dar." She viewed the milling caterers. "I think...wait." She turned and found one of the crewmen edging past. "Excuse me."

The man looked at her warily. "Yes?"

"This stuff's all for the crew. Where can they put it? Is there a kitchen near the main dining room so, uh..." Kerry watched bemusedly as they were instantly surrounded by crew. "So they can keep it warm for you?"

"For us?" The man asked. "You're kidding, right?"

The crewmembers started peeking into the trays on the cart, whispering to each other in muted excitement.

"Uh, no." Kerry shook her head. "So, is there a place?"

"Sure," the man said. "C'mon, we'll take them to the elevator." He motioned for the caterers to follow him. "Taki, taki, let's go."

"Elevator?" Kerry queried. "They told us it wasn't working."

"Not for anyone but crew." The man cheerfully explained. "Sorry!" He started off leading the carts with many willing assistants. "Hey, is that alcohol?" He rattled the biggest cabinet. "All right!"

Kerry put her hands on her hips, then looked over at Andrew. The big ex-seal shrugged and half grinned at her. "You know something, that's not very goddamned funny," she said. "I had people lifting hundred pound switches up those stairs."

Andrew blinked at her in some mild surprise. The crewman also turned and looked at her.

"I," Kerry pointed at her chest, "paid for all that. So you can take your crew only rules and stuff it up your butt, buddy." She pointed at the crewman, whose eyes widened. "You better rethink that attitude right now!"

"Hey! Hey, relax, okay? It's not my rule!" The crewman stammered, backing off. "You can come on the elevator, okay? Take it easy."

Kerry glared at him, then caught motion in her side vision and turned to see Dar rambling down the last few steps in the stairwell. "Hey."

Dar walked right through the crowd, expecting it to part. It did. "What's going on?" She asked, giving everyone a dirty look. "Did all the food get here?"

One of the caterers came up to her. "Yes, ma'am," the man said, handing her a list. "It wasn't easy, Ms. Roberts."

"Or cheap." Dar reviewed the bill, then handed it to Kerry. "Why were you yelling?"

"Did you know there was an elevator?" Kerry asked. "A working one?"

"No." Dar looked at the nearest crewman. "Is there?"

The man nodded.

"Then get this stuff upstairs." Dar directed. "And let our people all know where it is so they can get the rest of your new computer gear in place."

The man nodded again.

"Scoot." Kerry nudged him. They watched the crowd start to sort out, and the now chastened crewman directed the carts toward a double set of doors at the end of the cargo hold. "Jesus."

Andrew cleared his throat. "Ah do not think they meant to be bad fellers."

"Oh, bull hockey, Andy. They certainly did. I know you seamen. If you don't have twenty voyages under you you're not worth a navy bean." Ceci snorted. "Please!"

Andrew managed a relatively sheepish look.

"You okay?" Dar took the opportunity to attend to more important matters. "Got our space squared away. Want to go see it?" She gave her parents a look. "They've got a room for you guys too."

"Bigger than a twenty four inch rack?" Ceci asked drolly. "Oh, be still my beating heart. I thought we'd camp out on the fantail." She indicated the stairwell. "Let's go watch this thing try to get out of the channel. That could be as entertaining as seeing Jerry Springer in Judge Judy's court."

Kerry squared her shoulders and let the tension flow out of her as she followed Dar toward the door. There would be time later, she hoped, when she could sit down and talk to her partner about what Michelle had said. For now, just the thought of changing her clothes, and relaxing for a little while was very appealing.

"You okay?" Dar asked again, lowering her voice.

Kerry exhaled. "Yeah." She put a hand on Dar's back. "I think I just need a protein bar."

"How about a roast beef sandwich?"

"That'll do." Kerry felt Dar's arm settle over her shoulders, bringing a very welcome comfort despite the humid air. "Matter of fact, yeah, let's go up on the deck. I want to wave."

"At the port?" Dar asked, puzzled.

Kerry merely chuckled, and kept on climbing.

The central atrium was a bit of a mess. Dar and Kerry stopped as they got through the stairway door, watching as their entire group was scrambling around trying to get the computer equipment in some kind of distribution order.

Everyone was sweating. The air inside had started to move around sluggishly, and by the strong scent of musky, musty mildew, Kerry deduced that the long absent air conditioning had been turned on. It wasn't helping much, however.

Mark spotted them and came over, his polo shirt grimy with sweat and dust. "Wow. Just made it, huh? I saw you run on with the chow." He grinned wearily at Kerry.

"You know me and chow." Kerry acknowledged with a droll grin of her own. "Everyone okay?"

"Wiped, but okay," Mark said. "We're gonna get this stuff sorted out, then everyone's gonna take a break and die for a half hour or something. John dragged his dad's cooler on with the gear." He pointed. "It's got ice and drinks in it."

"Good idea." Dar complimented him. "I ordered food for either five hundred normal people or two hundred fifty sailors and us," she said. "They're taking it to one of the big dining rooms. Let's get set up, let everyone relax and maybe go take a shower, then get dinner."

Mark nodded.

"Everyone should get a room." Kerry chimed in.

"Except you and me. We're sharing." Dar reminded her.

"Shucks." Kerry gave her a kindly 'duh' look, then returned her attention to Mark. "Let everyone chill out and get food. We can plan to start up again after that."

"Right." Mark plucked his filthy shirt. "So much for that light blue collar reputation IT has." He remarked.

"Wasn't what they advertised in my school either." Kerry took Dar's hand and they circled the atrium, exiting out the doors onto the deck outside. A breeze caught them, welcome even with its humidity, as they walked over to the railing and stood there, side by side, watching the pier recede.

The sun was setting. This far from the highway, there was no sense of the hectic scramble to get home that would be going on in the city, and over the engines they could hear the call of sea birds coaxing them out, away from the land, out to the sea.

Kerry looked down the pier to where Michelle and Shari's ship was also moving out preparing to follow them down the channel. There was a large cluster of people on the pier, and she wondered if the guards that chased them were part of it.

Would they get in trouble for letting Ceci on? Kerry figured they wouldn't get in any more trouble than they would for staying aboard with the rest of their staff anyway. "It's going to be a nice sunset."

"Yeah." Dar leaned on the railing after cautiously shaking it to test its strength. "Ah. There are our little friends." She mused. "Shari and Michelle. Left at the dock as usual."

Kerry peered down at the pavement. "Wave at them, honey." She lifted a hand and waggled it.

Dar gave her a look, but complied. "Why?"

Kerry watched intently, and smiled as she saw Michelle point at them, grabbing hold of Shari's arm and turning her toward the ship. "Hi there, you two little piles of horse manure." She crooned. *"Hasta la vista, cucarachas."*

Dar snickered. "Don't hold back Ker. It'll give you a hemorrhoid."

Shari pulled free and ran toward the ship, pointing and turning around to yell at the group behind her. This far away, all they could see was the motion, and the frustration in the woman's gestures.

Dar stood up to make sure she was recognizable. She lifted her arm and waved cheerily at them again, then let her elbow rest on Kerry's shoulder. "I think they're a little perturbed, Ker."

Shari turned and found Quest in the crowd. She pointed at him, yelled something, then turned and pointed at Dar's ship.

Quest made a hand gesture then he turned his back to Shari and started toward the gates of the pier, where a group of people had gathered.

"I think they're pooping stalactites, honey," Kerry responded. "Michelle just tried to get us to give up the bid and help them win it instead."

"What?"

The film crew pushed out of the crowd and rushed up to Michelle and Shari with Cruickshank in the lead. Shari turned around and shoved her away then she picked up a piece of pier iron and threw it at the retreating ship.

"Mm hm." Kerry leaned on the railing, almost smiling when she felt Dar's hand immediately settle on her back, her thumb snagging the back belt loop of her jeans to keep her steady. "She figures we can't win, so why not help them, and they'd toss us a few bones afterward."

Dar made a snorting noise.

"I told her I'd talk to you and see what you said." Kerry continued. "She accused me of being a bottom."

Dar started laughing, ending up sliding down the railing to sit on the deck holding her hands over her stomach as she continued to crackup. "Bwahahaha!"

"Dar, get up." Kerry tugged at her sleeve, muffling a laugh herself. "Oh, hurry. I think — look!"

Dar grabbed the railing and pulled herself up, turning around to peer at the port. She could see Shari now facing off against Michelle pointing at her with vicious, sharp motions, the redness of her face visible even from where she was standing.

"Wonder what that's about?" Kerry leaned on the rail next to her, shoulders touching.

Dar merely watched. "Think her head's going to explode?" She asked.

"Oh, I hope so." Kerry replied. "Did you know they're not sure when they're going to let the ships back into the port?"

"Really?" Dar said. "No, I hadn't heard that. Thought they were just coming in. Oh, wait. They couldn't." She changed thoughts. "EPA wouldn't work at night. They need time in the morning."

"Yeah."

"So, we scooped all of them." Dar laughed. "Son of a bitch. All I wanted was to catch up. We could end up ahead of the game."

"Yep." Kerry leaned her head against Dar's shoulder. "Oh, look!" She pointed.

Dar craned her neck, where the crowd of people around Shari suddenly convulsed, and chaos ensued. "Think her head exploded." She observed. "Either that, or she started hauling off on those guards. Or Michelle."

"Mm. Good. That'll make them forget about us." Kerry said. "Guess I owe her a thank you."

"Don't stretch it." Dar warned. "She's probably telling them we're terrorists."

Kerry snorted softly. "Wouldn't it be something if she went off on Michelle? Sometimes I think...you know, I think she projects onto you all the crappy stuff inside herself, Dar."

Dar fell silent, her eyes turning from the pier to her partner's profile.

"People do that, you know." Kerry added quietly.

There was another long moment of silence, and then Dar shifted, leaning over and giving Kerry a kiss on the cheek. "Yes they do, don't they."

"Yep." Kerry agreed. "C'mon. Show me our barracks for the night." She linked her arm with Dar's, but they both stood there watching the dock recede and the chaos with it. "We don't get to do this on our boat." She observed, steering the conversation downstream a little.

"No. I have to steer and that requires looking forward." Dar agreed. "I'd love to watch the sunset with you while we go out, but crashing into a billion bucks worth of motor yachts would just ruin my day."

"Mmm, true. But it's kind of nice." Kerry smiled. "The view, I mean."

Dar drank in the reddening sunlight, watching the glow outline the buildings on the horizon. "Kinda."

Kerry looked down at the churning water, now a somewhat frightening pea soup color from the engines wash. "Ew." She looked at the pier, spotting a group of men in identical dark windbreakers heading for the breakfront, along with some people in regular clothes carrying what looked like equipment. "That the government people?"

"I think so."

"Did mom really call them?" Kerry asked.

"Uh huh." Dar turned and gestured to the door. "We can probably watch the rest of the sunset from our cabin."

"We have a window?" Kerry was surprised. "I mean a porthole?"

Dar grinned. "C'mon."

"Cool." Kerry obediently followed her inside, and across the atrium to the stairwell. "I'm still pissed off about those elevators."

"I know. C'mon." Dar started up the steps. "Look at it this way; at least we get a workout from it."

"Hm." Kerry glanced behind her, satisfied at the progress the team was apparently making in organization. "I ever mention how much I hate the stair stepper?"

Dar chuckled and kept on climbing.

DAR'S CELL PHONE rang as they pushed open the door to the room they'd been assigned. She stood aside to let Kerry go in, and opened it. "Yeah?"

"Ms. Roberts!"

Ah, the Herald. "Yes?" Dar drawled. "What can I do for you?"

"You're on the ship." The reporter almost laughed. "Aren't you?"

"We are," Dar confirmed, entering the cabin and closing the door behind her. "With our team, and our gear, and we're getting a lot done. I'm quite pleased from a business perspective." She smiled. "Anything else?"

"A lot of people are pretty damn ticked off at you," the reporter said. "They're saying dirty tricks."

"Dirty tricks?" Dar's brows contracted. "What's dirty about it? I negotiated with the captain of the ship and got what I wanted. Not my fault they didn't."

"Quest told them they couldn't!"

Dar chuckled. "I never asked him if I could."

Another laugh. "Damn it, you should have taken me with you," the reporter replied. "What a story. See you when you get back."

Dar closed the phone and stood near the door watching Kerry explore their cabin.

It was definitely old. The place had the air of a patrician, yet far outdated and well worn, quality hotel. The fabrics were faded, the teak floors were water stained and in need of a refinishing. The wall bore gilt paper on it that almost visibly exuded trash into the room.

Yet, it had a certain rakish charm. There was a reasonable sized bed in it with clean, if threadbare, linens and a tiny sitting area with two chairs and a low table.

A cramped bathroom was near the door, but near the back was sliding glass panels that led out to what Dar considered to be the saving grace of the thing. A balcony with a view of some wide open spaces, and promised some air movement if nothing else.

Kerry had discovered this and pushed the doors open, sticking her head out and approving. She ducked back inside and faced Dar. "This isn't nearly as bad as I expected," she admitted. "I thought we might be sleeping on the floor, and I wasn't looking forward to it."

"Me either." Dar sat down on the bed and patted a space next to her. Kerry came over and they sat quietly for a minute, absorbing the rumble of the ships engines and the motion that was quite different from their boat.

"The ship moves." Kerry noted.

"It does." Dar concurred.

The sea breeze came in the open balcony doors and refreshed the stale air inside the room. Kerry lowered herself down until she was lying flat on the bed and let her hands drop to her sides. It felt good to be sitting still for a bit after the long day, and despite the fact that the night promised to be even longer, she was glad she was here. "We're going to do this thing, Dar."

Dar lay down next to her and folded her hands over her stomach. "We're going to do this thing." She confirmed. "Come low tides or high seas we're going to."

"They're going to be telling stories about this in the office for the next twenty years, you do realize that." Kerry crossed her ankles, noting the water stains on the ceiling.

"Yeah." Dar eyed her. "And speaking of that, have you heard the latest one about me?"

Kerry's green eyes narrowed, and she turned her head to face Dar. "No. What?" She growled. "So help me, Dar, one of these days I'm going to catch one of these people spreading all this crap and I'm—"

Dar put her hand over Kerry's mouth. "I saved your life from a cute, blonde woman eating shark."'

"Murph?" Kerry looked very surprised.

"Yes." Dar removed her hand. "So, now I'm wondering Kerrison, since I only told Mariana what happened, and I told her the truth, Frisbee and all, exactly how would the office have gotten that idea?" She rolled over and propped her head up on one hand, looking at Kerry inquiringly.

After a brief nibble on the inside of her lip, Kerry gently traced the outline of Dar's jaw with her fingertip. "I didn't say anything about a shark."

The blue eyes took on a twinkle that lent a distinct sweetness to Dar's expression. "Punk."

Kerry grinned impishly. "Hey, who better to spread stories about you than me? At least then I get to like what I hear." She tweaked Dar's nose. "Isn't it good to hear nice things for a change?"

Dar grinned. "Yeah. Shocked the hell out of me, but yeah, it was nice, even though it was an out and out lie."

"Weelll." Kerry waggled her hand. "It could have been true." She ran her fingers though Dar's bangs. "Does that bath-roomette over there have a shower in it?"

"Uh huh."

"Big enough for both of us?"

"No."

"Wanna try it anyway?"

Dar reached over and pulled Kerry into an embrace, rolling over so they ended up in a pile in the center of the bed. "Love to." She kissed Kerry on the lips, tasting a dusting of sea salt on them. "Know what else we never get to do while we're under way?"

Kerry chuckled, a deep, rich sound from her gut that fairly drooled sensuality. Then she paused thoughtfully. "How thick are these walls?"

Dar kissed her again. "I don't care." She ran her hand under Kerry's shirt and cupped her breast. "Least it'll get their minds off sharks."

Too true. Kerry surrendered to the enticing passion, the wound up tension in her easing as an ache of a different kind took its place. The shabby nature of the room became irrelevant as she focused instead on the warm smoothness of Dar's skin and the gentle touch that was gliding over her body.

So what if they had to work all night if the night started off like this?

BY THE TIME they climbed down the forward staircase and approached the dining room, it was well into twilight and the air conditioning had finally started making inroads into cooling the ship down. Dar felt comfortable in her short sleeved shirt and jeans, and after their improbably shared shower she felt refreshed and ready to take on the night.

Trotting along beside her, Kerry appeared to have recovered her energy as well, and was in a good frame of mind as they crossed the threshold and entered the dining hall. Instead of jeans, she'd chosen a pair of carpenter's pants complete with a hammer loop that Dar found almost too cute for words.

A buzz of sound made them both look up, and they realized they were joining a larger crowd than anticipated in surroundings that almost upheld the ship's tarnished glamour.

Dar slowed, and looked around, mildly surprised. The huge room was in better condition than she'd expected, its ceiling reaching up through two decks and the back wall entirely made of glass windows that showed a nice view of the receding Port of Miami.

The carpet was new, apparently freshly installed, and the tables were covered with linen and neatly set with silverware. Along the back side of the room a large buffet line had been set up, and behind that the caterers were busy setting up to serve the food they'd brought with them.

The room was filling up with crew, most of them fairly young, and all of them dressed casually. The atmosphere was relaxed and far friendlier than it had been previously. They had been treated with courtesy while they were onboard, but the crew had made it obvious that they were encroaching on their space.

The ILS staff was in small clusters, mingling warily with the crew and attracting the attention of the women especially. Dar nudged Kerry as Mark was surrounded by a pair of blondes and a brunette. "Think we should rescue him?"

Kerry chuckled. They started walking toward the small group, but then they were spotted and the ILS team started heading toward them at the same time.

It was interesting. Kerry watched the eyes of the crew follow the techs, detecting a touch of envy there. In a way, she could almost see a parallel between the two groups — like the ship employees, her techs had their own hierarchy, and like the officers of the ship, they looked to their leadership for direction, protection, and reassurance.

The big difference, of course, was that the ship's senior officers were all men. She and Dar were decidedly all women.

"Everyone get settled all right?" Dar stopped on the last step down into the hall, waiting as all the techs gathered around her.

"Yeah, pretty much." Mark answered for them. "It's pretty cool. We all got windows." He sounded surprised. "But man, those bathrooms are tiny! If you had your family with you, showers would freaking take all morning."

Dar looked at him, and cocked an eyebrow. She glanced at Kerry, who studiously gazed off into the distance. "Ahem. Right." She cleared her throat.

"Anyway, it's all cool." Mark assured her.

"Good." Dar put her hands on her hips. "Here's the plan," she said. "Everyone get a good dinner, relax, and then we start distribution."

"We've got everything lined up in the lobby." Mark said.

"Atrium."

They turned to see Kerry's old friend Talley standing there. He coughed and blinked self deprecatingly. "It's the atrium. We don't have a lobby," he explained. "We don't have bathrooms, we have heads, and we don't have rooms, they're cabins or quarters."

Some of the crew had drifted over and were listening.

"Okay, the atrium." Mark amiably corrected himself, then returned his attention to Dar. "We unboxed everything before we went and changed."

"Um, excuse me." Talley interrupted again. "Can I ask a question?"

Dar leveled her gaze at him. "Sure. Shoot," she said. "But if you want to have a jargon contest, I'm willing to bet I can beat you at it, especially since I grew up on a Navy base and know more names for the gear on one of these damn things than you have short hairs."

Talley blinked at her. "Uh."

"You had a question?" Dar pressed him, raising both eyebrows meaningfully.

"Dar." Kerry bumped her gently. "What is it, Talley? Dar's just grumpy because she hasn't been fed." She ignored the outraged look from her partner.

Encouraged, Talley turned to her instead. "What is all that stuff for?" He asked. "It looks like a computer warehouse in there."

Kerry laughed softly. "Well, it's for you," she said. "It's new computers for the ship."

The crew glanced at each other. "For real?" One of the women asked. "Even at reception? We've used manual manifests for twenty years. You're saying we're getting one of those too?"

Kerry nodded. "That's what they asked for," she said. "A lot of things will change."

"Wow." Talley murmured.

A clatter of footsteps behind them made Dar turn and see the ship's officers entering the hall. Unsurprisingly, her father was accompanying them with Ceci strolling along beside him with a very droll expression on her face. "Hi."Dar issued a general greeting as they stopped on the top landing with them.

The captain paused, regarding her briefly before producing a thin lipped smile. "Ms. Roberts, good evening," he replied. "I see you have kept your end of the bargain."

Dar glanced at the food line and the bar being set up, and half shrugged. "It's not the Waldorf, but it beats McNuggets™." She ignored the glare from the staff captain. "Shall we?"

The captain gestured toward the buffet graciously. "Please," he said. "You have met my officers I take it? Some of them, anyway?" His eyes fell on the staff captain, "And you also know, I believe, ah," he glanced at Andrew. "Commander..."

"Oh yeah, we've met." Dar drawled.

"Heh." Her father snickered. "Yeap. A few times."

Ceci rolled her eyes. "Obvious who genetically contributed to that sense of humor." She observed. "Can we eat now? I hear coleslaw calling my name."

They walked down the steps and into the room. The crew quickly separated to let the officers proceed unhindered, but as they approached the food line, several of them shyly joined up again. "Sir, may we take your plates?" One asked the captain respectfully.

"Certainly." The captain nodded. "We will be using that table, there." He pointed to one with conspicuously finer service on it. "Please have a bottle of red wine, and a bottle of vodka taken there."

"Sir." The man who had spoken ducked his head, then turned and walked purposefully toward the bar.

Mark approached Dar. "Uh, boss?"

"Don't you even think about it." Dar thrust her thumb over her shoulder. "Get in line, all of you."

The techs scuttled over obediently, muffling grins as they joined the growing string of bodies waiting to hit the chow.

Kerry craned her neck, then turned to Mark. "Tell you what. I'll grab your roast beef if you find a couple of bottles of Corona." She offered. "Deal?"

"Deal." Mark headed off toward the bar, with a grin.

"We brought on a case." Dar eyed her partner.

"Not taking any chances." Kerry put her hands behind her back and rocked up and down on her heels a little. "I know at least our part of this crowd."

"Mm." The line started moving as the captain finished perusing his choices, and Dar ran her eyes over the buffet critically. Given the short notice, the caterers had actually done pretty well. Besides the roast beef, they'd gotten hold of a roast pig, several turkey breasts that were being carved, some legs of lamb, what looked like pans of broiled white fish of some kind, pans of lasagna, some miscellaneous parmigiana, and tubs of assorted vegetables.

There were also mashed potatoes. Dar licked her lips in satisfaction and nodded. She was hungry, and she knew Kerry was also, since neither of them had brought along any protein bars to snack on, and they'd just used up quite a bit of energy with each other.

"My goddess, is that asparagus?" Ceci remarked. "Honestly I thought I was going to have to troll for seaweed."

Kerry chuckled. "Mom."

"Well, I did. I've been visiting on ships where they thought meatballs were a vegetable because they had chopped parsley in them."

"I see lots of vegetables." Kerry observed. "Look — there's carrots." She looked again. "Or maybe they're sweet potatoes."

"Long as they aren't barbequed pig livers." Her mother in law sniffed. "So, are you feeling better now?"

Kerry took a plate and handed one to Ceci, Dar having similarly equipped herself and Andrew. "Huh? Oh." She cleared her throat. "Yeah, I had a chance to relax for a while up in our cabin." She virtuously placed a piece of bright green broccoli on her plate. "Sorry I was so grumpy before."

"I've got Mark's beef." Dar turned her head to advise Kerry. She had two plates, and was dexterously juggling them while adding items, something Kerry wouldn't have dreamed of trying.

"Okay. Thanks." Kerry bumped her gently with one shoulder. "Careful."

Dar chuckled and continued her balancing act.

Ceci piled her own plate with flora. "Well, to be perfectly honest, Kerry, if I'd found out I'd been lugging hundreds of pounds of gear up a set of metal stairs when there was a perfectly good elevator to ride instead, grumpy would have been the least of what I'd been."

Mildly vindicated, Kerry merely grunted, as she served herself a little of everything saving space for a few grape tomatoes before she followed Dar toward a nearby table.

Ceci sat down next to Andrew, eyeing his plateful of meat and potatoes with wry resignation. "Thought they had peas."

"Ah do believe they did." He allowed. "Did you want some of them?"

Ceci sliced off a bit of asparagus and bit into it. Of all the differences she had with Andy, this one usually caused the most need for workarounds in their daily lives. In the years he was in the Navy, she really hadn't had to worry about it since he ate in the mess, or was aboard ship, and she pretty much was left to her own vegetarian devices and could cook as she wished.

Or not.

So, of course, she'd been chagrined when her daughter, who after all had more experience eating her cooking than the Navy's, turned out to hate vegetables just as much as her father did.

Genetic? Ceci seriously doubted it, but there were two identically laden plates on the table, and neither her husband nor her child had ever seemed to suffer physically because of it. Kerry, on the other hand, was much more vegetable friendly and, in fact, she kept cutting off bits of her flora and depositing it on Dar's plate when Dar wasn't looking.

Dar, of course, carefully navigated around the intruding bits of color. Ceci could have told Kerry it was a lost cause since she'd tried it along with every other trick she could come up with. However, she noticed Kerry kept at it, and eventually Dar ate one of the chunks just to get it out of her way.

Hm.

Maybe she just hadn't tried hard enough. Ah well.

The boat moved gently under them, and slowly the line cleared the buffet and the low rumble of conversation started up around the room. The bar was getting good action, and everyone seemed happy with the food selection.

Some of the ILS techs had mixed in with the crew, and Ceci watched the reactions as the two very different groups mingled. Given their ages were pretty close, she figured they'd be able to find something to talk about.

They were still a little civ. "Hey, Andy?"

"Yes, ma'am?" Her husband peered at her.

"We should go on a cruise."

One grizzled eyebrow rose. "We live on a boat," he said. "Ya'll want to go on a bigger one?"

"Mm." Ceci nodded. "One of those huge floating monstrosities where they put mints on your pillow and you can play golf on the top deck."

Andy winced.

Well, maybe not. Ceci went back to her vegetables. Or maybe she could find one where they'd let you fish off the fantail. Andy would like that.

Now that everyone was seated, the captain stood up at his place and tapped his knife against his water glass. The room quieted, and all eyes went to him. "I am glad we have this opportunity to enjoy a good meal together," he said. "You all have been working very hard, and it is good that we have seen progress, and that we have an evening free of the sound of jackhammers, yes?"

The crew clapped immediately, but said nothing.

"So get a good rest tonight. Our guests will, unfortunately, be working, but I am thinking they do not make as much noise as the metalworkers, is this not true?" The captain looked at Dar.

Dar was glad she'd just taken a sip of beer to clear her mouth out. She swallowed it quickly. "We can make noise if we have to," she said. "But we generally don't."

"Excellent." The captain turned around. "And let us hope the government finishes their investigation quickly, as we cannot return to port until they do." He sniffed. "However long that will take. So enjoy this meal as best you can."

Dar blinked, and looked at Kerry.

The captain sat down, and picked up his wine glass, sipping from it with a calm expression.

Ceci scratched her jaw. "I hope I didn't just throw us into a bad Flying Dutchman nightmare."

"Yikes." Kerry covered her eyes. "I've got a bad feeling about this."

"Wall." Andy continued plowing his way through his dinner. "Ain't life just one little kick ass after t'other."

Chapter Five

KERRY LEANED AGAINST the granite fountain in the center of the atrium checking off items on her clipboard. It was very quiet around her since it was well after midnight and her team was all out delivering gear to various parts of the ship.

She could hear the faint slap of water against the outside of the hull and she could feel the motion under her legs, but, otherwise, the silence around her leant timelessness to the moment.

The ship creaked a little. Metal plates under long strain from holding back the water protested the surge of the waves that was very apparent to Kerry as she stood in her solitude.

After dinner the crew had vanished to their quarters, or to some other place on the ship she figured, someplace *they* weren't welcome. That was fine with her since they had a lot of work to accomplish and it was much easier without everyone underfoot.

And yet, the emptiness gave the ship a ghostly quality she wasn't entirely comfortable with. Another creak made her look quickly around, and then she mentally slapped herself for being over imaginative. "Okay," she spoke aloud. "So that takes care of all the PC's. Now we have the POS systems to do. Right?"

"Right."

Kerry jumped, unable to stop herself in time even though her ears readily recognized the voice. "Yow."

Dar sauntered down the central steps, brushing her hands off against her dust covered jeans. "We are talking."

"Ah." Kerry put a neat check on her checklist. "Got the satellite going, huh?"

"Yeap." Dar seemed very satisfied with herself. "Took some persuasion, but we got it going. They're surfing the web up there."

"Oh really," Kerry said. "Bet that's a new experience for them."

"Mm." Dar leaned against the marble column next to Kerry. "It's slower than hell, but it's something." She peered at Kerry's list. "Not bad. All the PC's out there?"

"Yep."

"Hm." Dar pulled out her PDA and keyed it on, watching as its wireless card picked up the signal from one of the devices she'd installed. She started her analyzer and observed the results. "Servers are up."

"Finally." Kerry groused. "Have I mentioned lately how much I hate picky whiny server operating systems?"

"No."

"I hate picky whiny server operating systems."

"Hm."

"Can't you write a better one?" Kerry asked, tucking her clipboard under her arm and giving Dar an inquiring look.

Dar's eyes opened up wide. "ME?" She asked. "I haven't finished writing your network security robot yet." She bumped Kerry with her shoulder. "Why don't you write one?"

"Uh uh." Kerry thumped her back against the column. "I'll stick to messing with your gopher, thanks."

Dar snickered.

Kerry looked at her. "You know what I mean."

"I do." Dar agreed. "But anyone else around probably doesn't."

Kerry peered around the vast emptiness of the atrium. "There's no one here. But even if there was, I bet no one would ever question me about your gopher, Dar."

Dar snickered again.

"Dar."

Slowly, Dar slid down to the ground, snickers evolving into almost silly giggles.

Kerry only hoped the tech team wouldn't come back for their next assignment for a few minutes. She slid down next to her partner and stuck her legs out, tapping her pen against her thigh as she waited patiently. "Dar."

"Ahh. Sorry." Dar stifled a last chuckle. "It's just too damn late."

After midnight, in fact. Way too damn late. Kerry slid over and pressed her shoulder against Dar's. "Want to stop for tonight? We can put out the POS systems tomorrow."

It was very tempting. Dar was tired. She knew Kerry was tired, and she suspected the rest of the crew was equally tired though none of them would admit it in front of their bosses. Could they risk waiting? They didn't know when the ship was coming back in, and while they were out here they had the advantage.

But it was also true that the later they worked, the more tired they'd be and the more mistakes they'd make. Now that all the computers were delivered, the major part of the work was done and the delivery of the dumb POS terminals could be performed early in the morning, couldn't it?

Dar gazed at the dark sky visible in the windows on either side of her. She acknowledged silently that her decision was being influenced by her own desire to break off, but as she looked up and saw the first of the techs coming back, weary and dust covered, she bowed to her gut inclination and gave Kerry a brief, decisive nod. "Let's can it."

"I love you." Kerry rested her cheek against Dar's shoulder. "Have I told you that lately?"

If she needed an exclamation point to that decision, well, she'd gotten it. Dar clasped her hands together and rubbed a bit of adhesive off her index finger as she waited for the crew to finish trudging up to them. "Time to take a break, folks."

The crew looked exhausted, and to top it off the ship had started moving a lot more pitching a little and rolling from side to side. More than a few faces were a touch green. "Boss, those are magic words," Mark said. "But hey, we got a ton of stuff done tonight. All that's left is to dump those things out there and run them up."

Dar nodded. "Right. So we do that in the morning," she said. "Go and get some rest."

"Everyone did a great job." Kerry added. "You guys are superstars."

Their eyes brightened despite the late hour. "It was pretty cool," Carlos said. "Especially with everybody out of our way—man, I was tired of tripping all over those guys with the welders."

"Yeah." Several nearby techs agreed. "We should work at night all the time."

"Hey!" Mark objected. "Speak for yourself, dude! Some of us have a life!"

Everyone started to chuckle. Dar got up and extended her hand down to Kerry hauling her up as well. "I don't know what the story's going to be tomorrow, if we're going back in, or what. So let's meet here at nine, and play it by ear."

"You got it, DR." Mark was covered in IT grunge and dust. "Man, I wouldn't care if that bed was a plank, I'd sleep on it right now."

"Hell yeah."

The group dispersed, heading off toward their assigned cabins. Dar and Kerry strolled along behind them, taking their time in mounting the stairs and climbing up to the level where their relatively palatial digs were located.

"Wonder where your folks were all night?" Kerry commented, as she nudged the door open and they went inside. "I didn't see them after dinner."

"Maybe they went to bed." Dar suggested.

"They went to sleep that early?" Kerry seemed skeptical.

"I didn't say that."

Kerry turned from where she was peering out the closed balcony door. "Oh, this is one of those 'think of that and go blind' things, isn't it?" She slid the door open and walked outside, surprised at the force of the wind. "Whoa."

Dar joined her. The balmy night air now tasted only of sea salt and a whiff of diesel. As they leaned on the balcony, the moon came out and painted a stripe across the tossing waves, showing up whitecaps as the ship ploughed through them. "Hm."

"Rough." Kerry noted grabbing hold of the rail as the ship pitched sideways. "Dar, you didn't..."

"In my bag," Dar said. "You feeling it?"

"No." Kerry said. "Just a precaution. The one time I got really seasick was on the Staten Island Ferry."

Dar looked at her. "You're kidding."

Kerry shook her head solemnly. "Calm day, barely any waves, Statue of Liberty in the background, me sick as a dog over the railing. Pathetic."

Dar chuckled. "Figures." She poked Kerry and pointed back inside. "C'mon. View from our aft deck's better, and it's hot out here." She herded her partner back inside, where the air conditioning had grudgingly reduced the humidity and provided a relatively comfortable temperature for sleeping.

Around them on this upper deck, they could really hear the creaking. Kerry listened for a moment as the ship rolled and groaned, and then she turned to Dar. "Is this thing going to fall apart? It sure sounds like it."

Dar peeled her t-shirt off, examining the stripe where her sleeve had been. "Nah." She turned the shirt inside out, and then folded it neatly, setting it to one side. "It'll last at least another night or two." She removed her jeans and did the same thing to them, rolling her socks up in a ball and setting them on top of the folded clothing. "Now."

"Now." Kerry had been leaning back enjoying the show. "Shower?"

"Mm."

"Bed?"

"Mmhm." Dar extended her hand. "Get the duds off, Yankee. Been a long day."

Yes, it had. Kerry agreed, pulling off her shirt. But now it was over.

Dar winked at her.

Well, almost over. Kerry shed her jeans and joined her partner at the door to the incredibly small bathroom. "If the ship rolls over, does the shower go sideways?"

Dar turned on the shower and pulled her inside.

"Just a question."

SHE WAS RIDING a horse. Kerry could feel the motion under her, and the exhilaration rush of wind against her face. She was sitting in the front of a big, strangely crude saddle with the security of a warm body behind her and a strong arm looped around her middle.

A long, long road stretched out before her, seemingly without any end she could see, and on either side, a beautiful forest spread out with no signs of human habitation.

It was beautiful.

She was filled with a simple happiness that wanted nothing else but the warm sunshine and the two sets of laughter rising up into it.

Then the horse bucked.

Kerry's eyes popped open, dragged from a sunny day into pitch blackness. The ship moved violently under her again, and tossed her up off the bed and back onto it. "Dar?" She yelped.

"Yes." Dar sounded barely awake.

Kerry grabbed hold of the edge of the bed as the ship tilted alarmingly to the right. "Is this normal?"

For an answer, Dar wrapped one long arm around her and a leg for good measure pulling her closer. "Well, it's open water."

The creaking had grown quite ominous, and they could hear thunder rolling outside. The pitch of the vessel had become pronounced, and the cabin was moving sharply from side to side as the ship rolled in the waves.

"Ah." Kerry swallowed audibly.

Dar lifted her head and peered through the darkness. "You okay?"

"Uh, sure." Kerry said inhaling sharply as the ship tilted to one side again.

"Sure about that?"

Her partner swallowed again. "Well, possibly not."

"Hang on." Dar carefully disentangled herself from both the bedclothes and Kerry's grip and eased off the bed, grabbing hold of the bathroom door latch as she was almost pitched right back down next to Kerry. "Whoa!"

"Whoa." Kerry repeated in a subdued voice. She clamped her jaws shut after that and tried not to think about how her stomach felt.

Dar hit the light switch. Nothing happened. She hit it again, then in a fit of unreasoning technical mindlessness flipped it back and forth rapidly. "Goddamn it."

"Mmph." Kerry wasn't inclined to add anything useful. She was just glad that if the lights weren't working, at least the AC still was. The thought of the room being clammy and warm and... "Oh god that was stupid."

"Ker?"

"Mmprh."

Dar felt along the wall until she found the desk, cursing as she almost tripped over her backpack that had fallen to the floor in the pitching. "Ouch."

"Ermp?"

Dar dropped to her knees and unlatched the pack, yelping as a rolling motion knocked her off balance and sent her tumbling across the carpet to land near the bed. "Son of..." With a growl, she crawled back and grabbed the pack, sitting down on the rug with her legs sprawled out.

That seemed to solve the motion problem for the moment. Dar untied the top flap and dug inside the bag, yelping a little as she poked herself with a pair of diagonal cutters. "Damn dykes."

Silence. Then Kerry cleared her throat. "What did we do now?"

"Not us." Dar dug further, and discovered a small vial. With a satisfied grunt, she drew it out.

"You have some other damn dykes in your backpack? Wow."

"Ha, ha." Dar scooted over to the bedside and reached out searching for Kerry's hand. "I have something for you." She blinked as warm fingers curled around her wrist, a little startling in the darkness despite her knowing how close Kerry was to her. "Think you can swallow a pill?"

"Gimme a minute," Kerry muttered.

Dar waited, pressing her back against the bed and grabbing hold of the frame as the ship moved up and down again.

Kerry made a small groaning noise.

"Easy." Dar grimaced in sympathy. She'd been relatively lucky so far in life with her experiences of seasickness, but the few times she'd suffered from it had convinced her never to travel without medication for it. "Ready?"

"Nuh uh."

Dar frowned. "Need some water?" She felt the grip on her wrist tighten and Kerry's forehead came to rest against her shoulder. "Hon, if you can get this down, it'll help. I promise."

Kerry merely stayed there for a moment, then she exhaled warming Dar's skin. "Move."

"You're not going to throw up."

"Dar, move."

Dar grabbed the bottle of water and got up onto the bed, hauling Kerry up to a sitting position mostly by feel. "Breathe." She felt her partner's body jerk and she steeled herself to deal with being thrown up on, but Kerry's jaws locked shut and she could feel the tension in the muscles of them as she laid her hand along her cheek. "It's okay. Just do what you need to do, Ker."

For a long set of pitching rolls, Kerry just stayed where she was. Then the ship settled a little, and as it did, she straightened up. "I think you got ten seconds." She inhaled sharply. "But don't hold me to that."

Dar felt for Kerry's lips and put the seasickness pill against them, feeling them part as Kerry trustingly accepted it. Then she applied the squirt nozzle of her water bottle to the same place, and squeezed gently. "Incoming."

Kerry made a somewhat strangling noise, making Dar wince and close her eyes, despite the darkness. Then she heard the sound of over-exaggerated swallowing. "Please." Dar addressed the ship. "Stay fucking still, okay?"

"Gurph." Kerry protested faintly.

"Not you." Dar growled. "This godforsaken piece of rusted metal held together with duct tape and old piss we're floating in."

A shudder went through the vessel. Dar growled again, almost as though a battle of wills was being conducted.

Kerry reasoned the thought alone was ridiculous.

But the ship, as many other things had before it, bowed to Dar's will and cruised along peacefully for a time until Kerry finally relaxed and slumped against Dar's body. "Ugh."

Dar stroked her arm gently, leaning back and easing Kerry with her until they were both half reclining. Wind blew rain against the balcony doors startling them, but the ship's course remained, at least for now, relatively steady. "Hmph."

Kerry wasn't ready to unlock her jaws just yet. The queasy feeling, though it had subsided, was out there on the fringes and threatening to recur at any moment. Throwing up now would not only be extremely yucky, it would also eject the medicine Dar had given her, and if there were two things she didn't want to do, those were them.

Dar seemed to sense that. She shifted her grip and gave Kerry a comforting light rub on her belly. "Just take nice, deep breaths."

Kerry tried a few. "You've gone through this before?" She guessed. "I can't believe it."

"Mm. A few times," Dar admitted. "First time I took the Dixie out was one of them, matter of fact. That damn thing's a bitch to drive when you're tossing your cookies, let me tell ya."

Kerry chuckled faintly. "You're just saying that to make me feel better." She accused.

"Nuh uh."

"Yes, you are."

"Am not."

"Are too."

"Feeling better?"

Kerry could barely see the outline of Dar's face in the dim light from the window, but her imagination filled in the angles and planes without effort. "Yes." She let her head rest against Dar's collarbone. "Oh, that sucked."

"Mm."

"What time is it?" Kerry asked. "Were we sleeping long? I didn't think it was raining before we went to bed."

"It wasn't." Dar confirmed, reaching over and picking up her cell phone. It showed no signal, which she expected, but also provided her with a clock. "Four a.m."

"Ugh." Kerry winced. "Two hours. No wonder I feel like something a cow stepped on."

Dar wondered if the ship was going to begin pitching again. Being out here in the dark, not knowing where they were heading didn't exactly make her comfortable, and the fact that parts of the ship didn't seem to be working well made it all the worse. "Wonder what the deal with the lights is."

"AC's on," Kerry commented.

"Hm. Yeah." Dar felt the ship roll a bit, and she glanced at Kerry. In the faint light, she could see the pale lashes fluttering a little, but her partner's body remained relaxed. Not surprising, since the industrial strength pill she'd given her usually knocked Dar out in fairly short order. "Doing okay?"

"Uh huh." Kerry closed her eyes. The sick feeling seemed to be receding further and she was getting sleepy again. The ship started to move, but the motion was slower and less violent now, and rather than make her queasy, it seemed to be relaxing her.

Weird.

Dar cradled Kerry against her, finding a smile somewhere as Kerry snuggled up willingly. She let her fingers comb through the disheveled blonde hair and knew a moment of ridiculous contentment despite the circumstances.

Thunder cracked outside. As though in signal, the ship started pitching again, but one quick look confirmed that Kerry was now safely asleep and oblivious to it. Dar braced her bare feet against the wall and the bedframe to keep them in place and hoped sincerely the damn captain was steering them out of the storm instead of into it.

IT WAS STILL dark, it was still raining, and it was still rocking like a hammock when Kerry woke again. She was fuzzy and that had her blinking her eyes a few times before she could make them focus on the gray shadows surrounding her.

How long had she been asleep? Beneath her ear, she could hear Dar's heartbeat, steady and even and she remained still so she wouldn't wake her up. After a few seconds of staring at the inside of the cabin, she let her eyes close again and tried to get back to sleep.

Problem was she could now hear all the creaking around her again. Outside the cabin in the hall, she could also detect the sounds of someone moving around, crashing against the walls as the ship moved restlessly in the waves.

Despite the size of the ship, it felt very fragile. Its bones screaming and complaining as the sea pressed in on all sides.

Paradoxically, however, here in the loose circle of Dar's arms Kerry felt completely safe, regardless of the ominous clatter around her. The ship could fall apart she mused, and as long as she and Dar were together she was sure they'd come through it just fine.

How did she know that? Kerry didn't really understand how, but she knew at some deep level that it was true. She'd known it since they'd been trapped in that hospital together, when Dar had brought them both out from under the collapsed wall refusing to allow mere concrete and metal to stop her.

At the time, she'd been stunned and overwhelmed, in pain and a state of high anxiety over what was going to happen to them as well as what might have happened to their friends and family. But one thing she hadn't been was afraid, though she hadn't realized that until much later.

Kerry listened to the noise in the hallways, a muffled drone slowly resolving itself into a pair of voices, male ones, obviously upset. One had a heavy accent, and she couldn't understand a word of what was being said, but the other had a clearer, sharper tone.

"Bloody bastard, I'm not hiding you no more!" the voice said. "No wonder you had to shut the bitch up. She probly got as sick of you as I am!"

Kerry's eyes opened. She glanced up at Dar, to find the faint glitter of her partner's eyes looking back at her. "You hear that?"

Dar nodded.

"Shaudup." The other voice growled. "Put you inna trunk and toss you over."

Kerry's nostrils flared. "Oh no," she whispered.

"What?"

"We're in a bad television movie."

Dar chuckled soundlessly. "Probably drunk," she uttered softly.

A loud crack made them both jump, then something crashed against the outside of their door, followed by the sound of a violent scuffle.

They both sighed simultaneously. "Excuse me." Dar disentangled herself and got out of bed, heading for the door as she pulled her t-shirt around her. She slapped at the light on her way, grunting when it stubbornly refused to produce anything but a sodden click.

Kerry hesitated, then scrambled out from the sheets and followed, getting behind Dar as she yanked the cabin door open and glared out into the dimly lit corridor.

Two figures were struggling, having swung across the hall and slammed into the door across from them. Far down the corridor, there was a sound of a second door opening as well.

"Hey!" Dar let out a bark. "What in the hell do you think you're doing?"

The two men stopped fighting, and turned, staring at her. "What are you doing here?" the smaller of the two demanded. "What are you doing on this ship? Get out!" He advanced on her. He was burly, and had had a rough, scraggly beard along with an ugly face.

Dar straightened to her full height, easily eight or nine inches over his, and braced her arms on the doorframe, not backing down an inch. "Buddy, if you know what's good for you, just stop," she warned him. "Who the hell are you, and what are you doing up here?"

The other man stayed back in the shadows, wiping a sleeve across his mouth, but saying nothing.

"Estavan."

The men turned at the sound of the captain's voice. He was standing at the end of the corridor, near an almost hidden panel half obstructed by his body. "Captain." The smaller man backed off, and half ducked his head. "I found these women here!"

Kerry was now peeking out from behind Dar. Her eyes fell on the other man, who was starting to edge his way back down the corridor. Something familiar in his profile caught her attention, and she leaned forward a little, sliding her arm across Dar's back to keep her balance.

He was taller than his companion, and thinner, but he had an air of general seediness that reminded her of the backwater carnival workers she'd occasionally see when the yearly church fundraiser was on up in Michigan.

Which reminded her of something she hadn't thought about in years.

The man caught her looking at him, and scowled, ducking his head and heading off at a more rapid pace, half shielding his face with one arm despite the darkness making him nearly invisible. Kerry watched him go with a very thoughtful expression.

"You did not find anything here but trouble, Estavan. Please go to your quarters, or take yourself down to the engine room where you belong. Do not bother our guests or myself with your noise any longer," the captain stated firmly.

"But captain..."

"Go." The captain raised his voice slightly.

"Aye." The man turned and trudged off after his erstwhile adversary, disappearing into the darkness as he turned the corner.

The captain glanced at them. "My apologies. He is my senior engineer, and has been on this ship a very long time. He does not like strangeness and changes." He turned to go back through the portal. Then he paused and turned, peering back at them curiously. "They did not assign you private quarters?"

Dar looked him right in the eye. "We don't need them."

Surprisingly he merely sniffed and nodded. "Very well. Good night."

"Captain." Kerry spoke up. "Are the lights not working for any particular reason?"

The captain reached out and flipped a switch in the hallway, apparently surprised when nothing happened. He flipped the switch a few times, much as Dar had done earlier, then grunted and shook his head. "I will find out. They are functional where the officer's quarters are." He turned and disappeared through the portal, which closed behind him with a definite snick.

There was a sign on the door but it was too far for them to read and too dark in any case. Crew only, Dar suspected. With a sigh, she glanced down at Kerry's head, which was tucked under her arm. "Bed?"

"What, and miss all the excitement around here?" Kerry asked in a whimsical tone. "Dar, did you see that other guy?" She pulled back as Dar turned and they shut the door leaving the darkened hallway behind them. "The one he was fighting with?"

"No, not really," Dar said. "I was too worried the little skunk in front of me might start grabbing."

"Hm." Kerry latched on to the back of Dar's shirt and followed her back to bed. "Yeah, he looked stupid enough...scary considering he's the ship's engineer."

"Explains a lot," Dar muttered.

They collapsed into the mussed bedclothes again and sorted out themselves, the sheets, and the pillows. Dar stretched her body out and rolled half onto her side as Kerry did the same, both of them facing toward the balcony windows. Dar wrapped an arm around Kerry's middle and they put their heads down at roughly the same time.

It was quiet, and the sound of rain lashing against the window sounded very loud.

"That guy's bothering me," Kerry spoke up suddenly.

"Hm?"

"That other guy. I've seen him before, and I'm trying to remember where," she explained.

"Um...not to be a smartass, but maybe it was here on this ship we've been working on for days?" Dar suggested. "Chances are you've seen him, Ker."

"Mm yeah, I know, but..." Kerry exhaled. "He was acting really funny—sneaking away like that when he saw me looking at him."

"Sneaking?" Dar asked. "Did he really?"

"Yeah. He put his hand over his face and walked off."

Now that was a little strange. "Well," Dar mused. "Maybe he buys into that 'looking at gay people causes blindness' theory."

"Dar!" Kerry snickered. "Yeah, you're probably right. I probably saw him on here—maybe down in the loading bay." She settled down, enjoying the warmth of Dar's body tucked up behind her. "Or on the dock. But what do you think they were talking about?"

Dar shrugged. "Sounded like they were just talking BS to me," she admitted candidly. "Guys do that."

"Girls do it too," Kerry agreed. "Yeah, maybe." She pondered further. "The captain didn't seem whacked out at all about us."

Dar chuckled.

Kerry turned her head and peered at her partner. "Does that mean I need to bring my gaydar back to Sears for retuning AGAIN?" she asked. "Jesus, I feel so clueless sometimes."

"No." Dar gave her a little squeeze. "It's just that I think it's more accepted on these kinds of ships than maybe what we're used to. I saw some of the guys up near the bridge having a little party when I was working on the SAT dish."

"Oh."

"I looked at them, they looked at me, and we all sort of went, yeah..." Dar lifted her hand and waggled it.

"I get the picture." Kerry in fact did, and it made her smile. Gay women and gay men were so different at so many levels sometimes.

She'd talked to some of the people at their church about that and found, to her bemusement, she often knew less about other gay people than she'd imagined. "Oh well. It'll come to me." She finally decided. "Where I've seen him."

"Uh huh." Dar pulled her a little closer. "After all this, I'm gonna be toast tomorrow."

"Me too."

Finally, it really was quiet. Even the rain found something else to hit other than their windows.

MORNING FOUND THEM out at sea with gray skies surrounding them and the water a sullen dark blue. Dar leaned on the balcony railing and looked down noting the whitecaps ruffling the surface, and the forbidding appearance of a world she usually found so welcoming.

Maybe seeing it from a higher perspective did that. When they were on the Dixie, the surface of the water was mere feet away, and she always felt far more a part of it than she did now towering so far above.

The sound of the cabin door closing behind her made her turn, and she leaned on her elbows as Kerry crossed the interior and emerged on the balcony next to her carrying two steaming cups. "Ah." Dar observed. "You found coffee."

"I found coffee." Kerry handed her one. "I found the crew mess, actually. It was pretty empty." She peered at the sky. "So much for that 'sailors rise at dawn' thing."

Dar chuckled sipping cautiously at the beverage. It wasn't good, and it wasn't bad, the mediocre norm of bland hotel coffee, but it was hot and caffeinated and that really was what counted. "It was probably quite a party last night. Did you happen to bump into the caterers?"

Kerry joined her at the rail, the wind ruffling her blonde hair. "Matter of fact I did. They're slightly freaking."

"I bet."

"I told them to just try to reuse the stuff they brought as much as they can, and put out little buffets for our folks at least. But I hope this doesn't last long."

"Me too," Dar agreed. "I just want the whole damn thing to be over."

Kerry studied her over the rim of her coffee cup. "You really do, don't you?"

Dar nodded.

Kerry slowly took a sip and swallowed it. "Know what I want?"

After a moment's hesitation, Dar gave a half shake of her head. "What?"

"Nothing." Kerry leaned forward and gave her a kiss on the lips. "I have everything I need right here."

"Aw." A charmed smile appeared on Dar's face. "You say the nicest things to me." She returned the kiss easing back to look into Kerry's eyes and finding the most pleasant mix of passion and affection there. "So."

"So." Kerry recalled the time with some regret. "Guess we better go get our job done, huh?" She let her hand rest against Dar's hip. "Get those POS machines out, then we can certify the system."

"And after that..."

"After that, it just is what it is." Kerry finished for her. "C'mon."

They left their cabin together and walked down the empty hallway seeing no one until they were halfway down the stairwell where they bumped into Mark. "Morning." Dar greeted him. "Sleep okay?"

Mark stifled a yawn. "I'm not a great sailor," he admitted. "Man, I'm freaking lucky I ran into your dad last night boss. He fixed me up."

"Hm." Kerry dropped down the steps two at a time. "Must be a family trait."

Several other techs came out of the hallway on the next landing and joined them heading down. Most still looked tired, a few still looked a little green around the edges. The ship wasn't moving nearly as badly as it had been the night before, but there was still a perceptible rocking and everyone held on to the handrails with the exception of Dar.

They entered the atrium, which appeared to be as they'd left it — boxes neatly stacked near the walls and machines lined up in rows awaiting deployment. A few of the boxes had tumbled across the floor during the night, but otherwise everything seemed undamaged.

"All right." Mark cracked his knuckles. "Let's check out the plan, dudes." He walked over to where a blueprint had been tacked up on one side of the elevator stack that was still taped off and out of service. The print had deck plans of the ship along its length, and there were blue and red dots to indicate where the equipment went.

Dar drew Kerry to one side and they listened quietly, allowing Mark to do his job without interference. Kerry looked around noting the lack of crew. "It's so quiet," she whispered.

Dar nodded in agreement. "Not much for them to do I guess," she uttered, then paused as Talley appeared from behind the front desk and headed their way. She nudged Kerry who turned and spotted him. "Here comes your buddy."

"My buddy?" Kerry gave her a poke. "Hi," she greeted Talley.

"Hi." The young man gave her a brief smile. "Did you guys hear the news?'

Uh oh. "No...what's up?" Kerry asked. "Don't tell me we're being hijacked to Cuba. If we are, I'm swimming home."

That got a smile from Talley. "No. They cleared the port. We're headed back." He glanced at the techs. "So if you guys need to finish stuff you probably better do it fast. From what I hear, the builders are on the docks waiting to jump on as soon as we tie up."

Dar frankly didn't know whether to be relieved or disappointed.

"Short vacation for you all, I guess," she commented.

Talley snorted. "It's all a big crock anyway," he said. "We all know the truth—soon as Quest finishes with his scamming, they're going to scuttle her, and we'll all be dumped somewhere. So give me a break."

Dar and Kerry exchanged startled glances. "You know that for sure?" Dar asked. "He's putting a lot of money into these ships."

Talley stared at her. "You're joking right?" he asked. "You don't think he's laid a dime out yet, do you? Everything's contingent on all you people finishing. He hasn't risked a cent, and he won't!" The man put his hands on his hips. "He's just playing you people to the hilt, and you all fell for it."

Kerry was aware of some of the techs listening surreptitiously. "Don't sell us short." She looked directly at him. "You don't think we haven't thought about that?"

Talley looked around, then at her. His expression was plainly skeptical.

"Maybe we're playing him." Kerry suggested. "Maybe we're using this project to advertise ourselves to the real ship companies who are watching...ever think of that?"

"Besides," Dar interjected. "Think about it—what if he's looking to get these hunks of junk bought by one of those real ship companies. You might want to clean up your acts."

Talley looked warily at them. "They won't touch her." He indicated the ship. "She'll end up in a scrap heap. We all know it."

Dar shrugged. "You don't know it until it happens." She shook her head. "So I wouldn't try to sink her yet."

The man stiffened, looking around quickly before he stared intently at Dar. "Where did you hear that?" He hissed. "Did they tell your old man? Those..." The sound of a door slamming filtered into the atrium, causing Talley to turn and look. With a last glance at Dar he headed toward the sound, breaking into a trot as he disappeared behind the front desk again.

"What in the hell?" Kerry blurted. "Dar, did you hear..." She stopped, her lips stilled by Dar's fingertips.

"I heard it," Dar murmured. "Stay here. Let's get this damn equipment out. I'll go find Dad and see if he's got any idea what's really going on."

Kerry frowned, a protest bubbling up. Dar cocked an eyebrow at her, and she squinted, triggering a rakish grin from Kerry in return. "Okay," she reluctantly agreed. "But if you're gone more than fifteen minutes, I'm coming after you."

Dar ruffled her hair. "Deal." She pushed away from the staircase and headed toward the front of the ship, figuring the bridge would be a good place to start looking for both her father and the truth.

Kerry watched her disappear, and then she turned her attention back to the group of techs. They all were carefully looking ahead, not at her, but she knew at least some of them would have heard Talley's conversation.

She reviewed their response, and decided it wasn't something to worry about at the moment. Or at least, it was something to worry about, but it had to take its rightful place after the other things she had to worry about.

"Boss, you got anything to add?" Mark asked. "We're gonna start on the bottom floor and work up for a change."

"Sounds good to me." Kerry moved toward the lines of equipment. "Don't know if you all heard, but we're headed back into port, and we've got to really get moving with this stuff. I want to certify it before we tie the ship up."

The techs started moving faster, a buzz of noise arising as they reacted to Kerry's statement. "Man, that's sorta too bad," Carlos said. "Those guys on the ship were gonna invite us to a party tonight."

Kerry eyed him. "They were?"

Carlos nodded. "Yeah. They got a bar downstairs," he explained. "That's where they all went last night." He picked up one of the POS systems, then appeared at a loss as to how to juggle its associated printer and assorted cables.

Kerry resolved the problem for him by picking them up. "C'mon," she said. "There are sixty of these things. If we go in pairs, it's only four trips for each team and we're done." She started toward the steps, glancing at the chart on the way. "And see? You'll get to see the crew's bar anyway. That's where we're going."

Carlos trotted after her, carrying his armful of POS station. They went to the stairs and started down, going past the last passenger floor and entering the crew spaces. It was still quiet, and their footsteps sounded very loud on the linoleum. Carlos' sneakers even squeaked a little whereas Kerry's hiking boots merely scuffed.

On either side of the wall, aged bulletin boards carried notices and announcements, and lining the inside of one long space was a map of the ship marked off into cryptic zones. To either side, they passed doors labeled with chipped and peeling name plates.

They continued on down the hall toward the front of the ship going down another half staircase and then down a narrower corridor. Ahead of them was a steel, gray door without a nameplate that had a very worn handle and a chipped and scarred surface that had been painted over many, many times. "That it?" Kerry asked.

Carlos nodded. "They showed me last night," he explained. "So I could find it again. They seemed pretty nice about it," he added. "We got to talking about computers and stuff."

Of course. Kerry tucked the printer under her arm and reached out to grasp the door handle turning it and pulling the door open. She stood back to let Carlos enter, then realized the room was occupied. She followed him inside and looked around, spotting perhaps twenty crewmen in various states of repose around the room, all of them turning to look at them. "Hi."

Two men were at the pool table. They straightened and turned, looking her over brazenly. One of the men sitting on a threadbare couch near the wall whistled.

Oh boy. Kerry continued across the room toward the small bar. Her shoulder blades itched, feeling the eyes on her, and she was glad she'd put on a relatively staid blue t-shirt instead of anything more revealing.

Carlos put the POS system down and went behind the bar, oblivious to the men around them as he searched for a place to plug it in while Kerry concentrated on connecting the receipt printer. She removed a small screwdriver from her back pocket and connected the cables, aware of some motion around her and the fact that several people were coming closer.

Carlos looked up. "Oh, hey," he remarked casually. "So how are you guys? Did you have a good party last night?"

One of the men slipped onto the barstool next to where Kerry was standing. "You shoulda come," he answered, "and brung your lady friend here. Hey honey, what's your name?"

Kerry didn't even look up. "Eleanor Roosevelt." She finished tightening the screws on the cable.

"So' kay if I call you El?" The man didn't miss a beat.

"Hey, chill out man. That's my boss," Carlos protested. "Don't talk like that."

"You work for a woman?" The man laughed and his friends joined in.

"Sure," Carlos responded, cheerfully unruffled.

The man leaned on the counter and tried to get Kerry's attention. "Hey, can I buy you a drink? C'mon, look up beautiful." He tapped on the surface right next to Kerry's arm.

Kerry obliged straightening up. The man sitting next to her was around her age with short, cropped dark hair and honey colored eyes. He wasn't unattractive, and there was a brazen sensuality about him that she suspected some women might find attractive. "Thanks." She tried the polite route first. "But I really don't drink anything but orange juice before dinner."

The two pool players came closer leaning on their sticks. None of them seemed threatening but they were definitely interested in her. Kerry accepted the flattery of the notion, but she didn't much care for the assumption that she'd welcome it.

Belatedly, Carlos seemed to realize things were sliding into the uncool zone. He stepped around the bar and came to Kerry's side, a little unsure of what to do next.

"We've got some orange juice," the man said. "We'll just add a little something to it. How about it? We can get the music going here and start the party early."

"Sounds good to me," one of the pool players said.

"Well, not to us." Kerry added a touch of firmness to her tone. "We've got work to do. So have fun with your party, gentlemen." She pocketed her screwdriver and started to move away from the bar. "C'mon, Carlos." She was suddenly aware that the room had no windows and only the one door visible and the walls seemed to close in on her as more bodies started to move her way.

"Yes, ma'am." Carlos stepped back out of her way and turned to follow Kerry.

"Pussy." The man at the bar laughed.

"Hey, c'mon. What's the rush?" The brazen pool player moved to get in Kerry's way. "We've got time before we hit port, and I like my ladies a little on the spicy side."

"Really?" Kerry didn't even stop to think. She planted her left leg and half turned whipping her right up in a roundhouse kick that took the pool cue out of his hands and sent it clattering to the ground.

"Hey!" the man yelped, and lifted his now empty fingers. "What the hell!"

The man came off the barstool. Kerry lifted her hands up into a defensive posture, curling her fingers into fists.

"Dudes, you should like back off." Carlos advised them. "She's like a black belt kick boxer."

Kerry's brows jerked up.

The men looked at Carlos who looked back at them with devastating earnestness. "No shit," he added. "She's got like a hundred trophies."

Kerry almost laughed biting the inside of her lip as the men backed off a little, watching her warily. She relaxed her pose and started toward the door again, this time unimpeded. "Gentlemen. Have a nice day." She called back over her shoulder as she opened the door and saw the blessed light of the empty corridor ahead of her.

Carlos followed her out and pushed the door shut behind them. "Was that okay?" he asked. "I didn't know those guys were such ass — er — ."

Kerry stopped and turned putting her hands on her hips and regarding him with mildly twinkling green eyes. 'Trophies?"

He shrugged sheepishly.

"C'mon." Kerry turned and headed for the stairs up. "Dar has trophies y'know." She made a mental note to find something nice to do for the unexpectedly resourceful Carlos.

"Yeah?"

"And she really is a black belt. I'm just a blue."

"Yeah?"

"Yeah." Kerry got to the top of the steps and continued up the hallway. Her knees were shaking, and she made a mental note to warn the other female techs to watch out for trouble. The ship chose that moment to roll to one side, and she was caught off balance, her shoulder smacking into the wall as the floor pitched under her.

Carlos hit the paneling next to her, and they hung on, waiting for the ship to steady and right itself. Kerry became suddenly aware of the fact they were below the waterline, and just as suddenly, she wondered where Dar was.

A low rumble sounded along with the hooting of horns.

She could see a flashing light down the corridor. The ship was still listing. "Carlos?"

"Yes, ma'am?"

"Run."

"Ma'am?"

Kerry grabbed his arm and started for the stairs.

"WHAT'S—UH—GOING on?" Carlos yelped, as they slid to one side on the steps and nearly toppled over them. "This isn't normal, right?"

"Right." Kerry grabbed the railing and hauled herself upward with fierce determination. "C'mon, just keep going up." She grabbed a door handle at the top of the steps and pulled. She was sent sprawling as it opened abruptly and swung inward. "Yah!"

"Hey!" Carlos grabbed at her. "Hey!"

Kerry scrambled to her feet and got her balance just as the ship decided to assist her and rolled back in the other direction. She and Carlos went catapulting through the door and across the hallway, slamming together into the wall as the door behind them slammed with a huge bang. "Son of a..."

"Hey!" Carlos grabbed for a handhold as the ship continued on its roll and went in the other direction. "Whhooooaa!!!

Kerry started up the tilting corridor gripping the railing along the wall tightly. "C'mon." She halted suddenly as a luggage cart broke free of its bindings and careened across the hall nearly crashing into them. "Jesus." She fended it off with some difficulty, then continued to the next doorway that led into the main stairwell.

The tilt made the lunge across the hall almost impossible, but she got hold of the doorframe with her finger tips and pulled herself inside. "Hurry up!" She called back to Carlos. "We've got to get out of here!"

"Yahhh!" Carlos had leaped after her, but missed the hold on the door and was now sliding back toward the opposite wall. "Go on...I'll catch up!"

Kerry didn't even think twice. She turned and headed back, hanging on to the frame and extending her arm out across the slanting floor. "Here!"

Carlos gathered himself and shoved off from the wall, only to have the ship tilt suddenly back to center. He was unable to stop his momentum, and he plowed right into Kerry, taking them both to the ground near the bottom step. "Oh!"

Kerry landed on her back, her hands reaching out to grab hold of anything she could in preparation for the next motion of the vessel. Carlos ended up sprawled over her, his head thumping against the riser as he pinned her to the ground. "Oof!"

"Ow." Carlos winced.

Kerry glanced at the curve of his ear inches from her nose. She cleared her throat gently. "No offense, Carlos, but this is definitely not my idea of fun."

"I am so sorry, ma'am." Carlos rolled off her quickly, his face a brick red.

Kerry sat up cautiously but the ship remained steady. Far above them, she thought she could hear laughter, and the sound of tinkling glass, and she wondered how many things had broken during the bizarre tilting. "Okay." She got up, grimacing as she felt her shoulder pop back into place, an uneasy sensation she'd been prone to since she'd dislocated it in the hospital.

It wasn't exactly painful, but there was motion in the joint she didn't have in her other arm, and remembering how that felt when it came all the way out always made her inwardly cringe.

"Are you okay?" Carlos asked hesitantly. "I didn't hurt you or anything did I?"

"No. I'm fine." Kerry started up the stairs. "Let's go find out what the hell's going on." She took the steps two at a time, rounding the landing and looking up ahead of her as she started to hear voices, along with the sound of rhythmic footsteps heading in their direction.

Could have been anyone really, but there was something about the pace and the weight of them that struck a chord of instant recognition with her. She turned the corner on the stairs and had to stop short as Dar flew toward them without regard for her own safety. "Hey!" Kerry got her hands out in front of her, ready to jump aside if Dar couldn't stop in time.

You really didn't want Dar plowing into you. She was solid as a rock and with any momentum you could easily end up on your butt with no effort at all. "Whoa!"

Dar bounced to a halt, taking in both of them with quick, darting looks. "You all right?" she asked crisply. "Mark said you went down to the bottom deck."

"We're fine—just a little shook up." Kerry nodded. "You?"

Dar waggled a foot. "Banged my damned toes on a door," she admitted. "Bastards."

"Your toes?" Kerry took her arm and they started up the steps once again.

"Damn crew...thought it was funny."

Uh oh. Kerry could sense the prickling of her partner's pride, never a wise thing to ruffle, at least in public at any rate. She sometimes realized she was treading a fine line, even in private, with Dar on that issue. She certainly could be silly at times, and she had a great sense of humor, but she really didn't like being made fun of.

Even by Kerry. "Bastards." She agreed with Dar's sentiment. "It's not funny. Someone might have gotten hurt. We had guys all over the ship carrying heavy stuff."

"Yeah." Carlos spoke up somewhat timidly. "I'm sure glad we got that machine installed before that happened."

"Me too." Kerry gave him a smile.

"Hey, maybe those jerks ended up against the wall in there, huh?" Carlos went on. "They sure deserved it."

Dar stopped walking and turned to look at Kerry, one eyebrow lifting. "Jerks?"

"Later." Kerry urged her forward. "Let's see if we lost anything."

Visibly reluctant, Dar peered down the steps before she grudgingly followed Kerry back up. She suspected there was more to it than just a tossed off 'later', but Kerry appeared completely undamaged so whatever it was couldn't have been too bad.

Could it? Dar exhaled, and kept climbing. Her foot was well on its way to healing, but now was throbbing painfully again, and her temper was heading toward the ragged side. She kept that in mind and bit her tongue as she caught up to Kerry, suppressing her desire to find out what the 'later' was right now.

No sense in taking it out on Kerry, was there? She put her hand on her partner's back as they walked up the last set of steps into the atrium, and relaxed a trifle as she felt Kerry lean back into the touch.

Several of the techs were standing in a group, and Mark was just coming down from the next floor up. All of them looked shaken, and they turned in relief as they heard her approach. "Everyone all right?" Dar asked.

"So far." Mark was sucking on the side of his thumb. "Got my hand caught in a freaking door, that's the worst I heard so far." He surveyed the chaos in front of them. "Crap."

The gear that had been so nicely lined up was now tumbled everywhere, some leaning against the glass wall to the outside, some upside down near the stairs, and the parts that went with them were strewn about haphazardly.

"What the hell happened?" Mark asked.

Kerry walked over and knelt by one of the machines, tipping it back over and checking the screen for damage. "Yeah, me too." She called back over her shoulder. "Those must have been some waves."

Dar put her hands on her hips and frowned, glancing aside as some of the crew appeared behind the reception desk, obviously amused. "Something funny?" she inquired of them.

They didn't answer, but they didn't leave either.

Dar's eyes narrowed. The door from one of the offices opened and the staff captain appeared, smirking as he watched the techs clean up the mess in the atrium.

A thought occurred to her. "Son of a bitch."

Kerry glanced up. "What?" She got up and walked over. "Not that I thought you were addressing me, hon, but you've got the most bizarre expression on your face."

Dar waited for the staff captain to stroll over. "Morning."

"Good morning, Ms. Roberts." The man smiled charmingly at her. "Are you having a good day so far today? I see you have some disarray here. So sad."

Kerry just barely held herself back from stomping on the man's foot with her hiking boot. The sudden desire for violence surprised her, but somehow the reaction didn't seem overly wrong. "The ship nearly turned over. What did you expect would happen? I'm sure you have things in a mess in places too."

The crew behind the desk laughed.

"Not at all, Ms. Stuart," the staff captain replied. "You should really be more careful with all your machines, yes?" He walked past them and laughed, as the techs struggled to right the gear. "Perhaps we will hit more high seas."

The techs looked around apprehensively, some of them grabbing hold of railings as though expecting the ship to tilt again. This amused the crew, more of whom had appeared behind the desk, and the laughter rang across the atrium.

Kerry put her hands on her hips. "You know something, Paladar?" She turned to her partner. "There's something not right about this whole thing."

Dar gave her a wry look, but was spared from answering as Andrew appeared and crossed the atrium to where they were standing. "Hi, Dad."

The big ex-SEAL was chuckling. "You all right, Dardar? See everything got knocked puss over keester up here."

"Look out, here she goes again!" The staff captain suddenly yelled.

The techs all scrambled around, trying to hold on to something and their gear at the same time, while they looked around frantically to see which way the ship was going to tilt next.

Now the crew was clustered in the hall and they all broke up laughing.

Kerry let out a breath. "Dar…"

Dar turned to Andrew. "Stability test?"

Andrew was also chuckling. "Yeap. It surely was that." He glanced at his daughter. "Figgered they'd play a little seaman's joke on ya'll."

Dar's expression didn't change. "It wasn't funny." She looked her father in the eye, her voice quiet. "Especially if you knew about it and didn't tell me."

"A joke?" Kerry repeated. "My god. People could have been seriously hurt!"

Andrew blinked at them. "Wasn't really that bad." He started to protest.

"That bad?" Dar's voice rose now taking on an edge. She pointed at the gear. "Those weigh sixty pounds. If Kerry had been carrying one when they pulled this stupid little prank she could have broken her neck!"

The rage was very evident, and Andrew was caught completely flat footed by it.

"Jesus Christ. What the hell is wrong with you people?" Dar was talking directly to him. "You think this is some kind of game?" Now she turned and pinned the staff captain with a hard stare. "Mister, you better have a nice bank account, because every piece of broken plastic's going to be taken out of it." She headed right for him. "You think it's funny? You all think it's funny?" She let her eyes sweep the crew who had stopped laughing.

The techs stayed very still, even Mark merely kept his head down and waited.

Just then, footsteps sounded on the steps above, and they all looked up to see two of the techs easing slowly down the stairs supporting a third. "Oh man...glad we made it down here," one of them said in obvious relief. "I think Darcy's leg's broken."

There was a moment of silence. Then Dar turned toward Andrew. "Funny," she commented briefly, before she headed toward the stairs. "Okay, get him down here. I'll go find out how long it'll be until we get to port."

Mark shook off his paralysis and got up, hastening over to help the injured Darcy along with a couple other techs. "Easy, dude. Just relax."

Kerry exhaled. "Jesus Christ," she murmured, gathering her wits. "What in the hell were they thinking." She turned and looked at Andrew, who was still standing there in something of a stunned silence. "That was really supposed to be a joke?"

Andrew's face took on an expression Kerry had seen but a very few times on his daughter's face. It was the one she got when she knew she'd done something outstandingly stupid, and it was a look that always touched Kerry's heart.

This time was no exception. She took a step closer to her father in law and put a hand on his shoulder. "I'm sure they didn't really mean to hurt anyone." At least, she sincerely hoped not.

"Scuse me," Andrew murmured before he turned and headed off in the direction Dar had gone.

Kerry watched him go, and then she exhaled heavily before she walked over to where the injured tech was sitting and assembling a plan as she walked. "All right," she said. "I don't think that's going to happen again. So let's get the rest of these things where they belong, so at least we get that much done." She knelt next to Darcy who was biting his lip in an attempt not to cry. "And don't you worry. We're going to get you some help even if Dar has to get a helicopter out here."

Darcy managed a faint grin. He was a dark skinned Cuban with a faint moustache and dark, curly hair. Kerry knew he had a talent for working with servers and he knew lots of really bad jokes. She put a hand on his uninjured leg and returned his grin. "Just try to take it easy. It hurts more otherwise."

"Yeah," Darcy managed to get out. "You broke your leg too? Sounds like you know." He looked down the length of his leg, visibly twisted around the knee under his thick jeans.

"Dislocated my shoulder," Kerry said. "When I was in that hospital explosion...if you remember that."

Several techs made sympathetic noises. "That hurts," one of them said. "My brother had that happen. He screamed like a, um..."

Everyone chuckled nervously.

"I did too," Kerry admitted, "when Dar had to put it back in place."

Wide eyes looked at her.

"In the dark, under a collapsed ceiling, in a building on fire." Kerry went on. "So you know," she patted Darcy's leg, "things could always be worse."

"All right." Mark stood up. "C'mon, you guys. Let's get this stuff moving. You three stay here with Darcy, all right? Get him some water or something." He looked at the crew, now standing in silence behind the desk. "From our catering guys. At least we know where it's from."

"I'll stay here," Kerry told him.

Mark looked at her. "This sucks."

"I know."

"This just totally freaking sucks."

"Yeah, I know."

Mark led the techs out again, arms full of hastily righted machines. Kerry waited a moment, then she sat down on the cold floor crossing her legs up under her and leaning her elbows on her knees. She stared at the marble with unseeing eyes, trying to absorb all that had just happened.

"So. Uh. That burning building...that was scary, huh?" Darcy asked.

Kerry looked up at him. "Yeah," she said. "Want to hear about it?" She figured anything that would take his mind off his leg would help.

"Sure."

Kerry straightened up and ordered her thoughts, pulling up her memories of that far off terrifying night. There was something just faintly familiar about the act — some chord the looks in the eyes of the techs that struck her as she got ready to tell her story — that almost made her pause.

Almost. Kerry shrugged the feeling off. "Well, it all started with a baby..."

Chapter Six

DAR HEADED DOWN the hallway toward the bridge, feeling her temper simmering as it hadn't for a long, long time. She was mad at a lot of things, the stupidity of the prank, the possibility of Kerry being injured, her father's complicity…

Gah. She stiff armed the door to the bridge and walked inside, her eyes sweeping right and left in search of the captain.

Two of the officers turned to look at her, startled. "Yes?" one said. "What is it you want?"

"Ah." Dar spotted the captain in his tiny office. "Found it. Thanks." She headed for the room. "All right, mister." She shoved the door open. "What in the hell do you think you were doing?"

The captain, who had been leaning on his desk with both hands, straightened up and stared at her in utter shock. "Pardon?" He snorted. "What is the meaning of this, you bursting into my office?"

"What's the meaning?" Dar went right up to the edge of the desk and pointed at him. "I'll tell you what the meaning is, Captain. The meaning is I'm going to sue your sorry ass for deliberately endangering my staff." She let her voice build to a bark. "Got it?"

The man's jaw actually dropped.

Dar turned. "But that's not why I'm here." She glared out at the horizon. "How long until this piece of junk gets into port? I've got someone that needs medical help."

"Ah, one hour. But Ms. Roberts… The captain started around his desk.

"Don't bother." Dar snapped. "Save the sanctimonious crap for someone who gives a damn about your stripes. Just radio ahead and tell them to have that gangway ready when we get there." She turned and walked out, slamming his door behind her and leaving him inside.

The entire bridge staff was staring at her in slack jawed disbelief, but Dar barely saw them. She continued on through the bridge and out the door, pulling up short as she almost crashed into the staff captain outside.

Maybe her stare warned him. He stepped out of her way and let her go past, then turned to watch her leave. "You really should work on that sense of humor, Ms. Roberts."

Dar didn't even bother to answer. She turned the corner of the corridor and headed down the damn steps again, tired of the ship, tired of running up and down stairwells, and very, very tired of obnoxious ship officers with bad hair and worse manners.

Spotting daylight, she got off the stairs at the eighth deck and went out onto the exterior promenade that circled the ship and gave access to the fresh air. She gripped the railing and stared over it, her guts still churning with anger.

Moving around seemed like a good idea. She turned and started to walk down the promenade deck, the wind buffeting her as the ship rocked slightly in the waves. The deck was empty, only the lifeboats swung over her head in creaky counterpoint to the ship's motion.

Bloody bastards. Dar felt like throwing up. She'd been safe enough when the ship tilted over, having just come back into the atrium and close enough to the stairwell to just grab hold of the railing and hang on. But the thought of Kerry being down in the lower decks, with all that gear, and all those guys...

Okay. Dar stopped and stood near the rail again, gripping it lightly with her hands. Just relax a second, yahoo. Nothing happened. She exhaled. Nothing happened to Kerry, anyway, except for...

Except for the 'later'.

Dar leaned her head against the metal cross brace, staring bleakly out across the sea.

"WHAT HAPPENED?" CECI knelt down next to Kerry giving the injured tech a concerned look.

Kerry had just handed him a glass of water and some Advil. It was all she had to offer for what was surely a tremendously painful injury. "He was carrying one of the terminals when the ship tipped over and he fell down the stairs." She gave Darcy a sympathetic look.

He grimaced back at her.

"Ow." Ceci grimaced too. "I was busy being green in my bunk. That little roller coaster seems to have fixed me up permanently. What happened? Have you seen Andy?"

Ergh. "Well." Kerry exhaled. "Apparently the ship was doing some tests that they sort of forgot to tell us about."

Ceci's brows both lowered. "Forgot?" She snorted.

Kerry half shrugged. "Anyway, looks like Darcy was the only one hurt," she said. "Dar's upstairs yelling at the captain and finding out how long it'll take us to get back."

"Hm." Ceci pursed her lips. "Sorry I'm not there watching. Nothing like a little deserved tongue lashing to perk up the morning." She shook her head. "Unbelievable. Someone could have gotten killed." She glanced at Kerry. "Bet she's pissed."

Kerry nodded. "Very," she agreed. "So was I, but I think she's more pissed at Dad than she is at the guys running the boat."

"Andy?" Ceci frowned. "But w..." She stopped. "He knew?"

Kerry nodded again, unhappily. "Dar went off on him big time."

"Did she? Good." Ceci announced firmly. "Let me tell you I've had my fill of that brotherhood of the sea nonsense, and if he knew and didn't tell her it was going to happen, he deserves a spanking."

Well, that was probably true Kerry acknowledged. But she also knew Andrew felt a kinship with these travelers, ratty though they were, that she probably would never understand. "I know," she said. "But I've been at the other end of that tongue lashing and it's no fun."

"So have I." Ceci commented. "But in my case, the real surprise was what it was like when she wasn't mad." She got up. "Let me go find my husband." With a pat on Kerry's shoulder, she wandered off, heading for the stairwell.

Kerry wrapped her arms around her knees and fought the desire to go with her.

ANDREW PAUSED AT the doorway, looking out. He waited for a bit, but Dar didn't seem disposed to move, so after a few moments he gathered his wits about him and pushed the door open.

The warm air blew against his face, a feeling so familiar it raised ghosts that had no place on this ramshackle cruise ship. He dismissed them, needing a clear mind to deal with the trauma ahead of him.

He had seen Dar mad on many occasions. She had a temper, hell, she had his temper and he knew to an intimate degree what that anger felt like inside. He'd seen her stand her ground fearlessly in front of situations she damn well should have run from, and though he valued his daughter's safety above all else, he knew where that courage came from and couldn't fault her for it.

But he also never had that anger turned on him before, and he wasn't really sure what to do about it. So, as he always had in all kinds of bad situations before, he just stepped up to it and walked over to where Dar was standing.

As he came even with her and put his hands on the rail, she turned her head and looked at him. The few things he'd thought about saying died on his lips, and he just stood there looking into those stormy eyes.

He'd seen them before, matter of fact—every time he'd turned his back on his family and climbed up that gangway to go back to sea.

'Specially that last time. There really weren't no words to say that meant anything faced with that, was there?

So he didn't say any. He just reached over and put his hand on Dar's shoulder. Dar looked away. Then she exhaled and pushed away from the railing. "I've got work to do," she said, briefly, before she eased out from under his grip and headed back toward the doors to the interior.

"Dar." Andrew called after her.

Dar raised one hand, but didn't turn around. "It's all right," she said, before she pulled the door open and went inside.

Andy leaned back against the railing and folded his arms across his broad chest, turning his head slightly as Ceci wandered up to him from the direction of the front of the ship. "You fixing to yell at me too?" he asked testily.

His wife rubbed her nose, suppressing a wry smile. "She should have kicked your ass, not yelled at you for that Andrew."

"Ah did not do anything."

"Exactly," Ceci said, seriously. "You should have. You know better."

Andy scowled.

Odd, to be on this side of the fence. Ceci mused. "Well, just let her be for a little while. Let Kerry work on her and turn her back into a pile of goo, then you can give it another try."

Her husband eyed her.

"Or go kick the captain's ass." Ceci suggested. "And by the way, I'm feeling much better. Thanks for asking."

He sighed. "Hell fire day all round."

"Mm." Ceci relented and put her arm around him. "And it's just starting, too."

KERRY TURNED HER head toward the hall just before Dar appeared in it. Some of the techs were straggling back in as well, and the atrium was becoming somewhat crowded. And yet, when Dar lifted her head and sought Kerry's eyes for that moment it was as though they were the only two people in the entire place.

"Excuse me." Kerry got up and threaded her way through the crowd. "Hey." She reached Dar's side and walked right into her personal space, ignoring the room full of employees and wrapping her arms around Dar's waist.

Dar, unsurprisingly, stopped walking and returned the gesture circling Kerry's shoulders. "Hey," she responded quietly. "We'll be in port in an hour."

"Darcy's doing okay. He's just in a lot of pain. I gave him what I had, but it's not helping much." Kerry said. "Did you see the captain?"

"Yeah."

Kerry waited, but nothing more seemed forthcoming. "Did you see Dad?"

"Yeah." Dar rested her chin against Kerry's head. "Did all the stuff go out?"

Kerry nodded. "Most of it. They just came back and got the last round. Then we're done. You want to test it?"

"No."

"C'mon." Kerry nudged her toward the steps. "Let's just get it over with."

"To hell with all of them. I hope the damn ship sinks in the harbor."

"C'mon."

"Jackasses."

Kerry really couldn't argue with that. "Okay, I really want to just get you alone in a dark room. Humor me?"

That got her a smile. Only a tiny, grudging one, but a smile. It was a start.

KERRY PECKED AT the keyboard, sparing a glance every few seconds to her silent partner. Dar was standing in front of the server racks, leaning her hands against them and staring into the blinking LED's with an expression of dour anger. "Well."

Dar grunted.

"At least we know the rack mounts all work right." Kerry commented softly. "You know, Dar—"

"Fuck them."

Kerry exhaled and continued typing, shaking her head a little. "Okay, the POS server's up." She got up and walked over to where Dar was standing, putting a hand on her back and giving it a little, friendly rub. "C'mon, sweetie."

Dar glared at the rack a few seconds, then she turned abruptly and slammed her fist into the back of the door, a sudden surge of violence that caught Kerry totally by surprise.

She pulled back, uncertain of what was going on. "Dar?"

"How," Dar growled, "could they be that stupid." She pulled back away from the door and studied the healthy dent her fist had made in the metal. "Son of a..."

Kerry acted before she thought it through. She jumped forward and grabbed hold of Dar's arm before she hit the door again and held it, wrapping both hands around her partner's wrist. "Hey! Hey! Hey!"

Dar turned and glared at her, but after only a few seconds did her expression soften. She leaned back against the wall with a thump. "Pah."

Reassured, Kerry moved up next to her and let Dar's hand rest on her shoulder. "Honey, take it easy, please. I know you're really upset, but beating up the ship isn't going to help." She put both palms flat against Dar's belly and looked up into her stormy eyes. "Take it easy."

Dar drew in an unhappy breath. "I'm just so pissed."

"I know." Kerry crooked her fingers and leaned forward. "Believe me, I'm mad too, Dar. It wasn't bad enough I had some creeps hitting on me in the bar, but then to have...Dar?"

"Hitting on you?" Dar's mental train jumped tracks without any effort at all and continued merrily along its way. "Is that the 'later? Why the hell didn't you say something? I could have..."

The agitation was wearing on her nerves. "Dar." Kerry repeated, pushing her very gently against the wall. "Would you please chill? You're giving me a stomach ache."

Dar sighed. One hand lifted and scrubbed at her face. "Let me go sit down." She circled Kerry and took a seat in the one utilitarian chair next to the racks, letting her elbows rest on her knees. "Sorry, Ker."

Kerry knelt beside her. "It really wasn't that big a deal," she explained gently. "Just a couple guys who thought any girl would fall for their masculine charms." She clasped Dar's hand with her own. "Carlos was with me, and I ended up kicking a pool cue halfway out the window. Nothing big."

Dar looked up through shaggy bangs at her. "Pool cue?"

"Uh huh. I kicked it out of the guy's hand."

"Ah."

Dar's fingers were chilled. Kerry lifted them and pressed them against her cheek to warm them, her thumb running over the faint swelling on the knuckles from where she'd punched the door. "Hey."

"Mm?" Dar now seemed exhausted rather than angry. Dar asked, "Can we just go home now? If we jump overboard as they get to the mouth of the cut, we could swim to the condo in about ten minutes."

Kerry wished she knew what was really going on with her partner. The violent mood swings were beginning to scare her more than just a little. "Sure." She combed her fingers through Dar's hair, encouraged by the way her shoulders relaxed at the touch. "Can I get you a drink or something?"

"Do I look like I need one?" The touch of wry humor was very welcome.

"Yeah," Kerry told her. "You really do."

Dar exhaled heavily. "I can't figure out if I'm more pissed at the jackass captain, the smartass crew, my father, or myself."

Kerry kept up her riffling. "You? What'd you do?" she asked. "Or is this whole tipping over thing a tradition of the sea you knew about and forgot to tell me?"

"No...well, I don't know, it might be," Dar admitted. "Hazing at sea is. I knew that. I just didn't figure on them pulling a stunt like that on a trip like this."

"Were you a haze-ee at some point?"

"No."

"Everyone was scared of your dad?"

A faint smile. "Something like that." Dar sighed. "But you know what? He knows better too. I can't believe he didn't tip me off that they were up to something. Damn, that hurts."

"Hon." Kerry murmured sympathetically.

"I feel like such a jackass," Dar said suddenly. "Letting that happen to all of you."

Ahh. "Sweetheart, it's not your fault."

"It is."

"No, it isn't." Kerry was gently insistent. "Don't take that on yourself. You couldn't know what that Captain was going to do, and if Dad lost his mind and didn't tell you that's not your fault. That's his fault."

Dar gazed ahead of her. "Ow."

"You know he didn't mean to hurt you, or me, or any of the guys," Kerry said. "Dar, he didn't even know where we were before it happened. Maybe he didn't think it would be that bad."

"Peh."

Kerry leaned forward and kissed her on the forehead. "Honey, I love you more than life. Please don't chew yourself out like this."

Under this onslaught of mushiness, Dar really had very little defense. As much as she really wanted to stay upset and angry, it was impossible in the face of Kerry's solicitous endearments. She let her forehead rest against Kerry's and gave into it, releasing the fury still churning inside her. "Eh," she uttered. "What would I do without you?"

"You'll never find out, so who cares?"

That produced a genuine, charmed smile on Dar's part. They stayed like that, just touching each other, listening to the creak of the deck plates until finally Dar cleared her throat slightly. "Guess we'd better get this done, huh?"

"Before the server guys come trooping in here and find us snuggling? Uh, yeah." Kerry gave her another kiss on the forehead, before they both straightened up and Dar faced the terminal. She reached over and typed in a few commands, opened her mouth to say something...

And the lights went out.

Kerry slumped against her and just started laughing.

"HOW MUCH TIME do we have left?" Kerry asked typing away as Dar sat on the floor near the rack's UPS systems.

They had propped the door to the hallway open and some small amount of light was creeping in from the stairwell—enough to outline Dar's profile and cast a silvery dull shadow across the keyboard Kerry was working on, but not enough to really be useful for anything other than dispelling claustrophobia.

"Um." Dar poked her flashlight around the front of the panel. "About fifteen minutes," she announced. "Glad you spec'd out sixty minute runtime models."

"Me, too." Kerry wiped the sweat out of her eyes, then dried her hand off on her jeans before continuing to peck away. "You know something?"

"Hm? No. What?" Dar seemed content to sit on the linoleum floor with her legs pulled up crossed under her.

"I so want a glass of cold raspberry ice tea, our couch, and a pair of gym shorts right now."

Dar reached over and patted Kerry's leg sympathetically. "How's it going?"

"Almost done," Kerry said. "I just used the demo database we used for the proof of concept on it, Dar. There's no real point in customizing it, is there?"

"Not really," Dar replied. "Well, you might want to put their name on the front screen."

"How about I put S/S Jackass of the Seas, instead?"

Dar chuckled, and scratched her chin. "I dunno, Ker."

"You could do an animated jackass, right? Couldn't you have it sort of bucking around the screen while we do the demo?" Kerry mused, as she set up the screens. "I know you could."

Dar scooted over and peeked at what Kerry was doing. The monitor she was in front of was plugged, like the servers, into the UPS and it seemed hard to believe she'd actually finish before the power was drained to the point they had to shut everything down.

"We should almost be in port," Kerry said.

"Almost."

"Want to go check if we are?"

"No."

Kerry kept typing, but a smile appeared on her face. Now that Dar had stopped being furious, she'd subsided into a quiet peacefulness, not really helping Kerry in what she was doing, but not hindering it either. "Do you think you should call an ambulance?'

"Mark did," Dar replied. "It's waiting for us on the pier." She held up her PDA that was stuttering gently. "They're done putting the machines out, not that it does one damn bit of good without any power."

"Okay." Kerry stopped typing. "I'm done."

Dar leaned an elbow on her thigh and peered at the screen. "Nice."

"Pointless."

"Pointless, but nice."

Kerry saved the configuration, and then sat back. "It's done." She looked around. "We're done. Dar, we did this."

"Yep, we did."

"Everything's installed, the servers are up, the PC's are out—the network works. We did it."

Dar swiveled around and extended her legs out, letting her head drop back onto Kerry's thigh. "Uh huh." She agreed idly. "We did finish it all. Freaking incredible."

Kerry patted her on the shoulder. "Let's go congratulate our troops. No matter what happens, they came through for us, didn't they?"

'They sure did." Dar sat up, letting out a sigh as she pushed herself to her feet and held her hand out for Kerry to grab on. "Let's do it." She kept hold of Kerry's hand as they left the server room walking together down the darkened hallway toward the stairs. "Know something?"

"You've had enough of ships for a while?" Kerry hazarded a guess. "When we first started this thing, I was going to suggest a cruise but now...."

"Mm."

"I mean, our boat's nice. I like it."

"Glad to hear that," Dar commented. "I was thinking maybe we could take a ride up the Eastern Seaboard, just check stuff out and see the coast." She swung their linked hands a little. "Visit New England. How about it?"

Kerry was momentarily speechless. Dar wasn't talking about a week vacation, she realized. She was talking about something far more extended. Far more, and though the suddenness of the request shocked her, the fact that she had an eager agreement on the tip of her tongue surprised her even more.

"Just something to think about," Dar added, a touch awkwardly. "Sorry. Didn't mean to dump that idea on you right now. Anyway, we should figure out how we're going to do this proof of..."

Kerry squeezed her hand and stopped walking. "Yes."

Dar stopped also and looked at her. "Yes?"

"Yes. Wherever you go, I go," Kerry said. "Wherever you want to be, that's where I want to be, just so long as wherever we go, we go together." She felt an enormous sense of peace after she said it, and it was nice just to stand there and absorb the look of absolute delight on Dar's face on hearing it.

Just let the future happen. She wasn't going to worry about it. "C'mon." She started down the stairs toward the atrium where she could hear a buzz of voices. "We're done. Let's get everyone and get the hell off this thing."

Dar didn't answer. She merely followed, a rakish grin on her face.

ALL THE TECHS were gathered in the atrium, with their overnight bags at their feet. Darcy was laying in the center of it, propped up on a pile of folded blankets with two pillows under his injured leg and a set of solicitous attendants nearby.

They all turned around and looked as Dar and Kerry approached, most scooting around so they could face their bosses as the two came to a halt near the center of the atrium. Dar looked around at the darkened space, then at the techs, then she lifted both hands in exasperated appeal.

A soft chuckle answered her.

"How's the leg?" Dar asked Darcy.

"Well," the tech said. "It hurts, but I think it may just be cracked or something, cause it doesn't hurt as bad as my arm did when I broke that."

Dar rubbed her elbow in far off memory. "Yeah, that's pretty memorable." She agreed. "Well we're almost back home, so just take it easy." She produced a grin for the injured tech who bravely grinned right back at her.

Kerry leaned back against the central marble column very content to let Dar be the focus of attention. Of the two of them, she was very aware that Dar was the more charismatic. Heck, she'd fallen under that magnetic spell the moment she set eyes on the woman after all, hadn't she?

"Okay, folks." Dar paused, considering thoughtfully. "We'll be back in port shortly. I want everyone to get their stuff, and get the hell off this damn thing as fast as you can. We've got medical waiting to get Darcy off, but after that, just grab and run."

Everyone nodded, but said nothing.

"I want you all to know how much we appreciate you being here." Dar went on. "No matter what happens with this contract, we completed the task we were asked to complete and nothing can change that."

Kerry smiled, but remained quiet as well.

"So I want all of you to take next week off, on us."

Everyone's eyes widened including Kerry's. She turned and looked at her partner in some surprise. Dar had put her hands behind her back and was rocking back and forth a bit, pleased at the response to her announcement.

"I think you all deserve it after the last few days." Dar went on. "So take off, have a blast, and don't think about this damn ship, okay?" She half turned to Kerry. "Remind me to send a note to Mari," she added under her breath.

"I'll send it," Kerry murmured back. "I only wish we were included on that," she admitted. "Boy, a week off sounds good right now. That was a nice touch, hon."

"Thanks." Dar glanced out the windows where the port of Miami was beginning to come into view. "Let's get ready to move out. I'm not too damn happy with the hospitality on this junk barge."

A couple of the techs got up and went over to the pile of cardboard boxes they'd taken the equipment out of, now neatly flattened and stacked near one wall. "Should we take these, ma'am?" One of the techs turned back to Dar. "Are we going to have to take all this stuff back out again?"

"Leave it," Dar said. "They're just getting one big bill for this, no matter how they decide to award the contract."

"But I thought..." Kerry nudged her.

"I don't give a damn what he said," Dar replied. "He'll get a bill, and I'll toss it to legal. Let them handle it."

"Hm."

"Ham'll love it." Dar wandered over to the glass wall and looked out as they passed the island they lived on. "Sure you don't want to just jump?"

Kerry joined her. "Don't tempt me."

Dar continued watching the scenery pass. In the window's

reflection, she caught sight of her parents entering the atrium, but she resolutely kept her back turned and pretended she hadn't seen them.

She wasn't really mad anymore, but now she felt very awkward about the whole thing.

Kerry nudged her. "Dar?" she whispered. "The Captain's heading for you."

Another mental train derailment. Dar turned in the other direction and spotted the officer, who was indeed, headed directly her way. "What do you think? Toss him overboard?"

Kerry patted her arm sympathetically. "I want to go home with you today, not bail you out."

Dar rolled her eyes, but assumed a mild expression as the captain came up to them. She held back a greeting, however, and waited for him to speak his peace instead.

"Ms. Roberts," the Captain said. "I owe you a very big apology."

Wasn't what she'd expected. "Mm." Dar responded noncommittally.

"Along with some small drills, we had expected that stability test this morning," the Captain continued. "I had instructed my staff to inform you of it. They did not."

Ah. "Now that's what I'd call insubordination," Dar commented.

The captain nodded. "So it was. I am sorry your employee was injured. Of course, we will take responsibility for his medical expenses." He clasped his hands behind his back. "Please understand, there was no harm intended for any of you."

Dar allowed herself to be mollified. She'd halfway liked the old salt, and had been very disappointed to think he'd deliberately put any of them in danger. "On your part, no." She wasn't ready to let him all the way off the hook, however. "I think your staff feels otherwise." One hand sketched the air around them. "Was the power going off another 'oversight'?"

The captain remained relatively unruffled. "I wish it was, since I was in my cabin shaving when it went off," he said. "We managed to burn out our transformer. It's very old. My engineer's one of the few men in the world still able to sort it out, but it will take time."

"How much time?" Kerry asked. "We have to demonstrate this system to your owners, and we need power to do that."

The captain shrugged. "Impossible to tell. We need parts, and those are not easily obtained. We will do our best, however." He gave them both a nod then turned and walked off, circling around the techs seated on the floor and heading forward toward the reception desk.

"Hmph." Kerry put her hands on her hips. "Dar, if they don't fix that power, we can't prove our concept."

"I know."

"Can we run a huge extension cord from the pier?" Kerry asked. "Or something?"

"Let's worry about that when the time comes." Dar took a seat on one of the low benches that ringed the atrium. She noted her parents had done the same nearby, and now she raised a casual hand and waved at them.

Kerry stood by a moment, and then she clasped Dar's shoulder with one hand. "I'm going to go get our stuff. Be right back."

"Sure that's safe?" Dar asked.

"Dar, please." Kerry chuckled. "Just make sure they don't tip the boat over again, okay?"

"Okay." Dar stifled the urge to follow her, and merely watched as she walked through the crowd of techs on her way toward their cabin. They all looked at her too, and Carlos approached her shyly. Kerry paused, then glanced back over her shoulder with a humorously accusing look before she lifted a hand and nodded, and walked on with the young man following her.

Heh. Dar only had a momentary reprieve however, as her father got up and walked over, sitting down next to her on the bench. It creaked a little under his weight. Dar took a breath to speak, and then let it trickle through her lips.

"Paladar Katherine," Andrew said.

"Yeah?" Dar had laid her hands on her knees, and now she studied them, her eye catching on the subtle sparkle of the ring on one finger.

"That was a damn fool thing to do, and ah was a damn fool not to cotton to it."

"S'allright." Dar exhaled. "I don't really think they were out to kill us. Just embarrass us." She leaned back against the wall. "Bunch of jackasses."

"Well." Her father folded his hands together. "Ah do not think most of them folks wanted to do bad by you all. Ah do think most of them cottoned to you," he said. "Few bad apples."

Dar shrugged.

Andrew was quiet for a bit as they both watched the activity in the room. "Been on this side of the fence a damn long time."

"I know."

"Didn't matter. Ah should have tracked you down and told you," her father said quietly. "Instead of being one of them jackasses."

Dar turned her head and studied his profile. "You can't be a jackass."

Andy's eyebrow cocked and he peered back at her with patent skepticism. "Ah most certainly can be, young lady."

"Nah." Dar disagreed. "You're my dad," she said. "If you're a jackass that makes me a jackass too. You calling me a jackass?'

Andy's lips twitched. "You ain't no jackass," he said. "You're a damn smartass, though."

Dar chuckled wearily.

"You get all the stuff done you need to?" Andy asked. "Fellers worked hard enough all night. Helped them carry some of them big boxes around."

Dar hiked one boot up and rested it on her opposite knee. "We got everything in. Problem is we can't prove any of it works without power," she said. "I've about decided the whole damn project is just one big curse with my name on it."

Andrew tapped the back of his hand against her thigh. "It'll work out. Always does."

Would it? For one of the few times in her career, Dar had to admit that she really didn't think it would this time. And, for the first time, she had to admit to herself that she honestly really didn't care. She would hammer right to the end to get it done, get it right, get it proven, because her personal honor demanded that. But if it ended up that ILS lost the contract, well, then they did.

Dar wondered if she should call Alastair and warn him. She owed him that.

Didn't she?

KERRY FOUND SHE was damn glad to get back on solid ground again though part of her inner ear was insisting that the pier concrete was still shifting underfoot. She was standing out in the hot sun near the ship, watching as her techs unloaded their gear and themselves. Darcy had already been transported out by a waiting ambulance.

Down the pier, the other ships were also tying up and the amount of activity around their gangways was roughly three or four times what it was around their own. She spotted Michelle and Shari down there at the next ship, and despite their lack of power onboard, she was glad their part of the task was at last over.

Unlike her rivals, she could now snag Dar and go off to get some lunch, then sit back and wait for the power to come back on so they could sign off on the system and be done with it. Kerry would, of course, have to work on presenting the official bid for the project, but that was just paperwork and it could be done in a pair of shorts and a t-shirt with her feet up in her home office.

"Hey, Kerry?" Mark detoured toward her. "We're all gonna go over to Bayside for some eats. You up for it?"

"Maybe. Where are you guys going?" Kerry asked.

"Hooters." Mark had the grace to at least blush. "I know it's all sexist and corny and stuff but you know they really do m..."

"Make killer chicken wings. Yeah." Kerry chuckled. "Let me see what Dar wants to do. Maybe we'll meet you over there." The irony of it poked her in the butt, and she had to laugh at herself as Mark trotted off to help with a couple of large tool boxes.

She spotted the Herald reporter headed her way though, and so she stifled the giggles and assumed what she hoped was a professional expression as the woman came up to her. "Well, good morning."

"Good morning to you too, Ms. Stuart." The reporter greeted her with a smile. "I'm guessing it's a much better morning for you than for most."

Kerry had a flash of a completely inappropriate memory of Dar, their cabin, and a comment about sea motion from the previous night and couldn't quite repress a blush. "Ah...yeah, probably," she agreed. "We got a lot done last night, and now, pending some electricity, we're ready to show off the results."

"Really? You finished?" The reporter exclaimed. "Everything?"

"We did." Kerry agreed. "We put out the point of sale systems this morning, and I finished the server configuration just before we made port. I'm very pleased with how everything turned out."

"I bet you are." Eleana said. "That was a pretty slick maneuver you pulled off...getting aboard. I don't think Mr. Quest really approved."

Kerry shrugged one shoulder as she watched the gangway. "You know, I think Mr. Quest really wants to have his cake and eat it too. He wants to control every aspect of this contract bid, and yet he keeps telling us we have to be creative and deal with all the setbacks as best we may. "

"Hm." The reporter made a note on her pad. "You know, that's a darn good point."

"Well, we were creative, and we did what we had to do to complete this project." Kerry concluded. "So I would hope he has nothing to complain about."

"Hm. And now the ship has no power, is that what you said?" The reporter glanced up. "Convenient glitch."

Kerry had been thinking that very thing not long ago. "Well, according to the captain, they blew the transformer. He's got someone working on it." She looked toward the gangway as the rude little engineer appeared, furtively peering out and motioning for one of the crew on the dock to come over.

A bit of sunlight hit him, outlining his face, and suddenly Kerry knew where she'd seen him before. "Oh." She inhaled in surprise.

"Excuse me?" Elena gazed at her in puzzlement.

Was it really the same guy? Kerry focused her peripheral vision on him and tried hard to recall that fleeting glance she'd had outside the drugstore. The man started berating the dockworker, and with that, she was sure. It was that same twisted face, the same sneering expression.

"Ms. Stuart?"

"Sorry." Kerry collected her wits. "I was just thinking about something."

"What's going to happen if they don't get power on? You do have to demonstrate those gizmos, don't you?" the reporter asked.

"We'll come up with something." Kerry assured her absently. "If Dar has to hire three hundred hamsters and make an interlocking power wheel, we'll get it done."

The reporter started laughing. "Oh, that's a quote," she said. "You know they had a big meeting last night, the rest of the companies bidding and Quest."

Kerry forced her attention back to the woman. "No, I didn't," she said. "What happened?"

"Don't know. They didn't invite me in, and no one's talking," the reporter said, cheerfully. "I was hoping you'd find out, and let me in on it too." She looked around, then started backing up. "Matter of fact, I think I see an interview opportunity right now...catch up with you later, Ms. Stuart."

Kerry turned toward the ship. The little engineer had disappeared back inside, and now she trotted over to the gangway and climbed up it, edging past a few workers coming from the other direction. She entered the ship's hold and looked around, but the man was nowhere to be seen.

Andrew was, however. He walked over to meet Kerry, his overnight bag slung over one shoulder. "Hey there."

"Hi, Dad." Kerry greeted him absently. "Hey, did you see a little guy...kinda scruffy looking in here a minute ago?"

"Wall." Andrew considered. "I think I know what feller you mean. He's the engine guy on here."

"Right." Kerry turned and faced him.

"Believe that feller went off to get the lights on. Said he's expecting a part or something," Andy said. "That's what you all need, right?"

Right. Kerry took a step back and leaned against the wall of the ship. "Yeah." She agreed. "Guess he's the one who knows what to do, huh?"

"Yeap," Andy said. "Talked to him a little bit. Old timer."

"He looks a little creepy." Kerry remarked.

Her father-in-law shrugged. "S'allright feller, I guess. Been with this here ship for most twenty years." He moved closer to Kerry, clearing the way for a flood of electricians and other craftsmen to pile onboard cursing and shoving.

"Stupid assholes," one man said. "How in the hell do they expect us to do shit with no power? What a bunch of..."

"Ahh. Shutup," his companion said. "Who the hell cares? They're paying us."

Kerry shook her head. "You know, they're right. What the heck are they going to do in the dark, Dad?" She asked. "Darn if this entire thing just makes less and less sense the longer it goes on." Her eyes flicked to the stairs, where a familiar figure was fighting her way down against the tide. "Ah. Good."

Dar emerged from the stairwell and spotted them. She walked over, shoving her way through the line of workers in complete disregard to the complaints and outrage she left behind her. "You two ready to get out of here? I saw mom get off before."

"Waiting for you, sweetie." Kerry told her, setting aside her new revelation for later. "The guys are all going over to Hooters for lunch. You up for it?"

Andrew snickered. Dar cocked her eyebrow at Kerry. "Hooters, huh?"

Kerry shrugged sheepishly.

"You hungry?" Dar asked Andrew. "I'm not sure mom can get anything but celery sticks and French fries there, but..."

"Naw. We'll head on back home." Andy responded. "Catch up with you all later." He gave Dar a pat on the arm, gave Kerry a wink, and ducked under the edge of the shell opening that held the gangway.

"Hooters?" Dar grinned.

"Okay, okay. You win. You were right. Can we go eat now?" Kerry asked. "And, there's something I need to talk to you about, but not until we get away from here."

Dar appeared intrigued, but she refrained from questioning Kerry and instead steered her toward the gangway. They worked their way down past the line of workers and walked together across the pier, both glad to leave the ship, its hot chaos, and the busy dock behind them.

They passed through the gates and across the short stretch of grass between the terminals, glad of the shade from the palm trees as they headed for the parking lot. "Should we find Quest and talk to him?" Kerry asked suddenly.

"Want an honest answer?"

"I don't want to either, Dar, but I think we should."

"Well, you're probably right." Dar amiably agreed. "But it's a moot point, because the little bugsucker's headed this way right now." She jerked her head slightly to the right. "So hustle up your good manners, because mine took a hike and I just might kick him in the groin rather than speak to him."

"Gotcha." Kerry slowed her pace and turned, coming to a halt as Peter Quest intercepted them. He was wearing a sweat stained polo and chinos, and he had a very harried expression on his face. "Good morning, Mr. Quest."

"Where do you think you're going?" Quest asked.

Kerry decided to take the question at face value. "To get some lunch. Would you like some?" she answered politely.

"What about your project?" he asked. "Giving up?"

"Finished," Dar supplied dryly.

"What?"

"We're done." Kerry confirmed. "We just need for them to get power back on the ship to demonstrate it to you, and we can close the book on it. You'll have my financial bid paperwork shortly thereafter."

Quest looked honestly stunned. "You mean it? He asked. "You really did finish?"

"We did."

Quest started laughing. He backed away from them, and then turned and jogged off, still laughing. He waved a hand at them as he went back through the gates, then turned and moved in the direction of Michelle and Shari's ship.

Kerry turned and faced Dar. "If you at any point figure out what the hell's going on here, you will tell me, right?"

Dar tipped down her sunglasses and peered after Quest. "Uh, sure," she said. "But you know what? I'm gonna enjoy showing off that system to that bastard. Maybe he'll invite the rest of those jackasses to come see it too."

Kerry bit her lip, her conscience wrestling with her desire to take the project out on top.

"Ker?"

Kerry leaned against the palm tree they were standing under. "Yeah?"

"What's up?" Dar rested her hand against the trunk. "You all right?"

Should she even tell Dar? If she did, Dar would be as responsible for this decision as she was. Did Kerry want that? Wouldn't it be better to just keep it to herself and have total control over it?

"Kerry?" Dar moved closer, and her voice dropped in concern.

Did she really want to lie to Dar? Kerry tipped her head up and met her partner's eyes. No. She didn't want lies between them. It wasn't how she'd decided she wanted them to live their lives together. "That guy," she said. "That little nasty guy...the one we saw in the hall last night?"

Dar cocked her head. "The engineer?"

Kerry nodded. "Remember I said I knew him from somewhere?"

"Yeah."

"He's the guy from the drugstore. That guy with the car and the woman in the trunk?"

Dar's jaw dropped. "Are you sure?" She put a hand on Kerry's shoulder. "That was the guy?"

"I'm..." Kerry exhaled. "Dar, I really think it was. Am I absolutely positive? It was dark, and I just saw him for a minute or so, but I think it was him."

Dar removed her sunglasses and studied Kerry seriously. "He goes off the ship, we'll never get power. Not in time. Not after what I heard about him."

"I know."

They looked at each other. "What are we going to do?" Kerry finally asked.

Dar nibbled the inside of her lip briefly. "We're going to go to lunch," she said. "This guy's not going anywhere. Let's just think it through and then we'll decide."

Kerry thought a moment, then nodded. "All right. That sounds good."

They turned and continued walking toward the parking lot, getting to their car just as a group of people came out of Michelle and Shari's terminal, arguing. They paused to watch them.

"Ah." Kerry murmured. "Guess we found out where our little friend Jason from New York went."

Dar watched Quest apparently make a final point, then walk off, leaving Michelle and Shari standing there with the newcomer, and the Army captain, and the Travel Channel filming crew. "Know what I think?"

"Hm?"

"Everything just went to hell." Dar opened the doors. "So let's go to lunch, and maybe they'll all have sunk on that thing before we get back."

Kerry climbed into the car and almost appreciated the hot leather as it eased the suddenly tense muscles in the back of her neck. Just when she was convinced things couldn't possibly get any worse...

"Hey Ker?"

"Uh?"

"Love you."

Kerry smiled, reaching across the console to give Dar's arm a squeeze.

Hell with 'em.

Just straight to hell with 'em.

IN THE END, they decided against Hooters. Dar suggested a quieter spot so they could just sit and digest everything that had happened. So they ended up at the little Thai place near the office in one of the back booths that afforded the most privacy.

Kerry leaned back against the banquette seat, and relaxed a little in the cool air and dim lighting. "Good choice." She half turned sideways and rested her elbow on the table, propping her head up against her fist. "Wow." She let out a breath. "I'm wiped."

Dar folded her hands together and rested her chin on them. Kerry did look tired, she realized, and her eyes were a bit bloodshot. "Been a long week."

"I vote we sleep in tomorrow." Kerry picked up her iced coffee and took a sip. "How's your foot feeling?'

"Eh." Dar waggled a hand.

"Mm. That about covers how I feel too." Kerry gave their waitress a smile as she put down a steaming plate of curried shrimp in front of her. "Thanks."

The woman put down Dar's meal and then a bowl of fragrant brown rice, giving them both warm smiles before she backed off and left them to eat in peace. "Much as I appreciate Hooters," Kerry said, "I'm a lot happier to be here." She scooped some rice onto her plate, and mixed it with some curry sauce.

"Me, too." Dar turned and motioned to the waitress. "Can we get a couple of glasses of the plum?" she asked. "Thanks."

Kerry checked her watch. "Isn't it a little early for that?" She teased gently. "Last time I had alcohol with you this early was when you got cleared at the heart institute."

"We can handle it." Dar smiled, remembering that morning with utter clarity. "We went to work after that."

"Oo yeah. I remember twirling around in my chair for a while counting the seagulls when we got back. I was about as useful as a pig with a PDA."

"So was I, but it had nothing to do with the damn champagne." Dar picked up a bit of chicken and ate it. "I was just in there thinking...'man, what can I do to make her hug me again'"

"You were not!"

The waitress put down two glasses of plum wine. Dar lifted hers and toasted Kerry. "I sure as hell was. It's a damn good thing I turned out not to have a heart problem, because mine was flopping around like a beached fish that whole day."

Kerry picked up her glass and touched her partner's with it. "Well, I don't know what mine was doing, because you'd already stolen it and had it somewhere in your desk drawer, I think." She took a sip of the cold wine, enjoying the sweetness against her tongue and the warmth as it traveled down into her stomach. "We're such a couple of hopeless mush balls, you know that?"

"Yes, I do know that." Dar settled down to her lunch. "But I think I like it that way."

"You think?"

"Mmhm."

They munched away in a companionable silence for a little while, having learned through experience that eating their food while it was still hot was worth forgoing the pleasure of talking to each other while they were consuming it. Kerry, especially, tended to go off on verbal tangents and since her upbringing would not allow her to chew while speaking, she often ended up with a plateful of chilly ingredients at the end of her meal.

Besides, it gave them a chance to think, and Kerry used that to think about the ship's engineer. There was no question in her mind that she was going to call the police, but she knew the unspoken question between her and Dar was when she was going to make the call.

Now? If they took the man off the ship, chances were they'd never get to test their solution, and by default, they'd lose the bid.

Kerry knew it was more important to bring the man to justice than for them to win the bid. But she also had enough of her shining altruism knocked off to know that one more day of freedom wasn't going to make a material difference to anyone. She really had no desire to shoot herself, Dar, and the company in the foot by turning him in before he got the power back on.

She took another sip of wine, allowing it to relax her, and continued working on her plate oblivious of the blue eyes watching her from across the table.

Dar was right. It had been a very long week, and now here at the end of it, she was really feeling the strain. The usual stress of her job combined with the stress of actually doing the nuts and bolts of it, combined with the emotional overload of dealing with all the bull hockey, had left her feeling like she'd been run over by one of the eighteen wheel trucks busy delivering to the ships.

She really just wanted to go home.

"Ker?"

Ah well. Kerry looked up to find Dar gazing back at her, chin propped up on one fist. "Yeees?"

"Listen." Dar cleared her throat slightly. "My foot's killing me and I've got a headache that could drop Godzilla. You mind if we just go back to our place and wait for them to call us when the juice is on?"

Kerry blinked in surprise. "Um — w — uh, sure." She stuttered. "Yeah, sure. That makes sense. No reason for us to stand around the pier, right? We'd probably only end up being the subject of more snitty video."

"Yup." Dar drained her wineglass.

"Good idea, Dar." Kerry felt a distinct sense of relief. "Especially if you're not feeling well," she added. "We have to take care of you. Last thing we need is for you to get a bad infection or something."

"Mm. Yeah." Dar worked on clearing her plate. "Maybe we can just hang out in the hot tub for a little while. That might help."

Oo. The thought of the warm water, a cold ice tea and Dar next to her perked Kerry up considerably. It also did nice things for her mentally, and she finished her last bit of rice with a touch of impatience. "Sounds great." She wiped her lips. "You going to tell Mark to give us a call?"

Dar had already signaled for the bill. "Sure." She agreed amiably. "Bet Chino will be glad to see us."

"Cheebles." Kerry grinned in reaction. "Yeah, bet she will." She found herself looking forward to crossing their threshold and getting out of the heat of the day into the placid chill of the condo's interior. She scooted out from behind the table and followed Dar up to the cashier's booth, leaning against the taller woman's shoulder as Dar paid the lunch bill.

She'd gotten past giving her grief about that. Now they generally took turns, since all their joint income was deposited, appropriately, into a joint account. Didn't really matter then, did it?

They walked out into a blast of sunlight, pulling down sunglasses over their eyes and heading quickly for the car.

Chapter Seven

KERRY TOSSED THE mail down on the table as they crossed the living room, stifling a yawn as she did so. "We get a lot of junk mail." She noted. "Hey Cheebles, honey, c'mere." She sat down on one of the dining room chairs and greeted their pet, who was dancing from paw to paw in excitement. "C'mere sweetie...I love you. Yeah."

Dar paused at the door to the bedroom, then ducked inside to rid herself of her hiking boots and their overnight bag, tossing both into the closet with benign disregard. Wiggling her toes against the cool floor, she then unbuttoned her jeans and folded them neatly tucking them into a wash pile and adding her shirt to them a moment later.

"Dar?"

"Huh?" Dar called back. "I'm getting undressed."

A blonde head poked itself around the door microseconds later. "Ooo...can I watch?"

Dar turned and put her hands on her hips, giving her partner a droll look. "Yankee hedonist."

"Dixie nerd." Kerry slipped around the door and joined her in the closet, pulling her shirt over her head and folding it over so it could join Dar's in the laundry bag. She was about to unbuckle her belt when Dar's hands slipped around her and pulled her close and she abandoned her undressing for some skin on skin contact instead.

"Ungh." A small sound escaped her as Dar's fingers traveled gently up her spine, kneading the knots she could feel along it. She closed her eyes and wrapped her arms around Dar, breathing in her scent and reveling in the heat of her body against the cool of the air conditioning. "You are walking wonderful."

Dar wrapped her arms around Kerry and lifted her up a little, tilting backwards until she felt Kerry's back relax. Then she let her down and gave her a hug, ruffling the hair on the back of her head as she gave her a kiss on the top of it.

Kerry felt awash in affection. It was a very nice feeling, and she smiled giddily into the skin near Dar's collarbone. "Boy that feels great," she said. "Glad we came home."

Dar steered her out of the closet and drew her over to the waterbed. She released Kerry's hand and dropped down onto the bed's surface, rolling onto her back and regarding her partner with half lidded eyes. "I'm glad too."

Kerry unbuckled her belt and slid off her pants. She started to fold them, then found them yanked from her grasp and tossed against the far wall. "Hey."

Dar crooked a finger at her. "C'mere."

Jesus. Even after all this time, it made her go weak in the knees. Kerry climbed into bed to prevent herself from collapsing into it and took a spot next to Dar in the hollow her weight made in the surface. "Okay. I'm here."

"Know what I was thinking?" Dar rolled half onto her side and traced a teasing line down Kerry's belly.

Thinking was probably down on her list of things to be doing at the moment. Kerry reached over and threaded her fingers through Dar's hair pulling her gently closer and kissing her.

"Ah. Reading my mind." Dar chuckled. "That's exactly what I was thinking."

It felt amazingly good to be right where she was. The linen was clean and smelled of sun and sea air. The room was cool and dark, and Dar's lips were nibbling along the edge of her jaw as her hands stroked Kerry's skin.

Something occurred to her, however. "Hey," she whispered. "What about your foot? Shouldn't we take care of it?"

"It's fine." Dar growled softly into her ear.

Oo. "Oh." Kerry laid her hand along Dar's cheek. "Was there really something wrong before?"

"No."

"You just wanted to come here?"

"I just wanted to take you home." Dar kissed her on the lips. "And take care of you."

"Of me?"

"Of you." Dar enfolded Kerry in her arms.

Oh. Kerry smiled giddily for a completely different reason. "Thanks." She rolled over and snuggled up to Dar, letting her body press against her partners. "I'm not sure what brought that on, but I'm not complaining."

Dar dismissed the bid without much further thought, assigning it to that category of problems that she had limited control over. Whatever happened now happened, and she wasn't going to waste time worrying about it. She had something more concrete to worry about wrapped up in her arms right here.

This mattered.

She slid her hands under Kerry's bra strap and released it, smothering a faint chuckle as Kerry tickled her, returning the favor.

Kerry's hand touched her hip, fingertips sliding under the fabric of her underwear and easing it down. Then her hand stilled and Dar heard a faint sniffle.

She eased back a bit, cupping Kerry's cheek and finding the faint dampness of tears sparkling in her eyelashes. "You all right?"

Tired green eyes peered back at her. "Perfect."

"Yeah?"

"Yeah." Kerry turned her head and kissed Dar's palm, and then let her touch slip lower, giving her body over to the passion building in it. Everything else would wait.

THEY ENDED UP passing on the hot tub. Kerry was laying on the couch, one bare knee propping up her diary as she wrote in it when Dar came back from the kitchen folding her cell phone up. "Nothing yet?" Kerry asked, as she reached out to scratch Chino's ears.

"Nothing yet." Dar confirmed. "And I just spoke to Alastair."

Kerry nibbled the end of her pen. "Yeah?"

Dar dropped down onto the couch near Kerry's socked feet. "Yeah. I told him what's going on." She paused. "Well, I told him a little of what's going on. He knows we completed our part of the deal, and that we've had a ton of challenges."

"What does he think?"

Dar slouched down and put her feet up on the coffee table. "He doesn't understand why this has been such a tough case."

Kerry put her diary down on her chest and stared at Dar.

"Told you I didn't get into details." Dar idly plucked at the toe of Kerry's sock. "But I thought I owed him a heads up."

Kerry studied her partner's expression which seemed quite relaxed, almost mellow. "Is he worried?"

"Eh." Dar grunted. "I hinted to him that it might not be a good idea to hang so much off this one. He said it wasn't Quest he was concerned with."

"The other guys."

"Mm."

"Well." Kerry pressed her foot against Dar's thigh, pushing gently against her. "All we can do is our best, Dar. I think we've done that."

"Have we?"

"Yes." Kerry sounded quite positive. "Outside my not accepting a dinner invitation here and there, I don't think there's anything I would have changed in terms of business decisions. Would you?"

Dar gazed across the living room, staring pensively at the far wall with its neatly framed pictures. "Besides socking Quest in the kisser when I first met him, no, probably not," she admitted. "You're right, Ker. We did a good job."

"We did." Kerry agreed. "We pulled together the bid requirements, implemented them, and achieved our goals within the time limit, despite having to practically FedEx ourselves to hell and back doing it. I say that's pretty damn good, Dar."

Dar draped her arm over Kerry's legs and patted her knee. "Know something?"

"What?" Kerry favored her with an indulgent grin.

"You really did a hell of a job the last few weeks," Dar responded seriously. "From taking care of that power outage, to setting up the pier, to working with the guys to get everything set. Very well done."

Kerry smiled even more broadly. "Thanks, boss."

Dar returned the smile. "I watch you do your job and it makes me damn proud."

Kerry's nostrils flared a bit, and she shifted, visibly surprised. "Gee, honey," she murmured. "It really wasn't that spectacular, y'know."

The cell phone rang. Dar glanced at it, debating with herself on chucking it across the room. Then she sighed and opened it, checking the caller ID and finding Mark's name there. "Hell."

"DR?" Mark ventured.

Dar's inner child whined, not wanting to go back to work. "Yes, hello." She sighed. "They make any progress?"

"Um...no, listen, Dar...I think we've got, like a big problem here."

Another one? "And that would be?" Dar gave Kerry a warning look.

"That engineer guy, the one everyone was talking up? He took off," Mark said. "They can't find him, and nothing's getting done here."

Oh, crap. "When did this happen?" Dar covered the speaker of her cell with her fingertips. "Your fugitive ditched us.

Kerry sat up abruptly, putting her diary aside. "What?"

Mark sounded half disgusted and half embarrassed. "Beats me. I just heard a couple of them come through here yelling about ten minutes ago. I guess they thought he was getting some parts or something. They're pretty pissed. That captain guy actually came off the ship and was looking around."

Dar took a breath, held it briefly then let it trickle out of her lips. "Okay." She finally intoned crisply. "We'll be right there. See what we can do."

Kerry swung her legs off the couch and stood up, reciting several carefully enunciated curses that certainly would have surprised her Midwestern family as she headed for the bedroom and presentable clothing.

"Thanks. See ya." Mark had the grace to sound apologetic. "I know this sucks, boss."

"Yeah, it does." Dar stood up and examined her reflection, then shrugged and sat back down, picking up a sneaker from where it had migrated half under the couch. "But that's the breaks. See you in a few, Mark." She closed the phone and dropped it on the table, then concentrated on putting on her shoes. "No, Chino. You can't help me. Thanks anyway." She nudged the Labrador out of the way, getting a wet kiss on the nose in return.

"You going to wear that?" Kerry queried from the doorway.

"Uh huh."

"Dar."

"What?" Dar got the other sneaker on and carefully tightened the laces around her still tender foot. "There aren't any holes in it, are there?" She glanced down at her ragged and cropped coveralls.

"Huckleberry Roberts." Kerry sat down on the loveseat and pulled on a boot, her legs now covered by sedate denim. "Put some pants on, will you?"

"But I already have my shoes on." Dar frowned. "C'mon. I don't give a crap. It's a damn shipyard."

Kerry gave her a plaintive look, but merely shook her head and continued tightening her laces. It wasn't that Dar looked bad; on the contrary, the faded shorts overalls were stunningly adorable on her—at least to Kerry's eyes.

It was just that they were going to work after all. She spared another glance at her partner, who was once again sprawled on the couch. Oh well. If anyone could carry off being an outraged executive in cutoffs, it would be Dar. "Okay, let's go." She stood up and ran her fingers through her hair. "You think he's really gone?" She asked suddenly looking up into Dar's eyes.

Dar pursed her lips briefly then she put her hand on Kerry's shoulder and turned toward the door. "Let's go find out. He could have taken off any time before now, Ker."

"But he didn't." Kerry sighed, as she reached for the door latch. "Goddamn it, I don't want that on my conscience for the rest of my life." She walked down the steps and headed for the car. "I'll drive."

"Okay." Dar gave the now woebegone Chino a sympathetic look as she closed the door. "Be good, Chi. We'll be back soon. Promise."

"Whine."

Know exactly what you mean. Dar locked the door and followed Kerry to the Lexus, getting into the passenger side of the already running car. She settled her sunglasses onto her nose and closed her eyes as she began the familiar process of considering their options.

If, of course, they still had any.

THE TERMINAL WAS in chaos. Now that a good percentage of the IT people had left, the crew had wandered in out of the heat and into the air conditioning, and had taken over most of the big room near the back. Most were sitting on the ground with their backs to the walls, some had cards out, and some were merely sleeping, oblivious to the commotion around them.

Mark was behind the desk on the raised platform, and he looked up as the door opened for the nth time, on this instance finally revealing the outlines he was waiting for.

He started around the edge of the platform then halted, gazing in bemusement at Dar's more than casual outfit. "Hey boss," he continued on regardless. "Glad you're here."

"I'm not," Dar told him. "You send everyone else home?"

"Sure," Mark said. "No sense keeping them here."

"All right." Dar looked around the room giving her head a little shake. "Let's go find our friend, the captain, and see what the hell he's doing about this cluster." She headed for the back door, clearly expecting them to follow her.

They did. "Hey," Mark whispered. "She wear that just to tweak these guys?"

"Don't go there." Kerry held up a hand.

"Okay." He cleared his throat. "Missed you guys at lunch."

Kerry glanced at a sleeping lump of humanity, and realized there were three heads entangled in the sheeting. "Uh, we did Thai," she murmured, an eyebrow lifting. "Then we swung by home."

"Ah." Mark murmured.

"Wish we were still there."

Mark looked at her in surprise.

Dar hit the back door and powered through it, angling across the bleached white concrete toward the gangway at the side of the ship. There was little activity around the opening, unlike in previous days. In fact, only a few workers sat around the ground near the ramp, most giving her cursory looks and then double takes as they approached.

Okay. So wearing cutoffs that short was a stupid idea. Dar marched up the metal ramp and into the ship, putting that thought firmly behind her. The heat inside the ship immediately vindicated her choice, however, and she heard the grunts of displeasure from her companions as they started up the steps.

It was dark, it was stinky, and she was over it.

Over it, over the project, over the ship, over its crew, over the heat, over Quest, and about to go over the top. Just finish it, Alastair had said?

Well, all righty then. She would.

THEY DIDN'T HAVE far to go this time. They could hear the yelling in the atrium as they climbed up the stairs to the seventh deck. Dar headed for the sound, her sneakers giving her stride a touch more bounce than usual as she strode through the archway and rounded the center column.

Kerry kept right on her heels, already feeling a touch breathless from the oppressive heat and the fast climb. She hoped whatever Dar had in mind to do she'd do quickly, so they could get the hell out of the ship and back outside where, at least, there was a little bit of a breeze.

"Are you telling me you don't have a single person on this damn ship that can get it working?" Peter Quest was facing off against the captain, his arms flailing in time with his words. "What kind of bullshit is that?"

For once, Kerry found herself in total agreement with the man.

"Come now, Mr. Quest." The captain, however, remained calm. "You knew when you purchased these vessels, that they were old and their technology out of date. That was no secret to anyone, else why would you have gotten them so cheaply?"

Abruptly, Kerry found herself switching sides, as she agreed with the captain wholeheartedly too!

"That's not the point!" Quest argued. "You're responsible for keeping the damn things running! That was the deal I made with your prior owners."

The captain shrugged. "You made the deal with them. Not with me. Or my crew. They are not indentured slaves, Mr. Quest. If they decide to leave, they leave."

Dar had pulled up near the circular stairway, and now she stood quietly listening. Kerry was glad to join her, putting one hand on the relatively cool brass railing and easing her foot up onto the first step. She was a little surprised that her partner had put a hold on all that angry energy, but she understood that this conversation they were listening to would probably dictate what Dar would do next.

"You have to get this ship running," Quest stated. "Get one of the engineers off those other ships."

Ah. Good idea. Kerry complimented him silently.

"Yes, we are attempting that." The captain agreed. "But they also are busy, and in any case, our electrical systems are not like the others."

Figures. Kerry sighed.

"Bloody hell!" Quest barked.

"Something like." The captain seemed unperturbed, despite the fact that he was in full uniform and it was stained horribly with sweat. "My prior company purchased the electrical systems for this vessel from a shipyard in Romania, and they were — how shall I say — made with a horseshoe."

Quest's eyes seemed about to bug out. Dar took the opportunity to move closer and join in the conversation. "You mean shoehorn," she said.

"Yes."

"Ms. Roberts." Quest almost seemed glad of her presence. "Maybe you can offer some helpful suggestions on how to resolve this."

"Me?" Dar's eyebrow cocked. "I'm an IT executive, Mr. Quest. What makes you think I have any suggestions, helpful or otherwise, on how to get forty year old diesel electric turbine converters working?"

"Because your reputation depends on it," Quest responded. "If you don't show me the goods, it's as good as you not doing it." He held up a hand. "Don't bother whining to me about how unfair it all is. I've heard it all before."

Kerry rested her chin on the railing and simply listened.

Dar put her hands on her hips, but her expression was thoughtful rather than pissed off. "Know what I think?" she asked.

Both men looked at her in question.

"I think you're a horse's ass," Dar remarked. "And you're not worth my standing here sweating. I couldn't give a damn if you get this piece of floating garbage working or not." She exhaled. "I'll send a bill for my time, my gear, and my removal costs to your headquarters Monday morning. Until then, Mr. Quest, you can most cordially kiss my ass."

With that she turned and started heading back to the stairs, extending a hand toward Kerry as she did so. "C'mon, Kerrison."

Kerry knew her eyes must have been the size of tennis balls by Dar's expression. She straightened up and started to move toward her, her ears ringing with what she realized was the end of the project, and quite possibly, the end of their tenure at ILS.

No matter what their history, Alastair couldn't stand by this time. Even she realized that.

"Ms. Roberts!" Quest spluttered finally. "You've got to be kidding!"

Dar turned her head, expression still quite mild. "Nope." She clapped a hand on Kerry's shoulder. "I've had enough. Enough of your games, enough of the press, enough of the bullshit, enough of the shady dealings going on around this port. Enough. I did what you asked. It's not my problem if you can't produce enough power to see the results. That's your problem, mister."

"My problem!" Quest said. "The hell it is! You have to prove you finished, or you don't make the terms of the deal, Roberts!"

"Your problem." Dar confirmed, half turning. "You're the one who didn't fulfill the terms of the contract, Quest. Maybe you should read it. You agreed to provide sufficient physical plant for the installation." Dar gestured at the ship. "You didn't."

"He didn't!" Quest pointed at the captain. "I had nothing to do with it!"

"I didn't sign a contract with the captain, Mr. Quest." Kerry spoke up for the first time. "I signed it with you." A loophole. Had Dar found really found one? "Dar's right. It's not our responsibility to make sure the ship works. It's yours."

The captain chuckled.

Quest took a step back, his expression almost stunned.

"So," Dar said. "When you've got your act together, give us a call. I seriously doubt you will." She added, "And, Quest? You might be able to bluster and bullshit the rest of these people about what you're going to get from them, but I've got a legal department the size of Alaska you're not going to enjoy dealing with."

It was a good exit speech, and Dar took advantage of it. She nudged Kerry toward the door and followed, refusing to wait for whatever lame retort she was sure Quest would come up with.

"You'll look like a fool on television!" Quest shouted. "How about that!"

More lame than she expected. Dar merely shook her head and ducked around the stairwell door, hustling Kerry in front of her. "Jackass."

"You're amazing," Kerry told her. "Have I told you that lately?"

"Am I?" Dar wiped a sheen of sweat off her brow. "It's just all bullshit, Kerry. Smoke and mirrors. This whole damn thing hasn't been anything but smoke and mirrors since the moment it started. I just can't figure out who the hell wins by it."

"Quest?" Kerry suggested. "He gets systems for his ships."

"Yeah, but it's all cosmetic, Ker." Dar finally put her finger on what had been bothering her. "They're not upgrading the engines or the mechanics. What the hell are they doing to do with them when they're done? They can't keep them in service."

"Huh." Kerry skipped off the last step and headed through the hold, now silent and empty. "But all this upgrading and all the, wait..." She murmured. "You're right. It's paint, and carpet, and us and wall sconces. Not plumbing or..."

"Yeah." Dar nodded, as they reached the gangway and started outside, glad of the moderately cooler breeze. "Just what exactly is the whole point here?"

A blast of light hit them and Dar threw up her arm instinctively to block it. "Hey!"

Kerry stopped behind her, shading her eyes as she stared at the cluster of people on the pier, surrounding the filming crew who had them pinned in a pair of movie lights as they came down off the ship. "What the heck?"

Dar continued walking slowly down the ramp, blinking against the powerful lights as she reached the pier concrete. "What is all this?" she asked, her eyes finding Cruickshank in the crowd. "Don't you have anything better to do?"

"No, we sure don't," Cruickshank told her, cheerfully. "Now, Ms. Roberts, we understand you've completed your install, is that right?"

Dar eyed her warily. "Right."

"But the ship has no power, so you can't demonstrate it, right?"

"That's right."

"So here we finally come down to it," the reporter said. "Everything that's gone on for the past few weeks comes down to this. You're the only ones finished, it's near sunset, everyone else is killing themselves to get done, and now you have to find a way to overcome this one last huge obstacle, and bring it home. Right?"

Dar cocked her head. "No."

"No?" Cruickshank said. "C'mon, Ms. Roberts. This is where we see that famous never say die, win at all costs reputation of yours. We're all waiting for it. How are you going to pull this one out?" She asked. "This

story has become your story. How you got involved, how you fenced
with your rivals, how you overcame all the roadblocks. So, what's the
plan?"

Dar slowly removed her sunglasses that were hanging from one
earpiece in her hip pocket. She settled them onto her nose, blocking the
harsh light along with the sun. It gave her a moment to think, and a
moment to regret thinking because of what her mind was coming up
with.

"Two hundred extension cords and fifty pounds of gerbils," Kerry
spoke up unexpectedly. "So, if you'll excuse us, we've got exercise
wheels to put together. Dar?" She took her partner by the elbow. "We
better make sure the plans for those haven't gotten out."

Dar kept her silence, allowing Kerry to lead her off through the
crowd. She was aware of the rattle of the camera as it turned to follow
them, but for once Cruickshank had been caught speechless. They
managed to get to the gate and through it before they heard footsteps
behind them, and Dar had the presence of mind to slam the gate behind
her, hearing it lock. "Ker?"

"Eighty pounds of gerbils? We should really over engineer it a bit
just in case. Way our luck's been running." Kerry muttered. "You know
something? You know what I just realized, Dar?"

"We're being played."

Kerry turned her head and looked at Dar. "You knew?"

"I just figured it out," Dar admitted. "But it's the only thing that
makes sense. We're being played. We all are, Shari and Michelle
included. This is a scam, Ker."

"I'm not so sure it is." Kerry took hold of her forearm and slowed
down. "I think —"

"Hey!"

They both turned to see Michelle headed toward them at a jog.
From another direction, the Army guy was approaching them. From yet
a third direction, Cruickshank and her team had managed to get around
the gate and were headed their way.

Kerry exhaled. "We can outrun them."

"Sure. But it won't help," Dar replied. "We're going to have to
come up with a plan."

"No gerbils?"

"No gerbils."

"But I thought you told Quest it was his problem?" Kerry said.
"Why can't we just tell people that?"

They could, Dar privately acknowledged. But it was obvious that
everyone here was expecting her not to, they were expecting to see a
miracle. Her famous resourcefulness. That ILS magic. Alastair expected
it. The reporters did.

Hell, Michelle and Shari probably did too.

So what the hell was she going to do? She felt very off balance having to think about coming up with a plan that fixed something that really wasn't her fault or responsibility. It would play right into Quest's hands, for one thing.

For another thing...

"Dar?" Kerry lowered her voice. "Do you think Dad would know someone who could fix this?"

Ah. Then again, there was a reason beyond the obvious Kerry was where she was. "Tell you what," Dar said. "You call and ask him, and I'll keep these guys busy. Okay?"

"Got it." Kerry gave her a pat on the side and escaped, angling away from the oncoming crowd toward the terminal. Despite the suspicions that had suddenly erupted in her mind, she focused on this new plan anyway. If it turned out to be what she'd thought...

Well, they'd look good, at any rate.

THE OFFICE WAS a definite refuge. Kerry slowly moved the cell phone around in a circle as she waited for Andrew to call her back. It was quiet in the room; she'd shut the door for some privacy, and the only sound was the hum of the computers and the cycling of the central air.

She wondered how Dar was getting on out there with the press and their adversaries. Dar could easily handle anything this lot was likely to throw at her, but Kerry was bothered by a sense that both she and her partner were missing out on one major clue in this whole crazy scene.

A soft chime caught her attention, and she swiveled around to review the screen on the PC next to her. Her mail inbox was up, and a new message was blinking placidly on the top line. Kerry clicked on it, seeing the name of their chief of security in the send column.

Inside, she found a terse recap of the breach from the other night that had allowed the army woman to gain access to their systems. Kerry reviewed it, decided there was nothing new there she didn't know, then clicked on the attachment.

Another standard process, current background checks on the cleaning staff, the cleaning supervisor, and last but not least, their invasive little friend.

Curious, Kerry opened the last one and reviewed it. After a moment, she leaned forward and stared at the screen, her brow creasing over her fair eyebrows. "What the..." She read the first section again, and then went back up to make sure the name on the report was right.

She had expected the report to outline the woman's military background, of course. They wouldn't pull any records besides that from the government, but that would be there, plus any outstanding police activity.

But this report didn't show anything of the kind. There was no mention of the military at all. Kerry sat back. "Well, I know she's on the creepy side of the service, but sheesh." She gazed in puzzlement at the report. According to what she was looking at, the woman was no more an Army officer than Kerry was.

In fact, it was hard to say what she was, aside from the fact that she'd gone to college for drama.

Drama?

Kerry scrolled down the report to where it listed clubs and affiliations. Thespians and Kiwanis. Could the security department have made a mistake? She scrolled back up and looked at the photograph pulled from the woman's driver's license record, and compared it to the shot they'd taken that night.

Well, given the usual horrendous nature of government photos, it was the same woman. So, was her military career just completely obscured by its secretive nature, or...

Or was it much simpler. Kerry clicked on the mail and forwarded it, typing in an address and a short, but very polite request. She sent it on its way and closed the attachment. "Let's see where that gets us," she decided, and then on a whim, opened another new message, this time to the security chief. "And, while we're at it, let's check out her boss."

She sent that request as well, and then settled back in her seat, moderately satisfied. "Something stinks like a three day dead mackerel here and darned if I'm not going to find out what it is."

DAR AND MICHELLE sat on the steps of the terminal while the filming crew waited in the shade nearby. "So." Dar examined her kneecap. "What can I do for you?"

"Decided on civility for a change?" Michelle asked.

Dar chuckled mildly. "You come over here to ask me for something, and start off by insulting me. Ever consider maybe that's why you never get anywhere?"

Michelle sighed. "You bring out the bitch in me, Dar. What can I say?" she said. "You bring out the bitch in everyone."

"Not everyone."

"Ah, that's right." Michelle shifted and extended her short legs, crossing them at the ankle. She'd finally given up on the power suits, and was wearing crisply pressed black chinos that were sadly covered in dust and pier grime. "Your little missus. How could I forget? You do know everyone thinks she's just a pretty ornament of yours."

Dar realized Michelle was trying to piss her off. She wasn't sure exactly why, but she was determined not to let her succeed. It wasn't easy, however. "Yeah, most people do think that," she agreed. "Until they either get slam dunked by her or she saves their ass."

"Mmph." Michelle grunted.

Dar waited a moment more, then retrieved a weed from between the cracks in the cement slabs and plucked its leaves contentedly. "So, let me ask again. What do you want?"

"I want to make a deal."

"Call Monty Hall. Maybe he'll let you squeeze by without a candle up your ass," Dar suggested. "Michelle, no deals. We're down to the last day of this damn charade... just let it play out."

Michelle appeared to consider this. She circled her knee with both arms and gazed out across the dusty parking lot. "I can't just let it play out. I'm not going to be able to finish this thing without help. Your help."

"My help?" Dar's voice rose incredulously.

Michelle sighed. "It's a bitch being so damn wonderful, isn't it?"

"What in the hell do you need my help for?"

Michelle half turned, her expression acknowledging the irony of the situation. "We can't get that damn satellite working. The idiots who installed it have been at it for four days, and they're just clueless. Their bosses are clueless. The people on the other end of the satellite are clueless. It just won't work."

Dar's eyebrows crawled up her forehead to lodge somewhere near her hairline. "And you think I can make it work?" she asked, with a slight chuckle.

"Yup. I do." Michelle confirmed. "You got yours going. No one else has gotten that far yet."

"No one?" Dar looked around the port, at the stolidly perched ships around it. "You're kidding me."

"Nope. We had a big meeting last night. Don't ask me why anyone thought it would be a good idea to get forty people who really disliked each other, and who'd been sitting in the hot sun all day in a room without gags, but we did." Michelle reported. "With the cameras. Could only have been better television if you'd been there, trust me."

Dar scratched her ear, momentarily at a loss. "Okay." She let her hand rest on her knee. "So, you want me to come fix your satellite, so you can..."

"Finish. Beat you. Leave. Get the hell out of this mud bowl. Yes." Michelle nodded. "Don't worry. You'll get full credit for it with the TV people. Starring role, they'll get you on camera saving our asses. Great stuff."

Dar got up and dusted her legs off. She was aware of the close scrutiny of the television people, and she suspected she was being filmed by the busy cameraman.

"C'mon Dar. I know there's an innate sense of fairness in there somewhere." Michelle also got up. "You know this has been the worst of the worst. You know you can't beat our pricing because whatever it takes to get this bid, I'll do it. You can lowball me, but everyone's gonna know you did, because we all know how much it cost you to pull off that stunt yesterday, and all the rest of the bull crap this whole week. At least you come out of it with great press for being the hero. What do you say?"

"What do I say?" Dar repeated. A motion caught her attention, and she looked up to see Kerry exiting from the terminal, pausing, spotting her, and breaking into a jog in their direction. Something about her expression made Dar wait, and as she came closer she could see those green eyes snapping with indignation. "Uh oh."

"Uh oh?" Michelle looked up at her, puzzled, then she realized what Dar was staring at. She got up just as Kerry reached them. "Ah."

"Those piece of shit mother pluckers." Kerry stated as she came to a halt.

Dar blinked. "Um."

Kerry turned and pointed at the television crew. "It's all been a fake, Dar."

"What?" Dar and Michelle both spoke at once.

"We're in a bloody twisted farce of Candid Camera," Kerry said. "It's all the television people. They're behind it. They're paying Quest off big time and that guy from the Army? He's an actor!"

"What?"

"He's an actor, Dar. So is that crazy woman I found in your office," Kerry said. "I just got a note from Gerry Easton. He checked them out for me. They're no more Army officers than Chino."

Dar put a hand on Kerry's shoulder. She could feel her partner's entire body shaking with outrage. "Are you saying this whole damn thing was staged?"

"Yes," Kerry said. "That's exactly what I'm saying. Those people were hired to break into our office and make a scene, Dar. That's why they didn't really know what went on there, and they couldn't explain what they were after."

Dar appeared thoughtful. "Huh."

Michelle grabbed her head with both hands. "Wait. Wait. Wait. This is nuts," she said. "This bid is real, those freaking ships are real—c'mon now, Kerry."

Something clicked. "No." Dar put her hands on her hips. "It's not nuts. It explains a lot."

Michelle was still holding her head. "Well, maestro, then explain it to me, because I just don't get any of this at all."

Dar made a decision. She tapped Michelle on the shoulder. "C'mon," she said. "Let's go back into our office here, and have a chat. In private." She turned and headed back for the terminal, a still bristling Kerry at her side.

After a moment, Michelle followed, catching up to them on the steps and not looking back at the cameras even once.

"OKAY, SHOW ME." Dar circled Kerry's desk chair and perched on the edge of the desk itself. "I've been kicking myself trying to figure out why nothing's been adding up."

Michelle took a seat at the next desk and watched attentively.

"Here." Kerry clicked on her mail, then got up and got out of Dar's way as she slid into the mildly squeaking chair. She traded places, perching on the desk as her partner moved the mouse impatiently, scrolling through the long, and somewhat detailed messages. "Bloody little pissant buggers."

Michelle snorted softly. "You Midwestern repressed types."

"I got over that," Kerry replied, folding her arms over her chest. "I can't believe this crap. Didn't you pick up on the slimy fakeness? You guys have been in bed with those camera people for weeks."

"Damn." Dar shook her head.

"Well." Michelle crossed one leg over the other. "You know, Dar. I didn't really expect to find out that you're the nice one of your little partnership."

"Toldja." Dar muttered.

"Told her what?" Kerry asked. "Look, I'm sorry. It's been a lousy month, and a lousy week, and a lousy day. Finding this out at the end of it just sucks."

Dar reached over and patted Kerry's thigh. "Easy, Ker."

"Okay, so let me get this straight." Michelle changed course. "You're telling me that you think this whole deal is one big made for television melodrama?" Her tone was incredulous. "You do realize how insane that sounds, right?'

Dar sent the mail to the printer. "Yeah." She turned and leaned back. "Problem is Ker's right. That Army captain who was hanging out with you all this morning's a fake. Got his security records right here."

"What was he doing here this morning?" Kerry suddenly asked.

Michelle drummed her fingers on the chair arm, the nails clattering softly against the padding. "He said he was evaluating the technology we were all using, on behalf of the government," she admitted. "Sounded like something the military might do. After all, we all are pretty high tech."

Dar snorted.

Michelle got up and peered over her shoulder. "Pardon me for being nosy."

Dar handed her the sheet from the printer. "Don't strain your eyes. Here."

"I have a headache." Kerry sighed. "Dar, I'm going to get a soda. You want?"

"Sure."

Kerry slid between the chairs and headed for the door, fishing coins from her front pocket as she left. Dar rummaged around in her mailbox for a few minutes, leaving Michelle to read the report in peace. She read Gerry's answer, hearing her old friend's gruff voice quite clearly in the words and reflecting that Gerry really had handled her coming out to him a lot better than she'd anticipated.

He'd seemed somewhat disappointed, but, she realized, it wasn't so much in her as in the fact that she and Gerry's son would never be getting married to each other. That touched Dar, because Gerry had always treated her like an adopted daughter, and when they'd been at odds over the Navy base she'd really felt it.

Even more so than with Chuckie.

Ah well. "So."

"So." Michelle wrinkled her nose. "Well, frankly, that actually does suck, Dar. Your Kerrison was right. This guy's fake as a perfect nose on South Beach." She tossed the report on the desk. "But I don't get it. You knew about him before this. What's up with that?"

"You didn't think it was a little odd for him to show up?"

Michelle shrugged both shoulders and made a face. "Given what we've had here the past week, with the EPA, and Customs, the police, immigration, the Coast Guard...no, frankly. I didn't think it was strange at all, or at least, no stranger than anything else that's gone on here."

Michelle did have a point there, Dar had to concede. "He showed up at that damn show in Orlando." She paused, considering her words. "I thought he'd picked up on that security seminar I did."

Michelle snorted in mild amusement.

Dar got up and paced around the small office, restlessly wishing Kerry would return. "He wanted to buy out some new technology I was working on."

"What a surprise."

Dar turned. "He ended up getting someone to sneak inside our office, pretending to be a cleaning person."

Michelle laughed, covering her eyes. "You're kidding, right?"

"No." Dar went to the equipment rack and studied the machinery mounted in it. "Tried to put some pressure on us with that, saying it showed lack of security for the government."

"Doesn't it?"

"Well, not if there's no government traffic going through the Miami office, no." Dar remarked dryly as she turned and crossed her arms. "Apparently he forgot to do his homework. Anyway, I got him to back off, but the whole thing just didn't make any sense."

"Still doesn't" Michelle got up and prowled after Dar. "I just can't believe this whole thing's a setup. It's just impossible."

Dar settled back against the desk and ticked off points on her fingers. "You have four ships," she said. "All of them are wrecks."

"Yeah, but they're being fixed over." Michelle objected.

"Only on the surface." Dar leaned forward a little. "Think about it—new carpet, new paint, new wallpaper, but same old engines, same old machinery, same old crappy plumbing."

"Heard you had a problem with that." Michelle smirked.

Dar looked at her.

"Okay." Michelle held up a hand. "I get your point. So, they're only doing cosmetic changes. So what?"

"So what?" Dar's voice rose in incredulity. "What the hell do you think they're going to do with the damn things when they're finished with the frills? They can't sail them in the US. They don't meet maritime code, much less public health! They've got kettles in the kitchens older than I am!"

Michelle appeared puzzled. She folded her own arms. "You know that for sure?"

Dar rolled her eyes.

"Oh yeah, I forgot. Navy brat," the other woman said. "Okay, well, maybe Quest was going to do that next. Maybe he got funding to do the cosmetics first."

The door opened and Kerry returned, bearing several bottles. One she handed over to Dar. "Cruickshank is outside, wanting to know where you two are. I kicked her out of the building."

Dar examined her offering with interest. "Double fudge Yoohoo?"

"What?" Michelle started forward. "Hey, you shouldn't piss that woman off. You know she's got all our asses on tape and she can...what the hell's wrong with you, Stuart? You lost your mind or the vestiges of common sense you used to have?"

"Both are intact thanks; but then, I guess we weren't being paid off by them so I have less to lose by being a meanie." Kerry replied evenly.

Michelle stopped on the way to the door and looked at her. "Who told you that?" She demanded.

Kerry merely smiled, and took a sip of her soda.

"It's not a payoff," Michelle told her stiffly. "It's an all access fee."

Dar started laughing, almost spitting a mouthful of her delightfully chocolate beverage across the room.

"It is." Michelle insisted. "They wanted twenty four hour access to us, well, they got it. But at a price."

Kerry patted Dar on the back. "Easy, hon." She was chuckling herself, though. "I guess that explains why we're behind in this whole scheme. We've been chasing her ass away from us from day one."

"Hey, it's subsidizing the work," Michelle said. "It's going to make my bid pretty damn unbeatable, so you can stop laughing now, wonderkind." She headed for the door again, shaking her head.

Dar wiped her eyes. "Michelle, you ass. The bid's a fake. What the hell difference does it make what your numbers are? You don't get it. You're not going to get a contract. There is no deal. It's all for television!"

Michelle paused with her hand on the door latch. "You don't know that."

"We do, and you know it too. You're not stupid," Kerry said. "C'mon, Michelle. You called me on my common sense. Where's yours?"

Their erstwhile adversary stood in silence for a bit, her eyes flicking between them as she considered.

Dar and Kerry waited side by side, sipping their drinks and obvious in the solidarity of their partnership. "How is that?" Kerry inquired, indicating the bottle.

Dar offered her a taste, tipping the beverage to her lips.

"Mm." Kerry considered. "Definitely chocolatier than the regular kind."

"I like it."

Michelle turned fully and leaned her back against the door. "You know something? You two are obnoxiously goopy."

"Kiss my ass," Dar replied pleasantly. "At least we don't act like two biddies at a cockfight."

Even Kerry blinked. "Pithy, sweetheart." She bumped shoulders with Dar. "Very pithy."

Dar shrugged. "Are we done posturing? You want to work with us to end this without everyone looking like jackasses, or do you want to leave?" she asked Michelle. "Pick one. But make it fast."

Michelle definitely looked both tempted and very frustrated. It was an odd mixture on her face. "Why in the hell should I trust you?" she suddenly asked. "You could be just looking to screw me over."

Ah. Good question. Dar took a mouthful of her soda, rolling it around a minute before she swallowed it.

"After all, wouldn't it be to your advantage to have me suddenly backing out of my deal?" Michelle asked shrewdly. "What if you're the one who's scamming this time, and you've just fed me a lot of BS?"

Kerry put her drink down and walked over to Michelle. "Sure, we could be doing that," she agreed, stopping just short of the other woman. "I could have made up that email, and we could be lying." She put her hands on her hips. "But you know what, Michelle? We aren't."

"So you say."

Kerry tilted her head and gazed down at her, enjoying the experience with a good deal of guilty pleasure. "Think about it. If what we're saying is true, then the only purpose for what Quest did was to make all of us look like fools."

It was apparent that the notion had occurred to Michelle, and her face twisted into a wry grimace. "That's one interpretation of what might happen," she answered. "However, hypothetically speaking, if this crazy story you came up with were true, what do you intend on doing about it?"

Gotcha. Kerry smiled at her with a touch of genuine warmth.

"And why would you want my cooperation?" Michelle added cannily.

"Because those television people made us the story." Dar interjected from her spot across the room. "So if we're going to get out of this without looking like crap, we've got to do it together."

Michelle gave her a look of patent disbelief.

"Trust us," Kerry said, catching her eye and holding it.

"You've got to be kidding"

"Trust us," Kerry repeated. "Or we'll both end up screwed and you know it."

Michelle studied those clear green eyes for a long moment. Then she turned and opened the door. "If I'm not back in ten minutes, I'd start looking for a plan B." She left and closed the door after her without looking back.

Kerry returned to Dar's side and sat on the desk, kicking her feet out idly. "Do we have a plan B?"

Dar drained her bottle of Yoohoo. "Ker, we don't even have a plan A yet."

"Ah."

"This changes every damn thing."

"Yeah."

"Goddamn it."

Chapter Eight

THEY WENT OUTSIDE, finding a place in the shade in front of the terminal where a stone bench and table were perched. Dar took a seat on the unevenly slanted bench and rested her elbows on her knees, gazing thoughtfully back at the ship as Kerry joined her.

For a little while, they just sat there together watching the foot traffic pass in front of them. There was a slight breeze, enough for the heat not to be unbearable, and the soft sound of nearby crickets was almost soothing.

Kerry shifted a little, bringing her shoulder into contact with Dar's. She propped her chin up on her fists and rocked back and forth, swaying them both.

Dar turned her head, and then leaned over and gave Kerry a kiss on the top of her shoulder.

Kerry smiled, and rested her head against Dar's.

"Did you hear from Dad?" Dar asked, after a few more quiet minutes.

"Not yet, no," Kerry replied. "But it was kind of a bizarre request, so maybe he can't find anyone."

"Maybe," Dar agreed. "Should we call him and tell him to stop looking?"

Kerry was quiet for a few breaths. "Well, I guess," she said. "There really is no point in doing this anymore. Is there? Can we just...go home? What are we going to do, Dar?"

Dar stuck her lower lip out, and scrunched her face into a wry expression. "That's what I've been sitting here trying to figure out."

"Hm. Yeah, me too."

"I just have really no idea how to turn this around. What the hell are we going to do?" Dar asked. "Do we just call Quest over and say forget it? Call the press? Call the Marines? How do we get out of this without looking like total idiots?"

Kerry watched a snail make its leisurely way across the concrete between her boots. "Well, we could play along with it."

"Bah."

"Yeah, my feelings too, but you did ask," Kerry said. "I mean, if we did play along, and we got all our stuff done and all that, what's the worst that could happen? The television show would just show us doing what we do."

"Mmph." Dar grunted.

Kerry waited, but the look of stubborn disagreement didn't fade from Dar's face. She exhaled, understanding the emotion behind it. "Okay, so, what does blowing them out of the water get us?"

"Immense personal satisfaction," Dar replied in a decisive tone.

Kerry sighed. "Aside from that."

Dar was quiet for a minute, then shifted. "It lets us turn the tables and not let it be seen that they pulled one over on us completely," she said. "Think about it, Ker. Here they all are, laughing their asses off at us behind our backs."

"Hm."

"So, does it look better for us to have them figured out, and play them in the end rather than be the ones who have to stand there like jackasses when they decide to reveal themselves?" Dar asked. "I think I'd feel a lot better about how this comes out, regardless of how it comes out, if I can salvage at least a little of my dignity."

Dar was right. Kerry could feel it, and she found herself nodding in agreement even before her partner stopped talking. "Okay, so where do we start?" she asked. "I don't think we should just come out and tell them we're on to them. Or should we?"

From a personal standpoint, Dar liked that idea. It meant the entire ordeal would be effectively over, and they could just go home. She really wanted that to happen, because frankly, the project was seriously getting on her nerves.

Unfortunately, Kerry did have a point, and she didn't think just blowing them out of the water was a good strategic idea either. Also, it didn't really satisfy her need for some revenge on Mr. Quest and his personal circus.

Ah well. "No, I don't think we should just spill their little story," Dar said. "Let's think about it a minute. What's the purpose for what they did? To get a good piece of television, right?"

Kerry shrugged. "I suppose, though a show about a bunch of geeks running wire— gotta wonder what demographic that's aimed at, hon."

"Eh." Dar looked around. "Miami, sun, fun, bare-chested sailors, lesbians...probably be a hit," she remarked in a droll tone. "But the point is they're hoping to get a fight to the finish, right? All of us going full out until midnight— maybe even a couple more cat fights along the way."

"Probably."

"So what if we all just cooperate and work together instead? Help each other to finish, so that everyone ends in a tie?"

Kerry looked at her. "Sweetheart, you know I love you with all my heart, but do you think you can really get all these people to do that?"

Dar shrugged. "I dunno. Haven't tried yet."

"Yeesh." Kerry rested her head against Dar's shoulder again. "Well, I guess we can give it a try, but if Michelle blows us off, that kind of blows that up, right?"

"Right. However..." Dar nudged her.

Kerry looked up and saw Michelle and Shari headed in their direction. "You think they're going to cooperate with us?"

Dar studied the approaching women. "Possibly." She got up and ran her hands through her hair, then let them fall to rest on her hips as she waited for their adversaries to arrive.

Kerry got up and came to her side, but her cell phone rang as she did so. She opened it, and glanced at the caller ID. "It's Dad." She murmured, before she answered it. "Hi Dad."

"Hello there, kumquat," Andrew answered. "You all doing all right?"

Kerry eyed the oncoming devilishly dykish duo. "Oh, fine, Dad...you? Have any luck?"

"Ah do believe I might have." Andrew sounded pleased with himself. "Got me a feller used to hang around on subs with me and he's willing to poke an eyeball at that damn thing."

"Great," Kerry said. "Are you coming over here?"

"Yeap, that we are. You by that concrete pillbox of yours?"

Kerry chuckled. "We're here. See you in a bit." She closed the phone hastily and cleared her throat, wondering what would be left on the steps when he got there.

Left of Shari, of course.

"Well?" Dar asked, as Michelle and Shari stopped in front of them. She noted Shari's skeptical expression, but realized suddenly that other than that, the sight of her old lover no longer held the slightest emotional charge for her.

It was an interesting revelation, given the circumstances. It was seldom that Dar actually got to experience a moment of personal growth when it happened, but she was actually glad she'd gotten a chance this time.

"Michelle's convinced this bullshit story of yours is true," Shari said, bluntly. "I think she's nuts, and I think you're a fucking liar." Like Michelle, she'd given up on business formal, but she'd opted for a canvas colored outfit that didn't show the dust quite as much.

"And you're here because?" Dar inquired.

"If you think I'm going to let you rob us of this bid, you're dead wrong, Dar." Shari warned. "I don't know what your game is this time, but I'm going to sink you, no matter what it is." She advanced and stuck a finger out pointing it at Dar's chest. "You are not going to bullshit me or intimidate her. Got me!"

Dar waited for the shouting to fade. She cocked her head to one side. "And you're here because?" She repeated mildly, allowing a hint of a smile to cross her lips.

Kerry folded her arms to prevent the temptation to whack Shari.

"You're not listening to me." Shari took a step closer and this time, poked her finger right into Dar's chest.

"You're not saying anything intelligible." Dar replied. "But if you don't want to end up in Jackson, take that finger back."

Michelle sighed.

"You don't scare me." Shari scoffed, leaving her hand where it was.

"That's your problem." Dar reached up and fastened her fingers around Shari's wrist. "I should scare you." She tightened down suddenly, the tendons on her arm jumping.

"Jesus." Michelle started forward, only to have Kerry put a hand out and stop her.

Shari tried to pull her hand back, but found it wouldn't budge. The skin on it was starting to turn red, and as Dar's grip clenched down further, the veins popped out on it.

"Let me the fuck go." Shari yanked her arm back. It got her nowhere, but off balance. Dar's body didn't even quiver—her half extended arm stayed still as iron, the curve of her biceps very visible under her tanned skin.

Now Dar stepped closer and pinned her with both icy eyes. "Now you listen to me," she growled softly. "You want to cut the crap? Fine. Cut the crap, Shari. Either you want to cooperate with me, or you don't. If you don't, get out of here. If you do, then shut up, and just start being a part of the solution instead of a windbag excuse for a person." She released Shari's arm and stepped back, and then waited. "Choose. Now."

Kerry let her hand drop as she also waited. There was nothing she could add to the situation, no words of wisdom that could help, or in fact, any words at all that could do anything productive—though she could come up with some that would probably degrade the confrontation to a fistfight.

She really wanted it to become a fistfight. She really wanted to punch Shari, and wipe that obnoxious look right off her face. It shocked her a little.

Shari stared at her hand that was still an angry red with vivid marks where Dar's fingers had been. She looked back up at Dar's face, which was still and watchful and as serious as a heart attack.

"Just think." Kerry found herself speaking up anyway. "If what we're saying is right, and you cooperate with us, we all end up winning. If you don't..." She shrugged a little. "We'll win anyway."

Shari really looked like she was sucking a lemon. "What if you're lying?" She addressed Kerry, no longer looking at Dar at all. "How in the hell can I be sure you're not just taking us for a ride?"

Kerry smiled at her. "You can't. You just have to either trust us, or not. But if you look at the facts, I think you can see the truth. You're not stupid."

Michelle's nose wrinkled and she rubbed her face with one hand.

Shari flexed her hand, then let it drop to her side. "All right," she finally said. "You're right. I'm not stupid, and I've been saying something stinks around here for a while now. I just thought it was you." She regarded Dar coldly. "But over the last day, I've started thinking something smells even worse than you do, and if I have to put up with you to find out what it is and kick its ass, then I will."

A frosty silence fell. Kerry broke it by leaning over and sniffing Dar's neck delicately. "Different strokes for different folks, I guess. I love the way you smell," she remarked.

Dar puffed a bit of air into Kerry's bangs. "Thanks." She took a breath, letting her jangled nerves relax a bit. "Now that all the bullshit's over, I suggest we go somewhere not out in a public parking lot and figure out where we go from here."

"Good idea." Michelle finally chimed in. "Nothing south of the Mason Dixon is neutral territory, so why don't we go find an anonymous dive with enough table space to have a meeting." She faced Dar. "I'd ask your other half to pick a spot but the last time sucked."

Kerry had the grace to look mildly abashed. She clasped her hands behind her back, and gazed off into the sunlight.

Dar remained silent for a moment. "Not smart to go far," she commented. "I know a place about ten minutes from here. It's quiet, and there's space to work."

Shari looked suspicious, but Michelle nodded. "Sounds all right," she agreed. "Directions?"

"Just follow us." Dar laid a hand on Kerry's back. "It's our place."

"Ah." Michelle murmured. "Isn't this just one of life's bowls of cherries?" She took Shari's arm as they followed. "And what kinds of pits are we getting ourselves into, hm?"

Shari snorted, but kept her mouth shut.

"SO." KERRY GLANCED sideways at her beloved, if sometimes obscure, partner. "This was a good idea, right?"

Dar looked into the rearview mirror to where Shari and Michelle's car was parked right behind hers on the ferry. "I have no idea," she admitted. "It's just...Ker, if we're going to really do this, cooperate with them, I think we need to get all the bullshit out of the way first."

Kerry groaned. "Haven't we been getting bullshit since Orlando?"

The ferry rocked under them a bit as it traversed Government Cut. Dar tapped her thumbs on the steering wheel of the Lexus and watched the choppy water ahead of them. "Yeah, I know." She sighed. "But listen."

"I'm listening." Kerry tucked her legs up under her and leaned on the center console, resting her head against Dar's shoulder. She barely kept herself from checking the rearview mirror, where she was sure her comfy position was being noticed behind them.

Dar nuzzled Kerry's hair, nibbling at a few strands, and planting a kiss on the top of her head.

Kerry waited for a few seconds, then she cleared her throat. "I'm listening," she repeated.

"Huh?"

"Dar."

"Oh. Yeah. Sorry," Dar said. "The way I see it, the only chance we've got to turn this thing around is to take away their big ending."

"Huh?"

"They want this big ultimate finish, right?" Dar stopped speaking, as she felt Kerry's breath against her ear. "Ker?"

"Yeees?"

"Are you listening to me?"

"Every word, hon." Kerry reassured her. "They want a big finish. You're right. They figure we'll dog and cat fight to the very end, scrambling to get everything done."

"Right."

"So we're... going to do what?" Kerry asked, as the ferry nosed up to its dock and the ramp started to lower. "I mean, we are done, right? So do we win by default?'

Dar let her head lean against her partner's. "No, because we haven't shown Quest anything."

"So?"

Reluctantly, Dar straightened up. "Time to roll." She put the Lexus in gear and steered it carefully up the ramp and through the solicitous water spray that removed the salt from the front of the vehicle. "Let's see how it goes with them," she said. "I've got sort of an idea, but it's still raw at the moment."

"I like raw." Kerry remained where she was, even though the car was now in motion. "Tell me what you're thinking, Dar. I hate having to sit there wondering what's going on."

Thus prompted, Dar cleared her throat. "Michelle told me they can't figure out how to get their satellite up. She wanted to pay me to do it."

Kerry started giggling.

"Yeah, it was pretty funny." Dar chuckled along with her. "But it gave me an idea...what if we all decided to help each other?"

"Um."

"We've got no power. She's got no satellite. From what I hear, Mike's network backbone won't come up. Instead of fighting, what if we all worked together?" Dar asked. She turned into their complex, rolling down the window and pointing at a visitor's spot as she headed for her own.

"You mean make it a tie?" Kerry's brow creased. "How does that work out, Dar? Who wins?"

"No one." Dar turned off the engine. "Kerry, remember this is all a farce. Who really loses are the television people. They're the ones driving this."

"Hm." Kerry opened the passenger door and hopped out. "Okay. Yeah, I lost track of that. I'm still in that 'win the bid' mode." She waited for Dar to come around the side of the car, and then they both waited as Shari and Michelle came up the drive to where they were standing. "Go for it," she added, softly. "I'll be in there hanging with you."

Dar put a hand on Kerry's back, her thumb rubbing her shoulder blade. "I'm counting on that." She straightened a little as their two adversaries approached.

"Okay," Michelle said, briefly. "We're here."

"Inside." Dar turned and headed for the steps. Kerry stepped back and gestured Michelle and Shari forward politely, following them as they all trooped up to the door.

Dar coded it open and walked inside, pushing the door back to allow the rest of them to enter. "Watch out for the dog." She cautioned as Chino bounded up to greet them.

"Ugh." Shari backed up rapidly. "I'm not into dogs."

Ah. Now doesn't that just figure? Kerry continued inside the condo and sat down on the loveseat, allowing Chino to squirm around and greet her. "C'mere Cheebles. Who's my sweetie?" She ruffled the Labrador's ears.

Dar closed the door and stood there a moment, apparently trying to decide which of her few social skills she'd try to engage next. "Siddown." She compromised between practicality and grudging politeness. "I'll put some coffee on."

Michelle and Shari took a moment to look around before they took spots on the couch next to each other.

It wasn't a comfortable moment. In fact, Kerry could seldom remember being so uncomfortable in her own living room. She sat back and regarded the two women, watching their eyes roam around the space in wary curiosity.

They'd worked very hard to keep the entire situation out of their personal space, and now they'd brought it right into the center of their private world, and Kerry suddenly realized she hadn't been prepared for it. "So."

"So." Michelle rose to the social occasion. "Nice place." She peered at the walls. "Someone takes decent shots."

"That would be me." Kerry sprawled out a bit on the loveseat. "Thanks," she responded graciously. "I like our cabin down south better, though. Less busy." She smiled. "But the view's nice here."

Shari looked like she'd swallowed a lemon. She edged back as Chino wandered over to investigate her, and jumping as the dog sat down and barked. "What does it want?"

"Relax." Michelle advised her. "I don't think that kind bites."

"All dogs bite." Kerry cheerfully contradicted her. "But Chino's pretty peaceful, unless you piss her off."

"Like you?" Michelle inquired, with a smile.

Kerry considered that. "Something like that," she agreed. "Yeah.

We can both be bitches when we have to be."

Shari got up and moved away from where Chino was sitting. She circled the room, examining the art, and the pictures on the entertainment center. "Guess old Dar is lucky you took her in," she commented, giving Kerry a bitingly sarcastic smile over her shoulder. "Nice of you."

Curiously, Kerry didn't find herself getting angry. She lifted her hand and rotated her finger in a circle. "Other way round." She disagreed. "This is Dar's place."

"Not anymore." Dar entered from the kitchen. "You own half." She barely spared Shari a glance as she perched on the arm of the loveseat. The scent of brewing coffee wafted into the living room. "CIO's of multinational corporations don't live in two room rentals."

Shari turned and regarded her. "Oh, right. I forgot you weren't white trash anymore."

Dar's eyes narrowed. "Go to hell."

Michelle sighed audibly. "Okay, tell you what." She put on a voice very much like that of a game show hostess. "Dar, I'm sure...in fact I'd bet on the fact that you have some boxing gloves somewhere in a closet here."

Dar's brow creased. "And?"

"Get them." Michelle stood up. "Because we're going to have you two put them on and just get this adolescent whore bitch issue between you out and over with because I am over it!" She yelled the last three words at full volume. "Grow the fuck up already!"

Silence fell when she was done. Chino sneezed, and trotted over to press herself against Kerry's leg.

Shari remained where she was, staring at Michelle in shock.

Kerry slowly turned and studied Dar, looking her over from head to foot. "Well." She finally broke the silence. "I think Dar's about as grown up as she's going to get in this lifetime, so I guess I'd better go get the gloves." She patted her lover's knee. "This won't take long, sweetie." Her impish grin took any sting from the words. "Try to aim away from the big screen, okay?"

Dar shifted and took a seat on the couch next to Kerry. "Nah." She extended her legs, crossing them at the ankles. "Michelle's right. Let's be grown-ups for a change." She tipped her head back to look at Shari. "So, sit down and let's save the insults for later."

Kerry got up. "I'll grab the coffee." She disappeared into the kitchen.

Shari stubbornly remained standing for a bit, examining the pictures on the shelves. Then she went back to the long couch and sat back down. "All right." She didn't look at Michelle. "Let's get this over with. What's your scam, Dar? Just lay it out."

"Okay." Dar extended one long arm along the back of the loveseat. "Here's the deal. None of us is finished with this goddamned charade."

"Not what I heard," Shari interrupted, but in a mild tone. "Michelle said you were done."

"We are." Dar agreed. "But we can't demo anything because we have no power."

Shari nodded. "Bad luck."

Dar shrugged. "Bad luck? At this point, knowing what I know I'd be surprised if it was any kind of luck. My guess is someone on the ship was paid off to throw a wrench in."

Michelle got up, a restless energy emerging. "You really think so?"

"I do." Dar stroked Chino's fur. "I think the goal was to keep everyone even to the very end, then have it be a horse race to the finish."

Michelle paced around, pausing at the entertainment center to look at the pictures also. "Quest." She turned. "He told us explicitly not to ask or try to stay on the ships when they left. Did he tell you?"

"No." Dar shook her head. "Never said a word."

"Wait." Shari leaned forward. "What did you have to give up to stay on?"

"Dinner," Dar replied.

"What?" Michelle turned and stared at her.

"Dinner." Kerry returned from the kitchen, bearing a tray with a coffee pot, cups, and a plate of cookies. She set the tray down on the table and knelt next to it, fixing cups for herself and Dar. "That's all they wanted. A good meal and some alcohol."

Shari sat back, ignoring the coffee service. "Mike said he could have sworn someone cut his fiber," she said.

"And Albert told one of my guys they were making great progress until someone broke into a container and stole some switches," Michelle added. "Holy hell."

"Mm." Kerry handed Dar her cup and sat down next to her. "It's been like that. One step forward, two steps back."

"And all of it with those damn cameras..." Michelle added. "You could really be on to something, Dar."

"Gee, thanks." Dar replied. "Glad those several billion brain cells ILS pays a premium for turned out to be good for something after all."

Shari fell silent. She edged forward and took a cup, keeping her attention on the coffee as she poured herself some.

Michelle tapped her thumbs together pensively. "Okay," she finally said. "So let's put the cards on the table. I thought it was a little strange that the filming people latched onto us, but I wasn't about to turn away that kind of publicity. They wanted angles, I gave them angles. They wanted controversy I gave them that, too."

Shari snorted a little.

"So now we're caught." Michelle got up and walked over to where Dar and Kerry were sitting. "Either we blow you off and play their game, and look like idiots when they reveal everything, or we cooperate with you in some unknown plan of yours that might, or might not be, on the level."

"Not only that." Dar smiled. "You're going to help us get the rest of them onboard too."

Michelle put her hands on her hips. "Maybe Kerry should get those gloves," she remarked. "I've got a black belt."

"I've got a shotgun," Kerry countered. "So why don't we table the issue, and hear what Dar's got in mind, because frankly, I've had it up to here with being manipulated." She held a hand up near her forehead.

Shari snorted again and shook her head.

Michelle turned and selected a sugar cube, placing it between her teeth and crunching it. "All right." She agreed. "Let's hear it."

Dar leaned back, and smiled.

"YOU ARE INSANE," Shari said. "I always knew that, but you've just proved it. How in the hell are we supposed to pull this off?"

Dar had left the cozy sanctuary of the loveseat and was pacing back and forth near the sliding glass doors. "The filming people are expecting a showdown," she repeated for the third time. "That's what they've based this whole deal on. David and Goliath. A battle for the bid with Quest dangling either carrots or daggers over our heads."

"Yeah. So?"

"So, what we want to do is turn the story around and make it what we want. Not what they want." Dar said.

"Do we?" Michelle was munching on some pretzels Kerry had brought out. "Wouldn't it be easier just to play along with them? If it's all bogus, who cares?"

"Sure." Kerry had taken over the loveseat and was laying across it with her feet up. "It would be a hell of a lot easier even if we all left the pier, and let them wander around looking for us and wondering where we all are."

"Now, I like that idea," Shari said.

"Actually, so do I," Michelle agreed. "I bet they're looking for us now. Wonder if anyone saw us leaving together."

Dar inspected the late afternoon sunlight gilding the water outside. Was it a better idea to do as Kerry said? It got them out of the situation, and hell, she didn't even have to go back out there. The idea of Quest and the television team standing there bewildered actually really did appeal to her.

Hm.

"Yeah." Dar leaned on the glass. "But it really doesn't get us any satisfaction, does it?" She turned and faced them, her hands behind her back. "After what Quest put us through, don't you want to see him get his?"

Michelle leaned back. "You want to hear the absolute truth?" she said. "Sure. I'd like to see him dumped into the ocean off that pier, and wave bye-bye as he floats out to sea."

Dar crossed the room and perched on the arm of the loveseat. "So then the plan is we get everyone together." She ticked a finger off. "We find out what needs to be done, and do it." She ticked another finger off. "We coordinate it so we all finish at the same time."

"Okay." Shari folded her arms. "So let's say we do that. We all finish. Then what? How does that get back at Quest?"

"He's counting on there being one winner, and the rest losers. If we all win, he has to pay for all four jobs," Kerry said, quietly. "And that has nothing to do with the filming. That's in the contract."

Shari looked at Michelle. Michelle looked at Shari. Both of them made identical thoughtful grunts.

"And, if we all work together, the filming people don't get their story. That means..." Kerry smiled. "I bet Quest doesn't get the publicity he was banking on."

"Exactly." Dar ruffled Kerry's hair, bemused by the fact that her partner had picked up on her plan without even knowing the details beforehand. Kerry looked up at her, lifting her eyebrows slightly. Dar grinned, and winked. "Nice summation."

"Thanks." Kerry's eyes twinkled. "Do I get a cookie for that?"

"Absolutely." Dar got up and headed for the kitchen, glad to be out of the intense scrutiny at least for a moment. She figured it would take a while for Michelle and Shari to decide what to do, so she took her time rummaging in the cupboard for just the perfect cookie to bring Kerry.

She had a lot to choose from. Dar gazed at the selection Orange Milanos? Traditional chocolate chip? Some grahams and milk?

"Hon?" Kerry appeared at her elbow and circled her waist with both arms. "Whatcha doing?"

"Picking cookies for you," Dar replied. "Did you give our guests some space?"

"Uh huh," Kerry said. "I sent them out onto the porch. You think they'll go for it?" She rubbed her cheek against Dar's shoulder blade and exhaled, enjoying the pleasure of the feel of Dar's body within her grasp.

Dar selected a bag of key lime, white chocolate, and macadamia nut cookies. She closed the cabinet and turned within Kerry's arms, draping her own over her partner's shoulders. "I don't know," she said. "Still a lot of hard feelings there."

"Mm."

"I was tempted to just go with your idea."

Kerry chuckled softly. "As I was saying it, so was I."

Dar gave her a quick hug, then stepped back. "Milk," she said. "How about we go sit on the couch and make a spectacle of ourselves when they come back in."

"How about I hide a dog biscuit in the couch where Shari was sitting and watch the fun when she comes back?"

"You're a rascal sometimes, you know that?"

"Bet your pooters I am."

"THIS IS INSANE." Shari shook her head.

"I know," Michelle agreed. She leaned on the railing and gazed out over the water. "But we knew something was going on. You've been saying that all week. It was just all too over the top."

Shari nodded. "I thought she was at the bottom of it all. Still not sure if she's not somehow."

Michelle sighed and dropped her head.

"Look, I know you think I'm off my rocker when it comes to Dar. Maybe I am." Shari turned and looked at her. "But you don't know her like I do and..."

"Stop." Michelle held a hand up. "Shari, let's be honest. Do you really think the person inside that million dollar bit of concrete is the same person you knew in college?"

Shari turned and looked back through the glass doors. Inside, she could see Dar walking back in from the kitchen with Kerry next to her their arms draped around each other.

She tried to remember, really, what Dar had been like back then. Awkward and rough around the edges, definitely. Almost anti-social and cocky as all get out. Sexy, in a very primal way that had appealed to Shari back then, but with an overwhelming complexity of character she had no idea what to do with.

Some things hadn't changed. Dar still had that earthy sensuality about her, but the awkwardness of youth had been replaced with a rock solid self confidence and, while she suspected Dar still wasn't a social butterfly, she handled herself far differently now than she had back then.

Back then, Dar's blunt honesty had scared Shari. She'd been faced with the potential deepening of a relationship she didn't really know if she'd wanted at all, and her reaction had been...

Okay, she knew she'd been harsh. What she hadn't expected was to have that be it. The end. Dar had walked out and she'd never come back. Shari had tried to call her a few times, but never gotten an answer, and eventually, she just found someone else to go with, and tried to forget.

The next time they'd met, she was being fired and she'd taken away the knowledge that one thoughtless brush off on her part had come back to bite her in the ass when she'd least expected it. She'd been so sure Dar would never amount to anything hadn't she?

Well.

"I think she's the same person, yeah," Shari finally said. "I just have no idea who that person was way back then."

Michelle pondered that, as she peered through the glass. Kerry was wrapped up in Dar's arms on the couch, and was indulgently feeding her cookies and milk. It was insanely precious. It was sappy. It was disgustingly romantic.

She sighed. Damn, Kerry was one lucky woman. "Okay. So what the hell are we going to do?"

"We go with them," Shari said, bluntly. "Because we have no real goddamn choice, and you know it. At least if we play into what Dar's up to, we come off looking like we have at least six brain cells between us."

"True," Michelle agreed ruefully. "I hate looking like an idiot. And you know what? That goddamn Cruickshank played us like a pair of first class ones. I think she really had the hots for her." Michelle pointed at Dar.

Shari rolled her eyes. "Doesn't everyone? Jesus Christ I am so tired of hearing every walking dick on that damn port talk about her. You'd think they'd caught a clue already she's gay and give the hell up."

"Mm. Well, let's go and get this rolling." Michelle tabled the discussion. "I think we need to have a frank discussion with our new colleagues and put a few truths on the table. I don't mind working this charade with them, but I want to know exactly where we stand first."

"Right," Shari agreed. "Let's clear the air."

Michelle stopped in mid step and turned. "Does that mean you're going to cut out the bitch for a while? I think if you do, she will."

"Me? You're the one who offered to put gloves on in there." Shari snorted. "And do yourself a favor and don't wave that belt of yours in front of her. She's got a couple of her own and she didn't learn to fight in a gym."

Michelle shrugged. "She doesn't scare me." She started to pull the sliding glass door open. "Now on the other hand, Stuart I wouldn't turn my back on." She cut the last word off as she stepped inside and gave Dar and Kerry a brief smile. "All right. We're in."

"Good." Dar licked a few crumbs off her lips. "Then let's get back to the pier. We don't have that much time."

"Fine." Michelle looked at Kerry. "Why don't you ride with me, and Shari can ride with Dar, and hopefully, when we get to the pier, everyone will be alive and capable of working together."

Kerry felt Dar's entire body tense. She sorted through her possible polite responses, discarded them, and went on to the rude ones.

Dar forestalled her, however. "All right." She gave Kerry a pat on the thigh. "Let's go." There was only a touch of resignation in her tone. "Get this over with."

Kerry got up reluctantly, wondering if she could figure out a way to sneak Chino into Dar's car.

Just in case.

IF IT WAS going to happen, at least it was happening on her turf. Dar settled her sunglasses onto her nose as she started up the car, watching Kerry reluctantly enter the passenger side of Michelle's rental.

Kerry did not like it. Every line in her body explicitly spoke about how much she didn't like it. Dar found it a little funny, and more than a little comforting to see her partner's visible agitation on her behalf and it formed a warm, friendly sensation in the pit of her stomach.

The passenger door to the Lexus opened and Shari climbed in warily, closing the door with the same reluctance as Kerry had displayed only a moment ago.

In that moment, Dar realized something. She realized that Shari was more intimidated by their being in the same space than she was, and once she'd realized that, everything changed. She relaxed into the leather of the driver's seat and put the SUV in gear, backing it out carefully and turning for the outer road and the ferry. "So."

Shari glanced at her, then looked back out the side window. "So," she repeated. "Looks like you got what you wanted."

Dar turned into the ferry dock, and pulled up in line to wait for the next boat. "That was the goal." She leaned her knee against the door and rested her arm on it.

Shari made a small, rude noise. "You know something, you really are an asshole."

Ah, at least the beating around the bush would stop now. "Sometimes," Dar agreed. "When I have to be." She finally turned and regarded Shari through her dark lenses. "But you knew that."

"I knew that." Shari confirmed. "When do you intend on letting Blondie in on your little secret?"

Dar chuckled. "Kerry saw that side of me first," she said. "She was a part of a consolidation I did."

"Guess she slept with you, so she kept her job, hm? Pity you didn't give me that option." Shari replied caustically. "I'd have given you a roll to avoid that round of resumes."

Dar regarded a seagull circling around the security kiosk, searching for dropped tidbits. "Kerry was worth keeping," she finally said. "You weren't."

"Fuck you too."

It only made her smile. "You're assuming it was personal. The fact is," Dar faced her, tipping the sunglasses down to expose her eyes, "I needed more marketing bullshit artists about as much as I needed a case of the hives."

The ferry pulled in, and Dar put the Lexus into drive, as the ramp started down.

"You're so full of shit. Business decision? Give me a break, Dar," Shari replied heatedly. "You enjoyed every damn minute of canning me."

Dar steered the car onto the ferry, taking the last position on the first lane. She set the parking break to give herself a moment to collect her thoughts. "Sure I did," she answered. "But the fact is your position was redundant."

"Bullshit."

Dar shrugged.

"You just fired me because I blew off your little declaration of love," Shari said. "So don't pull that crap with me, Dar. Lucky for little Stuart she was more receptive."

Strangely, it didn't even hurt anymore. "Know what your problem is, Shari?" Dar lazily watched as the next line of cars filled up, her brows lifting as Michelle's rental pulled in even with them and parked, despite the fact that they'd been right behind Dar, and should have been at the front of the next line.

How had Kerry arranged *that*?

"I'm sure you're going to tell me," Shari answered sarcastically.

"You're a bigger asshole than I am." Dar lifted a hand and waved at Kerry, who waggled her fingers back, then circled her thumb and first finger in an OK gesture and raised her eyebrows. Dar made the same gesture, then twitched her head slightly in Shari's direction, and switched to a lifted middle finger instead.

Kerry started laughing, inaudible behind the glass.

"Well, I've..." Shari started.

"You've been trying to get me back since then. Give it up." Dar advised her. "I don't give a shit. There's nothing you can do to me, including taking over fucking ILS, that I would give two cents for." She turned and faced her again. "Do you understand me?"

Shari stared at her. "No," she said. "I never understood you. You're from goddamned Mars."

Dar was unable to stop from producing a wicked smile. "That must make you from Uranus," she drawled pleasantly. "Are we done now?"

Shari glared at her in silence.

"SO." MICHELLE SNIFFED reflectively. "Hard as we tried to kill each other here we are."

"Here we are," Kerry agreed. "In the middle of the biggest piece of horse poop I think I've ever seen in my life."

Michelle digested that. "You know what? That's true," she agreed. "I've been part of some really screwed up deals before, but this one's in a class by itself."

And that was definitely the truth. Kerry ordered her thoughts and tried not to give in to the urge to open the car door and climb into Dar's Lexus instead. She could see Dar's shoulders from where she was, and they seemed relatively relaxed.

She hoped things were going okay. It was so hard for her to judge where Dar's head space was right now.

"And your little tricks didn't make it any easier," Michelle added.

"My tricks?" Kerry looked at her. "I don't know what you're talking about, unless you mean Andy," she said. "And that wasn't a trick, it was just insurance."

Michelle laughed. "Okay. So let's just say you putting a ringer into the loading crew was...insurance."

"He did a good job, didn't he?" Kerry countered.

"That's not the point." Michelle sounded a bit testy now.

"It is the point. He did exactly what they were paying him to do," Kerry said. "And while he was there, he found out about your dirty tricks for us."

"My dirty tricks?"

"What are you calling putting in duplicate orders?" Kerry asked. "And what are you calling trying to prevent deliveries to our ship?"

Michelle studied the passing cargo yards. "That was strategy."

Kerry snorted. "Strategy my ass."

"Insurance my ass," Michelle countered. "Shall we count that as even?"

Should they? Kerry allowed that the two tricks pretty much counteracted each other. "All right. Fair enough." She decided. "What about all the rumors being spread around our office?"

Michelle shrugged. "Shari's idea."

"Why?"

"She figured she could knock Dar off balance if she caused trouble between you two."

Kerry felt herself getting a little lightheaded with anger. Her breathing quickened and she felt her hands start to twitch, the fingers of them curling unconsciously into fists as they rested on her denim clad thighs. "That's something I'll never write off," she stated quietly.

Michelle looked at her, in some surprise. "Just talk. You must get that."

Kerry took a breath, and then released it. "Oh, sure, we do," she said. "But it's not the talk. It was the intent." Slowly, she turned and rested her elbow on the console between the seats, looking directly into Michelle's eyes. "I couldn't give a damn about this business, about this bid or about you."

Michelle blinked

"But if you or she ever do anything again that's meant to try and destroy our relationship, I'll come after you, and they'll have to arrest me to stop me." Kerry's voice was dead serious. "Am I coming through loud and clear here?"

"You're threatening me?" Michelle sounded incredulous.

"Yes," Kerry answered. "And it's not idle."

"You realize how that sounds don't you?"

Kerry nodded. "If you think I'm crazy, you're right. I am," she said. "Dar means that much to me."

Michelle cocked her head, her eyes searching Kerry's face with a new interest. "You know something? That's the one thing we really didn't count on," she said. "And I should have. All along I wanted to believe that you were just like we were."

It was Kerry's turn to look surprised.

"Two dykes with a common business motive," Michelle clarified. "Who also like hot sex," she added. "But that's not what you two are about at all."

"Um...well, actually..." Kerry found herself blushing.

Michelle pursed her lips. "I apologize for the scuttlebutt. That was dirty."

Progress, at last. "Thanks," Kerry said.

Michelle was quiet for a second. "Now you can apologize to me for bugging our offices,"

"Huh?"

"Stealing our client list?"

Kerry cocked her head in puzzlement. "We didn't," she spluttered. "I thought you did that to us!"

They both folded their arms and stared at each other.

THEY HAD, APPARENTLY, run out of insults and for a few minutes the ride across the water was quiet. If she looked to her left, Dar could see the ships squatting at their piers and she wondered what they'd find when they got there.

Chaos? Definitely. Her cell phone rang, and she checked the ID before she answered it. "Hi, Dad."

"'Lo there, Dardar," her father answered. "Got us some good news."

"Yeah?"

"Feller here, he got the juice on."

Ah. Dar gazed at the oncoming ferry dock. "Great," she said. "I'm on my way over."

"See ya." Andrew hung up.

Dar folded her phone up and set it on the center console. She hit the window switch and opened her window, leaning her elbow on the sill as Kerry did the same. "Dad," she said briefly. "They're good to go."

"Ah." Kerry said. "Does that change our plan?"

"No."

"Okay." Kerry pulled her head back inside the car. "See you in a few."

Dar closed the window and leaned back. She pondered a moment, then she turned her head and looked at Shari. "We have power."

Shari looked back at her warily. "So does that mean the deal's off? You kept us distracted long enough to get what you wanted, I guess."

"No." Dar shook her head. "Doesn't change anything." A faint, quirky smile appeared. "I just wanted you to know if I really wanted to end this right now..." Pale blue eyes peeked from behind the wraparound shades. "I could."

Shari folded her arms over her chest. "Fuck you."

Dar's smile spread into a charming Cheshire imitation. "Had your chance once. I've developed a sense of taste since then."

Shari's face twitched.

"At any rate." Dar relented, deciding there was just so much fun she could stand at any particular moment. "That's one boat we don't have to worry about completing. We can concentrate on the other three." She watched through the window as the ferry docked, glad of her sunglasses as they turned and faced almost due west.

Shari stared at the angular profile at a loss on how to counter the mixture of Dar's cool business and sarcasm. What else could she say that she hadn't already? For a month she'd been digging at Dar, poking and prodding and savaging her every chance she got.

It had gotten her exactly nowhere. For all the time she'd spent with the reporters, smearing Dar's character, her reputation, and anything else she could think of here she was at the end of the goddamned project and the bitch had still come out on top.

What the hell?

What the freaking hell? She suddenly realized that even if Dar lost the bid, lost the publicity, and lost the business, she'd still come out on top because her goddamned son of a bitch charisma would just make everyone not give a flying crap.

Goddamn it.

GodDAMN it.

She glared at Dar who remained immune to her scathing thoughts, apparently relaxed and content with whatever was going through her mind, her fingers drumming lightly against the steering wheel. One finger held a ring, and for the first time she looked close enough at it to see the details.

It was a beautiful piece of jewelry that screamed expensive, but in a refined and understated way. Purchased, she was sure, by the well bred Midwestern bitch in the next car that had certainly been born with several silver spoons shoved up her ass.

She'd tried very hard to sell Cruickshank on the idea that Kerry was sleeping with Dar for her career. On the surface, it made perfect sense. But watching Dar's little bedmate work over the last few weeks made even Shari grudgingly accept that if she wanted to go anywhere else, she could.

Work anywhere else. Live anywhere else. Sleep with anyone else.

Then she'd tried to convince the reporter that Dar was a little psycho that possessively dominated and abused the smaller woman.

Why? That was what Cruickshank had asked.

Because Dar was a psycho. Shari had seen enough of her as a young

woman to know that. She had a cold, vicious side to her that had scared
the crap out of a lot people when they'd gone to school together. Raised
on a military base, poor, anti-social...

Dar started whistling softly under her breath, a gently melodic
sound that broke Shari's mental conversation with herself. She had her
head turned away from Shari, and in the reflection from the window her
expression was visible as she looked over at the other car.

Something had changed. Shari shifted and turned the other way,
staring out her own window as the ferry ramp started to lower. Or
maybe Dar had simply grown up and out of her past.

Maybe the reporter had been right. Shari had thought she was
simply stupid.

Now she was faced with the realization that there was no way she
was going to beat Dar. Not in any realm. So. Screw it. Time to get out of
this piece of shit situation with anything she could. "Dar."

"Yes?" Dar turned her head, her pale eyes safely hidden behind her
shades.

"Truce." Shari held up a hand. "I'm over it. If this is going to
happen, let's just have it happen and get it over with." She worked at
keeping any sarcasm or sting out of her voice.

Dar started the Lexus remaining silent for the length of time it took
her to release the parking brake and put the car into gear. The offer of a
truce didn't fool her any, she knew all Shari wanted was to avoid any
more of her wit until she was far enough away to pitch a grenade at her.

But, Dar believed in taking whatever advantage was offered to her,
and having some peace and quiet would definitely be an advantage.
"All right," she said. "Truce."

Shari seemed a little surprised, but she shrugged it off and leaned
back as they rolled off the ferry.

It remained to be seen, of course, just how long it would last.

Chapter Nine

"SO, WHAT WAS that all about?" Michelle asked, as Kerry rolled the window back up. "Or do you two talk in code regularly just to piss people off?"

Kerry leaned back in her seat, stifling a yawn. "Oh, sure. We talk in code. Sometimes Dar builds a fire on her desk and sends me smoke signals if she's really bored."

Michelle eyed her suspiciously. Kerry had extended her legs and crossed them at the ankles, and she didn't appear to be considering being any more forthcoming than that. Kerry's eyes were hidden behind silver sunglasses and it was very hard for Michelle to tell exactly what it was she was up to.

Maybe she'd be better off not knowing. She decided to return to their prior conversation instead. "So. You didn't put someone inside our company. That what you're saying?"

"Wasn't us." Kerry agreed. "Now. You tell me about anything you might have left behind in our offices after that meeting."

Michelle started the car, her brow furrowed. "Excuse me?"

So. Had Dar been right all along? "We found something inserted into our network after you all left—a piece of spying technology."

"Really?" Michelle sounded fascinated. "What'd it get for—whoever it was?"

A smile. "Nothing." Kerry chuckled. "Dar found it."

"Wasn't us."

Kerry nodded. "Dar didn't figure it was...said it was too sophisticated." Zing. "But with everything happening all at the same time, it was a tough call."

They followed Dar's Lexus off the ferry and started toward the pier. "Well, after we found out about your little trick with Dar's father, believe me, lots of things occurred to me to get back at you." Michelle admitted frankly.

"Like getting our pier supervisor to quit?"

"Huh?" Michelle darted a look at her. "I said occurred. I didn't say I did any of them."

Was Michelle telling the truth? Kerry had a feeling she was.

"And after that phone line scam." Michelle added suddenly. "Not to mention that bait and switch ploy at what you jokingly called a restaurant."

Kerry sighed, lifting one hand and propping her head up with it, her elbow resting against the car window sill. "It's pointless for me to bother saying neither of those were planned, isn't it?"

Michelle snorted. "You're seriously expecting me to believe you didn't take up four telephone lines on purpose?"

"No, I did." Kerry said jumping a little as a cab nearly cut them off. "I just didn't know they were the last pairs out of that CO. I put them in every terminal because those bastards wouldn't assign any specific one to a specific ship."

Michelle thought about that for a few minutes. "Hmph."

"Sorry," Kerry said. "Honestly, at this point, if I'd done it to screw you, I'd just say so. What's the point in not?"

"Hmph." Michelle wrinkled her nose. "So you're telling me you and Blackbeard the pirate over there are total innocents? C'mon."

Kerry's lips quirked. "We're not," she admitted. "

"Hah."

"We scared the crap out of you both in the Living Seas."

Michelle almost stopped the car. "What?"

"Dar and I were diving in the tank."

Luckily, a red light was at hand. Michelle turned and stared at her. "Are you serious?"

Kerry nodded. "Yeah," she said. "But other than that, honestly Michelle, we haven't done a damn thing to you. That's what pissed me off so much because all you've been doing since we met in Orlando is come after us with a hatchet."

Michelle jumped as a car behind them honked impatiently. She started forward, visibly rattled. She remained silent for a while, then abruptly cursed. "You have no idea what that caused."

Kerry eyed her warily.

"You have no damn idea."

KERRY TROTTED ACROSS the tarmac to Dar's car, pulling up short as the driver's side door opened and her partner emerged. "Hi." She studied her body language with a touch of anxiety, but relaxed when it was obvious that Dar was okay.

"Hi." Dar shut the door behind her. Shari had already left the car, and was headed across the lot to where Michelle was standing waiting to go inside the administration building. "How'd it go?"

"How'd it go?" Kerry asked at the same time.

Dar muffled a chuckle, and ran her fingers through her hair. "Me first. It sucked."

"Hm."

"We halfway agreed on a truce at the end, but I think she just wanted me to shut up," Dar admitted. "You?"

"Bitchfest." Kerry joined Dar as she started to walk toward the building. "Hard to read, really. I think you were right though."

Dar glanced at her. "I was?"

"Yeah. You said you didn't think they were behind a lot of the stuff at the office, and I think that's true," Kerry admitted.

"They were behind the crap talk."

"Yeah, Michele told me." Kerry wrinkled her nose. "But not the cell thing, or Duk's little defector apparently." She walked a few steps, regarding her scuffed sneakers soberly.

Dar moved a little closer as they walked. "I, um..." Don't know? Not true, since she certainly did know. "Shari was trying to cause problems between you and me."

Kerry did a little shrug and nod movement. "Duh," she uttered. "You figured that."

"She figured if she could break us up, I'd be distracted enough to forget about the bid," Dar added.

"Is she really that stupid?"

Dar had to smile. "Yeah."

"I mean, I always knew she was an idiot." Kerry added. "But apparently she's lost even more brain cells over the years."

That was, Dar realized, a not too obscure compliment. "Weeell..." She put her hand on Kerry's back as they walked up the steps to the admin building. "I can't say I was much of a catch back then."

"Bull poodles."

Dar chuckled.

"Dar, I've seen pictures. If I'd met you in college, you'd have saved me a week of gender orientation hell on South Beach, let me tell you." Kerry paused before the closed door.

"Thanks. I think," she said. "I guess from her viewpoint there was a certain logic to it." She exhaled, frowning a little.

"You mean, if something had caused a problem between us?" Kerry asked gently.

Dar nodded.

Kerry kicked at the concrete with the toe of her sneaker, then looked up. "I can't speak for you, sweetheart, but it would take one hell of a lot more than some bullshit talk for me," she said. "Because even the thought of that makes me want to start crying."

Dar stepped forward and put her arms around Kerry hugging her. "Me too." She whispered into Kerry's ear. "I'd rather die than lose you."

Kerry inhaled softly, dismissing the world around her as she buried her face into Dar's shirt. After a moment though, she pulled her head back and smiled. "Can we continue this discussion later?"

"Sure." Dar released her and stepped back, glancing around with a faintly embarrassed look. "My luck they got that on camera somehow."

Kerry chuckled, giving her a pat on the side. "I hope so."

Dar graciously opened the door, and stood back to let Kerry enter. As she followed her partner through the outer lobby to the room where Quest had set up his base of operations, she took a moment to consider what she'd have thought of Kerry if they'd met earlier.

Would Kerry have been her type? Did she even know what her type was back then? Dar didn't think she had. Shari had attracted her more because of her domineering personality than her looks, and Kerry wouldn't have had that kind of attitude back then.

Or now, for that matter. Kerry wasn't shy, but she did have an air of gentle reserve in public that often made people assume she was until they really knew her.

She also had a wicked sense of humor that still sometimes caught Dar by surprise.

Kerry was, she realized, completely different than anyone else she'd ever gone out with, as well as being completely different than Dar herself.

Opposites attract maybe? Then what the hell had she been doing with all those other high class Type A's she'd been going with? Wasting time waiting for the chance to walk in that scruffy little IT manager's office, apparently.

"Dar?" Kerry was standing near the door, hands on her hips, looking at her. "Hello... earth to Dar?"

"Sorry. Just thinking." Dar reached for the handle. "C'mon...let's get this started." She was a trifle surprised that Michelle and Shari hadn't waited for them, but on second thought...

Maybe she wasn't.

They entered the room, only to find pandemonium inside. Not that they weren't used to chaos around this project, Kerry mused, but groups of people standing around, apparently randomly, yelling at each other was new even for them.

Quest wasn't there. The other bid teams management was, though, and no one seemed happy. The two other bid teams seemed to be yelling at each other, and Michelle and Shari were trying to make them stop. Dar observed the waving arms for a moment, then put her powerful lungs to good use. "Hey!"

Mike turned and pointed at her. "You son of a bitch!" He yelled at the top of his voice.

Everyone else stopped, and shut up, as the words echoed for a moment.

"Wrong gender, and if you talk about my mother like that again, I'll pull your cock off," Dar replied, in a normal tone. "Assuming I could get a grip on it."

"You screwed us all over!" Mike dropped his volume considerably.

Kerry perched on one of the tables, crossing her arms over her chest. "Oh, this should be good," she said. "Wonder what we did now?"

"Okay, hold on." Michelle gamely stepped in. "Just everyone take it easy. There's stuff..."

"You shut up too!" The man whirled on her. "You're just as bad!"

"Hey!" Shari frowned. "Chill out! We didn't do jack to you."

Kerry got back up and wandered around the office, spotting some ship diagrams on the back wall and going over to study them. Where was Quest, she wondered? This close to the deadline, she'd have expected him to be crawling all over them, not to mention his filming crew.

So, where was he?

"Okay, if everyone's done venting hot air, shut up and listen." Dar's voice overrode the muttering.

Ah. Nothing like her partner's own brand of diplomacy. Kerry idly opened the top of a cookie jar sitting on the desk and looked inside. Not surprisingly, it appeared empty. "Y'know, there's nothing in the world more useless than an empty cookie jar, and that just nails this stupid project to a T."

"You say something?" Michelle asked her, turning at the sound of her voice.

"Me? No." Kerry muffled a grin. She closed the jar.

"I'm not listening to crap from you!" Mike said. "Quest told us what you did!"

Kerry turned. "He did?" She inquired.

"Yes." The man turned and looked at her. "He told us all about you buying off the workers, and sabotaging us."

Oh, Jesus. Kerry was about to answer, when she felt her cell phone start to go off. She unclipped it from her belt and glanced at it, frowning when it just showed a couple of half numbers. That rang a half bell in her head.

"Get real," Dar answered for her. "We didn't do anything to anyone. Let me clue you in on what's really going on here."

The cell phone rattled again, and Kerry lifted it to her ear, hearing a sort of popping noise. She studied it in puzzlement, racking her brains to remember where she'd seen the device behave in a similar fashion before. Was it in the office? No...

"Like we'd believe you?" Mike responded sarcastically.

"Okay, now hold on." Shari threw her bra into the ring. "I realize this might be tough to swallow, but you really should listen to what Dar has to say."

"What?" Both of the other bid teams turned to face Shari. "Have you lost your mind? You told us yesterday she wasn't anything but a lying two-faced bitch!" Mike spluttered. "Now you're pitching her bull?"

"Shari's right." Michelle stepped up to the plate. "We've got some new information. Remember information? It's the stuff you use to make decisions?"

"Holy crap," Kerry whispered. "What in the heck..." She started looking around, peering curiously at the items on the desk until she focused once again on the cookie jar. It was set on top of a bookcase behind the desk chair, with an unobstructed line of sight of the whole room. "Huh."

"Give me a freaking break! I'm not interested in a pack of bullshit!"

She squinted at the front of it, then turned. "Dar?"

Dar looked around, raising an eyebrow at her.

Kerry faced away from the jar, pointed her thumb at herself, then lifted her right hand and made a shutter snapping motion with her index finger and thumb.

Dar's eyes widened slightly.

"What?" Michelle watched them, her glance going back and forth. "This is no time for charades, guys."

"Well, you know, you just never can please everyone now can ya?" Kerry spread her arms wide abruptly, taking a step back as she did so. Her elbow hit the cookie jar and it smacked against the wall, then bounced off and fell from the bookshelf, hitting the linoleum floor and breaking into several large pieces. "Whoops."

Michelle stepped over and looked at the debris. "Pronghorn antelope in a china shop?" She suggested wryly, then her eyes focused on something. "Whoa...hold on. What's that?" She leaned over to get a closer look at the pottery shards.

Kerry curled her finger at the rest of the room. She pointed down at the jar shards, then held her finger to her lips. Dar joined her immediately, almost bouncing across the room as the others more reluctantly followed.

Buried in the shards was a small webcam mechanism, with gears and pulleys intended to allow it to be controlled remotely. The ornate design in the front of the jar bore a small hole which the lens had previously been subtly poking through.

The lens was now facing down, and they watched the pullies move feebly, trying to refocus it. The radio control affecting it made Kerry's cell phone pop again, and she held it up. "Picks up the weirdest things."

"Remote?" Michelle mouthed, her ginger eyebrows lifting.

Kerry nodded.

Mike knelt down and picked up a shard, moving the cam gingerly with one fingertip. Shari stood back, crossing her arms with a thoughtful expression. She looked around the room more carefully, her eyes searching the corners looking for something.

"So, what's the deal?" Mike looked up at Dar. "What are we missing here?"

The attitude had changed so quickly it almost gave Dar whiplash. However given what Kerry had found she had no doubt there were microphones to go with it. "Tell ya what," she said. "Let's take a walk outside, and get some fresh air. "

"Good idea." Shari instantly agreed. "It's getting stuffy in here. Air conditioning's out again, probably." She added, "We can catch a breeze near the water." She headed for the door with a determined expression. "Coming?"

They all filed out after her into the lobby that was conspicuously empty. The closing of the outside door echoed after they left.

Then footsteps rang out and several people rushed across the lobby, entering the office with rapid steps and muffled curses.

THEY FOUND A place to sit down on the seawall overlooking the cargo channel on the far side of port. Nothing was around but a few hopeful seagulls that flapped off in disgust when they discovered there were no sandwich crusts to be had.

The wind was blowing across the pier with some force, blowing offshore and conveniently taking their words out over the water for them. "Okay." Dar rested her elbows on her knees. "Just do me a favor and listen until I stop talking, then you can tell me how full of crap I am. Deal?"

Mike grunted.

Dar laid it out for them in crisp sentences. Kerry merely sat quietly next to her watching the faces of the two men as well as Michelle and Shari as they listened. No one really wanted to believe her, Kerry could tell. After all, realizing they'd all been played like a banjo wasn't the most pleasant thing going now was it?

Dar finished her briefing. "So that's what we've got. The last piece you saw yourselves—that damn camera. I'm sure they had tape running too. It was a nice scene we were having."

Mike stared off into the distance, then shook his head. "Well, shit," he muttered. "I wish to hell I could say you're just full of crap, Dar, but to be honest, something hasn't been adding up. Graham and I were talking about that yesterday." He indicated the fourth bid member, who so far hadn't made peep one.

Shari nodded. "We noticed, too," she admitted. "There was just too much insanity." Her eyes flicked to Dar's face, then away. "Even considering everything."

Mike held a hand up. "But you brought those filming people in," he objected. "So is this your scam?"

Interesting question. Kerry unconsciously leaned against Dar's shoulder as she waited for the answer. There was just something amazingly comforting about the solidity of her partner's presence, and she just barely kept herself from putting her head down on that same shoulder as they sat there.

Michelle stepped up. "The television people contacted me," she said. "Seemed like a good deal at the time, so I said sure. Free publicity? TV exposure with no outlay? Anyone would have said yes." She pointed at them all. "You all would have. Even you two."

"Probably." Kerry graciously agreed.

"But you bought their pitch hook, line and sinker." Mike reminded her. "They played you good."

Michelle shrugged. "Just as good as Quest played us all."

"Excuse me," Graham spoke up at last. "What is it we intend to do about this?" he asked. "It is almost end of the day. We are not complete in these projects, and it is all apparently to no purpose."

Now, here was the tough part. Dar glanced at Kerry, and raised her brows slightly, the invitation implicit in the motion.

Good nerd, bad nerd? "Well, we had an idea." Kerry gamely went forward. "We thought that this whole thing was apparently designed to get on film a knock down drag out fight to the finish, right?"

"Yeah," Shari agreed. "Preferably with the good guys winning."

"Define good guys," Mike muttered.

"So, what if no one wins?" Kerry asked. "What if it's a tie? What if we all join together and level the playing field, and just make sure everyone finishes successfully."

Momentary silence. "What the hell would that do?" Mike asked.

"Screw them over," Shari said, bluntly.

Graham rubbed his face with one hand. "You are telling me that we should help each other? Why should we trust you?" He indicated both sets of women. "Why should we trust any of you? You've been cat-fighting each other for weeks. Now you are standing here, and you want us all to work together? It's insanity!"

Kerry glanced past them to the admin building. She spotted Cruickshank emerging with Quest, both of them looking around. "Uh oh."

Dar focused on what she was looking at. "We're out of time," she said. "Listen, I don't really give a crap if you trust us or not. The fact is we're done."

"But powerless." Michelle interrupted her.

"No." Dar shook her head. "We have power. I could have just grabbed the jackass over there and been done with this if I wanted to." She stood up as Quest discovered them. "So here's the plan. We go to our areas, and whatever you need done, call me. If you had your crews bought out from under you, I'll send people. Got a technical problem? We'll find a way to fix it. We've got two hours."

They only had seconds to decide. Quest and Cruickshank were headed their way.

"Call you." Mike looked like his head was going to explode. "This is nuts, Dar."

"Lose or tie. Pick one, but do it now," Dar said, as she already started to edge away from the group.

"We're in," Michelle said, briskly. "Expect my call about our satellite."

"All right." Mike scowled. "I'll need techs." He backed off and checked his watch, then turned and hurried off, breaking into a jog toward the pier his ship was in.

Graham stuck his hands in his pockets. "Not sure you can help us," he commented mildly. "We're short a bit of gear — supplier ran out."

Kerry cleared her throat, loudly. "Hey, Michelle?"

Michelle had halfway turned around to beat a hasty retreat, then turned back around to face him. "Call me." She lifted a hand, and then turned again, heading off in the opposite direction.

Dar and Kerry were left alone to face the music. Kerry suspected it would be an exceptionally tuneless polka, and she decided maybe retreat was a better option. "C'mon, Dar. We've got stuff to do." She took hold of her partner's arm and started tugging.

"Roberts!" Quest yelled.

"Ms. Roberts." Cruickshank moved to intercept them. "Wait...I've got some questions for you!"

"Dar, we better get out of here. Anything we say could blow it." Kerry uttered.

"Right." Dar lifted a hand. "Sorry. We've got work to do." She turned and urged Kerry ahead of her, heading down the strip of grass that bordered the seawall.

"Stop! Roberts! Get back here!" Quest called. "Stop!"

"Glad the wind's so noisy." Kerry broke into a trot, then a jog. "Did you hear anything?"

"Nope." Dar loped next to her. "Not a damn thing."

"Me either."

"Roberts! God damn it! Stop!"

Don't like it when someone else takes charge, eh? Dar smiled grimly as she let the echoes fade behind her. Well buddy, get used to it.

KERRY WAS STANDING in the raised middle platform; the central figure in a sea of milling techs. The front doors to the pier building were locked, though she thought she'd seen one of the camera crews loitering around outside a moment ago. "Okay folks, listen up."

There was a palpable air of anticipation in the room. Mark leaned on the counter she was standing behind, a look of almost smug triumph on his face. "It took a lot of busting ass, but damn if we didn't do it, huh boss?"

Yikes. Kerry now faced a completely different dilemma. They'd pushed their team to the limit, and the guys and gals hadn't disappointed them. Now she had to tell them that basically, their efforts had been for pretty much naught. "Guys, I've got something a little difficult to explain here."

Her team settled down and looked up at her trustingly. Kerry had a moment of flashback, to the day she'd stood in front of a very different team for a very different reason, with much the same looks directed back at her.

Then, she'd saved them from unemployment, and in the process saved herself from going back to a life of oppression at home. This time? Well, this time, she just had to tell them she'd led them down a slightly crooked path. Not really so bad, was it?

"First off, I want to thank you all for all the killer work you've done over the past week," Kerry said. "I appreciate it, Dar appreciates it, and not least, the company appreciates it. You made it all happen."

Everyone grinned.

"However." Kerry leaned on the counter, giving them all a very wry look. "There were some things going on here that we didn't know about."

"Uh oh," Mark said.

"So, the bottom line is, now that we've gotten our stuff done, we need to help everyone else get theirs done too."

Everyone stared at her, jaws dropping open a little. It would have been comical if Kerry wasn't so conscious of the minutes ticking away. "Guys, please just trust me on this one. I'll explain later, but we're almost out of time. I need to split up some teams, and send you all over to the other ships."

Mark covered his eyes with one hand. "Ohmyfriggengod."

"Holy crap." Carlos blurted. "We're going to help them now?"

"Yep." Kerry shifted a few pieces of paper. "Once we all finish, I can tell you the rest of the story. It's quite a story. But Dar wanted me to let you all know — despite what we're going to have to do — the only real winners in this entire shebang are standing right here in this room."

The techs fell silent, the buzz in the room dying out as they absorbed the compliment.

"We are the best. We proved that." Kerry went on. "Now, we have to take it a step further, and take this project to a different level. So," she exhaled, "let's get going. Grab yourselves a pop, and your gear, and I'll call out names in a minute."

The techs stirred, and started moving. Mark waited for some space to clear, then he propped his chin up on his fist. "Um, Kerry?"

"I know." Kerry held a hand up. "Just go with it, Mark. The whole thing's a farce."

"Huh?"

"It's fake. It's a whitewash. It's not real. The ships aren't going to sail anywhere. It was just one big charade for the cameras."

"No shit?"

"Ma'am?"

Kerry turned to find their security guard standing there. "Yes?"

"Those people at the door are not taking no for an answer." The guard pointed. "They're starting to get real mad." Past him, Kerry could see the filming crew, Cruickshank, Quest, and others all clustered near the door, banging on it. "Yikes."

"Whoa." Mark blinked.

"Take this list and get these guys over to the ship in slot 12." Kerry handed Mark a piece of paper. "Hurry, and whatever happens, tell everyone not to say anything to anyone about what we're doing. Just keep quiet."

"Huh?"

"Mark, we've been in the dark for weeks. Now it's our turn to pull one over on these people." Kerry told him. "Got me?"

Mark hesitated, then grinned sheepishly. "Not a clue boss, but if you say shut up, no problem." He took the paper and scanned it. "Okay!" His voice rose. "Following names get your asses over here!"

Right. Kerry ran a hand through her hair. "Okay." She faced the guard. "Let me just get a mouthful of something and I'll go take care of those guys. They say what they want?"

"Ms. Roberts." The guard supplied promptly.

"Well, there you go. She's not here." Kerry gratefully accepted a bottle of grape soda from Carlos. "Thank you." She took a sip of the cold beverage and considered what she was going to tell the reporters. A grin crossed her face, and she chuckled a little. "You want a story? All right. I'll give you one."

She stepped down from the platform and headed for the door. "Time for you to chase *your* tails."

DAR DUCKED BEHIND a container, watching as one of the filming crews hurried past her toward the entrance to Michelle and Shari's pier building. She slunk out after them and waited for them to pass the crew gangway, then she scooted up the metal walk and into the ship's hold.

It was dingy, smelly, and as ratty looking as theirs was, only it was painted slate gray inside rather than the worn blue she was used to. There also seemed to be fewer rust stains on the steel plate walls.

Other than that, same old, same old. A few crewmembers were morosely shoving boxes around, and they glanced at her as she entered. After a moment's interest, they returned to their tasks, apparently having seen enough.

Hm. Should she feel insulted or grateful? Grateful, she decided with a nod, as she edged past two men carrying a large crate that gave off a scent of burnished copper.

What would happen to them? Dar wondered. If this entire thing was a farce, then all their hopes would have been raised for nothing. She paused inside the door and looked at the crewmen, seeing something in their attitude that made her realize that they'd never been fooled at all.

They'd known all along. In fact, Dar remembered, some of the crew on her own ship had even told her, but she'd been too focused to really listen.

Damn. When she sat back and looked at it, how much of this farce had been there in front of her all along? How much of her attention had been distracted to the point where she'd almost missed it all?

Ah well. Dar knew she had to shrug it off, since there was no way to go back and change it. At least now she did know what was going on, and was doing something about it. Better late than never?

Something like that.

She thought that the bridge and the mounting point for the satellite system would be in relatively the same place as theirs, and so she started up the steps two at a time. On the way up, she passed a few more of the crew, who brushed by her without much interest and kept going.

Nice guys. Dar reached the main deck and left the crew stairwell, crossing through a propped open watertight door, and entered the atrium. Unlike her ship, this one seemed to be in a little better condition, and the crew on this deck was busy polishing the brass railings and doing other cleaning chores.

One of the women behind the reception desk looked up as Dar headed for the main stairs. "Well, hello there," she called out, in an almost cheerful tone. "You're new."

Dar gave her a brief smile and a half wave.

"Smashing shorts!"

Ah. Ugh. "Thanks." Dar wished for the stair landing, wanting to be out of the woman's line of sight. Kerry told her not to wear the damn shorts, and Kerry had been right, as she usually was. How could she really expect anyone to take her seriously when she dressed like a half assed redneck?

Jesus. Dar sighed as she rounded the stairs and headed upward. I really do need to get the hell out of here. My head's so screwed up I'm going to sink the goddamned company if I don't. With that somewhat daunting thought on her mind, she jogged up the steps, dodging several officers strolling in the other direction.

The hallways were empty up on the top deck, though. She headed down one long, long corridor freshly laid with carpet, shaking her head at the seemingly pointless expense. Ahead of her, she spotted the locked door that on her ship lead to the bridge and she headed for it, wondering if banging on it hard enough would eventually gain her entry.

Fortunately, she didn't have to. As she came within a body length of it, the door opened and Michelle's head appeared. "Ah." Michelle spotted her. "Just who I was about to go looking for. Kerry said you were heading here."

Not exactly what Kerry had thought, regardless of what she'd said, Dar reckoned. "Here I am." She agreed. "Let's get going. The damn reporters are crawling all over the pier."

"I know I saw them." Michelle held the door open. "This way."

Dar followed her through the senior officer's hallway, noticing that this ship, at least, had retained quite a bit of its glitzy interior. The walls were paneled in wood, and the carpet was new and expensive looking.

They stopped in front of a door that Michelle shoved open. Inside was the cramped communications center. This room was pretty much identical to the one on Dar's vessel. She entered, ducking around a rack of satellite gear to find two men standing in front of the console, frustration apparent in their faces.

"God damn it, Steve...I've already tried that."

"Yeah, but did you get those guys on the phone with you? They said they had a fix for this." The shorter of the two men retorted. "I think they're full of crap, but if you don't have them do it, they won't admit they're wrong.'

Dar took a moment to examine the equipment, as she listened to them argue. It was more or less the same as what she was using on the other ship, but there seemed to her to be too much of it. She turned and regarded Michelle with a single cocked eyebrow. "Three routers?" she asked, lowering her voice.

Michelle held her hand up. "We paid to have a network design engineer come in here and give us the definitive solution. That's what he gave us." She edged away from the two men, and motioned Dar to follow her.

Amiably, Dar did. "He gave you cat crap on a stick." Dar advised her. "Let me guess...did he work for the hardware vendor?"

Michelle nodded.

"And you didn't catch on to him wanting to sell pointless hardware to you?"

Michelle sighed. "Sometimes you have to trust the experts." She looked pointedly at Dar. "Like now, for instance. So since we're short on time, mind rolling out your brain cells and dusting that possibly redundant hardware with them?"

"Kennel your puppies." Dar returned the banter, and turned, standing back and waiting for Michelle to clear the riffraff out of the way. She spotted a laptop and went over to it, flipping it open and reviewing the screen, as well as the cable that connected the back of it to the equipment rack.

"Hey." One of the men finally noticed the scruffy vagabond in their midst. "Can I help you?"

Michelle took him by the arm. "Not even if I bought you an Einstein injection, kiddo. Take your buddy and go find some ice cream somewhere, hum?"

"But, ma'am," Steve protested, pointing at Dar who had already oozed into position in front of the gear and was pecking at the laptop contentedly. "Who is that?"

"Shoo." Michelle gave him a gentle push toward the door to the communications room.

"But..."

"Shoo."

Dar smiled, as she got to work, getting into the configuration of the equipment and studying what it was supposed to be doing. She typed a command and reviewed the results, frowning and shaking her head a little. "Jesus."

Michelle had taken a position up around the corner of the rack, where she could watch without standing on top of Dar. "That doesn't sound good." She glanced at the small porthole in the room. "And we're running out of time."

"Well." Dar stepped back and looked at the rack. "I could spend a few hours untangling that configuration."

"We don't have a few hours."

"I know." Dar reached for the cables in the rear of the rack and started ripping them out in handfuls. "So I guess I'll do it the easy way."

Michelle covered her eyes. "Oh crap." She sighed. "It took that guy four days to put that stuff in."

Dar snorted, finishing ripping out the cabling and ending her destructive activity, only to dive into the laptop with a piratical chuckle as she reset everything to its defaults. "Look at it this way. It wasn't working."

Michelle sat on the edge of one of the desks, rubbing the back of her neck. "Yeah, that's true," she muttered. "Story of my life lately. Nothing's working."

With her back turned, Dar was sure her widening eyes were hidden from view. She hoped against hope that Michelle's comment wasn't the beginning of a sensitive chat because she knew that definitely was not her forte – at all.

So she kept her nose in the screen, starting the configuration of the main unit as she tried to assemble a new design on the fly and crossed her fingers she wasn't going to have to call Kerry for help.

"HI." KERRY SLIPPED through the front door and closed it behind her, facing the reporters with a neatly dredged up pleasant smile. "What can I do for you folks?"

Cruickshank was caught by surprise. She'd been banging on the door and had turned away to come up with some better method of getting attention and hadn't expected Kerry to come out. "Well, ah, yes. Ms. Stuart. Right."

"That's me." Kerry agreed.

"Well, thanks for the offer, but we're really looking for your boss," Cruickshank said.

"Really? Me too."

"What?"

"Me too." Kerry drew the woman aside and lowered her voice. "She's missing. I can't find her. After we got back from being at sea, she disappeared."

It was the last thing the reporter expected. "But, I saw her with you not twenty minutes ago!"

Kerry didn't miss a beat. "That was after we got back," she said. "Anyway, if you find her, can you let me know? The hyperbaric thermoelectric generator she built is giving us a little problem. I think it needs adjusting."

"The what?"

"Well, we had to get power somehow," Kerry told her. "Dar didn't want to wait for the ship to fix it. We're coming up on a deadline here."

Cruickshank collected herself. "Uh, okay. So, let me make sure I understand you right . You mean to tell me Ms. Roberts..."

"Please, call her Dar. She hates formality."

"Uh huh, okay. So you're telling me Dar built this, uh, this power generator from — from what exactly?"

"Oh, odds and ends," Kerry said. "Yes, she just finished it, and we tried it out, fried a few things, but we seem to have it settled down now, but like I said, it's acting weird and I really want her to look at it." She turned and pointed at the ship that now, in the coming sunset, had a few lights shining in the windows. As they watched, one sputtered out. "See? I don't dare put the computer system on that — might blow up."

"Uh, okay, right," the reporter said. "So, if this works out, does...I mean, you'll win, right?"

"Uh huh."

"Okay. Well, that's very exciting!" Cruickshank said. "I mean, it could be over. Listen, can we get some film of this, uh, whatever it is? How long will it take Dar to fix it? Could it be in the next ten minutes or something like that?"

Gotcha. "Well, it's hard to say." Kerry confided. "We have to find Dar first — and you know, that's a proprietary piece of hardware. I'm not sure she'd want it filmed, but maybe you can ask her."

The reporter was already backing away. "Ah, yeah, I'll do that. Listen, I'm going to go, uh, talk to someone. I'll keep my eye out for her, okay?" She turned and rushed off, nearly shoving the two cameramen ahead of her.

Kerry waggled her fingers amiably. "Bye." She checked her watch, wondering how long it would be before Quest and his scumbags made an attempt on her hyperbaric thermoelectric generator. "Hm. Wonder if they have any of that old plumbing around still."

She ducked back into the building and shut the door, giving the guard a wink.

THE COMMUNICATIONS ROOM had gotten relatively quiet. One of the officers had come in a time or two, but after glaring at Dar's back with completely no effect, they'd left the two IT professionals in peace to muck with the cables to their hearts content.

At least one of them anyway. Dar paused to study her screen, one hand lifting to riffle her bangs back off her forehead before she continued to type.

"Well?" Michelle asked for the nth time.

"Artesian." Dar replied.

"Very funny."

Dar looked up over the screen of the laptop. "Michelle, I'm doing this as fast as I can. You're not making it any faster if I have to stop and be inane with you every sixty seconds."

The shorter woman released a disgusted breath. She checked her watch then got up and wandered over to the porthole, staring out it and turning her back on Dar.

In that peaceful silence, Dar got back to work. She left the laptop for a moment and went to the rack, connecting a cable to the back of one piece of equipment and running it through the side of the rack to a second, plugging it in with a decisive snick.

After waiting to see the lights near the cable ports go from dark, to yellow, to green, she returned to the laptop and sat down behind it, cracking her knuckles before she got back to work on the keyboard. It wasn't that configuring the units was that difficult after all, she'd done it plenty of times before. It was trying to integrate the devices into a satellite system just different enough from the one she was using that was presenting its own set of unique challenges.

Dar frowned and tried another setting. "Hmph."

"You say something?" Michelle turned.

"Nope." Dar went over to look at the satellite gear, turning it on and watching the oscilloscope waver and settle into a pattern. "Where's the dish mounted?" she asked.

Michelle looked at her. "How would I know?"

Dar put her hands on her hips.

"Listen, not all of us are egghead tech huggers, okay?" Michelle replied to the implied derision. "I leave the technical installations to the experts. I don't ask my air conditioning repairman to let me inspect his filters either."

Egghead tech hugger. Dar liked that. It had a nice ring to it. "Ever consider the reason I'm as successful as I am at what I do might be the fact that I invest myself in the technology?" She went back to the laptop without waiting for an answer, coding in a second option.

Stubbornly, the device refused to cooperate with her and the results didn't change.

Damn it.

Dar pulled out her PDA and tapped in a message and then sent it. She continued on to a different area of the configuration, setting up some secondary sections to her satisfaction before she saved the configuration just in case.

You never knew when something might happen that could wipe your work out after all, and... Dar looked up as the lights went completely out, plunging the room into darkness relieved only by the fading light from the porthole.

The rack went silent as well. "Nice," Dar commented.

"Shit."

"Careful what you ask for."

KERRY READ THE PDA message twice before she rapidly shook her head and made a weird noise of astonishment. "I can't believe I'm reading this." She sat down at one of the desks in their small office and logged on, waiting for the network to validate her account as she tapped her thumbs on the desktop.

"What's up, boss?" Mark entered. "You get rid of the spooks?"

"Yeah." Kerry opened up a console window and logged into Dar's shares back in the office. She browsed through them until she found what she wanted, then opened the text file and viewed it. "I can honestly say I never thought I'd have to do this."

"What?" Mark eyed her curiously.

Kerry copied the contents of the file into a notepad file then transferred the file to her PDA. "Dar forgot how to do something."

"Huh?"

"Yeah, that's what I said." Kerry attached the text file to her reply message, and sent it back to her partner. "Sometimes she has these small flashes of plain old ordinary humanity and I'm never really expecting them."

Mark chuckled. "Yeah, I know what you mean. I remember one time we were working late in the ops center, and Dar had gone downstairs to get some cables or crap like that. I had to get some ends, so I went down after her and when I got to the door, I heard this cursing like crazy inside. I walked in and Dar was on her back on the ground and I couldn't figure out what was going on."

"Tripped?" Kerry asked, with a knowing grin.

"Yeah fell right on her butt. Man, she was pissed." Mark agreed. "Cause, like, she's pretty graceful normally, you know?"

"I know."

"So I was like—do I laugh? Commiserate? Offer her a hand up?" Mark shook his head. "Close the door and pretend I wasn't there? There weren't any good choices."

"Yeah," Kerry said. "I never really know what to do either. I usually just end up kissing her."

Mark's jaw clicked shut. "Uh," he said, after a moment's silence. "Wasn't really an option."

Kerry's cell phone rang, saving her from having to recover from her mild faux pas. She answered it, wryly scrubbing her now blushing face. "Hello?"

"This is Shari."

Ugh. "Hi."

"Michelle told me to turn over some of our spares to Graham."
Shari said shortly. "Which I'm willing to do."

Bet you're not. Kerry mentally stuck her tongue out at the phone.
"Okay, that's great," she said. "But what do I have to do with this?"

"You're supposed to have the answer to everything," Shari said.
"So here's the problem. They have no way of getting the stuff over to
their ship because all the pier people have vanished. They have no carts,
and the three people he has left over there have bad backs."

Kerry stared at the wall, her jaw working a little as she struggled to
get words out through her clenched teeth.

"Uh oh." Mark was watching her in fascination. "Should I get the
baseball bat?"

Kerry cleared her throat. "Why don't you help them take it over?"
She suggested mildly.

"We're busy."

You. Are. Such. An. Asshole. Kerry mentally articulated the words,
and almost duplicated the effort audibly. "Okay. I'll take care of it," she
said. "Thanks." She hung up the cell phone, shutting it with a vicious
click. "Stupid hairball piece of sea cow moosemeat."

Mark looked at her, his eyebrows hiking up. "Evil, boss. Evil."

"Bah."

Kerry opened the cell again, and dialed a number. She waited then
started speaking when it was answered. "Hi Dad. Listen. Do you have
the truck here?" She waited. "Can you bring it over here? I have to pick
something up over at the next ship, and drop it off somewhere." She
waited again. "Thanks. I really appreciate it." A smile. "You rock,
Dad."

She closed the phone. "You know something? People suck."

"Yeah, but other people don't." Mark suggested. "Was that big D's
pop? He's cool."

Kerry got up. "He's more than cool," she said. "He's the father I
always wished I had." She paused, a little surprised the words had
come out. "So anyway, we're going to go pick up some switches and
bring them over across the port to that other pier. Okay?"

"Want some help?" Mark asked. "Not that the big guy couldn't just
pick up that whole ship and put it in his shoulder, but y'know, we got
guys to do that stuff for you." He followed Kerry out the door. "Kerry?"

Kerry held up two fingers as she headed for the front door.

"Right." Mark turned. "Hey, Carlos! Get over here." He motioned
to the tech. "We got a gig, dude. Move it!"

"Yeah?" Carlos didn't seem upset by the command. "It's better than
hanging out here. Where we going?"

"With the boss."

"Oh. Cool." The younger tech grinned. "Poquito boss, yeah?'

"Yeah."

"Bueno."

They walked outside and joined Kerry, who was standing on the curbside rocking up and down on her heels. Sunset had begun in earnest and the light was growing golden, as a relatively cool breeze came up off the water and ruffled their hair.

"Getting late," Mark remarked.

Kerry gazed at the sky. "Can't spin fast enough for me," she admitted. "It'll be nice to get to the end of this particular day." She caught sight of Andrew's truck heading haphazardly in their direction. "Okay, so here's the deal. We have to go get some switches from that ship over there and bring them to that one across the way. Speed counts. We don't really have much time."

"There go those reporters again." Carlos pointed. "They're going to that other ship too. Hey, and there's people all running around over there."

Kerry looked, and sure enough, there was a lot of activity around the gangway. She tipped her head back and shaded her eyes, as she noticed something else. "It's pretty dark over there," she commented. "I wonder..."

Her PDA beeped. She pulled it out and looked at it.

> I'm stuck in a dark room with a bunch of wires,
> bad carpet, and Michelle.

Kerry quickly tapped out a message as Andrew pulled up in front of the pier.

> I'm about to get in the back of Dad's truck. Want
> to trade?

"Howdy there, Kerry," Andrew said. "You all want a hitch?"

Kerry vaulted into the bed of the pickup, finding herself a handhold as Mark and Carlos joined her. "Go for it, Dad."

"Sure you're hanging on back there?'

"Go."

The truck started into a 180 degree turn that aimed to take out a large patch of gravel and grass as Kerry hung on for dear life.

She hoped one of them remembered a flashlight.

Chapter Ten

THE DARKNESS CONTINUED, and Dar lifted her arm to wipe the sweat off her forehead as she stood in the middle of it. "Okay."

"Okay what?" Michelle asked.

"Okay this is not getting us anywhere." Dar reached over and, by touch, identified the piece of equipment she'd been working on. She pulled the screwdriver from her back pocket and using just her fingers and a mental image she unscrewed the rack mounts and yanked the piece of gear loose.

"What are you doing?"

"Making progress. "Dar grunted as she hoisted the router clear of the rack. "I'm going back to the office." She tucked the laptop under one arm and the router under the other.

"With that? No way!"

Dar moved past her in the darkness. "Michelle, I can't configure this in the dark with no power. If you can figure out a way to do that, we'll stay here. Otherwise, hasta banana, cucaracha." She pulled the door open and headed out into the pitch black corridors with Michelle's scrambling form right behind her.

"Hey!"

Dar just kept going. She figured she was making enough noise to warn anyone ahead of her to get out of the way, and she was moving with enough force that if Michelle was dumb enough to grab hold of her, she'd end up flat on her ass or dragging behind.

They were running out of time. "Why don't you go find out why the lights are off?" Dar suggested bluntly. "You're not going to help me with this thing."

"How do I know you're not sabotaging it?" Michelle countered.

"Would you know anyway, even with a damn searchlight focused on me?" Dar shot back. "I could be programming this thing to send packets to the moon for all you know." She spotted a bit of light and headed for it, turning the corner and getting to the stairs with a sense of relief.

"I'll get Shari to find out what's up." Michelle stubbornly stuck to Dar's heels, flipping open her cell phone as she trotted down the steps after her. "Hey. You know what's going on?" She spoke into the phone. "Well, find out. Let me know." She closed the device up and put it back into her pocket.

"Maybe they forgot to pay the bill." Dar tucked the router under her arm.

"What bill? My bill?"

"The electric bill."

"Very funny." Michelle skipped a few steps to catch up. "Why don't you just leave that here. Maybe we can just forget the whole thing."

Dar reached the main deck and headed for the upper gangway. "Forget it." She emerged into the sunlight and strode across the teak surface, hopping up onto the metal walkway with determined strides.

"Dar!" Michelle yelled in frustration. "Now stop!"

Dar glanced at the pier below, spotting the filming crew wheeling to focus on this new noise above them. She waved at Cruickshank as she passed over her head, then she broke into a run along the concrete walkway.

"Hey! Hey!" Michelle yelped, caught unprepared by Dar's escape. "Get back here! That's our router! Hey! Hey! Stop!" She chased after Dar belatedly. "Roberts! Hey!" She started running, pounding down the pathway as fast as she could.

Below them, the camera people rapidly swung the lens up to capture the action, Cruickshank barely getting her jaw closed in time to bring the microphone up to her lips to talk. "A new development is just breaking here. It looks like the ILS team has taken something from the Telegenics team!"

"Roberts! Damn you!" Michelle howled. "Get back here! Have you lost your mind?"

Heh. Dar spotted a familiar car heading toward the pier and she almost stopped, then thought better of it when she glimpsed the furious expression on Michelle's face. The absurdity of the entire situation suddenly became clear to her, and it almost made her double up laughing.

"Roberts!"

So what the hell, she might as well have some fun. Dar turned gracefully and ran backwards, sticking her tongue out at Michelle before she turned around again and picked up speed.

"Bitch!"

"Hard to say what's really going on—oh!" The reporter jumped back out of the way as a small pickup truck roared through the gates and headed straight for her. "Now what?' She glanced between the truck and the walkway, torn as to what to report on.

The truck skidded to a halt and Kerry launched herself out of the back with Carlos and Mark right behind her. "Excuse me." She gave the reporter a halfheartedly polite smile, motioning the techs toward the gangway. "Let's go people. We've got gear to move."

"Hey! Roberts!"

Kerry heard the yell, and only just kept herself from turning to look.

"Ms. Stuart, can you tell us what's going on here?"

"Nope." Kerry ran up the slanted metal platform. "C'mon guys." She had no idea what Dar was up to, but she knew they only had limited time to get things moving so her partner's shenanigans would have to wait till later.

Right now, she had a switch to pick up from a bitch. And speaking of...

Shari appeared at the top of the ramp at the last second, and Kerry only had a heartbeat to stop. Being covetous of her heartbeats, she decided not to, and instead plowed right into the taller woman knocking her head over keester into the darkness of the hold.

Ah. Kerry felt a sense of personal satisfaction she hadn't quite anticipated and loved every minute of it. Her body tingled with the release of energy. She stepped down into the warm space, aware of the techs that had stopped short behind her. "Oops. Sorry." She apologized. "Didn't see you there."

Shari leaned back on her hands and just glared.

"ROBERTS, DAMN YOU! Stop!"

Dar knew Michelle couldn't catch her. She got to the end of the walkway and shoved the door open with her shoulder, trading the humid late afternoon air for the cold briskness of conditioned dryness. She started down the stairs, rambling down them at a breakneck pace as she heard the door open again behind her.

She could hear Michelle cursing, too. Dar got to the bottom of the steps and entered the open space of the terminal, spotting a table set up near a wall that conveniently had a power outlet underneath it. She dropped the router onto the table and put the laptop next to it then knelt to plug it in.

Michelle was coming up behind her. Dar got the plug in and stood turning and quickly finding her center of balance just in case Michelle decided to do something really silly like try to kick her. "Ah, ah ah." Dar held both hands up in warning.

Michelle kept going, reaching out to grab Dar's shirt. "I've had about enough of you, goddamn it!" She suddenly found herself stopped, her fingers inches from their target as Dar simply used her longer reach to good advantage.

She grabbed Dar's arm with both hands and yanked at it. Under her fingers, the muscles bunched and stiffened as Dar's hand closed on the fabric of her shirt, and Michelle looked up to find ice cold, blue eyes regarding her.

The humor was gone. The light coming in the window flickered off the tanned planes of Dar's face and accentuated the slight flaring of her nostrils.

Psycho, Shari had said. Michelle had dismissed the charge, but right now, right here, she wondered. "What the hell was that about?" she finally asked, dropping her hands from Dar's arm. "You lost your mind?"

"Hey." Dar shoved her back gently. "I needed light. Chill out." She turned and opened the laptop, reconnecting it to the router that was gently blinking at her from its place on the table. Her heartbeat was still a little fast, and her knees shivered in reaction to the adrenaline seeping out.

Michelle was no threat. Dar knew that. No matter how many belts or how many wisecracks the woman had in her, there was no doubt in Dar's mind that she could kick her butt.

Hell, there was no doubt in Dar's mind that Kerry could kick her butt. In fact, if Kerry had come in the room while Michelle was pawing at her, she had no doubt she'd have been picking up armfuls of pissed off Midwestern Republican, and hauling her off before the Telegenics president ended up dumped head first into a garbage can.

Ahrg. How freaking professional. Dar now felt embarrassment overcoming her anger. "Okay." Now let me try this again," she said, glad at least that Kerry hadn't witnessed the childish standoff. What would she have thought?

KERRY STEPPED AROUND the still supine Shari. "Where's the boxes. We don't have much time." She glanced behind her as Mark turned on his flashlight and shone it around the hold. "There?"

"Bitch."

Kerry leaned close to the stack of boxes. "Yeah, here it is. C'mon, guys." She started pulling at a box. "Carlos, give me a hand, okay?"

"Ma'am! Ma'am!" Carlos scurried warily past Shari, who was slowly getting to her feet and rubbing her back. "Let us get that. It's heavy!"

Mark quickly joined him. "Yeah. Hey, boss, why don't you wait outside for us, huh?"

Kerry ignored them and held up her end of the box, as they edged it out of the stack and headed for the gangway. "Careful, guys," she warned. "All kinds of obstacles around here."

"You should know," Shari snorted. "Sure you don't know why the lights are out? According to the guys upstairs they went out while your precious partner was playing with something."

"Hm, well, yes, I can see that." Kerry grunted. "I've had that happen once or twice, but honestly, I don't think Dar did for the ship quite what she does for me. Scuse me. You're going to get stepped on."

Mark clucked like a duck, but kept walking backwards as they got the switch out of the ship. "Hey, look out."

Cruickshank thrust a microphone into his face. "What are you doing?"

Mark looked at her, looked at the box, and looked back at her. "Lady, this thing weighs a ton. Could ya move, please?"

"But this is the second piece of equipment your company has taken from the Telegenics ship. What's going on?" The reporter persisted. "What are you doing?"

"Dropping this." Mark grunted, hauling backwards and just pushing the woman out of the way. "Hey, Mr. Roberts? Can you give a hand here?" He called out.

"Roberts?" Cruickshank turned and spotted a new victim. "This gets even thicker. Over there boys! Get the shot on him, on that guy."

DAR STUDIED THE screen briefly, scowling. "Huh. Is that how I did that?" She muttered, then shook her head and copied in the configuration, reviewing the results with bemusement. "Guess it was."

Michelle had taken a seat on the table and was just watching her with a dour expression.

"Okay." Dar reviewed the configuration again, then looked up. "What's the deal with the power?"

"Is that ready?" Michelle asked.

Dar nodded.

Michelle opened her cell phone and dialed. There was apparently no answer, and she gave the phone an annoyed look before she got up. "Stay here. I'll go find out."

Dar's brows hiked. "Not afraid I'm going to run out the door with this?" She inquired. "Sure you don't want to chain me to the table first?"

Michelle gave her a withering stare. "You'd enjoy it too much." She stalked out, brushing past two of her workers as they entered shaking their heads and laughing.

Dar didn't really want to just stay where she was, but she really didn't want to go back out into the muggy heat either. She compromised by pulling out her PDA and tapping a message to Kerry, hitting send before she wandered over to the doors and peered through the glass at the lower part of the pier.

Her father's truck sped past. Dar blinked, seeing Kerry, along with Mark and Carlos, hanging on for dear life surrounding a crate in the back. "Whoa." She leaned against the glass, watching them go. Kerry had the straps holding the crate down in one hand with her legs braced and her free hand up in the air. She looked very much like she was riding a bucking bronco.

Cute. But dangerous. Dar frowned. She watched until the truck was out of sight, then turned and went back to her table, drumming her fingers on the surface of it. She'd been there only for a few seconds when the two guys that had come in from outside approached her, eyeing her warily.

She eyed them back. "Yeah?"

The taller one folded his arms over his chest. "So, you're that big shot everyone's talking about?"

Dar looked him up and down. "Probably."

"You the one who said nobody could break into your network?" The shorter one blurted. "You're that super nerd chick?'

Unsure of whether to be flattered or insulted, Dar settled on annoyed instead. "Yeah. Who's asking?"

"Man, you sure don't look like it." The two men walked away, shaking their heads again.

Huh? Dar quickly looked down at herself, half expecting to see paint or worse splashed across her ragged denim outfit or a rip in an unexpected place.

However, she looked reasonably acceptable so, who knew? "Thanks." Dar called after them, spotting Michelle and Shari entering from the back door and dismissing the two men without further thought. "So what's the story?"

"Somehow," Michelle paused, placing delicate emphasis on the word. "The main electrical panel seems to have blown a fuse. They're apparently..." She paused again, and grimaced. "Replacing it."

"All right." Dar ran her hand through her hair. "I'll go put this back in so it'll come up when the power does. I still have to work a few things out with it once that happens." She closed the laptop and unplugged it, tossing the cable to one side. "Thing we've got to be careful of is not tipping off the damn filming people."

"Little late for that," Shari remarked dryly. "Your father just tossed one of their camera rigs into the water. Hope you've got a nice size bank account to go with that condo."

The back door from the pier opened and the filming team entered, for the first time looking really, really pissed off. Two of the men were dripping wet, and a third was carrying what was obviously a very soggy piece of expensive filming gear.

"Hm." Dar picked up the router. "My guess is, time for us to go."

"Don't want to face the music?" Shari taunted.

Dar tucked the router under her arm and started walking toward the steps.

"Ms. Roberts!" Cruickshank spotted her. "Hold on just one minute, please!"

Dar just kept right on walking, but the room wasn't that big and the reporter caught up to her as she reached the stairs. "Excuse me a minute." Cruickshank said. "Can we talk?"

"Nope." Dar started up the stairs. "I don't have anything to say."

"What? You're turning this project upside down, and you have nothing to say?" The woman sounded angry. "You owe us some answers!"

"No, I don't." Dar didn't even turn around. "Except to say... how do you like being on the dark side for a change?" She rounded the stairway and headed up the second flight. "Michelle? You coming?" She yelled down over her shoulder.

"What?" Cruickshank spluttered. "Dark side of what? Where are you going? What are you doing?"

Quest entered downstairs, his voice echoing across the hall as he crossed it down below. "All right, Graver. It's time to pay up or shut up."

Cruickshank stopped, torn between following Dar and going to see what was going on. "Oh."

Dar stopped also, cocking her head to listen. Where she was standing they couldn't really see her, and she reasoned it was as good a time as any to get some dirt.

"Pay up? It's not sundown yet." Michelle's voice came back. "Come talk to me when it's dark out."

"I'm not waiting," Quest said. "I want what you promised me, NOW!"

"Screw you, ya little..." Shari burst in. "I'll tell you what I'm gonna give you!"

"Uh oh." The reporter reversed her direction and started downward. "Damn you, Roberts. I don't have a camera for this!" She cursed. "What am I supposed to do?"

"Take notes." Dar started down after her.

"MS. STUART?" CARLOS had one foot wedged between the crate and the lift gate and both his hands clenching the strapping with all his strength. "I have to say to you that you, for sure, make this job very exciting."

"Um, thanks." Kerry nearly pitched overboard as Andrew took a curve in the road on their way across the port. "Actually, I really didn't expect IT to be quite this, uh..."

"Whacked?" Mark supplied.

"Yeah." Kerry squinted into the wind, her blonde hair whipping wildly around her head. She realized her PDA was buzzing in her pocket, but faced with the choice of reading the message or possibly being tossed out of the back of the truck, she regretfully decided the note would have to wait.

Bummer, because she was fairly sure it was Dar.

"Hey, Kerry?" Mark inched closer. "That was pretty cool, you knocking whatserface on her ass."

"I enjoyed it," Kerry admitted. "I've just had enough. Honestly. This has just gone over the top for me."

"Yeah." Mark nodded. "This is not cool. I mean, actually doing it with you guys was cool, but the whole thing sucked otherwise."

"Yeah." Carlos agreed. "What he said."

They pulled up to the pier across from theirs and bumped to a halt at the ship's gangway. Graham was standing there waiting with three men at his side.

Also at his side was the Miami Herald reporter.

Kerry jumped out of the truck and opened the gate, as Andrew got out and ambled around to join her. Graham and his crew crossed the pier with the reporter following them, as Mark and Carlos started loosening the straps that held the crates down. "Hi." Kerry addressed Graham. "This what you need?"

Graham jumped nimbly into the back of the truck and examined the packing slip on the outside of the casing, leaning close to read it and rubbing some grease off with his thumb. After a moment, he straightened up. "It is." He seemed pleased. "Fellows, give a hand here. We may not be dead in the water after all." He looked up at Kerry with a puzzled smile. "I thought this was coming from your other friends. Did you have extras?"

"No. It's theirs," Kerry said. "I'm just your local FedEx gal."

The reporter leaned on the side of the truck. "Mind if I ask what's going on here?"

They all turned and looked at her. Kerry leaned closer. "Are you really sure you want to know?" she asked in a confidential tone. "Or have you figured out yet that the stink around here isn't from the fish in the channel?"

Elena's eyes twinkled. "Do tell?" she said. "Because all of a sudden, everyone around here who was more than willing to yap at me all day long clammed up."

Graham's men hauled the boxes off the back of the truck and started lugging them inside. He lifted a hand and waved it in Kerry's direction as he followed them, tactfully leaving her with the reporter out on the pier.

Kerry found herself in a mild dilemma. She knew it would all have to come out sooner or later, but if she told the reporter now, they all still looked like prize jackasses for falling for Quest's game. If she didn't let the reporter in on it, though, there was a chance Dar's instrumental part in exposing the hoax would be overlooked.

Hm. "Want a ride over to the other side of the port?" Kerry offered.

Elena looked at the truck, then at her. She grinned wholeheartedly and hopped up into the bed, giving Andrew a slap on the shoulder. "Stoke 'em up, Commander. I got a feeling this sucker's gonna get me either a Pulitzer or another career."

Kerry got into the back of the truck and settled herself on the wheel well, her booted feet braced against the ribbed bottom of the bed. She spread her arms to either side along the warm metal and gazed steadily at the reporter.

Elena removed a camera from the bag slung over her shoulder and focused it, taking a shot of Kerry just before the truck started to move. "So," she hastily put the device away and hung on, "what's the scoop?"

Kerry had pulled her PDA out and was reading it. "Hold that thought," she said. "It just went from one scoop to a hot fudge sundae."

She got up, balancing carefully and knocked on the window to the cab, sliding it open as Andrew slowed the truck. "The other ship, Dad. I think it's all coming down there."

"Ya'll know what?" Andrew replied. "Ah do believe this here whole damn thing's gonna owe all of us a case of damn beer 'fore it's over."

Kerry sat down and braced herself, blinking against the dust in the humid air. "Hell, Dad, if we can just finish this stupid thing, I'm buying."

The truck rambled over a speed bump and they all bounced.

"WE HAD A deal." Quest said.

"Yeah, we had a deal. You were supposed to make sure we had the best of everything." Michelle snapped at him. "So where is it?"

Quest spread his arms and turned. "You had the ship in the best condition, the best port, and the best loading crew. I did what I said I would. So now, it's time for you to give me what you owe me." He held his hand up. "I'm out of time on this farce. I want my check. Now."

"Bullshit."

"Bullshit nothing. You failed," Quest accused. "You dropped the ball, you little lesbo freak."

Dar stopped just short of entering the room, letting her hand fall against the corner wall that separated the stairs from the open area. Cruickshank stopped with her, and they both listened with remarkably similar expressions.

"What the..." the reporter whispered.

"Hm." Dar pressed against the wall, kneeling down to let the router and laptop rest on the floor before she stood up again and flexed her fingers. "That wasn't part of your script?"

Cruickshank gave her a quick, almost furtive look. "My script?'

Dar snorted softly.

"Wait a minute...we've got some issues with your 'keeping your bargain.'" Michelle argued. "In fact, after what I learned today, I don't think we owe you a damn dime." She paused. "You clueless breeder."

"What?"

"Yeah, you're the one who didn't keep up his end of the bargain." Shari pointed at Quest. "You were supposed to keep ILS in the dumpster, and screw them over. What happened to that?"

Cruickshank's jaw dropped. Dar's eyebrows lifted.

"What?" Michelle turned and stared at her partner.

"Insurance, baby." Shari smiled. "I always take out extra."

"Without telling me?" Michelle asked sharply. "This was my deal, remember? Who asked you to get involved in it?" She rounded angrily on Shari. "What the hell do you think you were doing making side deals without my knowledge?'

"Ooh." Cruickshank murmured. "Second thought, glad no camera. Fugly."

Dar found herself silently agreeing. The last thing on earth she'd ever want to get captured on film would be her and Kerry arguing. "No kidding," she muttered back.

"Give me a break. Someone has to look out for our money, because you sure as hell don't." Shari scoffed.

Dar chose that moment to emerge, circling the end of the stairwell and stalking across the scruffy gray carpet toward the group of arguing people. After a moment, she heard the reporter scurrying out after her and they both arrived at roughly the same moment that Michelle whirled and was about to let her partner have it. "Excuse me." Dar correctly interpreted the smaller woman's body language.

Michelle cut off in mid breath turned, her expression altering. "Thought you went to the ship."

Shari smirked at Dar. "Finally getting a real clue, redneck?'

"Roberts." Quest greeted her stiffly.

Dar halted and let her hands rest on her hips. She studied the three jackasses standing in front of her as she considered her options, a faint, yet unpleasant smile crossing her face.

Her options scattered as Michelle grabbed Shari by the arm and pulled her toward the small office in the back of the terminal. Shari looked like she wanted to protest, but then shrugged and went along, the two of them disappearing into the office as Michelle slammed the door closed.

That left Dar, Quest, and Cruickshank standing there in a dour circle looking at each other. "Okay," Dar finally said. "So now we know you never intended a level playing field."

Quest shrugged uncomfortably. "You said you were open to challenges."

Dar chuckled mirthlessly. "You never said you were open to being paid off. I could have afforded more than they could. You should have shopped around." She gave the reporter a sideways look. "Sure that wasn't part of your script?'

Cruickshank and Quest exchanged wary glances.

What now? Dar wondered. Everything seemed to be shifting and skewing, leaving her with only a few clear options at this point. Should she blow it all right now? Somehow doing it here, with no one else present didn't suit her sense of strategy.

"Okay." Cruickshank took over. "Well, we've got a new twist here it seems, Mr. Quest. You've been playing both ends against the middle. Interesting angle." She motioned the filming crew over, who had apparently just finished getting themselves a new camera. "Let's get some of this on screen."

Quest turned and just left. He didn't say a word; he didn't even look back at them. He just walked out of the building and let the door close behind him.

That left Dar to face the cameras, so naturally her cell phone rang. She glanced at the caller ID, then opened it. "Afternoon, Alastair."

"Hello there, Dar." Her boss sounded relaxed and cheerful. "How's it going?"

The outer door opened and Kerry slipped inside. She spotted Dar and headed over followed closely by the Herald reporter. The filming crew was approaching from the other side. She could hear shouting from inside the office Michelle and Shari had disappeared into.

It was almost sunset.

"Well." Dar sighed. "Alastair, about the only thing I can tell you right now is that we're at about one hundred percent suckage."

"Ah." Alastair cleared his throat. "That's bad, isn't it?"

"It's awful."

"Really?"

"Really."

"Ah. Well, is it going to get better?" Alastair asked. "We've got a board meeting on Monday, y'know."

"What's up?" Kerry mouthed, giving the approaching film crew a worried look. "Where is everyone?"

"Dar?"

If you have a plan Dar, stick with it. Dar heard the echo of a younger Alastair's advice way back when, at a time where the then VP of Operations had given advice to a new regional tech manager. "Yeah, Alastair. I'm here. Listen, we've got some stuff to do. I'll give you a buzz back when we're done."

"Ah. Okay, right," her boss said. "I know you'll take care of things. You always do."

Dar folded the phone and started backing up. "C'mon, Ker. Help me install a router, huh?"

Kerry gave the reporters a startled look, but followed. Elena kept right at her heels, a determined expression on her face.

"Wait, wait. Come back here." Cruickshank called after them crossly. "Don't make me chase you down. C'mon now."

"We've got something we have to do," Dar told her. "Maybe later."

Dar picked up the router and laptop from where she'd left it, and they started up the steps.

"What exactly do you have to do in this ship?" Cruickshank called after her. "Break something else?"

They kept going. "What are you doing?" Elena asked casually. "Sabotage?"

Dar held up the router. "Bringing their circuit up."

"What?"

"It's complicated." Kerry sighed. "And it's only getting worse.

Where's Shari and Michelle??"

"Fighting."

"Jesus."

"WHAT THE FUCK?" Michelle whirled as soon as the door closed, and faced her partner. "What is going on here?"

"I'm protecting my investment," Shari told her coolly. "Don't look so shocked. You'd have done it if you'd thought of it. That jackass was asking to be paid off."

Michelle went to one of the desks and stood next to it, her hands on the back of the chair and her back to the room. "No, I wouldn't have."

"Bullshit," Shari said. "You cut a deal for this place, remember? What was that, Miss White Shoes?"

"I paid for an advantage for us," Michelle said, through almost clenched teeth. "Not a wrecking ball for them. Don't you get the point, Shari? Did you ever get the point? I wanted to win. Not beat them."

"Give me a break." Shari rolled her eyes. "Take your morals and flush them. Beating them was the only way we were going to win you fool. We had to smash them into the ground, or else this whole thing was just stupid bullshit."

Michelle sat down in the chair and rested her elbows on her knees. "But we didn't."

"Well, if that fucker out there had..."

"He did." Michelle cut her off. "They bribed the loading crew. Paid off the foreman. Paid off the electricians and plumbers, and put a dozen road blocks in their way."

"Not enough."

Michelle laughed bitterly. "No." She shook her head. "Just be honest for once. They're just better than we are. Hell, they're better than anyone is. They're fucking unbelievable. You know I just watched Dar sit down and do in twenty minutes what it took that stupid guy we paid ten fucking grand to do in four goddamn days!" She stood up, her voice rising in frustration. "Jesus! Do you know what you set them up for? If this gets out—and that freaking reporter knows despite everything we tried to do—all the money we paid, all the crap you arranged for at god knows what price and, despite all that, they fucking did it all anyway? And then helped *us*? Do you know what that will look like?"

Shari shrugged, and looked away.

Michelle sat back down. "So, brain trust. What do you suggest we do now?"

Shari walked over and sat down on one of the tables against the wall. Shoved against one corner was the telecommunications gear, and there were a few computers scattered around haphazardly. "Fuck if I know," she admitted. "Only reason I said anything about the payoff was to get Quest to shut up."

"Yeah, sure."

"Go to hell."

"Already there, thanks."

There was a brief moment of silence. "You two have fun up there in the dark?" Shari asked in a sarcastic tone.

"No." Michelle seemed too tired to even be insulted.

"C'mon, you miss an opportunity to grab a little from a good looking woman? No way."

"Shut up and go to hell," Michelle said.

"Thought we were already there." Shari taunted her. "I don't know, up there in the dark, I'd have taken a shot at it." She leaned back on her hands. "What's the worst she could do? She was a good kisser way back when."

Michelle stared ahead of her. "You were right, by the way."

"What?"

"There was something in that tank at the restaurant."

Shari got up and walked over to her. "You have fucking lost your mind, you know that? What the hell made you think of that now?"

"It was them." Michelle looked up with a quiet, almost tired look. "They were diving in the tank and they deliberately tried to scare the shit out of us."

"Who — wait." Shari held her hand up. "You mean Dar?"

"Both of them. They dive." Michelle said. "Kerry told me about it." She paused, a trifle awkwardly. "So, if it means anything at this point, I'm sorry. I was wrong."

Shari seemed for once to be at a loss. "Shit," She murmured. "So I guess I wasn't a sicko fixated on Dar then, huh?"

One of Michelle's ginger eyebrows quirked. "No. You are fixated on her," she replied evenly. "But you were right, it was her in that tank, and they did screw with us."

"And caused us to break up. Nice," Shari said. "Fucking thanks, Dar. You did it again, you stinking whore bitch."

Michelle shrugged this time. "Well, that's what you were trying to do to them. I guess it's just some kind of half assed justice."

"Fuck that."

"Whatever."

"Fuck you too." Shari walked out and slammed the door behind her.

Michelle leaned back in the desk chair and put her feet up on the desk. She let her head rest back against the fabric and stared at the gray wall, wishing more than anything that she was back home and out on a sailboat somewhere.

The door opened, and one of the techs came in, stopping short when he saw her there. "Oh, sorry ma'am." He apologized. "I just need to get my kit."

"For what?" Michelle asked

The tech seemed taken aback. "Uh, well, the power just came on, and our stuff's coming up so, I mean, you want us to like, test it right?"

Michelle stared at him. "It's up?"

He nodded. "Yeah, the server guys were pretty surprised...the pipe's up. They didn't think that was gonna happen any time this century, no offense, ma'am."

"Yeah. I know. I didn't think so either, but I had..." Michelle exhaled. "Someone came over and worked on it. They got the power back on, you said?"

The tech nodded. "Talk about down to the wire. We don't got but like fifteen more minutes before the deadline."

Michelle got up and motioned to him. "Get your stuff. Let's get this project closed." She walked out the door and into the terminal, thinking so hard she walked right past the cameras bright lights, and didn't hear Shari's voice talking to them.

Chapter Eleven

"OKAY, OKAY OKAY." Elena chased them down the gangway. "Let me get this straight."

"That's your first mistake." Kerry muttered. "Nothing in this is straight."

"Especially us," Dar remarked.

"Dar."

"You are telling me that this entire thing, all these boats and all you guys, this whole thing, all of it is one huge Candid Camera stunt?" The Herald reporter sounded utterly incredulous. "Are you insane?"

"We've wondered that over the last few weeks," Kerry admitted. "But no, we're not kidding. It really is a made for television stunt."

Elena grabbed hold of Kerry's arm and hauled her to a stop. Kerry turned around, and Dar, sensing there was no motion at her back, also stopped and turned.

Seeing her partner being accosted, she marched back in the other direction.

"Easy, slugger." Elena held her free hand up to Dar. "Now you two listen to me." She added, "Do you realize the scoop you just handed over? How amazing a story that is? So I have to be sure it's true, because when I phone this one in, my editor's underwear's going to spin round three times and knit itself into a bootie."

Kerry was impressed with the colorful speech. "Sure, we know that," she answered. "After all, you looked out for us locals, stands to reason we'd return the favor, right?"

The reporter looked from Dar to Kerry. "It's really true?"

Dar nodded.

"So what's your plan then? What are you guys doing?" Elena asked. "You just fixed something on their ship, didn't you?"

"That's right. I..."

"Dar." Kerry reached past the reporter and grabbed hold of her partner's arm. "Look."

They looked over the railing to the pier. Shari was leading the filming crew out, heading for the ship with a determined expression.

Quest appeared from the left and hurried over to her, meeting the group of them at the end of the gangway. "What's going on here?"

"What's going on here?" Shari turned to Quest. "You gave us a challenge, and we beat it. Now it's time to show it off to you, and let the world see what we can really do."

"Dar!" Kerry's jaw dropped. "You just fixed it for them, and now that..."

The reporter rested her hands on the railing. "So, I guess she's not in on the TV plan?"

"She is." Dar experienced a sour taste on the back of her tongue. "But I guess she decided to take the low road. Damn."

"Stop her." Kerry urged. "C'mon, Dar. You can't let her take the credit for what you did!"

"Whoa." Elena was behind her, snapping pictures.

"Dar!"

Should she just let them do what they wanted? No, Dar supposed she really couldn't. With a disgusted sigh she edged past Kerry and the reporter and headed back down the walkway toward the ship. "I'm probably going to have to jump down off this thing too. That should make some good video."

Below, Shari marched up the gangway, the camera crew following her. Quest waited at the end of the gangway, watching them go by with a bemused expression on his face. "Guess this is the ending you were looking for," he remarked to Cruickshank as she passed.

"Well, I'll take it," the reporter said. "We'll need to go to the others after this and get some reaction shots. Don't tell anyone until we do. I want to see their faces."

Dar growled softly. "See this, you little..." She picked a spot near the end of the walkway and put her hands on the rail.

Kerry measured the distance from the second floor walkway to the ground and sped up, her hands reaching out to grab hold of Dar and prevent a possible vault over the railing to the ground. "Oh, bububhhh — w — "

Dar stopped unexpectedly. Kerry crashed into her. "Hey!"

"Shh." Dar pointed. Now, closer to the ship, they spotted Michelle in the gangway entrance, standing with her hands on her hips blocking the way.

"Can I ask what's going on here?" Michelle called out.

Shari stopped and regarded her warily. "We're going to show Mr. Quest our results."

Kerry wedged herself in behind Dar, who was leaning her elbows on the railing. She rested her chin on her partner's shoulder and watched intently. "Here's where you prove yourself fish or fowl, Michelle," she whispered.

"Mm."

"What results?" Michelle asked.

"The system." Shari looked at her like she was crazy. "I know it's done. Rafael came and told me. So let's go and show it off." She smiled, clearly expecting Michelle to join in. "Let's get Mr. Quest in there, show him what he's paying for, and then I'll buy a round for everyone!"

The cameramen cheered. "You're on." Cruickshank agreed, with a smile.

"C'mon." Shari moved forward and put her hand on Michelle's arm. "We've been working like idiots for weeks for this. Let's go enjoy it."

Michelle moved her arm out from under the touch. "Sorry," she addressed the others. "Rafael was wrong. We're not ready." She looked at Quest. "So, I guess you can come back later. Or we'll call you."

"Ah." Kerry breathed into Dar's ear. "Unexpectedly Piscean."

"Mm."

"What?" Shari barked. "Are you serious?"

Michelle's expression remained mild. "Sure am." She laid a hand on either side of the gangway railing, providing a diminutive, but effective roadblock. "After all the hard work, I'd hate to see us fall flat on our faces trying to show it off, hm? Give us a little more time." She told them. "Then we'll be ready."

Cruickshank seemed a little suspicious. "You sure you're not holding back on us? I heard some of your guys say you were good to go also."

"Yeah," Shari said. "Look, it doesn't have to be perfect. It's almost sundown. Let's get this over with Michelle." She lowered her voice and gave Michelle a meaningful look. "We both want that."

The redhead merely held her ground. "Nope. Sorry," she said. "I designed this, and I'll say when it's ready. Not Rafael, not Julio, and not George Barfing Washington. Me. I say it's not ready. Everyone got that?"

"Ooh." Kerry leaned on Dar's shoulder. "About time that side of her showed up."

"I didn't know she had a side like that." Dar mused.

Quest finally shrugged. "As you wish." He turned and started to walk away. "Just bear in mind, I have finite patience, and we have an agreement to conclude."

"Yeah." Cruickshank recouped the situation. "Let's talk about that deal, shall we?" She motioned the camera forward. The big lights came on, washing the side of the ship in bland silver, blanking out the golden sun. "You paid off Mr. Quest to help you win the bid. Is that it?'

"Yohoho." Elena chortled softly. "Arr...there be pirates around here, matey."

Shari turned. "That's right," she replied boldly. "The name of the game is winning, Ms. Cruickshank. That's what we do. We win." She added. "Now, excuse us. I need to talk to my—partner." She moved further up the gangway, forcing Michelle to step back.

"But, wait," the reporter said. "I'm not finished with you two."

"You're finished," Shari said. She walked off into the ship, taking Michelle by the arm and guiding her inside without any visible protest from the red haired woman. They disappeared into the dark inside of the hold, leaving the reporters outside.

Cruickshank put the microphone down, and the lights went off. She turned and looked at the lead cameraman. "What do you think?"

"I think she's lying," the man said, promptly. "I think she's in cahoots with those other guys."

"Who, Graver?"

The man nodded. "Yeah. Something's fishy. You said you saw that other woman bringing in some of their equipment? And we saw that other stuff being taken away in that truck."

"Hm. And we thought we were being so subtle." Kerry lamented softly.

"Well, I think you're right," Cruickshank said. "Something ain't gelling here. We've got all the ramp up film we need to make this story, and now when we're getting to the critical point, they're backing off."

"Right." The cameraman nodded. "Hey, you think maybe those other guys paid them off? They've got the dough."

Cruickshank tapped the mic against her thigh. "Maybe," she said. "Let me go talk to the boss. We've put too much of our cash into this to lose out due to some monkey business."

"Ook Ook." Dar hooted softly.

They watched the crew leave, crossing the pier and walking right under the walkway they were standing on. After they disappeared, Dar and Kerry straightened up and looked at each other.

Then they looked at the reporter.

"Okay," Elena said. "So, what's the endgame here, folks? What are you going to get out of this whole shebang? That's what I want to know. What's the goal?"

It was a very good question. "To go home," Kerry answered. "We've been wasting our time here for weeks spending god only knows how much money on this project, putting sweat and tears into it, and for what?"

"Hm," the reporter said. "Couldn't you go and get Quest, and take him to your ship, and have them show you guys as the ones that finished everything? Wouldn't that get you something? Good press? Yes?"

"We could," Dar agreed, turning to lead the way down the walk to a stairwell in the corner between their ship and this one. "Yeah, we could."

"So, why don't you?"

Dar was silent for a few steps, turning her head to watch Kerry's expression from the corner of her eye. Kerry was gazing ahead of them with gentle patience, waiting for her to answer for both of them. "What do you think, Ker? Should we just go do it?"

Kerry turned and looked at her, cocking her head a little. "No," she said. "I don't want to give those television people what they want. You said it the last time, Dar. The only way we win in this thing, is to take away their goal, not go for ours."

"So, let me understand this," Elena said. "You're deliberately forfeiting all this fun television notoriety, and wasting all those dollars, just to piss off the filming company for arranging all this?"

Dar considered that. "Something along those lines," she agreed.

"The thing is, I don't like being played. Neither does Kerry."

"No one does." Kerry interjected. "Michelle doesn't. Shari's—"

"Just an asshole." Dar completed the sentence. "So we told the rest of the teams what was up, and promised we'd help everyone finish on time. That gets their projects paid for by Quest."

"And by everyone finishing at the same time, cooperating like kids in the schoolyard, there's no drama," Elena said.

"Not even dyke drama. Yes." Kerry agreed.

"D'you feel like idiots that they got so far with it before you figured it out?"

Dar chuckled softly. "Yeah."

They walked down the stairs and headed for the terminal building. "So, why do you think Michelle Graver went along with the plan back there?" Elena asked. "Or was she telling the truth, and they're not ready?"

"They're ready," Dar said.

"You know that for sure?"

"I brought their systems up." Dar reached for the door handle and pulled the door open, standing back to allow them to enter. "So if Michelle chose to say otherwise, all I can assume is that she just decided to stand by her word."

"Ah huh." Elena entered, scribbling notes as she walked. "That surprise you?"

"Oh yeah." Both Dar and Kerry answered at the same time.

The terminal was mostly empty; just a few techs were sitting around, kicking their heels and waiting for something to happen. "Hey, Ms. Roberts." One of them, standing by the counter with a cell phone in his hand spotted them. "We're gonna do pizza. You in?"

The casual nature of the question charmed Dar to the core. "Sure." She agreed, reminded irresistibly of a much younger time in her life when she'd done what the tech did and lived on pizza and takeout Chinese. "Dominos?

The man nodded. "Yeah.

"Thin and crispy, half vegetarian half meat lovers, extra cheese." Kerry supplied succinctly. "And dots. Two cokes."

"You got it," The man grinned at her.

Dar walked over to him, tugging her wallet out of her pocket. She removed a card and tossed it on the counter. "Put it on that." She instructed. "Tell them they get a ten percent bonus if they get it here and I don't confuse the cheese with a box of rubber bands."

Elena chuckled, putting her pad down by her side as she stood next to Kerry. "You two are characters, you know that?" She said. "My boss told me this morning, after I let him in on some of what was going on, that he wants me to make this a banner story, front page in the business section, in three parts."

"Yeah?" Kerry said. "Is that good?"

The reporter chuckled. "He doesn't know the half of it. Wait till I call him," she said. "Mind if I use your office back there to do that?"

Kerry glanced at the back of the room that was echoingly empty. "No, go ahead." She agreed, watching as the reporter walked away from her. She waited a moment, then headed across the carpet to join Dar, who was sitting on the counter. "Sheesh."

"Long day." Dar agreed, with a sigh. "But it's almost over, sweetheart."

Kerry smiled at the endearment. "Know what? I've really enjoyed working on this with you. Despite everything."

Dar ruffled her hair. "Likewise."

They looked up as the front door opened, and Cruickshank entered, with an unexpected Jason Meyer strolling in with her.

"Ah." Kerry exhaled. "I've got a bad feeling about this."

"Oh yeah." Dar muttered. "Big time."

The two newcomers stopped in front of them. "We need to speak to you," Meyer said, with little trace of his former attitude in New York. "Can we have some privacy?"

Dar's eyebrow arched. "Sure." She slid off the counter and gestured toward the office. "After you."

Cruickshank also stood back. "Sir?" She addressed Meyer. "Please."

Sir? Kerry felt the situation tilt radically, and she was suddenly reminded of the test on the ship. Was this another test?

Or what?

"WHAT THE HELL was that all about?" Shari rounded angrily on Michelle. "You know damn well this thing's ready."

"It's not."

"Bullshit!" Shari said. "What kind of game are you playing now, Michelle?"

"Fuck you." Michelle enunciated the words carefully. "Like I told Cookie Puss, this is my design, and I say when it's ready. Not the techs and not you." She pulled away and started for the elevator.

"Yeah? How much did she pay you off with?" Shari yelled after. "Or did she promise you a three way?"

Michelle turned at the doorway and looked back at her. "You know what? If she asked me, I would." She turned and disappeared into the hall.

"Would what?" Shari shouted.

A door slammed, echoing in the hold.

"Doesn't make any god damned sense!" Frustrated, Shari picked up a discarded tube of cardboard and threw it across the hold, bouncing it off the wall. The heat and the dirt were getting to her, and she went to the edge of the gangway to get a breath of air.

She hated this place. The stink and the noise of the shipyard made her stomach churn, and as she looked out over the cracked pavement, even the color of the faded building made her sick.

Her attention focused on the gate that separated the pier area from the street. A tall figure had walked to it, opened the lock and entered, and she recognized him immediately as Andrew Roberts. "Asshole." She muttered, as the big man ambled across the concrete.

How had she missed that when she'd first seen him? His bastard kid looked just like him, so why hadn't she figured it out? Same body carriage, same eyes, same kiss my ass attitude. She knew Andrew had been in the Navy, and from what she'd been able to decipher from her brief time with Dar, she figured he'd been in some kind of Special Forces.

Well, he looked like it. He was wearing a tank top, and even though he was no youngster, he had an impressive muscularity that reminded her more than a bit of his daughter. As she watched, a short, furtive figure emerged from the shadows and intercepted him.

Andrew halted and looked at him, cocking his head in a listening motion.

Shari squinted a little, looking at the little creep as well. He seemed familiar to her, but she couldn't think from where. She walked out onto the gangway and headed toward them, but they saw her approaching and both turned and walked away.

She stopped. "Aw, what in the hell am I doing?" With a sigh of disgust, she turned around and started for the terminal building with its musty, if efficient, air conditioning.

Halfway there, she stopped, and turned around again. Both Andrew and the other man had disappeared beneath the gantries next to the other ship, but there weren't many places they could have gone. With a sudden narrowing of her eyes, Shari followed them.

MARK WIPED THE sweat from his eyes, surveying the work they'd just completed. "Skanky racks," he commented.

"Yeah." The tech from ship three answered. "Cheapos." He put a hand on one stanchion and shook it, demonstrating the relative flimsiness. "Sucks, but they're squeezing every penny out of this."

"Uh huh." Mark flipped the switches on the equipment and watched as the lights began to dance. The fans sounded almost deafening in the small space. "Loud suckers."

"Glad I don't have to listen to 'em." The tech agreed. "Where the hell did they come from? Johnny said they were hung up in customs coming in."

"We got them from Telegenics," Mark said.

"No shit?"

"Yeah."

"What the F?"

Mark shrugged. "They had extra. My boss kicked them in the ass and made them cough it up."

"Whoa!"

The equipment finished flashing and settled down to a more sedate blinking of its many lights. Mark began methodically plugging cables into the front of the device, following some obscure format known, probably, only to him.

The tech joined him and they inserted RJ45 jacks without speaking for a while. Halfway through, the tech cleared his throat. "So, what's it like working for them?"

"Kickass," Mark replied briefly.

"Yeah?"

"Yeah."

"How long you worked there?"

"Ten years," Mark answered. "You hear bullshit, bullshit, bullshit about ILS, but for IT jobs, it rocks. You get the best gear, the best new stuff, and cool bosses."

"Huh."

"When was the last time you brought a firmware bug to your CIO and they fixed it?"

The tech blinked at him.

"Like, they fucking fixed it. In NVRAM, in machine code." Mark clarified. "Those guys who develop routers? They call her for advice."

"Whoa."

"In fucking credible." Mark went back to plugging in cables. He looked up as the door to the small wiring closet opened, revealing Carlos. "Yeah? You done?"

"This is the last one." Carlos pointed at the machine Mark was working on. "Had some bad fiber patch upstairs, but Manny came over with the terminator and fixed it."

"Cool." Mark nodded. "You hear how it was going next door?"

"Manny said he took care of them. Whoever put that backbone in was sucking." Carlos reported. "He had to re-terminate all the strands. It took him a long time."

"Man, I'm glad we didn't go with those guys." Mark muttered. "They were pitching Kerry and telling her they could do it for half price, but what bullshit."

"But isn't the whole deal to do this as cheap as possible?" The tech standing next to him queried. "I thought that was the gig, to get the whole contract. Lowball. Right?"

Mark sighed. "Yeah," he admitted. "That was the whole point, but you know, Kerry just can't do it. We threw that around when she was looking at the vendor bids and it wasn't cool to compromise on that stuff. We lose contracts all the time cause of that."

Everyone was silent for a bit. Carlos was leaning in the doorway, scrubbing his hands and working a splinter out of the palm since there was no room in front of the switch for more than two people to plug things into it.

"So, is that cool?" The tech finally asked. "I mean, that's why Telegenics is so big now, right?"

Mark was quiet for a few moments, gazing at the switch as he thought. "For business? I think it's not really that cool," he finally said. "But for me, yeah, it's okay because I like to feel good about stuff I put my name on. I don't put my name on crap, and neither does she."

"Huhh." The tech went back to plugging.

"This whole thing is getting so crazy." Carlos picked up the conversational ball. "I really can't figure out what is going on."

Mark snorted. "Join the club."

"Yeah."

THE REPORTER WAS nowhere to be found. Kerry looked around the small office, then shrugged and closed the door behind her as she followed Dar and the two newcomers into the room. Maybe Elena had stepped outside instead of into the close, somewhat depressing space, and she could hardly have blamed her.

Dar took a seat on the top of one of the desks, trading the comfort of the desk chairs for the advantage of height as she faced Meyer and Cruickshank. She casually braced a foot on the chair though, and rested her forearm on her knee.

What role should she play? Kerry wondered, knowing she had only seconds to decide. Sometimes she and Dar swapped positions, and she took the lead, but she sensed that this would not be a good place to do that. Certainly, their two visitors were focused on her partner.

Hmm.

Kerry took a seat in the desk chair next to where Dar was sitting, and leaned back, resting her elbows on the chair arms and crossing her legs at the ankles. "So." She addressed the two. "What's this all about?"

They looked at Dar.

Dar remained silent, one brow lifted slightly.

"We don't really have the time to play around here." Kerry continued. "And I think you've wasted more than enough people's time, effort, and money already. So, if you've got something to say, go ahead." She read Dar's body posture from the corner of her eye, and exhaled, figuring she'd guessed right.

Dar lifted her arm and draped it over the back of the chair Kerry was seated in, her fingers casually brushing her partner's pale hair.

"Well." Meyer took the lead on his part. "First of all, I guess you can figure out that I'm not quite who I presented myself to be the last time we met." He leaned back against one of the desks, resting his weight on both hands. Cruickshank stood by quietly, her hands folded in front of her.

Dar considered the words. "Are you more or less of an asshole than you were pretending to be?" She asked bluntly.

Meyer chuckled. "Well, depends who you ask." He conceded. "Let me explain."

"Should I take notes?" Kerry inquired. "Because this scorecard's getting big enough to be mounted above the bleachers in Pro Player Stadium."

Meyer looked at her, but didn't respond. He licked his lips and paused a moment, then fastened his eyes back on Dar. "My name is, surprisingly, Jason Meyer. But I'm not an IT executive, though for a few months, I did play one on television." He smiled at Dar. "That's confidential, since the rest of the folks in New York didn't know they were on candid camera."

Dar just looked at him.

"It's a reality concept we're pitching called "Fooled Ya!" Cruickshank supplied quietly. "That was our pilot program," she added. "I'm not a newspaper reporter, either."

"Right." Meyer agreed. "Deal was, I'd get hired on, see how far I could take it. Fake credentials, fake background, fake previous employers. How much could I push it? Well, I pushed it to the limit, and just when I was about to take it over the top, you showed up."

Kerry leaned forward. "You risked a major corporation, and the jobs of thousands of people for a game show?"

Meyer shrugged. "They hired me," he said. "They took a risk, and so did we, and thanks to your interference, my risk didn't pan out."

"My interference?" Dar sounded incredulous. "You've got to be kidding me."

He shrugged again. "You blew my ending," he said. "But interacting with you gave me the idea for this project, and I was able to sell it to my money people. But this time, you're not going to do it again," he stated. "So let's start talking money, and drop all the other bullshit because as you pointed out, Ms. Stuart, we don't have time to play around."

He slapped his hand on the desk. "Cards on the table time, Roberts. Either we're both going to walk out of here winning, or we're both going to walk out of here losing, and trust me, baby, you're gonna lose more than I will."

Dar folded her arms. She eyed the two of them with a dourly shrewd expression. "All right. What's your deal?" She asked. "What exactly do you want?"

Meyer smiled. "That's the answer I wanted to hear. So listen up."

"OKAY, WE'RE DONE." Mark dusted his hands off. "C'mon, Carlos. Let's go. I bet they got pizza left back there."

"You got it." Carlos pushed off from the doorway and stood back as Mark left the room. "So, is this ship okay now?"

"Dunno." Mark turned back. "Is it?" He asked the tech.

The tech was connected to the new equipment via a laptop, and he merely gave Mark a thumbs up rather than be distracted from what he was doing.

"Good deal. Later." Mark was satisfied. He joined Carlos and they walked along the hallway, turning sideways as several of the crew passed in the other direction. "Y'know, I feel kinda sorry for these guys."

Carlos looked behind him. "Those guys?" He jerked a thumb at the crew. "Or the guys in the wiring room?"

"The ship guys," Mark said. "Cause if big D is right, and this is all a scam, it sucks for them, you know?"

Carlos was quiet for a few steps. "I am sorry," he said. "But after they did what they did to us with the ship I do not feel sorry for them. Ms. Kerry could have been very hurt, and one of us did get hurt."

Mark frowned. "Yeah, I know," he said. "That did really suck. If Kerry'd gotten hurt, Big D would have gone ape shit."

"She was very pissed off." Carlos agreed. "She even yelled at her papa."

"Uh huh." Mark thought about that as they walked. "Her pop's cool."

"Si."

"He's crazy about both of 'em. Did you know he was MIA for like, years? They thought he was dead."

Carlos blinked. "Really? I did not know that. How sad."

"Yeah. Big D's been through a lot of stuff in the last few years." Mark lead the way down the gangway to the pier, and headed to the fence gate. "But she's good people."

"Oh yes, I think so too." Carlos nodded. He looked around. "So is this it? Are we done now?"

Mark certainly hoped so. It was getting late, he was tired as hell, and it was Friday. He was looking forward to leaving the pier, getting a shower and a cold beer, and moving on to whatever it was they were going to do next.

Hopefully, it would have nothing the hell to do with boats. Maybe Dar would push out development of the new router thing she'd written. That would be a couple of development cycles at least, and working on Dar's stuff was always a kick.

It worked, even when it was only half baked and undocumented. He was still finding little scripts and programs of hers every time he rummaged around in the systems, nothing huge, but just scrappy bits of code that kept stuff running in the background with little fanfare.

Kind of like Dar, sometimes. "Yeah, I think we're done," Mark said. "Let's go find the boss and wrap this whole damn thing up."

"You know what I think?" Carlos said. "I think we should get together, and we should take our bosses out because they have been so nice to us. You think we could?"

Mark was briefly silent, as they crossed the roadway and entered the huge, now empty, parking lot that separated the two sides of the port. The sun was going down, and the breeze was now cooler, drying the sweat on the back of his neck as he walked.

Taking Dar out was tough. Her view was, she was the boss, and she made the big bucks. So she paid the dinner check. Mark knew it well, because he'd tried it often enough even with something as cheap as a freaking pizza.

But, who knew? Maybe they'd pull it off this time. Maybe he could grab the waiter before they sat down and give them a credit card. "Sure. We can try." He answered Carlos as they walked up the steps to the terminal behind their ship. "What the heck. Worst she could do is whack me one."

Carlos opened the door and they entered, getting several steps into the room before they both stopped and stared.

A huge crowd was gathered, surrounding a television screen on a cart. While they watched, several camera men roamed back and forth, shooting them.

"What the hell?" Mark spluttered. "What's going on?"

"Shh." One in the crowd hushed him.

Mark sidestepped around until he could see the television, blinking as he recognized Dar's distinctive figure on it.

A moment more and he recognized the room she was in as the back office not fifty feet from where he was standing, and as the picture shifted awkwardly, Kerry came into focus as well.

But what the hell was going on?

More importantly, did Dar know what was going on? It looked like she was being interviewed, but with the door closed. Did she have any idea that everyone was listening in?

The huge crowd blocked any approach to the back office door, but Mark knew that crowd wouldn't have stopped Dar, and it sure as hell wasn't going to stop him. "C'mon." He grabbed Carlos' arm.

"WHAT EXACTLY DO you want?" Kerry asked.

"Nothing much," Meyer replied. "Except a nice, suspenseful, dramatic ending that will suck ratings and pay off for my backers."

"Like what?" Kerry persisted. "Mr. Meyer, in case you hadn't noticed we're IT. Last time I checked, nerds weren't hip and trendy media darlings."

"Exactly. That's why this story turned out so interesting," Meyer said. "Because frankly, if you'd told me a bunch of geeks and a dirty shipyard would make good television before I was on this project, I'd have kicked your sorry asses' right out of my office."

"And?" Dar asked.

"And I've found there's drama in all this in very unexpected places," Meyer said. "Big drama in those old ships and the people on them, big drama in the idea of four companies going head to head to win something, and big drama in everyone fighting like cats and dogs, stabbing each other in the back at every turn. Lady, I couldn't have hired a top flight scriptwriter to make up something sassier than this has been."

"So what do you want from us?" Kerry asked, again. "If you've got such a great story here, I mean."

Meyer smiled at her. "We know what you're doing," he said.

"Do you?" Dar smiled back at him.

"Oh yes. Your friends at Telegenics were very emotive and detailed in relating your little plan to scotch my ending," Meyer said. "I know you've been helping the other ships to finish, and I know you coerced Telegenics into giving up some of their spare equipment for those other guys."

"Coerced?" Kerry gave him a puzzled look. "They offered."

"Ms. Stuart, please." Meyer gave her a condescending smile.

"And?" Dar asked again. "So you're right. We're not playing your game. We'll all finish dead even, present our bills, and go home."

Cruickshank had positioned herself carefully, standing to one side of her apparent boss and at an angle, so she could look at both Dar and Kerry. She kept her hands folded in front of her, her fingers moving restlessly as though playing with worry beads.

The motion caught Kerry's attention, and she watched the reporter from the corner of her eye. The conversation so far had seemed to her to be mostly just hot air. It was as though Meyer were merely spouting off for the record, as though...

Kerry's eyes narrowed.

"No, no you won't," Meyer said. "I've learned a number of things about you in the last few months, Roberts. At first I thought you were just a high priced jackass."

"Half right." Dar drawled. "Which half depends on who you ask."

"But you're not." Meyer strolled closer to her. "And that's the only reason I'm here, Roberts. Because I know you can deliver what I'm asking for."

Dar's eyebrows lifted.

"And I won't waste either of our time playing to your sense of fairness."

"My sense of fairness?" Dar chuckled. "I'm not the one who sweated my tail off trying to rig the contest here, Jason."

Kerry felt a slight buzz at her belt. Distracted, she glanced at her cell phone, but the vibration didn't continue. She lifted and examined it, a tickle of familiarity tugging at her memory.

"Most of the people here, they just didn't get what I was after," Meyer said. "They didn't feel what I felt, about how this story could really be a groundbreaker."

"I'm not sure why you think anyone would care." Dar finally got up, pacing around the chair and twisting to loosen a kink in her back. "I sure don't."

Meyer looped both hands around one knee. "Let me lay it on the line for you."

"Here's a first for this project." Kerry muttered, leaving her phone for the moment and concentrating on the scene before her.

Meyer ignored her. "It's really simple. There's a lot of money being put into this deal, money I'm not prepared to either risk or lose." He moved a little closer, facing off against Dar. "So here's the deal. You play ball with me, and I give you one million US dollars. In cash."

A small silence followed his words. Then Dar shifted a little. "I think you know that's not a big figure for ILS." She half shrugged. "That's the coffee budget for the year."

He smiled. "I think you know I'm not offering it to your company," Meyer replied. "And even someone who makes what you do, has desires that money could take care of, now couldn't it?"

Kerry's phone buzzed a little again, but she ignored it, her attention fixed on her partner's profile. She could hear her own heartbeat thundering in her ears as she strained to listen for Dar's answer, uneasily aware that for one of the rare times in their relationship, she really didn't know what that answer would be.

Fortunately, she didn't have long to wait.

Dar's eyes glinted gently. "You can't buy me," she said, with a quiet smile. "Even if I only had my last paycheck in the bank, I'd still tell you to kiss my ass."

Meyer didn't even look at Kerry. It was as though she wasn't even there. He nodded a few times, giving Dar a wry look. "I thought you'd say that. So, here's the real deal." He leaned forward. "The one you can't say no to."

SHARI WALKED PAST the back doors to the pier building, giving the guards with their noses plastered to the glass a puzzled frown as she passed them. What in the hell were they looking at? Free freak show, maybe? She gave her quarry a quick glance, then dismissed the windows and hurried on so as not to lose them. Probably wasn't interesting anyway. Probably just staring at Psycho Bitch's legs.

Well, to hell with them. She paused behind a stack of pallets as Andrew and the little guy stopped just short of the gangway. It appeared to her that they were arguing, or at least, the larger man was lecturing, and didn't that just figure?

Only thing you get out of a jackass is another jackass. Andrew's vicious attitude toward her left a nasty sting, and she'd decided if he was doing something shady, well, she'd just find a way to screw him over it, just like she had his pissant offspring.

"Let's play nice, huh? Let's end up even. Fuck that." Shari muttered, as she edged around the stack of pallets and skulked over to the next one, trying to stay out of sight and yet get close enough to listen. She'd agreed to hear Dar out only to see what the bitch was up to, and she'd figured Michelle was after the same thing, but after that last piece of crap...

Fucking Michelle. All she wanted was to be part of their little clique. She should have realized that since Orlando, with all that breakfast and dinner bullshit. She'd finally cut that out after they'd gotten stood up in that grunge pit.

Blew up the whole glamour, Shari had thought. But apparently she'd been wrong, since it was pretty clear that all Michelle wanted now was to suck up and probably get a job with them.

Asshole.

She watched the two men walk up onto the gangway and enter the ship, and after a moment to let them get past the rusted iron, she followed.

It was quiet now. Most of the dock workers had left, and the ships were sitting placidly in their piers with just a soft clanking sound coming from them.

Shari walked up the gangway and paused in the entrance, looking around the somewhat dark interior. She didn't see anyone, so she continued on and prowled inside the hold. Some boxes were stacked against the back wall, and she searched around them, but they were apparently towels or something equally boring.

There was no sign of the two men. She searched further, sticking her head warily into a small cul-de-sac before she reluctantly headed for the stairs. She'd gotten up two steps when she heard voices behind her, and she stopped, listening intently.

"Mister, ah am telling you that you cannot hide yerself in this here boat no more." Andrew's voice rumbled through the silence, almost making the dust motes on the stair railing dance.

"You listen. We go soon, and no more BS." Another voice answered, equally deep, but with an odd accent. "What you think you did here, to bring someone to touch my ship? I should kill you."

Andrew just laughed. It was an odd, out of place sound, and listening to it Shari could hear a clear echo of Dar.

"Little feller, ah am not going to mess with what you just said. Either you go tell the man upstairs you got you some trouble, or ah will."

"I come to you for help, because you know the sea and this is how you treat me?" The other man said, indignantly. "You are no sailor."

"Git." Andrew's voice sounded more stern. "Or ah'll pick yer ass up and tote you up there."

The voices faded, amid a few clanging, metallic sounds.

Shari popped out of the stairwell and followed the noise, ducking her head around a metal doorway and spotting two small staff elevators. One was just closing. "Damn."

Was it worth following them? Hell, whatever the dumpy guy was doing was probably something stupid like smuggling Cuban goddamn cigars. Not worth her time.

Shari drummed her fingers on the metal. No, that wasn't worth her time, but maybe she could cause some damage on her own. Wouldn't it be a kick if the bitch sisters went to demo their wonderful crap and it died?

With a smile, she went back to the stairwell and started up it.

Chapter Twelve

THE MEMORY CAME to Kerry with a startling fury. She reached over without thinking and took hold of Dar's wrist, her fingers tightening on the bones under the skin.

Dar looked at her and an eyebrow quirked.

About to speak, Meyer paused. "Something wrong?"

How to let Dar know? Kerry wished they really had the psychic connection she sometimes wondered about. There was nothing she could say that would clue her partner in, without also cluing in the other two.

Or was that a bad thing?

"You okay?" Dar half turned, her voice dropping in concern.

What, what, what, what...oh. "I just remembered something," Kerry said. "What we were talking about when you were hanging upside down in the closet."

Dar blinked, her face caught between puzzlement, and the obvious notion that Kerry had lost her mind. Then her gaze shifted slightly, moving past Kerry, before it came back and focused again. "And how this is different than that was?"

I love you. "Yes."

"Ah." Dar nodded. "Yeah." She turned back to Meyer. "You were saying?"

"I was saying this." Meyer gave her an odd look, but continued. "The bottom line is I want my company to come out ahead. You want your company to come out ahead. We all know this ship deal's a scam, right?"

"Right." Kerry murmured, trying not to look at Cruickshank.

"My brother's on the Board of Directors of the biggest cruise line on earth," Meyer said. "So what I'm prepared to put on the table is an assurance that ILS will get that nice, big, lucrative juicy contract that we all know you're lusting over, and that we all know you know is the only possible gain out of this."

"And?" Dar folded her arms over her chest.

"And, what you need to deliver to me is you taking the checkered flag. Is that so hard?"

"So, let me get this right," Kerry said. "You want to film us showing Quest our system, and 'winning' the bid."

"Exactly."

"And for that, you guarantee ILS that big contract?'

"Exactly."

"Mr. Meyer, if we 'win' this 'bid', we'll get that contract anyway." Kerry remarked simply. "In fact, even if we do nothing, we'll probably get that contract because the fact is, we're the best at what we do and everybody knows it."

Meyer stared at her. Dar bumped her gently with her shoulder, a grin tugging at the corners of her lips. "Got anything else? Because frankly, it's beer time." Kerry added. "And we're done here."

Cruickshank edged a little closer, then went still again.

"Not everyone in your company shares your confidence, I'm afraid," Meyer said. "Like your Board of Directors. They'll take a bird in the hand and leave you two in the bushes. Want to see?"

"Sure." Dar felt a jolt of unease.

"No problem." Meyer put his cell on the desk and dialed a number, the sound of the tones echoing softly in the room.

"HOLY SHIT." MARK had paused, halfway through the crowd. He'd gotten close enough to the screen to hear the last thing said, and everyone went quiet, to hear what would happen next.

He'd never get across in time. He knew it. Damned if he wanted to stand there and watch Dar get shafted though. He knew the board well enough to know if they were offered that much bucks, they'd toss Dar to the wolves.

He thought Dar knew that too, though you couldn't tell it from her face.

Man. This was gonna suck.

"What's happening?" Carlos whispered.

"Serious suckage." Mark uttered back. "Where the hell's their power cords. I'd love to yank them out of the...Jesus, is that a UPS?"

"Yeah."

"Guess they're smarter than they look." Mark realized glumly. He could start yelling and cause a scene, but he was stuck at the moment, not sure what to do. He didn't want his boss and friend to be embarrassed on tape, but on the other hand, breaking the crowd up wouldn't look great either.

"Can we do something?" Carlos asked. "I know where is the power and the lights. They are using the UPS for their cameras, but that television is coming from the wall over there."

Mark's eyes brightened. "Great. C'mon."

"The power door, it is for sure locked."

Mark smiled. "Buddy, that's the last thing you need to worry about with me around. Lead. Go. Move." He nudged Carlos, who started working his way through the back of the crowd.

"Hello?"

Mark stopped and grabbed Carlos. "Too late."

"What?"

Slowly, Mark turned toward the screen, recognizing the voice that had just echoed slightly in the room.

KERRY FELT LIKE her entire midsection was tied in square knots. She had a sick feeling that Meyer had trumped them, and now it would give him, the bastard, exactly the ending he'd been looking for.

They'd fallen for it. They'd been suckered.

Muskrats! Stupid, neutered, pissant muskrats!

"Hello?" A voice answered the cell phone. "Hello?"

"Ah, Mr. Maclean," Meyer said. "This is Jason Meyer. Remember me?"

"Absolutely! Sure do," Alastair replied. "Was just discussing what you told me with some of my colleagues, in fact. They're pretty darn excited."

Kerry looked at Dar, wondering how she could keep that stolid expression when she, more than anyone, knew what the score was here. Her partner's half smile and look of mild unconcern hadn't budged an inch. Dar was no actor; could she really think the board would back her?

Kerry knew the board. Some of them were okay. Some she even liked, and Alastair had a special place in her heart because she sensed in him a genuine caring for Dar that went past their business relationship. She suspected, in a way, that the CEO had gone out of his way to guide Dar as she was developing her skills and provided some needed support to her when things got tough.

But money was money, and business was business. Kerry eased closer so their shoulders made contact and just hoped it was over fast.

"Good to hear. Listen, I've pretty much gotten that deal sealed up here, but I've run into a roadblock, maybe you can help me with it," Meyer said. "In fact, I'm sure you can."

"Sure." Alastair agreed cheerfully. "What do you need?"

Meyer looked across at his adversary, and smiled. "Well, here's the problem. We're about done here. Your team's done a great job, and they finished first. Great job!"

Alastair chuckled.

"I told your folks here all I need is for them to let me get that on film, and the contract's yours." Meyer continued. "And they turned me down."

"Eh?"

"Seems they made a deal with the other folks here not to win." Jason continued. "So they're turning down my offer. Now you can fix that, right?"

"Well, I'm sure I can, but..."

"Now, I don't have time to waste on phone calls or meetings. It's sundown. Deal's done. Can you fix this, Mr. Mclean? I'm sure you can. Give me your word right now, and I'll consider it done."

Dar felt her throat go dry, and she was glad she wasn't speaking. Alastair would think she'd lost her mind, along with her better business judgment.

This was it. She'd crossed the line. Dar drew in a breath, and wanly wished only that Kerry wasn't there to have to witness this.

"Mr. McLean? Can I get your promise?" He gazed across at Dar with a look of quiet triumph.

Kerry put her arm around Dar's waist. To hell with the cameras.

There was a long moment's silence, then Alastair's voice came through the crackling connection with uncommon clarity. "Well, Mr. Meyer, no you can't."

Drawing in a breath to speak, Meyer halted. "What?"

Dar's lips twitched, just slightly.

"'Fraid I can't give you that promise." Alastair did sound regretful.

"Why the hell not?"

"Folks on the scene there made a decision," Alastair stated. "I respect that."

Meyer stared at the phone in utter disbelief. "Wait, you're telling me that I'm offering you a golden deal, and you're not going to take it because some idiot here who works for you, and who obviously doesn't have your company's best interests in mind, said otherwise?"

Alastair's voice dropped into a cold, startling crispness in a heartbeat. "You know something, mister? That idiot's been with me a long time. Never could get her to do anything she didn't want to do, but you know what? It's always for a damn good reason."

"Well, what about your board? I'm sure they don't feel the same way." Meyer rallied desperately, his eyes darting to Cruickshank.

"Have a great day, Jason. Sorry things didn't work out," Alastair said, just before he hung up, sending a solid click down the line.

A tenuous silence fell. Meyer looked up, finally, and met Dar's eyes.

Dar found a smile somewhere that she really wasn't feeling. She produced it anyway, just to watch Meyer grind his teeth in reaction, as she felt Kerry relax against her in relief.

The silence lengthened as nobody seemed to be sure what to do next. Then Dar caught the faint hint of light reflecting off something moving in the frame of Cruickshank's oversized sunglasses, and with a determined look, started toward her.

MARK STOOD IN the middle of the crowd, a grin on his face. The people around him were stirring and conversation buzzed louder, as the camera people stood in silence, now unsure of what to cover.

"That was..." Carlos hesitated. "Who was that, was that the big boss, yes?"

"Yeah." Mark saw a loosening in the throng, and took the opportunity to start moving toward the office door. "C'mon."

"He did a good thing." Carlos followed him.

"Buddy, you don't know." Mark edged past two tall men craning their necks to watch the television. Abruptly the picture cut off, fading to a glum black and the chatter level rose in reaction. They were halfway to the office door when it abruptly opened.

"Send me a bill for the damn camera!" A low voice carried out into the hall. "I'll pay the postage from hell, which is where you both belong!"

"Roberts!" A man's outraged voice answered. "Come back!"

"Kiss my ass!" Dar walked out, her brisk stride slowly turning to a dead stop as she spotted the crowd turning to stare at her. Both eyebrows jerked up in surprise. "What the hell's this?"

One of the camera people brushed by her and headed for the office. Another woman joined him, while the group near the television started to turn and gravitate toward Dar.

Quest appeared from somewhere and shoved through the throng, also headed toward Dar and the newly arrived Kerry.

Mark beat everyone to it. He plowed his way through the confusion and got to his boss's side, planting himself between them, and the buzzing multitudes. "Hey." He hesitated, not really sure what to say next. "Aum—"

"Hey." Dar glanced past him. "Were we the evening news?"

"Yeah," Mark admitted. "I tried to get back there to clue you, but it was like a zoo out here."

Dar glanced at the crowd. "So I see." She murmured. "We knew it was being filmed but..."

"Yeah."

"Son of a..." Kerry exhaled. "Did you hear Alastair? I'm flying to Texas and giving him a hug soon as we leave here." She raked a thatch of blonde hair from her eyes. "I can't even think of any good curse words to apply to this whole thing. Jesus!"

Quest shouldered through to them. "All right, Roberts."

"Dar!" Michelle appeared from god only knew where. Pleasantly enough, there was no sign of Shari, for which Dar was very grateful. The last thing on earth she wanted to deal with right now was her ex-lover.

Kerry seemed to sense it, because she eased closer, linking her arm through Dar's in an unconscious gesture. "Unreal!" She shook her head. "What a pair of jerkwads!"

Of course, the first thing on earth she wanted to deal with was her current one. Dar leaned against Kerry gratefully, wishing she had a bottle of Advil and a gallon of chocolate milk to go.

"Ah, Dar..." Graham appeared, and the fourth bid manager was right behind him. "That was quite spectacular."

Dar was still shaking inside. The sudden win had honestly surprised her, and she felt quite adrift at the moment, needing to ground herself in a world that had tilted half on its side again. "Thanks." She muttered. "Crock of BS ending to a crock of BS project."

"You can say that again." Graham agreed fervently.

"Roberts." Quest pushed forward. "Just what's going on here?" He looked around. "What's up with all of you being here? Given up, have you?"

Dar gathered her wits. She motioned Michelle, Graham, and Mike to join her, and then faced Quest. "We're done." She announced quietly. "We all finished your requirements."

"No." He shook his head. "No way. You can't have."

"Yes." Dar replied.

"You can't have." The man insisted. "I don't believe it."

"You're right." Graham said. "Left to our own devices, given your interference, we could not have." He rocked on his heels, his hands clasped behind his back.

"My interference?" Quest gave him a mock surprised look. "What do I have to do with it? I just want my project finished."

"But lucky for us, we had Dar here." Michelle continued the thought blithely. "And between us all, we managed. We're done."

"Are you sure?" Quest asked doubtfully. "Really finished? Really?"

"We're sure." Michelle told him with confidence. "We all worked together."

Quest looked at Michelle. "You double crossed me." He accused. "You made a deal with her!"

Michelle smiled. "Why, yes, I did." She agreed. "And you know, I enjoyed it."

"You double crossed us!" Mike pointed at Quest. "You brought us in here to compete for your bogus contract, and the only thing you really wanted was a piece of crap television show!" His voice rose. "So believe me, mister, you're not only getting my bill for the project, you're also getting a bill for my time, my people's time, my aggravation, my companies cell phone charges, and the bloody parking ticket the bastards just gave me outside this damn building!"

Even Dar was impressed by the outburst. "Hmp," she said. "Couldn't have said it better myself."

"Yeah." Michelle nodded.

"Quite,"Graham said. "Except I didn't get a parking ticket."

"You're a fraud, mister." Kerry pointed at him.

A soft hooting was heard from outside. Quest's head jerked up, and a not so nice smile pulled at his lips. "Well, it seems that the truth is...I'm not the fraud here." Quest said. "And you've all just made a pretty big mistake."

"You can say that again." Michelle commented. "Many of them. Meeting you was the first."

Surprisingly, Quest laughed. He slowly started to back toward the rear entrance to the terminal. "You all think you're so smart. You don't know jack." He gestured at Michelle. "And you're the biggest fool, but all of you are idiots."

"We're not the idiot, buddy!" Mike accused.

"She!" Quest pointed at Kerry. "She said it right in front of you! None of you even got it!

"Huh?" Kerry looked at Dar. "What did I say?"

Dar was as bewildered as everyone else. "No idea." She murmured. "Said when?" She asked in a louder tone.

"At the meeting!" Quest crowed. "I thought we were sunk right then, but none of you caught on. Not even you." He looked at Kerry. "You were dead right. I wanted these ships done, and I wanted them done for free. And you all did it!"

"The meeting?" Kerry said. "At the office!"

"What do you mean, we? What are you talking about, Quest! You were in it with the television people! It was never about the ships!" Michelle shouted in frustration. "You told me that!"

He reached the back door, just as ship horns sounded outside again. "I lied!" He laughed. "And you all just lost, big time!" He pointed at them. "Fools!"

"No we didn't," Dar said. "You're getting a bill, buddy. Trust me." She started toward the back door, Kerry at her heels.

"Four of 'em." Michelle confirmed. "And maybe a lawsuit for your little scam."

Quest smiled again. "It wasn't a scam," he told them. "The contract was real." He glanced behind him, then turned back, obviously enjoying the moment. "I got exactly what I wanted."

"Those ships aren't taking on passengers ever again," Dar said. "Don't tell me any different. I saw those engines."

"Not as ships, no." Quest agreed. "But they're not going to be cruise ships. They're going to be hotels." He opened the door. "In Europe. Hasta la vista, my little friends. Next stop for me is Barcelona, and you can chase my ass with paper all the way if you want."

He ducked out the door and shoved it closed, then bolted across the pier toward the ship.

"Where the...hey!" Dar ran across the carpeted floor, followed by the others. "Quest!!!"

They reached the back door in time to see Quest jumping aboard the ship, crossing a narrow plank that had taken the place of the metal gangway. The ropes tying the ship to the dock were already off, and they could hear the engines whining as they got up to speed.

"You thought you were screwing me!" The man yelled back. "You gave me exactly what I wanted! Thank you! Thank you! Assholes!" He shot them a bird, and then vanished into the darkness of the hold.

"Quest!" Michelle yelled at the top of her lungs. "Get back here!"

A crewman tossed the plank clear, and stood back from the shell door as the ship moved away, pushing off from the pier with a groaning creak of its old steel bones. He lifted a hand and waved lazily at her, then disappeared as the door ground shut, sealing with a metallic clang audible from where they were standing.

In shock, they watched the ships move off, unable to do anything but stare.

Saucily, the ship let off its horn again, in a 'shave and a haircut' pattern, as it jaunted slowly down the cut and out toward the open sea. The water chopped gently against the hulls, and a breeze had risen, puffing out a tattered American flag which had been run up the mast on the ship Dar and Kerry had worked on.

"Son. Of. A. Bitch." Michelle clipped the words off tightly.

Dar put her hands on her hips, truly at a loss. She turned her head and looked at Kerry, who was looking back at her with a completely stunned expression. "He got us," she said, simply.

"He got us." Kerry repeated. "Jesus P. Fish."

"That too." Dar covered her eyes, shaking her head in disbelief.

"Floating hotels?" Kerry said. "That's why the public spaces got fixed..."

"And not the engines." Dar looked over as the other door slammed open and Meyer appeared with Cruickshank at his heels. They gave her a dark look, but the chaos distracted them and they focused on the rest of the crowd instead.

"What happened?" Meyer asked brusquely. "What's going on?"

"What'd we miss?" Cruickshank added. "Where are they going? Is this another gag? What's the deal?"

They looked at each other. Kerry cleared her throat. "You missed your perfect ending." She advised them.

"What?" Meyer yelped. "What ending? What? Where?" He spun and looked around. "What in the hell's going on? You mean he tricked us? That bastard!"

"Irony, thy name is Travel Channel." Kerry uttered under her breath, finding the humor in the situation somewhere. A motion caught her attention, and she spotted Andrew walking across the pier toward them, his hands in his jeans pockets and a bemused expression on his scarred face.

Did he know? Kerry wondered. She hoped not. Misery did like company after all, didn't it?

Michelle exhaled heavily. "I'll be a monkey's uncle," she finally said. "Never thought I'd find a situation that warranted that old hoary saying, but damn it if this one doesn't."

Dar stared at the retreating ships, still mostly in shock. "Ook, ook." She agreed wryly. "Ook, ook, ook."

KERRY WALKED OUTSIDE the terminal and waited on the edge of the steps for Dar to come out after her. Twilight was on them, and the glaring light of the day had faded to a placid purple, returning the temperature to one of almost comfort.

Almost.

The other bid managers had come out ahead of her, and gone to their cars. They were heading over to Snappers in Bayside to sit down and talk it all out, but she was glad she had a few minutes here to try to clear her mind and consider what they'd gone through already today.

Ludicrous insanity was what it was. Kerry rubbed the back of her head, which was pounding with an annoying ache, and wished she'd remembered to stick some Advil in the glove compartment. Maybe Dar had some. "Oh. There you are."

"Here I am." Dar agreed, putting a hand on her back. "C'mon, let's go. I need a good stiff drink."

"I think we all do." Kerry started down the steps with her. "You don't have any aspirin, do you?"

"In the car, yeah," Dar said. "Dad's going to meet us at the front there and tag along." She added. "I think I owe him a beer, among other things." She nibbled the inside of her lip, lapsing into a pensive silence as they walked across the tarmac to the car.

Kerry was glad to slide into the leather seat of the Lexus and lean back, the residual warmth of the sun soaking through her shoulder blades and offering relief. "Ugh."

"You okay?" Dar asked, as she turned the key and started the engine.

"Tired." Kerry admitted. "Whacked out."

"Me too," Dar said. "Wish we could just go home."

Kerry laid her hand on Dar's thigh, rubbing her thumb on the rough surface lightly. "Me, too." She echoed. "Thank the Lord it's Friday."

"After what we just went through, it would have been Friday no matter what day we ended on." Dar pulled out of the parking spot and headed for the pier building, where Andrew was standing and waiting. "I'm so looking forward to a few days off." She glanced at Kerry. "You have anything in mind for tomorrow?"

"You and me in the waterbed all day, naked," Kerry said, as they pulled up and Andrew opened the back door. "That okay with you?"

Dar managed a rakish grin. "Dare you to say that again." She drawled, as Andy closed the door and settled into the back seat.

Pale lashes fluttered tiredly at her. "Dare me?"

Dar cleared her throat. "Hi, Dad."

"Lo, Dardar." Andy replied amiably. "Hell of an end to this here thing."

Dar snorted. "Did you know they were going to do that? Pull out?"

"Wall." Andy shifted, stretching across the back seat and leaning back on the door. "I knew they were fixing to leave, can't miss it when them diesels fire up. But you said they'd be leaving round sundown anyhow, so I figured that was it."

"They skunked us." Kerry half turned and peered at him over the headrest. "Even the TV people. "

"Yeap." The ex-seal gave her a wry look. "Ah did not see that one coming." He admitted. "I figgered it was what you said it was, with them television people. Got to give them sailors' credit, they kept their pie holes closed up."

"Maybe they didn't know." Kerry suggested. "Not the big guys, I mean, but the worker bees. The ones I talked to seemed to be pretty darn puzzled as to what the heck was going on."

"Yeap, that could be." Andy agreed. "Navy was like that. Don't know, don't ask, don't tell, don't get yer ass in the way."

Dar chuckled. "You always knew what was going on." She disagreed.

"Wall, I had me a monkey with their eyeballs inside them machines, now didn't I?" Andy reached over and ruffled Dar's hair. "But I sure fire know something about this here situation that you all do not."

"What's that, Dad?" Kerry glanced curiously at him. "About the ship, you mean?"

Dar concentrated on merging onto the bridge that would take them over to Bayside. She was tired, and she knew her reflexes were suffering because of that, but the traffic was thankfully light and she eased into the left hand lane with little trouble.

"About that ship. "Andrew sounded surprisingly smug. "It done sailed with the number of folks it spected to, but there's one that ain't there they're gonna miss, and one that's there they sure fire ain't."

"Huh?"

Dar glanced in the rearview. "What are you talking about, Dad?"

"Ah turned over that little engine feller to the police," Andy said. "He told me 'bout that thing he did to a lady he did meet. You were right, kumquat."

Kerry's eyes lit up. "Yeah?" She exhaled. "Wow...boy, I feel a lot better now. I thought he got away with the whole thing. Why'd he come back?"

"Ship guy." Andy shrugged. "Anyhoo, them folks ain't gonna appreciate taking on that big old bag of wind woman you all did not care for in his spot, I will tell you that."

Dar very nearly braked to a halt in the middle of the causeway. "What?"

Kerry got up on her knees and gripped the seat back, goggling at her father in law. "Shari went on that ship?" She squeaked. "You have got to be kidding me!"

Andy grinned, his blue eyes twinkling back at her. "Ah do not think she planned that, 'zactly." He allowed. "She was fixing to make some more trouble for you all, and ah did not see the value in troubling her to tell her that there ship was leaving."

Dar clapped a hand to her head. "Oh my god." She laughed

helplessly, steering into the turn lane for Bayside almost at the last minute. "Dad, they're going straight across the ocean."

"Ah do realize that, Dardar." Her father agreed equably. "Woman always seemed to be like she needed a rest of some kind. All that hollering and fussing and all."

"Heh." Kerry turned and sat down, a big grin on her face. "Who cares about Quest? That just made *my* day." She chortled. "Hope she ends up with crackers and water swabbing the decks for her passage." She wriggled in her seat, doing a little dance to some unheard tune.

Dar just kept laughing, shaking her head as she pulled into a parking spot near the stairs. "Know what I want to know?" She asked as they got out. "Which one of us gets to tell Michelle?"

Kerry snickered in a very uninhibited way. She walked around to the back of the Lexus and made a squeezing gesture, nodding when Dar popped the hatch for her. She reached inside and pulled Dar's briefcase over, tugging open the front flap and digging inside for the bottle of Advil Dar usually kept there.

Her mind was on Andy's news, though. She imagined Shari finding herself stuck on board and raising hell. She imagined the captain ignoring her — no, worse. She imagined the captain just locking her out of the control room and letting the rest of the crew laugh at her.

It was a very satisfying image. She wondered if Shari would whine all the way to Barcelona. "Hey, Dar?"

"Hm?" Dar leaned against the back hatch next to her. "Can't find it?"

"No, I've got it." Kerry fished out the bottle and opened it, shaking out a few pills and pocketing them before she tossed the bottle back in. She closed the hatch and they all started walking toward the mall. "So, what happens now?"

"Now we have dinner." Dar replied promptly. "Fish okay by you, Dad?"

"Long as they're cooked, Dardar."

"Not exactly what I meant." Kerry demurred. "But I guess that'll do for now."

Dar ambled down the half flight of steps and they crossed into the plaza, moving single file through the press of Friday evening shoppers. She knew she hadn't answered the question Kerry had posed, but she also knew she didn't really have an intelligent answer, so she was glad her partner had accepted the deferral.

What now? Who knew? It wasn't like there was a section in any business plan she'd ever done that covered the situation they'd just suffered through. They'd figure out something, she supposed — just like she supposed she'd be a while explaining to Alastair next week exactly what had happened.

Along with everything else she had to explain. Dar set the somber thought aside, and draped an arm over Kerry's shoulder as they entered the outdoor restaurant and spotted the others.

Being on the waterside and with a light breeze, it was reasonably bearable. They took a seat at the large table along with the rest, and for a long moment everyone just stared at each other.

A waiter appeared, and gazed inquiringly at the newcomers. "Whatever imported draft you've got." Kerry made a circling motion with her hand including all of them. "And I'd like a glass of water, too, please."

"Sure." The man disappeared.

"Thanks, Ker." Dar extended her legs under the table and folded her hands over her stomach.

"Figured you'd save the milk for dessert." Kerry replied, and then turned her attention to the rest of the table. "So. Here we are."

"Here we are." Graham agreed, and then glanced around. "Well most of us." He added. "Where's your boorish partner?" He asked Michelle.

Michelle shrugged. "I have no idea." She replied briefly. "Haven't seen her since before the Ringling Brothers Barnum and Bailey circus started over at their corral." She jerked her head toward Dar and Kerry.

"Well, no loss." Mike said, bluntly.

Andrew cleared his throat.

"Sorry, but it's true." Mike misinterpreted the sound. "I know it's not a gentlemanly thing to say, but if that witch drowned in the channel I'd clap. What an asshole."

Michelle pursed her lips, and her nails tapped each other as she steepled her hands before her chin. "Well, we're all assholes at one time or another." She said, diplomatically. "And we all have different ways of doing things."

Curiously, Kerry felt herself smiling when she heard Michelle say that, and she was pleasantly surprised when the red-haired woman refused to bow to the majority and join in with the bashing. That took character, which she hadn't frankly figured Michelle to have.

And it was true, really. They could all be assholes when they wanted to be, herself included. She debated telling Michelle where Shari was, then figured it could wait for later. Michelle didn't seem too concerned, anyway.

Very different from what she'd be acting in a similar circumstance, that's for sure. "Well, we figure they have to dock somewhere." Kerry steered the conversation to something more productive. "Maybe our international office can track them down."

"Is it worth it?" Graham asked. "I know it's a lot of money in gear, but I have to be honest, Kerry—I don't know if it's worth the recovery costs. I may just have to write this one off as a deal gone bad. Not going to make my people happy, but what to do?"

"You mean, just let them get away with it?" Kerry queried a mildly astonished look on her face.

Graham shrugged.

"Not all of us can afford that," Michelle said.

"Can any of us really afford it?" Mike asked, suddenly. "I don't mean financially either."

Everyone pondered that, and then as if in some accord, they all turned and looked over at Dar, who had been amusing herself by folding her linen napkin into the shape of a rabbit.

Sensing the lack of conversation, Dar looked up, her hands pausing in mid-motion. "What?" She asked, with a frown.

"What's your plan, ace?" Mike asked. "How are you going to pull the rabbit out of your ear this time?"

Dar looked down at her napkin rabbit, then merely shrugged. "Maybe I'm not." She pulled one end of the fabric and the bunny disappeared, becoming a mundane flat panel again. "Maybe we just lose this one." She looked up as the waiter approached, and accepted an icy mug of beer from him.

After taking a sip, she gave the silent crowd another shrug, and didn't say anything more.

AH. COOL AIR, no sweat, freshly showered, clean clothes.

Being home was like a small side trip to Heaven. Dar extended her arms across the surface of the waterbed and just absorbed the blessed silence, broken only by the snuffling of a Labrador nose and Kerry's soft humming from the kitchen.

"Hey, sweetie?" Kerry called in.

"Ungh?" Dar could manage only a grunt in response.

"Hot chocolate or ice cream?" Kerry's voice answered, from much closer.

"Yes." Dar replied, keeping her eyes closed.

With a soft chuckle, Kerry came over and sat down next to her, making the bed wiggle. She ran her fingers through Dar's hair, riffling the dark locks and smoothing them back from her partner's forehead. There was a crease there, and she rubbed her thumb against it, the motion getting a flickering of long, dark lashes as two pale blue eyes peeked out and studied her. "Tired?"

"Very." Dar admitted. "You?"

"Urrrgh." Kerry managed a grin. "I'm just so glad to be home."

Home. Dar grinned back. "I'm glad to be alone with you."

"Growfy."

"And you too, Cheebles." Kerry laughed. "Ahghr." She rolled over and put her head down on Dar's stomach, gazing up at the ceiling through half closed eyes. "I've got hot chocolate brewing, and the ice cream is in the fridge getting spoonable."

Dar sniffed. "So I smell." She laid her arm over Kerry's middle. "I think I would have rather had dinner with the crew."

Kerry covered Dar's hand with her own, and interlaced their fingers. "I think I would have rather had dinner with just you," she said. "I'm so wiped, Dar. I feel like my brain is in a spin cycle somewhere."

Dar's expression softened and she turned her head to study the woman resting next to her. "How's your head?"

"Still hurts." Kerry admitted. "Or maybe it hurts again. I think it was okay for a little while there."

"I think I should be getting you the hot chocolate instead of the other way around." Dar was glad of something to distract her thoughts from the bid, even if the something was her beloved partner's discomfort. "Want a neck rub?"

Kerry didn't even dissemble. She rolled over and exhaled blissfully as Dar's powerful hands began their work at the points of her shoulders and started toward her neck. She could feel the warmth of Dar's skin under her thin t-shirt, and hear the steady beat of her heart, and all of a sudden she felt like crying.

"Ker?"

"Ungh?"

"You okay?"

Kerry swallowed. "Just tired." She mumbled. "It's been a frustrating couple of weeks."

Dar understood exactly what she meant. Instead of continuing the neck rub, she hauled Kerry gently up and enfolded her in a hug. "Damn frustrating. But I'm very selfishly glad you were there with me for it."

Now, Kerry did start crying for a completely different reason. Or maybe it was the same reason, it was hard to tell. It was a relief, and it lightened her spirits, as she returned Dar's hug and they both started laughing, there in the middle of the bed.

Finally Kerry sniffled. "I'm glad too," she said.

Dar exhaled, the outside edge of her thumb idly tracing Kerry's ear. "I think I'm going to give us a week off too. How's that sound?"

"Can we do that?" Kerry asked, after a moment.

"I don't care. I'm going to." Dar replied. "I need a time out."

Kerry tilted her head a little so she could see Dar's profile. The low light in the bedroom didn't reveal much, but she realized that Dar probably looked as tired as she felt. If it had been stressful for her, what had it meant for Dar, who had to deal with all the emotional stress along with it?

"Sounds cool." Kerry gave her a gentle squeeze. "I'm there. In fact, how about we go down to the cabin?"

"Mm." Dar grunted approvingly.

They were both silent for a little while, communicating through gentle touches and hugs. Sometimes, Kerry found, that worked best with Dar. She felt the tension in her partner relaxing as she clasped her hand and placed a few light kisses on the back of it.

Love really was useful for a lot of things that you couldn't duplicate with drugs or other chemical assistance, she decided. It was free, and it was healthy, and you probably wouldn't end up on the cover of the Enquirer because of it.

Kerry considered that thought briefly, then gave it a wry grin. Well, maybe you could, but only if you were famous.

"I will have to call Alastair on Monday," Dar remarked.

"I'm going to send him a basket on Monday," Kerry said. "What's that brand of Scotch he likes, again?" She asked. "Because you know, it would have been real easy for him to have promised Meyer the world. He wouldn't have even had to dis you doing it. He could have just said he'd take care of it. But he didn't."

"He didn't." Dar agreed. "He trusted me."

"Yup."

Dar sighed. "And I didn't deserve it this time."

Kerry rolled her eyes. "Oh, bullshit, Dar."

A shrug. "Hon, I didn't," Dar said. "He trusts me because he's had good reason to before. This time he didn't, and I know it and you know it. I blew off the company, I was blowing off my job, and the only reason we were ahead at that moment was pure stupid luck."

Kerry squirmed up so that her head was even with Dar's, but she kept her limbs draped over her partner's body. "Do you really believe that's true?"

"Umhm." Dar nodded. "You should too, because it could have been a massive mess you'd have had to clean up after."

"Think I'd have cared?"

Dar turned her head and regarded Kerry. One eyebrow lifted. "You damn well should care."

"I don't."

Kerry's cheerful disregard surprised Dar a lot, especially since she remembered their discussion on the Disney bus not that long ago, when Kerry had worried about not abandoning her responsibilities in trade for a day of fun.

What changed? "Seems to me," Dar commented, deciding to find out. "I remember being chastised about playing in a water park instead of working."

Kerry's expressive face crinkled into a wry expression. "Busted," she admitted. "But that was a long time ago."

"Two weeks!"

"This project lasted half a lifetime. A lot can change in half a lifetime." Kerry protested. "I got a whole different perspective, Dar. I got over it. I got over myself, maybe." She finished, in a softer tone. "So many people were asking me what the hell I was doing running around on the pier hauling cable—maybe I got around to asking myself that."

"Hm." Dar made a small, thoughtful sound.

"I think we both need a time out, so we can figure out what our roles really are again." Kerry concluded quietly. "Maybe we rewrite them so they make more sense."

"Hm." Dar repeated her thoughtful sound, this time ending it on a slightly higher note that meant approval.

"They didn't make much sense the past few weeks."

"Nu-uh." Dar agreed. "You're right." She reached over to gently push aside the pale hair obscuring one eye. The skin around it creased as Kerry smiled, and Dar continued on to trace her lips with the tip of one finger. "They didn't make much sense."

"But we make sense." Kerry murmured, catching Dar's fingers between her teeth, and then releasing them. "So we'll work it out, won't we?"

Dar leaned over and kissed her.

Kerry took that as a yes, and returned the gesture, taking a leisurely amount of time about it. She took a breath, and felt her body press against Dar's as her partner did the same. Her headache began to fade as they lay there intertwined in each other's arms and she nestled her head down on Dar's shoulder, and just soaked it all in.

Dar stroked her face, and it was like drinking something warm on a cold day, a feeling of inner warmth that started inside, and spread through her, erasing the lingering shreds of the day still clinging to her. "Mm."

"Mm." Dar echoed the sound.

"Days can be as tough as they want as long as they end like this." Kerry leaned over and pressed her lips against Dar's cheek. "That's the only thing we had that no one else did y'know?"

Dar smiled, and nodded. "Uh huh."

"That and your sublime articulate-ness." Kerry kidded her. "I don't know what I'd do without that."

Dar pouted, batting her dark lashes and giving Kerry a mock wounded expression.

"Much less what I'd do without you." Gentle green eyes gazed over at her as a smile crossed Kerry's face. She smoothed her thumb over the pout, as it dissolved into a sweet, returning smile. "God, I love you so much."

Dar let her forehead rest against her partner's as she pondered the ironies of her life. Then she tilted her head slightly and indulged herself in a long kiss, rolling a little onto her back and taking Kerry with her until they ended up nose to nose with Kerry on top.

Waterbeds really had it all over regular beds for that sort of thing. Kerry was sprawled over her and it was merely cozy, instead of being anywhere close to suffocating. "Love you too," Dar said, lifting her head up and nipping Kerry's nose with her lips.

"Mm." Now it was Kerry's turn to resort to non-verbalization.

Dar cleared her throat gently. "Know what I just realized, though?"

"What?" Kerry answered.

"We lost track of that Herald reporter."

Kerry nibbled her lower lip, her brow contracting a little. "Yeah? Oh. Yeah. I know." She slipped one hand under Dar's shirt. "I looked for her when we went into the office, but she wasn't around. You figure she left? I didn't see her afterward, either."

Dar nuzzled Kerry's nearby ear, nibbling on the lobe of it before she answered. "Maybe we'll have to find out by reading Business Monday." She whispered into Kerry's ear.

"If she left before the ships did, we better call her and make sure she doesn't look like a nitwit." Kerry whispered back.

"We'd probably come off looking pretty good if we didn't."

"Until she had to retract the story." Kerry gave her partner a little smack on the hip. "Bad Dar. "

A low, throaty chuckle made her ear vibrate.

"C'mon. Let's go get our goodies," Kerry said. "We can't worry about Herald reporters right now." She gave Dar a quick kiss, and rolled out of the waterbed, hauling Dar with her. "There's ice cream to be had, and mucho BS to be forgotten."

Dar willingly followed, more than ready to throw the recent past right out the sliding glass doors and not look back.

Chapter Thirteen

THE WORLD INTRUDED itself into her dreams—pleasant and formless things of warmth and seashore that she allowed to slip free and be replaced with the comforting feel of Dar's body.

Ah. It was nice to wake up with someone, that's for sure. Kerry slowly let her eyes drift open, taking in the sunlight as her gaze fell to the bedside clock. Muffling a curse she started to bolt upright, only to be held in place by Dar's arm. "Augh!" She squawked.

"Saturday." Dar's voice enunciated clearly, from about an inch away from her ear.

"Buh." Kerry slumped back down into the bed, closing her eyes and willing her heartbeat to stop trying to give her a nosebleed. "Son of a bitch."

Dar settled back down behind her, one arm still clamped firmly around Kerry's middle. "Had a feeling you were going to jump."

"Urgh." Kerry moaned. "My head's spinning," she said. "I hate waking up like that."

Dar kissed the back of her neck.

"Now, waking up like this, on the other hand..." Kerry purred. "Is another story."

"Are we waking up?" Dar queried. "It's not that late."

Kerry eyed the placidly gleaming clock, which was edging past 10:00 a.m. For them, it was late, and Dar knew that, since they generally got up around 6:00 a.m. Even on weekends it was rare when they stayed in bed past eight in the morning. "Where's Chino?"

"Already let her out."

"Ah." Kerry pondered that. "How long have you been up?"

"A little while," Dar admitted. "I was just enjoying laying here being a bum."

Kerry rolled over onto her back, gaining an appealing view of her partner's profile. Shaggy, dark locks spilled everywhere out of control, prompting Kerry to rake them into a little better order with one hand. "You need a haircut."

"How about a Mohawk?" Dar suggested amiably. "That'd spark up the Monday morning meeting, huh?"

Kerry studied her, then lifted a few thick thatches of hair up over Dar's head and reviewed the results. She released the hair, then ruffled it. "No."

"No, huh?"

"No." Kerry shook her head positively. "Do you know how much paperwork that'd cost us with me having to fill out personnel incidents every ten minutes because I bitch slapped someone for commenting on your hair?"

"Hm."

"Mariana would flip out."

"Oh well." Dar conceded. "I guess it's just a trim again, then. Everything else I've ever tried with this mop has pretty much ended up looking like I stuck my thumb in a socket."

"It's so wavy." Kerry agreed, fluffing out Dar's bangs. "I like it."

Dar smiled. "Glad you do," she said. "Like the color?"

"Sure."

"Don't want me to change it?"

Kerry's brows hiked sharply. "To what?" She asked. "Green?"

"Hm."

"No, it's pretty. I like it this color." Kerry added seriously. "It makes your eyes stand out."

"They're like weird little blue marbles. They'd stick out anyway." Dar drawled.

"You're so funny." Kerry chuckled.

Dar grinned at her.

Kerry grinned back. "I guess we're up now, huh?" She mused. "I haven't slept this late in forever." She stifled a yawn, and stretched her body out, exhaling with a slight chuckle as Dar traced a teasing line up the center of her stomach. "Ooo."

"I was never a late sleeper." Dar admitted.

"I never was supposed to be." Kerry wiggled a little closer. "Even on weekends, you weren't allowed to sloth about in my father's house, that's for sure." She picked up Dar's hand and examined it, running her fingers along the palm. "So when I moved down here, boy, did I love weekends."

"But you don't sleep late on weekends." Dar objected. "Don't you want to?"

A faint smile crossed Kerry's face. "Well, I thought about that the other week," she said. "I guess the thing is, I love my life so much now, sleeping seems like a waste of time." She looked up at Dar. "It's much more fun to be awake."

Dar's face lit up, visible even with the sunlight pouring through the blinds. She held her hand out to Kerry. "So let's go live, then. I think someone's FedExing coffee."

They scrambled out of bed, and were joined by a frisky Chino as they walked into the living room and were dappled with yet more sunlight pouring in the sliding glass doors. "Oo, pretty day." Kerry ducked into the laundry room and snagged two long t-shirts, tossing one to Dar as she pulled the other over her head.

Dar opened the back door for Chino, then wandered over and started messing with the coffee machine. "Know what I want?"

Kerry closed her eyes and put one finger against her forehead. "Uhmm...scrambled eggs on cinnamon toast?" She opened the refrigerator and started removing objects from it. "Am I close?"

"Heh." Her partner snorted. "That, and you, but what I was going to say is that I want one of those spiffy automatic coffee makers we saw at the trade show. The one with the little cartridges?" Dar held her thumb and finger up about two inches apart.

"The one cup thing with all the choices?" Kerry asked. "Ooo, yeah, that had good coffee. Can we get it plumbed in here? What about one for the cabin? Do they come in colors?"

Dar started chuckling, as she pressed the button to start the coffee brewing. "I'll check."

"I think a blue one for here, and a green one for the cabin would be cool." Kerry set out a handful of eggs, and retrieved her favorite grill pan from the hanging rack just over the stove. "Grab me some OJ?"

"Sure." Dar opened the door and got out the juice, setting it on the counter and retrieving two glasses from the cupboard. Her shoulder bumped the LCD screen mounted to the cabinet, and she glanced up at it as it turned on and blinked at her.

Nothing was on the screen, so she nudged it aside and poured the juice, handing Kerry hers and leaning against the counter to consume her own.

Orange juice was all right she decided as she watched Kerry neatly crack the eggs. Apple juice was better, and she really preferred white grape juice, but both were too sweet for Kerry's tastes in the morning, so she accepted the orange beverage as well.

Life was full of compromises. Kerry got up early on weekends to make her breakfast, she had orange juice, they both took a step toward the middle and each other and, maybe in the process, discovered what had been hard and fast rules really weren't.

Maybe that was why she was now willing to let this one go. Dar pondered the thought. Let this bid go, and just recoup what she could instead of going after Quest and moving heaven and earth to get him — to stop him — to make him pay — for playing her for a fool.

"Honey?" Kerry glanced over. "Stop making bubbles in your juice. It sounds weird."

"Sorry." Dar finished the beverage and set the glass down. "Why don't I...whoops." A blinking light on the screen had caught her attention. "Huh, he hasn't done that in a while." She reached over and clicked the light, since they'd turned off the voice commands to keep the system from responding whenever they talked to each other. "Alastair."

"Oh?"

The picture box opened revealing Alastair's face. He was in his home office, she was surprised to note, and then she realized it was Saturday in Houston as well as in Miami. "Morning, Alastair."

"Morning Dar!"

"Hi, Alastair." Kerry called out, keeping her attention on her frying pan. "I owe you a bottle of something very expensive."

"Ah." Alastair peered around, not able to see Kerry who was out of camera shot. "Well, thanks, Kerry. Did I do something to deserve it?"

"Yes." Kerry responded, but didn't go further.

Dar realized Alastair didn't, in fact, know that they knew what he'd said the day before. "You probably don't know it, but your conversation with Mr. Meyer yesterday was being broadcast to an audience of hundreds." She told him. "Including Kerry and myself."

Alastair blinked, then turned a bit red. "Ah. Well." He cleared his throat. "Y'know, I thought about that after, and Dar, I hope you didn't think I meant you were an idiot when I..."

Dar chuckled and waved a hand. "Thanks for standing by us, Alastair." She overrode him. "Made my day."

"Ahah. Yes, well." He seemed abashed. "Well, the fellow was a stinker, you know, Dar? Made my hackles go from the start, and he got me at a bad time."

"Meeting?" Dar hazarded.

"Eh? No."Alastair said. "Caught my thumb in the car door."

"Ow. Sorry."

Alastair went silent for a moment, apparently absorbing the last bit of news. "Thought you might call me last night to give the scoop," he said, casually.

Now it was Dar's turn to feel abashed. "Yeah, sorry." She muttered. "We got home late."

"Yes? So what happened?" Alastair asked. "Been on my mind all night."

Oh. Ugh. Dar took a seat on one of the stools and hooked her feet on the rungs. "Well, nothing good, to be honest," she admitted. "After you blew off Meyer, I found out he'd staged the whole damn thing and everyone and their grandfather was watching it outside the office we were in."

"Tch."

"So then Quest showed up."

"He's quite an interesting fellow." Alastair remarked. "Did you know his father was a ringmaster in the circus?"

Kerry snorted softly. "Well, now doesn't that explain a few things."
"Eh?"

"How did you know that, Alastair?" Dar asked. "You know this guy?"

"Believe it or not, the wife does." He admitted. "Fifth cousin's third uncle's stepson or something like that. Called me up once and asked me to give him a job—had no skills, no prospects. I had to turn him down, unfortunately." He added. "Realized it was the same chap just the other day."

Kerry turned her head and looked at Dar.

"Interesting," Dar said. "Well, he showed up, we told him we were all finished, and the bastard took off and ran."

"Eh?'

Dar clasped her hands between her knees and looked at her boss. "He took his ships, and left. Apparently he was the one scamming all of us, including Meyer. He did it to get the upgrades. He's selling the damn things to some hotel consortium over in the EU."

Alastair's jaw dropped. Literally.

Kerry peeked around into camera range. "That was kind of how we felt, too."

"Buh." Alastair spluttered. "Good god, Dar! He took us? For all that?"

Dar nodded.

"And we...you...we...just let him go?"

Dar's brows quirked. "Alastair, I love the company, and you, but standing in the way of a forty thousand ton ship ain't my idea of how to go."

"B—"

"We're going to track them down over in Europe." Kerry cut in. "I'm sure legal can do something."

"All the good that'll do. Jesus, it'll cost twice what we spent." his voice trailed off. "My god."

"Everyone was in the same boat." Dar muttered. "He just scammed us, Alastair. I knew it was some kind of rig, but one inside another one..." She ended up just shrugging uncomfortably.

"Well, I'll be a son of a bitch," Alastair finally said, after staring at her in silence for a few seconds. "I'll be a son of a bitch." He seemed at a loss. "Ah, well. You know the funny thing there, Dar? That Meyer fellow called me back last night and didn't say boo about all that!"

Kerry finished the eggs and scooted them neatly onto the pieces of toast she had ready. "Jerk." She muttered under her breath. "Wonder what he wanted?"

"Really?" Dar shifted, leaning back against the counter.

Alastair now seemed a touch embarrassed. "He apologized, you know. Said he'd been under some horrible pressure, you know the story."

"Uh huh."

Alastair watched her face as though judging something. "Say, listen, Dar."

"Here it comes." But Dar half smiled, a touch of wryness in her expression. "What did he want, Alastair?"

Kerry picked up a piece of toast and walked over, handing it to Dar as she leaned on the counter next to her and moved into camera range.

"Ah." Alastair glanced at her. "Well, listen, he told me he's going to try to salvage something out of this whole mess, and I guess we all are, huh?"

"Mm." Dar grunted.

"So he wants to do a little wrap up with you, and the rest of those fellows, just to see what they can come up with," he said. "And hey, he did say you'd scooped 'em. Be good for us, huh?"

Ugh. "I don't want to give him a damn thing," Dar said.

"Well, Dar..."

"Did you tell him I'd do it?"

"Me?" Alastair pointed at his own chest. "Lady, were you not listening to that phone call? I gave up trying to tell you to do things ten years ago. I just...well, I just told him I'd ask, that's all."

"He's a skunk, Alastair." Kerry chimed in.

Dar glowered at the camera.

"Be some kind of offset, y'know, when I have to tell the board about this fiasco." Her boss reminded her, gently. "Not gonna be fun, Dar."

No. That was true enough. "I know," Dar said. "And I wish I could tell you I have a magic answer to how we're going to recoup that money, but honestly, Alastair, I can't."

"Ah."

Damn it. Dar sighed. "Guess some good publicity won't hurt." She conceded. "I'll try to come off as intelligent as possible given I was taken in just like the rest of them were."

Alastair looked marginally happier. "Well, good decision, Dar. And hey... I'm sure we'll come up with something to tell the board won't we?" He gave her a wry look. "He's going to call you tomorrow. See what you can get out of it, huh?"

"Okay." Dar conceded. "Do my best."

"Always do, Dar. Always do." Alastair gave her a more sympathetic look. "You two have a great day, huh?"

"You too, Alastair." Kerry said. "Sorry we couldn't make it come out better."

Alastair waved a hand at them then the picture went off, leaving the kitchen in silence. Dar sighed, and started chewing on her egg sandwich. "Wasn't as bad as I expected," she said.

The nonchalance didn't fool Kerry a bit. She gave her partner a one armed hug, and a kiss on the cheek. "We'll make it look good. After all, we did save all their butts, didn't we?"

"Bah."

Kerry gave her another, longer hug.

DAR LAY SPRAWLED across the couch, reading a diving magazine. She usually enjoyed them, glad of a chance to kick back and read about someone else's obsession.

In fact, they usually gave her ideas for vacations. She'd pondered asking Kerry if she wanted to do a live aboard dive cruise in some exotic place. Fiji, maybe. Or Palau. It was one more in a list of things she wanted to do with Kerry. She'd come to realize that at some level her growing dissatisfaction with work was related to her resenting their not being able to go and do stuff like that.

Dar flipped the page, and gazed at an inquisitive seal, caught in mid-bark. She'd always wanted to dive with animals, but somehow her trips over to the other coast had never seemed to have enough extra time for that.

A soft sound made her look up and over at Kerry, who was draped over the loveseat doing absolutely nothing but relaxing. She had her hands folded over her stomach, and her eyes closed. She appeared supremely content to be doing nothing more than occupying a comfortable spot near enough to Dar for her to touch if she reached out.

Dar reached out and stroked Kerry's hair with her fingertips.

A green pupil appeared and peered curiously at her. "Susan B. Anthony dollar for your thoughts?" Kerry said. "Magazine boring?"

Dar lifted one shoulder expressively. "My head's just wandering," she said. "I keep reading the same paragraph over and over again. I'm over it."

Kerry flopped over onto her side so she could see Dar better. "Something bothering you?"

Dar didn't answer.

Kerry waited, her head resting on the loveseat arm as she reached down and gave Chino's head a pat. She already knew the answer, and in fact, she was pretty sure she knew the answer behind the answer, because she was bothered by it too.

"Pah." Dar set the magazine down. "I'm gonna go take Chino for a walk."

Chino jumped up and came over to her, tail wagging as she recognized the word. She nudged Dar's knees as she stood, and followed her to the door, then out and down the steps as they left the condo.

Kerry considered joining them, but then reconsidered, reckoning that her partner needed a little space. Dar usually signaled that pretty clearly, and usually it took the form of her going out onto the beach to wander a little by herself.

In the early days of their relationship that would have intimidated Kerry a little. Even later on, she'd felt a sense of apprehension when Dar had taken up one of her funks, and it had taken her a long time before she'd come to understand that when it happened, it wasn't that Dar was mad at her.

Most often, Dar was mad at Dar, and she knew if Kerry was around, she couldn't be mad at herself for long because Kerry would nibble away at her mood until it evaporated. Sometimes, Dar just needed to stew a little, and when she was ready to be humored, she'd show back up and find a spot somewhere near Kerry.

So Kerry decided to stay where she was, and picked up Dar's

discarded diving magazine and began to flip through it. "Oo." She murmured. "Palau. Man look at those fish." She read the article with more than a touch of envy. "How in the heck do these people all take off weeks and weeks to go out on those boats? Don't they work?"

It wasn't as though the people in the picture were retired vacationers, either. They were all around her age. "Hmph." She shook her head and turned the page. "Man, I wish we could do that. For like two or three weeks, just go out there and see everything. That would be so cool."

So why didn't they? An internal voice asked. "Because we both work for the same place, and we can't be gone at the same time." Kerry lectured herself absently. "And you know, that's really getting to be major suckage."

She turned another page, and absorbed an ad for a new kind of wetsuit. It was cool looking, and Kerry tried to imagine herself wearing it. "Hm."

They didn't wear wetsuits much, but as she'd noted in Disney World, they did have the advantage of making you look sort of sexy in a Sea Hunt kind of way. Maybe she'd get one of these for the night dives they did off the back of their boat on long summer nights.

Kerry flipped the page back and studied the dive charter again. Okay, so the people in it got away for three weeks. Her lips twitched. She could do it anytime, and had a custom yacht to do it with. What was the whining for again?

Sometimes it was easy to fall into the trap of that whole greener pastures thing, and you lost sight of the lawn you were sitting on.

Kerry put the magazine down and closed her eyes again, letting her thoughts continue to wander. It felt like she had a lot of extra fragments in her head, making it difficult to concentrate on anything and rather than strain to pay attention, she just chucked it all instead.

DAR WALKED DOWN to the east end of the island, where there was a small spit of land that jutted out. She sat down on a patch of sand, curling her toes into the grainy warmth as she gazed out over the sea.

Chino trotted over and deposited a turtle on her foot. She sat down and looked expectantly at Dar, who made a grab for the animal as it scrabbled upside down, its tiny feet waving in the air. "Hey, Chino. That's not a toy."

"Growf." Chino nosed the turtle, obviously hoping Dar would toss it for her to retrieve.

"C'mon." Dar examined the creature and found it unhurt. It was a fresh water one, though, so she knew it hadn't swum up out of the nearby Atlantic Ocean. "Were you someone's pet?" She asked it. "I had a turtle just like you once."

Chino sniffed at the turtle, which pulled its head in.

"He doesn't like you, Chi." Dar smiled. "I don't think Brownie would have liked you either. She hated cats."

Carefully, Dar put the turtle down under a piece of driftwood. She had no idea if the animal could survive out on the beach, but she wasn't sure he'd survive if she took him home, either.

This bit of business taken care of she returned her eyes to the sea, one hand absently scratching Chino's neck. She wondered where the ships were by now, probably many miles out to sea. Were the crews partying?

Had Quest told them what their fate was?

Were they all laughing at the four companies they'd duped, and left back in Miami?

Had the Captain, whom Dar had taken a liking to, thrown Shari overboard yet?

So many questions.

So many open issues.

That's what was really bothering her, Dar realized. Well, that and the fact that she'd been made to look like a bloody idiot in front of her boss, her partner, and god knows how many other people.

She fished a shell out of the sand and examined its cracked, ridged edge. It had a dry feeling from the salt and the sand dust and she smelled it, detecting the faint, buttery scent she remembered well from her childhood.

She had, briefly, collected shells. They were interesting, and she'd spent hours finning up and down the beach shoreline, half in and half out of the surf as the sea alternately tugged and pushed her, teaching her the rhythm of its heartbeat.

Most of her friends had no use for them. Her father had no use for them, except for the mahogany olive she'd found once—an old soldier of the sea that he'd taken from her and kept in his uniform pocket for god only knew how many years.

After a while, she'd been at a loss as to what to do with them, so on a whim one morning, she'd gathered them all up—all their colors and varied shapes—and presented them to her mother as a gift, suspecting she'd quietly eject them into a hole in the backyard at the very first opportunity.

To her bemusement, Ceci had absolutely loved them. The textures and patterns had really captured her artist's eye and she'd spent hours arranging and studying them on mats in the little corner she'd set up for a painting studio.

Confused the hell out of Dar, but it was the best reaction she'd ever gotten from a gift, so she wasn't about to question it.

People surprised you sometimes. Shari had surprised her, and after that experience Dar had tried very hard not to let anyone surprise her ever again.

Kerry sometimes did, but that was okay. Kerry only surprised her in good ways. She'd never yet surprised her in a bad way even when she herself thought she might be, like with the tattoo.

Dar sighed, and rested her chin on her forearm. The one thing Shari had accused her of that she knew hit home with a vengeance was the fact that she never gave in. She always had to win—always had to pull one out of her hat.

She could never take losing. Wasn't that what Shari had said? She couldn't take it because that would prove she was just another loser like all the rest of her friends.

Shari being the exception, of course.

She was going to prove Shari wrong this time. Dar tossed the shell into the water. She was going to lose gracefully, take what credit she was due for doing a decent job, and move on. No pulling rabbits out of anywhere, no last minute heroics, no making it happen.

"Right Chi?"

Chino trotted back over to her and re-deposited the turtle in her lap. "Growf." She nudged Dar's hand impatiently.

With a sigh, Dar collected the animal and stood up, brushing sand grains off her leg. "Okay. Let's take it back to mommy Kerry, and see what she says about keeping it," she told the dog, as they started back toward the condo.

The sun was starting to slant down toward the west, and the breeze off the water made it very comfortable. Even the heat wasn't that overbearing, though Dar stifled a yawn as she walked, kicking bits of beach trash ahead of her as she wandered.

Then her steps slowed and she came to a halt, her brow creased.

Chino stopped, came back and grabbed the edge of Dar's shirt in her teeth, tugging in the direction of home.

Slowly, Dar gave in to the motion, starting to walk again, but this time with an extremely thoughtful expression on her face.

THE CONDO WAS very quiet when Dar entered and her eyes went to the love seat where Kerry was now curled up on her side, fast asleep.

She closed the door carefully and edged across the living room, trying not to make any sound as she settled down on the floor next to Kerry, just watching the slow, even motion of her breathing.

Chino ruined all her stealthy work by clattering over, and poking a cold wet nose right into the hollow of Kerry's eye socket.

"Chi!" Dar made a grab for the dog, but it was too late and Kerry jerked awake, her eyes nearly coming out of her head. "Damn it. Sorry, Ker."

"Yow!" Kerry coughed. "What in the hell was that? I felt like a raw meatball hit my face!"

Dar pointed at Chino's black nose.

"Jesus." Kerry hauled herself half upright. "That's twice today."

She rubbed her face with one hand. "Boy, I must have been more tired than I thought."

Dar released Chino and leaned back against the couch. "Sorry about that. Why don't you go back to sleep? Not like we've got a lot planned for this afternoon." She tipped her head back and regarded Kerry. "Ker?"

"What on earth do you have in your hand?" Kerry was leaning forward and staring at Dar's closed fingers with intense fascination. "Is that alive?"

Dar brought her hand over and opened it, revealing the turtle. "Yes, it is."

"Ooo." Kerry crooned at it. "It's so cute!"

The turtle cautiously extended its head, and scrabbled at Dar's skin with its four small feet. "Chino found it on the beach." Dar explained. "It's a freshwater—I used to have one when I was a kid."

"How'd it get here?" Kerry looked up from petting the animal on the head with the tip of her finger. "It didn't swim the cut, did it?"

"Nah. Probably some kid got it, and let it go." Dar replied. "I was going to leave it, but Chi kept bringing it back to me, so..."

"So...we're going to PetSmart." Kerry concluded with a grin. "Rocking. I've always loved turtles."

"Tortuga." Dar pronounced, rolling the R sound a little. "Yeah, we can bring Chino. She loves PetSmart."

"She loves the toy aisle." Kerry sat up. "Okay, let me go throw water on my face, and we can go get Señor Tortuga a house."

"Can we get a hermit crab to keep him company?" Dar asked ingeniously.

Kerry paused, and leaned an elbow on Dar's shoulder. "Tell you what." She whispered, confidentially. "I'll get you a hermit crab, if you tell me what we're going to do to fix this whole stupid mess."

They were pretty much nose to nose. "Are we doing something?" Dar asked, quietly.

"There is no way," Kerry leaned forward and gently kissed her on the lips, "that I'll believe you don't have some plan, some way, some amazing solution to keep you, and I from looking like jackasses in front of that camera tomorrow."

"No way?"

Kerry rested her forehead against Dar's. "Dar, one of the things I admire most about you is the fact that you never give up. You never back off, you never quit, and you never, ever lose," she said. "That's what caught my eye about you from the moment we met."

Dar watched the turtle march across her palm, averting her eyes from her partners briefly. "Some people might not think that's a positive trait."

"Some people might not." Kerry readily agreed. "Anyone who has to compete with you, in fact. But I don't, and I love it."

Ah. An unexpected revelation. "You do?"

"I do."

"You love me being a bitch?" Dar questioned. "Because that's what I am when I do that." Her eyes searched Kerry's. "I'm not sure that's really desirable in a long term relationship, is it?"

And, there it was. Kerry found herself speechless as she stared at her partner.

Dar gave her a tiny shrug, her lips pressed together tightly.

"Y'know." Kerry finally found her voice. "I grew up having to hide who I really was and I didn't half realize just how mind obliterating that was until I met you."

Dar blinked, looking unsure and a little apprehensive.

Kerry stroked Dar's cheek gently. "Please don't tell me you think you have to change for me to keep on loving you. Please." She paused, swallowing. "Don't tell me that."

Dar hadn't expected this conversation to happen like this, so soon, or to hit so hard. Her heart was pounding so fast she could see the flashes from the beats as after images in her eyes, and her tongue felt three sizes too big for her mouth.

But here it was, and there was no point in holding it back any more. "Well." Dar took a breath. "Everyone in my life's always told me the reason I pushed everyone away from me was because I was who I was." She took another breath. "So I'd rather change that than take a chance on losing you."

Kerry glanced at the turtle, who had settled down into the palm of Dar's hand. "Don't change." She whispered, looking back up into Dar's eyes. "Don't change a damn thing, Dar. I love every single thing about you."

"Everything?" Dar sensed the directness in Kerry's rapt attention.

"Everything."

"Everything?"

A touch of sweetly amused exasperation entered Kerry's tone. "Honey, I fell in love with you when you were in the act of firing my ass. How much more everything do you need?"

Hm. Dar thought about that. "Am I being a stupid, insecure jackass again?"

"No." Kerry leaned forward and kissed her again. "We both have questions sometimes. We just have to remember to ask them and not keep quiet."

Sure. Easy for her to say. Dar felt a lot better, though. She still felt like an insecure jackass, but it was hard to be too hard on herself when Kerry's lashes were fluttering against her skin and they were eyeball to eyeball over a turtle.

"Feel better now?" Kerry gave her a kiss on the nose.

"Eh." A sly twinkle appeared in the blue eyes so close to hers. "I get a hermit crab?" Dar asked.

"With a painted house." Kerry promised. "But you have to spill the plan, remember."

Ah, the plan. Well, Kerry's faith in her notwithstanding — Dar kissed her. "Well, I don't have a plan." She admitted. "But I do have an idea, so we'll see how far it goes."

Kerry grinned. "I knew it." She did a little seated dance on the couch. "You know what I'm hoping?" She asked, as she got up and started around the end of the couch toward the bedroom. "I'm hoping you found some way to pull a bathtub stopper on those things and they're now stuck in place bailing to beat the band."

Dar got to her feet and looked around for something appropriate to deposit their new pet in. "Hey Ker? Where'd you store that old fish tank of yours?"

"You didn't comment on that." Kerry called in from the bathroom. "It's in the closet there, bottom shelf."

Dar retrieved the tank and set it on the dining room table. She placed the turtle inside, then went into the kitchen to find it something to eat. "Actually, I'm counting on them making it in one piece." She called back, taking out a piece of lettuce and a few shreds of carrots.

"Really?"

Dar chuckled softly. "Really." She carried the vegetation back to the tank and put it down next to their new resident. "There you go, buddy."

The turtle seemed a bit overwhelmed by its new environment, his feet scrabbling against the glass. But the lettuce attracted him and he munched a bit of it. Dar watched him for a moment, and then she retreated into her study, sitting down behind her computer and giving the trackball a whirl.

Her desktop came up, with its background of an underwater scene. Dar opened her mail program, briefly reviewing some new entries. One made her frown, and she opened it, scanning the contents before she hit reply. "Kiss my ass." She hit send, shaking her head. "Brainless gitwads."

"Did you say something?" Kerry entered, pulling a clean t-shirt over her head.

"Not to you." Dar fished in the small wooden box near her monitor, and removed a business card. She opened a new mail and typed in an address from it. She paused to think, resting her chin against her laced fingers as she considered what it was she wanted to say.

Kerry settled on the couch, tucking her feet up under her. "Can we get Dad to sink them?"

Dar chuckled.

"You know he could."

"We probably could get them stopped." Dar flexed her fingers, then started typing. "Hold on a minute, I'm thinking in German."

German? Kerry's ears perked up. "Hans?"

"Ja."
Hm.

"YOU HAVE GONE out of your head." Hans' voice sounded remarkably clear, given it was coming from a continent away. "Do you know what time it is here?"

"You called me." Dar reminded him dryly.

"Do I know what time it is?" Hans asked, not missing a beat. "How could I know when I get these very strange emails in the middle of the night?"

Dar gave her trackball a whirl, studying the information on her screen. "So you're sure it's Gilberthwaite? Intercontinental Holdings?"

"As sure as anything in this business can be sure," Hans said. "My sources are respectable, and it seems they have quietly bought two hotel lines recently."

"Ah." Dar scrolled down. "They're pretty big."

"They are not Marriot Corporation, but yes." Hans agreed. "And so?"

And so. Dar reviewed the corporate data, her eyes searching for connections between the bland points. Intercontinental had picked up properties that were mostly older, mostly converted chateaus, castles, country mansions—you name it.

They were modestly successful. Customers liked them, and they'd gotten on the hotel A lists, pushing their theme of the grandeur of yesteryear.

That made the ships fit in with their corporate plan, all right. "Okay." Dar mused slowly. "This is the pitch. You listening?"

"Most surely, I am listening." Hans replied.

Dar felt her mind going a mile a minute. It was a feeling that had been familiar to her for a long time, but not so much recently. She'd almost forgotten how much she liked it. "I'm sure they already have a management system."

"They do. One of my competitors."

"So what we have to do is sell them yours, riding on my pipes."

Hans was silent for a long moment. "We have to do that?" He finally queried. "Why?"

"You don't want to sell your system?"

"I do." Hans protested. "But what advantage can we offer to these people? You cannot be thinking of going cheaper than my competitor. I will not allow it."

Interesting reverse psychology, Dar considered. "No, not for this guy." She reluctantly agreed. "He goes for quality, which is why he should go for us."

Hans laughed, but there was no mocking in it. "You know, I agree!" he said. "In fact, that is exactly how I will—what you call—pitch to him.

He should buy my system and your hardware because it is simply the best, and that is all there is to that. It is good. I will call them."

"Great." Dar paused to take a breath.

"I can go back to sleep now, yes?" Hans asked pointedly.

"Sure," Dar said.

"Then a good night to you, Dar. Please give my regards to your delightful wife."

"Thanks. Night." Dar hung up the phone, not entirely satisfied with the conversation. "Hm."

"So, what was that all about?" Kerry asked. "Did he go for whatever it was you were asking?"

Dar scowled. "Not sure." She half shrugged. "I think he did, but not with the urgency I really wanted." She sighed. "Well, we could just hint that we've got something in the works."

Kerry frowned. "I hate vague hints," she said. "Almost as much as I hate not knowing the plan."

Blue eyes blinked guiltily at her. "Sorry." Dar murmured. "C'mere."

Kerry got up and circled the desk, peering at Dar's screen. "Okay. I'm here."

"I asked Hans to find out who was in a position to acquire those four ships, and do something intelligent with them. After he made jokes about half the companies in Europe, he came up with three." Dar clicked on a window. "I ran analyses on them, and we came up with two that have balance sheets so bad they couldn't buy a Happy Meal, and this one." She pointed at the screen she'd been reading.

"Ah."

"They own a lot of old time, classy places."

Kerry grunted. "And you think they're after the ships?" She glanced at her partner. "Why them, and not Starwood, or one of the big multinationals from this side of the pond?"

Why, indeed? Dar found herself in the position of trying to explain a hunch, one of those intuitive decisions she often made and seldom regretted. Kerry had been one of them. "Just feels like a European company is in this," she said. "So anyway, I wanted Hans to pitch his distributed management system over a network we'd provide."

"Why?"

"Why?" Dar gave her a look.

"No..." Kerry held a hand up. "I know why, but I guess I mean, why us? What does this get us?"

Dar clicked on a page. "They have two hundred locations," she said. "What it gets us is a major European backbone, which we don't have right now, as a growth platform. It also gets us a foothold in the services sector, which we also don't have, and last but not least..." One more click. "It recoups all our investment in that ship as well as locks our competitors out."

It nearly took Kerry's breath away. "Whoa."

"Mm." Dar grunted. "If Hans can pull it off," she said. "He didn't sound too enthusiastic about it, but we'll see."

"Couldn't we..." Kerry paused. "We've got programmers, Dar. We could do our own system."

"We could." Her partner agreed. "But it'd take years, which we don't have."

"Hm."

"And, if this is Intercontinental Holdings, they're pretty fiercely Euro centric."

"Ah. We need Hans to front us." Kerry nodded. "It's a great idea, Dar."

Dar leaned her head against her fist. "Wish I'd thought of it a little sooner." She admitted. "Wonder if any of the rest of them caught on? We could be in a race and not even know it."

Kerry's cell phone rang, startling them both. She reached for it, flipping it open as a glance showed her an unfamiliar number. "Hello?"

"You bitch."

The voice was loud enough for Dar to hear it, and it brought her upright and reaching for the phone. "Give me that."

"Ah ah ah." Kerry scrambled out of reach. "Excuse me, there's no one here by that name." She responded into the phone in a pleasant tone. "You must have the wrong number. Goodbye." She closed the cell. "I don't remember giving her my cell phone number. Did you?"

Dar glared at the device, her eyes narrowing.

"Just kidding." Kerry assured her. "That was a marine line—guess she's still stuck out there, huh?"

The cell rang again. Dar imperiously held out her hand, palm up. "Give me that thing."

Kerry hesitated, then she meekly handed it over.

Dar opened it. "Yes." She answered, in a silken tone.

"Don't you fucking hang up on me again, you bitch."

"Different bitch." Dar replied. "And I'll hang up any time I like, so unless you've got something even slightly intelligent to say, goodbye."

Kerry snuggled up to her, wrapping herself around Dar's tall body and angling her head to listen. "You know something." She murmured. "She's the first person, including my father, I hate enough to wish something bad happen to her."

"I am going to fucking sue your ass!" Shari screamed into the phone.

"For?" Dar responded mildly.

"I'm stuck on this piece of shit ship!"

"And that's my fault how?"

Silence.

"Did I ask you come aboard it? Did I ask you to start playing around with the IT systems in an attempt to screw with us? Did I make you so stupid it's a wonder you can breathe and blink at the same time?" Dar went on. "Sorry to have to inject reality, not to mention logic, into the conversation, but frankly you screwed yourself, which is what you should have been doing all along so as not to give the rest of us migraines."

"Ooo." Kerry wriggled.

"You." There was a hiss of interference. "This is all your doing! I know it! You've been trying to fuck me over ever since I dumped you!"

"Stop blaming me, Shari." Dar's voice suddenly went very serious. "You want someone to blame for your troubles, look in a mirror. I don't need to screw you over. I've got everything. You mean nothing to me."

Silence.

"So stop wasting my time." Dar finished quietly.

The line went dead. Dar looked at the phone, then she closed it and let it drop onto the surface of her desk. She looked down at Kerry, who was still wrapped around her. "Well."

Kerry hugged her.

Dar exhaled. "You know something? I actually feel sorry for her."

"I don't." Green eyes peered wryly up. "And you shouldn't either. You were so totally right, Dar. Whatever happened to her, she did to herself."

"Mm."

"Not that she'll ever buy that." Kerry acknowledged.

"No. It'll always be my fault." Dar sighed. "Damn it."

Kerry sniffed. "Well." She concluded. "If that's the case, I hope they're in hundred foot seas every second they're out there, and run out of Dramamine."

"Ker."

"Sorry, hon, if she's determined to hate you, I'll just return the favor. I was never into that two wrongs rigmarole." Kerry stated stubbornly. "At least not where you're concerned." She added hastily, seeing Dar's hiked eyebrows.

"Not very Christian." Dar remarked diplomatically.

"Neither am I anymore." Kerry smiled, with a touch of bitter sweetness. "But seriously, Dar. I don't think there's anything you can do for her. I think she's talked herself into believing you're out to get her, and she probably doesn't realize she has a thing for you."

Dar blinked. "What?"

"Don't you remember? In North Carolina? She tried to get you to go out with her." Kerry poked Dar in the ribs. "I think she liked what she saw, and figured she could pick up from way back when."

"Except I wasn't interested." Dar murmured. "I blew her off."

"So, you switched places."

"And she was determined to bring me down, just like she thinks I was determined to do that to her." Dar sat down on the desk, releasing a breath in sudden understanding. "Holy crap."

"Crap, anyway." Kerry smoothed the unruly dark hair off her partner's forehead.

Dar stared off past her, through the window. "One of us has to stop this, then," she said. "And I think it has to be me."

Kerry absorbed that thoughtfully, but made no comment.

Chapter Fourteen

CECI STOOD BEHIND the captain's seat, her hair whipping back as they traveled across the dark sea. She felt a bit like a dog out for a car ride, except there were no traffic lights anywhere and Andy was actually driving in a straight line. "Why are we doing this, again?"

"Dardar done asked."

Ceci digested this for a moment. "And if she asked, you'd jump off a building?"

"'Pends on what I was supposed to squish down at the bottom of it."

His wife chuckled dryly. "You'd enjoy squishing whatever it was."

"Probly."

Ceci leaned against him. "How long till we get there?"

Andrew checked the watch strapped to his wrist. "'Bout two hours." He concluded. "Got some buddies of mine slowing things down."

"Hm." Ceci flexed her fingers. "How about some hot chocolate?" She tugged on her husband's ear. "You up for that, sailor boy?"

"Yeap." Andy nodded positively. "That'd be real nice."

"Be right back." Ceci made her way to the ladder and carefully climbed down, trading the warm, if whipping, wind for the peace of the boat's cabin. She waited for a particularly sharp pitching to stop, then walked over to the small kitchen and slipped behind the counter.

She wasn't much of a cook, and never pretended to be. Neither was Andy. They both subsisted on a mish mash of burgers and vegetable curries, with a lot of fresh fruit and what seemed to her an inordinate amount of peanut butter.

But she could manage hot chocolate just fine, knowing to make it with just the right amount of chocolate syrup and milk, and microwaving. She did so now, and took a seat on the weighted base stool to wait for it to finish heating.

The drone of the big diesel engines was almost inaudible inside, which always surprised her. She'd gotten used to the motion now, and in fact, the rocking of the boat even in dock put her to sleep like a baby. Every once in a while, though, she'd look around and slap herself when she realized that after all she'd gone through in her life, here she was now with it all.

Hilarious, really. Ceci leaned on the counter, listening to the whirring of the microwave heating up the chocolate. She could almost imagine running into a very early version of herself now, and informing that rebellious freak that she'd end up married to a sailor and owning a motor yacht anchored off South Beach.

She was pretty sure she'd have run screaming. Now, she just peacefully observed their neat, teak inlaid living space and stuck her tongue out at her younger self. At least her family still disowned her, right? That had to count for something to those crabby little memories.

Both their families had disowned them. She'd once broached the subject to Andy of trying to reconnect with his family, but he'd just shake his head without even a moment's hesitation.

Ah well. She'd reconnected with Dar, and that would have to be enough familial reconciliation for her for this lifetime, at least.

The ship rocked a little again, and she turned to peer out the porthole. It was getting very dark out there, and she was still really wondering what Dar was thinking when she asked them to come. It worried her a little, because insofar as she understood her daughter, she didn't understand this.

The radio crackled softly, whispers from hidden travelers on the sea like they were, talking into the silence.

"READY?" KERRY GLANCED at her reflection in the mirror, twitching a bit of blonde hair into place. "You realize they won't recognize us, right? After we spent the last week in rags?" She surveyed her silver blue linen sheath as she shrugged into her gunmetal gray jacket.

"Probably not." Dar appeared in the mirror's reflection behind her. She was dressed in a black business suit jacket and skirt, with a burgundy silk shirt. "You look gorgeous." She complimented her partner, giving her an approving smile as she twitched the shoulders straight on Kerry's jacket.

Kerry straightened in reflex, glancing in the mirror to meet Dar's eyes. "Thanks." She smiled. "So do you."

"Hm, this old thing?" Dar held her arms out, giving her suit a droll look.

"It's what's in it." Kerry turned around and traced a line down the front of her partner's neck. "Did I say anything about the packaging?" Her fingertip disappeared inside the collar of Dar's shirt. "Any word from Hans?"

"Nope." Dar reached past Kerry and selected a pair of earrings, fastening them into her lobes. "Not a word."

Kerry sprayed a bit of perfume on her wrists, and rubbed them together. "Well."

"It's Sunday." Dar shrugged. "Can't really expect much on the weekend." She picked up Kerry's arm by the wrist and rubbed the inside of it against the side of her neck. "Mm." She growled softly. "I like that."

Kerry almost sneezed, the sudden seduction sending confusing signals across her body. "It's new." She responded in bemusement.

"It's you." Dar relented, releasing her arm and giving her a pat on the shoulder. "We ready for our close-ups, Ms. Demille?"

Kerry rolled her eyes. "What are you going to do, since we haven't heard from Hans?"

"Bullshit." Dar replied amiably.

"Really?"

"Yup. C'mon."

Kerry followed Dar out the door and into the purple twilight of the summer evening. They walked together down the path and over to Dar's car. "You know where we're going?" Kerry asked. "I don't think I ever heard of the place."

"Ivan Tors?" Dar chuckled softly. "Yeah, I've been there."

"Really?" Kerry got into the Lexus and settled into the leather seat. "I thought your mom said you were too feisty for baby commercials."

Dar closed the door and started the car. "I was." She backed the Lexus out of its parking spot, leaving Kerry's smaller blue one sitting in lonely isolation. "But they used to film Flipper there, and we went on a school field trip to check it out."

Kerry leaned an elbow on the center console. "You're kidding."

"Nope." Dar shook her head. "They were doing some movie or something there when we were there—had the big tank filled up with water and I jumped in."

"Oh my gosh."

"Hey, it was hot." Dar turned onto the main road of the island. "Pissed off a lot of people, let me tell ya, but one of the guys doing the shots wanted me to stick around."

Kerry's eyes twinkled. "Ah. A gentleman of discerning tastes."

Dar smiled, but didn't answer. She pulled up and drove directly onto the ferry that was just about ready to cast off. Rolling into place, she set the parking brake and relaxed. As she looked off toward the west, toward a still crimson line near the horizon, she could sense the end coming and was glad of it.

"So you're going to bullshit?" Kerry changed the subject, watching her partner's fingers tap restlessly on the steering wheel. "What part do you want me to take up? How we're working to incorporate our international partners?"

"Mm. I like that." Dar gave her an approving grin.

Kerry leaned back watching the shoreline go past as the ferry crossed the cut. The last light was fading from the sky and she enjoyed the faint puffs of magenta still outlining the western clouds. "We driving down to the cabin tomorrow or taking the Dixie?"

Dar didn't answer for a few minutes, her brow tensing a little. Then she shrugged. "Let's take the Dixie. We can run down to Key West one of the days for fun if we want."

"Ooo, I like that idea." Kerry found herself really looking forward to it. "I really do." She added, in a softer tone. "And you know we can get some stuff done from there, Dar. I've got so much catching up to do."

Dar eyed her.

"I just really like the idea of working from there." Kerry caught the look and blushed a little. "I got so much more done that one day we were there."

Dar casually reached over and took Kerry's hand in hers. They both sat in silence as the ferry made a lazy u-turn in the channel and started to nose up to the landside ferry base. Then Dar turned her head and looked at Kerry. "I want to put together this deal." She sounded slightly surprised. "With Hans."

"Do you?" Kerry asked.

Dar nodded. "We can really make a move in Europe with this," she said. "We've got a lot of service contracts over there, but almost no infrastructure. That's why the international calls give me such a hive. They have no clue what I do."

"I think it's a great idea."

"Which one?" Dar half grinned.

"All of them. I like the idea of you expanding our business there." Kerry replied. "And to be honest, I think I need to pull back from that side of it a little. I need to get our house in order. There's been way too much suckage in the last few months."

They both studied each other as the ferry docked, and the ramp started to come down. "I was seriously considering quitting last week." Dar finally said.

"I know."

Dar started up the Lexus. "I'm not going to quit on a failure." She shifted her hands to the wheel, watching impatiently as the ferry deck hands began to direct traffic off the boat. "I'm just not going to do that."

Kerry settled back as they started up the ramp, nodding a little to herself. "I like that answer," she said. "It reminds me of something my father said once."

Dar barely kept from driving off the edge of the ferry base. "What?"

Kerry folded her arms. "He said, 'Kerrison, if you ever go out in public and do something, you better do it right. If it lands on page one of the Washington Post, you'll spend a year in the back room washing dishes.'"

Dar blinked. "Did I just say that?" She asked, in an outraged tone.

"No." Kerry nudged her. "Drive straight, hon. They won't believe us if we say we missed it because you drove off the causeway." She waited until they were underway again. "But his point was the same thing — when you do something, you should do it right, or don't do it."

"Oh. Okay." Dar drummed her fingers on the wheel. "Yeah, I guess it is the same general idea, isn't it?" She paused, then glanced at Kerry. "Did you listen to him?"

Kerry merely nodded, her expression shifting to one of quiet introspection. "One of the few times." She added, after a moment. "So I'm right there with you, Dar. I don't fail in public. Not if I can help it."

"Mmhm."

They traded the causeway for the highway, and headed north.

"WHY AREN'T WE moving?" Quest asked, as soon as the captain cleared the doorway. "We've been sitting here for an hour!"

The captain gave him a brief smile. "That is right." He agreed. "And we will be sitting possibly for some hours more. There is a defect in the engine."

Quest threw his hands up. "This piece of crap boat."

"Ship." The captain corrected him. "Mr. Quest, I am sorry if this disturbs you. However, we are outside the waters of the United States, and so you perhaps should just go and relax while we attend to this problem. I did warn you we could have some difficulties."

"Yeah, yeah." Quest grumbled. "I just want to be out of here. I can taste a decent glass of beer the closer we get to the other side."

The captain shrugged both shoulders. "I do sympathize," he said. "We too, are looking for some relief from the lives we've been forced to live these last few months." He walked over to the window in the dining room, peering out into the darkness. "I am looking forward to going home."

Quest snorted. "Hey, at least you had a break. I can't believe you conned Roberts into buying the whole damn ship dinner," he said. "Very slick."

The captain did not turn. "I think the lady was glad to do it."

"Lady?" Quest guffawed. "Get real."

"I rather liked Ms. Roberts." The older man twitched his jacket straight. "At any rate, I must return to the bridge. If there are further developments, I will inform you." He walked to the door and slipped through it, not giving Quest a chance to intercept him.

"Prick." Quest curled his lip. "You'll be going home all right, old man. I know they'll kick your ass right off this tub as soon as the check's signed." He put his feet up against the chair next to him and pushed back, rocking slowly in the rhythm of the ship's motion.

A shadow caught his eye, and he looked over toward the big entrance to see Shari entering. "What do you want?" He asked sharply. "I thought I told you to stay upstairs and stop aggravating everyone."

"Go screw yourself." Shari told him bluntly. "You don't tell me anything, you piece of shit."

"You better watch your mouth." Quest pointed at her. "You forget I can have you charged with being a stowaway. That's big time trouble for a skuzzy dyke without any passport."

Shari sat down near the window. "Don't threaten me. I finally bought my way into that comm office upstairs and got a phone call out." She told him, with a sneer. "So my passport's no longer an issue. You better hope you make this stupid trip worth my while, or maybe I'll charge you with kidnapping."

"Like anyone would kidnap you." Quest laughed. "What a piece of shit you are. Is there anyone in this thing you didn't screw over? Your partner? Roberts? Me? The media? Meyer? You were sleeping with everyone."

"Look who's talking." Shari taunted him right back. "If you switched sides any more times you'd have split yourself in half, you horse's ass."

Quest started laughing. "I was right. We're two of a kind." He announced, with a cheerful grin. "Maybe if you're not too obnoxious on the crossing, I'll let you work for me when I sign my contract with the new owners."

"Don't even think it." Shari growled. "I don't work for anyone."

"Yeah, you sure didn't do much for your little girlfriend. Bet she wishes she'd hooked up with your old flame."

"Screw you."

Quest laughed again. "Better think twice. I think you burned your bridges with your friend."

Shari sullenly stared at him.

"Who knows? Maybe you lucked out getting stuck on board." Quest went on, with a smirk. "Wouldn't you like a new start? I don't think you're leaving behind anything worth going back to."

One of the crew entered, and paused awkwardly. "Uh, excuse me."

"Yeah? What?" Quest seemed glad of a new victim. "What's your name again, Weenie?"

"Talley," the man said. "The staff captain asked me to tell you that dinner is being served in the officer's mess."

"Tell them I said to bring it to me here." Quest told him.

Shari got up. "If you're so stupid that you'd give those people a chance to poison the plate they're bringing you, I don't want to be here to see it." She looked at Talley. "Where's the place it's being served?"

Talley gave her a mildly accepting look, and indicated the stairs. "Down there. I'll show you," he said. "And I'll pass along your message, sir."

Shari followed the young man down the stairs. "How do you like working for a jackass like that?"

Talley glanced at her, then shrugged. "He's a clueless breeder. They're all the same. He'll get tired of the whole thing when we get to where we're going, and take off."

"Think so?" Shari asked.

Talley smirked. "I think he'll be lucky he's not hanging over the railing the rest of the crossing after I tell the staff they've got to bring him his dinner."

Shari chuckled dryly, but her thoughts kept going back to what Quest had said.

What, really, did she have to go back to?

Nothing.

But what if she could turn it all around, and make a deal with the new owners of the ships? Shari's eyes glinted. She could pull her own miracle out of her ass this time, and screw the rest of them. She'd show up Dar, and she'd prove she was the real driving force behind Telegenics.

Yeah.

DAR PAUSED INSIDE the back door to the studio to let her eyes wander over the space, trying to remember what it had looked like the last time she'd been there. After a moment, she shook her head and followed Kerry across to where a long table was set up against one wall.

Everything seemed to be painted black. Behind the table was a set of doors, one larger than the other, with a heavy seal and what looked like a police light mounted over it. It was flashing red, throwing annoying blurps of light around the room.

"Ah." Graham was already there, and he walked over to them as they approached. He was dressed in a well fitted, conservative gray suit and appeared to be the successful businessman he, in reality, was. "We were taking bets whether we'd see you two here tonight."

"Us, miss a party?" Kerry said. "Never. Besides, I don't know about you, but I needed some closure out of this thing."

"I agree." Michelle joined them. "They're doing individual interviews first." She indicated the door. "And they've catered us. Go have some television food. Guarantee that doesn't happen to any of us often."

Dar touched Kerry's back lightly. "I'll grab you a coke." She ducked away and headed for the table, leaving Kerry to fence with their rivals.

"Nice outfit." Michelle complimented her.

"Thanks. You too." Kerry replied, with automatic graciousness. "We got a call from your partner."

"So did I." Michelle didn't miss a beat. "Did you arrange all that?"

Graham was merely watching them, his eyes flicking from Kerry to Michelle with interest.

"Sad to say, no," Kerry said. "We were as surprised as you probably were."

"I wasn't."

Kerry's eyebrows twitched. "You weren't?"

"No. I mean..." Michelle backed up hastily as she saw Kerry's expression change. "What I meant was I wasn't surprised when I found out she'd gone on your ship to try and screw you over. Not that I knew she had."

"Ah."

"Don't start throwing things at me." Michelle warned, with a wary grin. "This suit costs a fortune to dry clean."

Kerry had to grin a little at that, lifting a hand and half shrugging to acknowledge the jibe. "We're just a bunch of radicals at ILS, what can I tell you? I do have to admit I wasn't expecting our admin staff to turn into culinary terrorists." She glanced aside as Dar returned with two cups. "Thanks."

"So, have you decided what you will tell them, Dar?" Graham asked, with a remarkable lack of artifice. "That's what we were discussing before you arrived. What lies we came up with."

Dar shrugged. "More or less." She turned to Michelle. "You going to tell them about Shari?"

The smaller woman's face scrunched up. "I'm on the fence."

Just then the red light went off, and they all turned as the big door opened. A slim, blonde woman with a pony tail and a huge clipboard looked out. "Okay, we're about ready to start. Everyone here?"

The front door shoved open, and a sweating Mike joined them, a look of overbearing aggravation on his face. "Traffic sucks." He announced crisply. "Sorry."

The pony-tailed woman looked at her clipboard. "Are you Mike?" She asked. "You're first."

"Figures." Mike dabbed at his forehead with his handkerchief. "This won't take long. Keep a beer cold for me." He edged past them and approached the woman, tugging the sleeves straight on his chocolate brown business suit.

The door closed behind him, and after a few moments, the red light went on. The rest of them lapsed into a pensive silence, standing in the middle of the depressingly dark stage.

SHARI JOINED HER new friend, Talley, at a Formica table, setting her tray down with its dish of god only knew what, and a glass of chemical punch, and taking a seat. The crew mostly ignored her and chattered to each other as they relaxed together.

Most were young, but some weren't, and there was a real mix of nationalities. In fact, Shari discovered, Talley was one of the very few Americans aboard.

"We don't like hard work." Talley explained, when asked about that. He selected a piece of mystery meat from the stew and ate it. "Americans don't like working seven days a week with no time off, and a crappy salary."

"I doubt anyone does." Shari offered, reasonably. "So why do it?"

"Travel," Talley said. "Different place every day, different people." He took a sip of the pseudo juice. "They give you room and board—

such as it is — so you can save money and put it away if you want to, or buy yourself stuff at every port."

It almost sounded appealing. "No attachments." Shari mentioned.

"Exactly." Talley nodded. "Which is why I think this whole hotel thing sucks so badly."

"Yeah." A young, willowy woman sat down next to him. "It's nasty."

"So you don't think it's a good idea?" Shari asked.

Both young people shrugged. "It's better than scuttling the ships, I guess," Talley said. "And we get to keep our jobs, which is more than the deck and engine guys got. They're pissed."

"They're weird," the girl said, her Australian accent rolling the words out. "But they'll go off and find some other bucket of bolts to cruise round in — you know it."

"Rather than working for — who was that?" Shari fished gingerly.

"Intercontinental Holdings, yeah." Talley supplied promptly. "I guess they'll be okay. Pretty good benefits."

"Yeah, those guys," Shari said.

"For me, it's good," the girl said. "I've wanted to move shore side and get in with these people, they've got a lot of good properties all over the continent."

"Hm." Talley nodded. "I guess. I'll just miss being at sea."

"Join the Navy." Shari suggested. "I hear the food's better."

The two looked at their plates, and then at her, and then at each other. Talley sighed. "Boy, I miss those IT guys. They really knew how to lay it on." He lamented. "It was nice to be treated like human beings for a change, wasn't it, Mandy?"

"It was." Mandy agreed. "I liked that lot. Clever boys and handsome girls. Wish they'd stayed on and I'm terribly mad at you all for letting them be tricked like that — with the staff."

Talley had the grace to look guilty.

Shari bit her tongue to keep from giving her opinion of Dar and her staff. She needed information right now more than the satisfaction that savaging the old bitch would give her. "So...Intercontinental — they a big outfit?"

Talley turned to her in relief. "Pretty big, for over there I guess. They've got a lot of unique places all around — castles and stuff like that. Exclusive."

"Yeah?"

"Maybe we'll get staying privileges." Mandy elbowed him. "Do a tour on time off and stay in a castle. I'd like that."

"I think they're going to do up each ship in a different era, or culture or something," Talley said. "Sounds pretty cool."

It did, actually. Shari felt a grudging appreciation for the idea.

"So are you part of Mr. Quest's company?" Talley suddenly asked. "I thought you were, but if you don't know about the new people."

Crap. "Nah. I'm from one of the other ships," Shari said. "I was just bringing something on this one when you all just up and left. I got stuck here."

"Oh!" Mandy looked concerned. "My gosh. Are you staying on the crossing? Don't you have clothes or anything? That's horrid!"

"Yeah, well, that's the breaks." Shari got up, picking up her mostly untouched tray. "Thanks for the company. See you later." She deposited the congealing food onto a dish cart and strode purposefully for the door, an idea growing in her mind that made her smile.

DAR HAD TIRED of standing around bullshitting, and she'd hunted around the big, empty stage until she located a few old folding chairs stacked against one wall. She called the others over, and they set up the chairs in a circle, near enough to the long table to replenish themselves when they wanted.

"Excuse me, we didn't rent those." The girl behind the long table cautioned them.

"You should have." Dar told her. "Just be glad we didn't come over there and sit at your table."

The girl retreated, reseating herself meekly behind the catering.

Kerry tucked her feet under her chair and let her hands rest on her knees. The big room was well air conditioned, at least, and with any luck they'd be done soon and they could get out of here. Her social gene prodded her, and she cleared her throat to get everyone's attention. "How about we all go grab some dinner and end this project on a civilized note?"

"You, civilized, and dinner scares me," Michelle said, but with a smile. "But I'll risk it. Graham?"

"Surely." Graham placidly answered. "My company is already sending hit men after me and I doubt I will survive Monday, so why not get a dinner out of it at the least? Perhaps we can all pass around resumes."

"Ah, yes." Michelle winced. "Isn't that the truth? Not all of us have as understanding an upper management as you do, Dar. That was a pretty impressive performance by your CEO." She took a sip of ice tea. "You have him very well trained."

"Alastair's not trained." Kerry hastily spoke up as she sensed the stiffening of Dar's body next to her. "He just trusts Dar implicitly."

"Hm."

"That is what I have heard." Graham said. "In fact, to be perfectly frank Dar, it's quite advantageous to your boss that your preferences are so explicit, otherwise many would assume something quite salacious between the two of you."

"They have." Dar shrugged. "He and I joke about it sometimes." She pulled her PDA out and checked it, then returned it to her purse with a sigh.

The rotating light went off, and the door opened. Mike came out, looking as though he'd drunk sour lemonade.

"Ah Graham?" The pony tailed girl asked, peering politely at them. "You're next, please."

Mike came over and took the chair Graham vacated, sitting down in it with a creak of protesting metal. "Hope you've got a cup on." He advised Graham.

Graham paused, made a face, then continued on, shaking his head as he walked through the door.

"Do they make cups for women?" Mike asked. "Cause I think there's a Wal-Mart nearby if you want to run out and get some."

Dar, Kerry, and Michelle exchanged looks. Kerry cleared her throat gently. "Are they wearing cups?" She indicated the now closed door.

"I'm wearing pointy shoes." Michelle displayed her fashionable stilettos. "This could be fun."

SHARI BROWSED THE internet, searching out details. She'd found Intercontinental's website easily enough, once she'd paid off the communications officer to give up his laptop for a few minutes. The man hadn't wanted to, and after she'd taken a quick look at his browser history, she could see why.

No wonder they had liked Dar. She gave them freaking internet. None of the others had done it, and they sure hadn't, since that would have cost money she wasn't about to spend on this shit ball bid. "Wonder if they even had any clue how badly they'd have lost this." She shook her head.

Intercontinental's site was boring as hell. She scrolled through pages and pages of bullshit, maps, site plans, and marketing crap so bland even she couldn't get through it. The one thing that didn't seem to be there was a contact number and address.

Figures. Shari kept hunting.

"Madame."

"Here." Shari held out another twenty dollar bill without looking. "Go away."

The bill was removed from her fingers, and a moment later, the door closed. Shari drummed her fingers on the keyboard, then thought of something else, and opened up a search page. "Don't want riff raff to call you, huh? Well, you issue stock, so you've got to have an address somewhere, baby. C'mon."

She ran a search against public companies, and found nothing. Then she tried against the SEC database, and finally, finally, there was something. She scanned the results, and leaned forward. "Ah hah." The company's officers were listed, most of whom were not familiar to her.

"Sir Melton Gilberthwait." Shari rolled her eyes. "Oh, give me a

break. Sounds like a cartoon character from Rocky and Bullwinkle."
She pulled out a pen and wrote it down nevertheless, and copied down
the telephone number beside it. "Okay, old boy. I'll just give you a ring,
and see if I can't make you a deal you can't say no to."

She checked her watch. "Well your office hours say 6:00 a.m., so I
hope that's not bullshit like the rest of your website is." She put the
piece of paper away, and closed the browser. With a glance at the door,
she walked over to the rack of computer equipment and looked at it.

A smoked glass door obscured the contents, and on the front was
taped a sign off sheet verifying that the gear behind the door was
operational.

It listed all the components. Shari scanned it, not really recognizing
most of the individual pieces of machinery, but knowing the major parts
from things Michelle had said. It was expensive stuff, and she had
fought tooth and nail with Michelle to get her to order the cheaper
components she'd found on the internet instead of the kind Dar had
used.

Michelle had flat refused. She should have known right then it was
all bullshit. It had nothing to do with competing with ILS, and
everything to do with impressing Dar. And Michelle had called her
fixated? What a blind fucker she'd turned out to be.

Shari got to the end of the list, and the signature line where ILS's
installer had guaranteed the install.

The name was familiar—a firmly scrawled D. Roberts. Shari stared
at the name for a long time, her lip curling up into an unconscious snarl.
She reached out and her fingers tensed against the paper, on the verge
of crumpling it.

Then she dropped her hand, and just spat on it instead. "I am going
to beat you." She told the page. "And you are never, ever going to
forget it."

DAR WALKED UP and down the cracked sidewalk outside the
studio. It was getting late, and the traffic in front of the building had
settled down to a steady trickle. The orange streetlamps were bathing
everything in an annoying color that strained her eyes to look at it.

She checked her PDA again, finding nothing in the in box. Hell,
Hans was probably out at the local pub. Dar checked her watch. No,
Hans was probably sleeping, without a care in the world for her
anxieties on this side of the planet.

She could bullshit the television producers, but there was a
warning bell ringing in the back of her head that reminded her that
Meyer was the type who'd pick up the phone and call the Europeans to
find out if she was lying or not.

That she didn't want to deal with. Dar paced down the walk,
dodging past two women jogging as she tried to work off some of her

nervous energy. It wasn't easy. She really felt like doing some sparring, and she felt bad about having left Kerry inside making small talk.

She stopped near a bus bench, and leaned against the telephone pole next to it.

What could she do? Dar sorted through her options. Maybe she could tell half truths, and just gloss over any specifics. Say they were working on a deal, which was true. Say she was working with a transcontinental partner — which was almost true since she had no real agreement with Hans.

But she was aware that this was going to be filmed, and that meant it could come back and bite her in the ass big time, if everything fell through or worse, if Hans found some European partner and they cut her out of it. She would look like an idiot.

Dar hated looking like an idiot. It might even be said that she'd made up the story just to make the company look good, and since that would affect the stock, there could be legal issues for her with that.

She was, as she found herself being reminded recently, a corporate officer and they were a public company.

"Hey lady."

Dar turned, to find an old woman taking a seat on the bench next to her. "Yes?"

"Is this the G bus?" The woman peered at Dar fuzzily, squinting through a pair of glasses with lenses at least a half an inch thick.

Dar straightened and looked around, spotting a sign tacked to the telephone pole. It bore a legend that probably required most of Dar's years of schooling to decipher and went a long way to explain why so few residents bothered using the transit system. "Yeah," she finally said. "Where are you going?"

"Hallandale."

Of course. "Yeah, that's the bus." Dar agreed.

"Good. Now if the stupid thing comes, it'll be a good thing. Are you waiting for the bus? You could sell that nice jacket and take a taxi, y'know."

Dar had to smile. "No, I'm not waiting for the bus."

"So why are you standing there? Go home!" The woman scolded her. "It's late! Does your mother know you're out here?"

Dar's jaw dropped a little, and she clicked it shut. "She does."

"She should be ashamed. Go on home, young lady."

Bemused and defeated, Dar left the safety of her telephone pole and escaped back down the sidewalk toward the studio. She got back to the door without any clearer idea of what she was going to do, but she was glad enough to trade the muggy night heat for the cold blandness inside.

Kerry looked up as she entered, and gave her a wry smile. She was sitting with Mike and Graham, and apparently Michelle was now undergoing the grilling.

Of course, Kerry was depending on her too. Dar felt the added weight on her shoulders. She didn't want to disappoint Kerry, or Alastair, or the board, or the company or her parents...

Jesus. Dar went back to her seat and dropped into it, feeling silently overwhelmed.

Kerry reached over casually and circled Dar's arm with her fingers, rubbing gently with the edge of her thumb. "Graham just told me they're being pretty brutal in there."

Dar lifted her brows.

"I think we should just keep our cool, and relax."

Sure, easy for you to say. Dar scowled silently.

"Actually I think we should tell them we bought the ships." Kerry continued blandly. "You know I had that budget I had to use or lose for this quarter."

Graham snorted wearily.

"Tell them your dad is going to re-commission them as a coastal defense."

Mike rolled his eyes, but laughed anyway.

A grudging smile appeared on Dar's face, as she looked into her partner's eyes. "He'd make a damn good Admiral," she said, understanding the banter for what it was. "Think you could keep a straight face if I pulled that on them?"

"No." Kerry admitted, with a grin. "But I'm sure you'll think of something, and if not we can start kissing each other. That should distract them."

Both men started laughing, mostly at Dar's expression. Finally, Dar started laughing too, because with the tension she was feeling, she needed to do something.

As Kerry had said, she'd figure out something. Dar took Kerry's hand in hers and squeezed it. And if not, well then, Plan B had its merits, too.

SHARI DUG MORE bills out of her wallet, glad like hell she'd stopped at the bank before she'd headed for the pier that day. She'd figured the last minute crap was going to cost, and she knew better than to trust in the altruism of her staff or the good will of the dock workers.

None of that, of course, would have been figured into the bid. She hadn't even been sure she was going to tell Michelle about it if she'd paid anyone off, though she knew her erstwhile partner had no real moral objection to the practice.

It was get it done that was all. That's what they'd decided to do when they'd gone into this whole rigmarole—to do whatever it took to win the contract—Shari counted out her money—to win the contract and beat ILS.

She thought Michelle was on board with her on that. Things had been going great for them, right up until fucking Orlando. They'd had it all planned out—starting with making a star appearance at the convention.

Then Dar had shown up, and it all started going wrong.

Just like always.

She tucked half the money away in her jeans pocket and folded the other half, glancing at the scrap of paper with the Intercontinental's contact name. "Well, not this time." She informed the scribbling. "Now, where's that little Ruskie?"

She opened the door to the communications office, but found it surprisingly empty. Every other time she'd come in she'd found the communications officer hunkered down over his desk, but this time the padded gray seat was barren, and she wasn't really one to look a gift horse in the mouth when it presented itself.

With a grin, she slipped inside and locked the door behind her, pocketing the folded twenties she'd tucked inside her right hand. No sense in wasting her resources, eh? She sat down at the console table and picked up the phone, pausing to straighten out the small bit of paper before she composed herself to dial.

She checked her watch. Only 3:45 a.m. in Europe, and she suspected her call would go unanswered. If it was a business number, though, she could leave a message and at least make some contact. She cracked her knuckles and paused briefly, considering what to say.

Despite the fact that it went against most of her personality, marketing was what she'd chosen to specialize in. She thought about what might make a good 'hook' for the possibly stuffy, probably stuck up continentals on the other end of the phone.

Should she be aggressive? That was her normal mode, and the mode she knew her rival felt most comfortable with as well. The only difference was, she admitted privately to herself, she'd never quite gotten that switch to sexy charm that Dar did so well—the one that could turn a frothing adversary into a drooling ape in roughly ten seconds.

She definitely hadn't had that when they'd been dating. Shari had been shocked to find herself snared by it long afterward.

So possibly not aggressive with the Euros. She turned her thoughts to something more productive. Her few contacts with overseas vendors had taught her they didn't really appreciate that American style approach, at least not very often.

Respectful. Shari nodded grudgingly, then she dialed the number, and waited, listening to the foreign sounding buzz in her ear.

THE DOOR LIGHT went off, and it opened so quickly afterward that it was obvious Michelle had started out before the session was over. One look at her face confirmed it, and if sparks really could fly from someone's eyes, the painted walls of the studio would have gone up in an instant.

"Uh oh." Kerry brushed a speck of dust from her sleeve. "That doesn't look good."

"Hm." Dar stood up as Michelle approached. "Problem?"

"Multiple sessions of triple digit jackassedness." Michelle replied succinctly. "Good luck Dar. For once, I hope to hell you take your reputation to the absolute limit and eunuch those people." She sat down in the chair Dar had just vacated and sat back, one toe tapping on the concrete floor in agitation.

"Hm." Dar shifted a little, unsure of whether to plant her hands on her hips or cross her arms to punctuate the statement.

"Ms...uh...Roberts?" The girl with the pony tail interrupted her dilemma.

Dar glanced over at her.

"Could you come with me, please?"

Dar put one hand on Kerry's shoulder, already sensing the motion as her partner went to stand up. "Depends," she replied.

"Ma'am?"

"I said, it depends." Dar repeated. "Tell your friends inside there I have no intention of coming out with an expression like Michelle's here. So if that's what they intend, forget it."

The girl stared at her. "Ma'am?" She peered behind her. "Do you want to be in this show?"

"No."

"Excuse me?"

"No." Dar began to wonder if the echoes in the big room were affecting the girl's hearing. "I don't want to be in this thing. So go tell those guys to either be civil or I'm outta here. Got me?"

The girl disappeared, though before she left she gave Dar a look usually reserved for the mentally deficient. The door closed behind her, but the light remained off, and the room fell back into uncomfortable silence.

"So." Dar addressed Michelle. "What's the deal?"

Michelle's lips were twitching slightly. "You only get away with that because you're really the one they want to get, you know that, right?"

"Sure."

"Dar, you're not going in there by yourself." Kerry interrupted.

"Listen, everyone else only had one representative." Dar told her, giving her shoulder a little squeeze. "If there are asses to be kicked, I can handle that."

"That's not the point." Kerry got up. "This was my contract."

And so it was. Dar inclined her head in concession. "True," she said. "Let's see what our little friend comes back and says."

"They actually asked me where Shari was." Michelle supplied. "I didn't tell them. It seemed to piss them off." She eyed Dar dourly. "You—" She paused. "Okay, let me be honest. We screwed them over for their little happy ending, so now the deal is scandal in corporate America. Get the drift?"

Dar cocked her head a little. "No."

"They went after some pretty dirty details." Mike spoke up finally. "Brought up a deal that went south for us, two bloody years ago."

"Skeletons, yes." Graham nodded. "Fortunately, most of ours are fairly benign."

Kerry scratched her jaw. "Hon." She patted Dar on the side. "I don't think we have any skeletons left that aren't either tattooed on my chest or were featured on national television at least twice." She looked at the rest of them. "Really."

"Hmph." Michelle snorted.

Graham pursed his lips and shrugged.

"You've got a skeleton tattooed on your chest?" Mike asked ingeniously.

"Let's go." Dar decided she was over it. "C'mon." She took Kerry by the arm and started for the inner door. "Let's get this over with."

THE PHONE WAS answered on what seemed like the thirtieth ring. "Intercontinental Holdings." A cultured voice echoed lightly through the phone. "How may I help you?"

Well, at least it wasn't a cleaning woman. Or at least, she didn't think so. "Good evening." Shari replied. "I know it's very late there, and I apologize for calling at this hour."

"Not a problem." The voice sounded a touch warmer. "We're quite used to calls at all hours."

Oh, really? Shari found that interesting. "Ah huh."

"The hostel business is round the clock, as it were." The woman clarified. "How may I forward your inquiry?"

"Of course," Shari said. "I was hoping to speak with Sir Melton Gilberthwaite? I completely understand if he's not available, perhaps I can leave word for him with an assistant?'

"Please hold one moment. I will see who's in at that location." The operator sounded almost cheerful. "I think they had a Far East meeting today, so let me just check."

A soft classical tune began playing in her ear, and Shari sat back, wondering if luck wasn't coming her way at last.

"LOOK, I DON'T know what the hell's going on, but I've got a schedule I need to keep." The woman with the pony tail was saying. "We've got this studio booked in an hour for a night shoot with MTV."

Meyer gave her a look. "All right, hold your tits, sister. I'll get this

straightened out." He brushed passed her and stalked toward the door.
"Pain in the ass little..." He stopped short, nearly crashing into Dar as
she came through the door with Kerry right behind her. "Oh."

"Oh." Dar didn't even slow down. She came right up to him and
poked him in the chest. "Oh, you've got about ten minutes of my time to
wrap up your game, Meyer, because I'm not wasting one minute more
than that on you."

"Hey, wait a minute!" Meyer backed up a step. "Just who do you..."

"You know who I think I am." Dar didn't let up. "So go over there
and put up or shut up." She gave him a shove for good measure, aware
of Kerry's close presence at her back. "Ten minutes!"

Meyer was caught off balance, and so he gave way, turning and
moving back toward the filming area. "Fine." He tossed back over his
shoulder. "Go with her. She'll get you ready."

Dar studied the space. Inside a ring of lights and two cameras on
dollies were two high director's chairs in dark fabric. It was all very
stark and utilitarian, and to her eyes, profoundly depressing. "Hmph."
She ignored Pony Tail and ducked between the two cameras, whose
operators were staring at her in fascination. "Think you could spare a
few dollars for fresh bed sheets for this?" She pointed at the backdrop,
which had several tears held together with gaffers tape.

Meyer just looked at her, then went back to studying a piece of
paper, murmuring to a slim, gray haired woman standing next to him.

"Okay...ah." Pony Tail hurried over. "Let's just get you, uh, both,
uh, ready."

Dar took a seat and leaned her elbows on the chair arms. "I'm
ready."

"Me too." Kerry hopped up onto the next chair.

Pony Tail stopped short. "Do you want us to..." She made some
vague hand gestures toward their heads. "Um. We usually want to do a
little hair, a little makeup."

"No, we're fine." Kerry responded in a kind tone. "But thanks
anyway. If we crack the lenses, I'll give you a credit card."

The girl shrugged, and walked off, shaking her head.

The two cameramen started to fiddle with their controls, making
the cameras bob up and down like some odd animals, moving in and
out on where Dar and Kerry were sitting. Dar put up with the show for
a minute, then cleared her throat. "Meyer? Nine minutes."

Meyer's head jerked up. "Wh—oh, shit." He glared at Pony Tail.
"You didn't say you were ready." He folded the piece of paper and
straightened his jacket before he walked over to them, sitting down in a
chair tucked up against where the cameras were.

"They wouldn't let me do anything." Pony Tail shrugged. "But that
works for me, because if you get out of here on time, I can go get some
tacos before Gloria Estefan shows up." She signaled to one of the camera
guys, who adjusted some lights and focused them on Dar and Kerry.

"Forgot my sunglasses." Kerry lamented.

"Please be quiet." Meyer instructed. "I'm going to start asking questions. I'll address you by name, and I expect the person I'm addressing to answer me."

Dar chuckled softly under her breath.

Meyer looked up. "Excuse me? Did you say something, Ms. Roberts?"

"Nope." Dar interlaced her fingers. "But I will. So let's get started."

Meyer gave her an unpleasant smile. "Hope you remember you said that, Ms. Roberts. Very well. Jenna, give me a clapper please, and we'll go."

His assistant moved around in front of him and held cliché quality film clapboard before the camera. "ILS takedown, first pass," she said in an unemotional voice. "Action."

"THANK YOU FOR holding." The woman's voice came back. "One moment, all right? Someone in that office can speak with you now."

"Thanks." Shari glanced at the door, which had just issued some suspicious rattling sounds as though the handle were being tried. She drummed the fingers of her free hand on the desk, and hoped it wouldn't take as long for the next secretary to answer. Last thing she needed them to hear was a bunch of those ship jerks yelling.

The line buzzed softly, then, thankfully was answered. "Good morning, Executive Operations. This is Patricia. Can I help you?'

The door rattled again. "Good morning." Shari half turned away from the door. "Yes, if it's possible, I would like to speak with Sir Melton Gilberthwaite?"

"Sir Melton's on a conference call at the moment." The woman answered promptly. "May I inquire as to what this is about?'

Hm. Good question. "It's a business matter," Shari said. "I was referred to him in regards to one of his properties – to possibly provide some services."

"Ah." Patricia cleared her throat. "I see. Well, I can't say when he'll be done. Perhaps you could leave your name and a contact number?"

Damn, damn, damn. Shari glared at the phone in frustration. Not only didn't she know what telephone line the damn thing was connected to, she had no idea how long she'd have possession of it. "I'm between locations at the moment." She temporized. "Could you maybe give me an idea of when I might try back?"

"Difficult to tell." The woman responded. "And there's someone waiting to speak with him here in the office. Perhaps two hours? He should have a few moments free before he breaks for breakfast."

Shari made a face, her fingers tensing on the paper. "That could be difficult." She sighed. "Thanks for letting me know. Can I leave my name with you, at least?"

"Of course." Patricia replied then hesitated. "Oh, wait. I hear them taking a quick breather. Maybe I can squeeze you in. Hang on." She put Shari on hold, leaving her to listen once again to transatlantic classical tunes.

"C'mon, c'mon." Shari glanced over her shoulder, hearing now a definite rattle, and the sound of upset voices outside. "Shut up you assholes. There's no one you need to call this late and your porn sites will wait a few minutes."

Vivaldi played on in her ear unrelentingly.

Chapter Fifteen

MEYER CLEARED HIS throat slightly. "Ms. Roberts."

"That's my name." Dar responded promptly. "Next question?"

Meyer waved his hand. "Cut." He leaned forward and rested his elbows on his knees. "Ms. Roberts, can you cut the bullshit, please?"

"Why? You won't." Dar twiddled her thumbs. "Six minutes." She caught a glimpse of Pony Tail out of the corner of her eye, smirking at Meyer. "Want your quote or not?"

The man sat back. "Roll." He rotated his finger in the air, waiting for the belated clap of the board as Pony Tail hurried back over and snapped it. "Ms. Roberts, your company's down thirty percent on contract renewals, your business outlook is lousy, and you've just spent a million dollars on a paper boat you can't even use to take pot shots at. What do you tell your stockholders, Monday morning?"

Dar had seriously been expecting a personal attack, and now she had to stop and consider what kind of answer she could give to a legitimate business one.

And it was legitimate, they all knew it. Even Kerry knew it. Dar could feel the sudden, small shifts of her partner's body close by, Kerry's unconscious fight or flight reflexes surging into action.

So here she was, right down to it. No more time to bullshit, no more time to wonder what the hell to do, just time to put on display why Alastair paid her as much as he did.

And why was that, exactly? Dar shrugged caution off to the winds. Hell, if she was going to go down, might as well go down in the biggest ass fireworks display she could come up with. "Me?" She inquired mildly. "I'm not going to tell them anything."

Meyer leaned forward, his eyes glinting.

"It's not my job to tell them anything." Dar cut him off before he could get another dig in. "My job is to take the company and its clients into the future of technology with confidence and competence, and that, Mr. Meyer, is exactly what I do."

Nice sound bite. Kerry complimented her partner silently.

"That doesn't answer that question, Ms. Roberts." Meyer replied mildly. "Because no matter who tells them, that answer comes from you. So, again, what is it you're going to say to justify what you did?"

Okay, so Meyer was pretty good. "Do I have to justify it?" Dar asked.

"Of course you do." Meyer answered, in that same, calm tone. "You're an officer in a publicly held company."

"Exactly. So what if my explanation breaks the confidentiality clause that office holds me to?" Dar delicately pulled out her thinnest, sharpest rapier and probed with it. "Surely you can't expect me to do that."

Warily, Mayer edged back. "Are you saying there is something you're holding back?"

"Am I?"

The man shifted, as though he wanted to get up and approach Dar. Dar merely smiled charmingly at him. There was doubt in his expression now, a frustrated wondering what Dar was up to. She knew she couldn't fence with him for long, but it was nice to have this one moment of sweet and very perceptible victory.

"You are, and I think you might want to let us in on it, because you might not get another chance, from what I hear." Meyer answered with a triumphant smile of his own. "So, I'll ask one more time, Ms. Roberts, what do you say to the people who trusted you with their money as to how you just squandered it?"

Ball. Her court. Shit.

Dar was very aware of Kerry's eyes on her, as well as the cameras, and suddenly she just relaxed and let the anxiety go. "What do I say? I say to them, count your dividends, ladies and gents. That million I tossed onto the table bought me back a deal from the new owners for a hundred times that, at least."

Oh. God. Kerry listened to the outright lie and fought to keep her face from reacting.

"Oh really." Meyer said. "Interesting, since I have it on great authority he doesn't deal with Yankees."

Dar's eyes twinkled gently. "I ain't no Yankee." She drawled.

"And we have many, many transatlantic partners." Kerry chimed in for the first time. "One of the great advantages we bring to our clients."

Without missing a beat, Meyer pulled out his cell phone.

"HELLO? YES, ONE moment please. I was able to get Sir Milton for you." The secretary sounded somewhat smug and pleased with herself. "It's only for a moment, though."

"Perfect, that's all I need." Shari assured her. "Honest."

The line clicked through, and she heard a deep throat clearing. "Hello?" She ventured.

"Yes? Hello? What is this?" A gruff voice barked at her. "Who's speaking?"

"Good morning, sir. Thanks for taking a moment to chat with me." Shari got out quickly. "My name is..." Her head jerked up as the door slammed inward, and the captain appeared with the communications engineer right behind him. "Ah, just a second..."

"Get that." The captain pointed at the phone. "You men, take hold of her, and quickly."

"Wait!" Shari got up and started to back away, but the engineer was too fast for her. He grabbed the phone, its end issuing broken snatches of puzzled outrage. "Wait! No! Stop!"

The engineer slammed the phone down, shoving her away and cursing at her in Russian.

"Get away from me." Shari warned the two big seamen who now headed for her. "Don't you touch me!" She hit the wall with her back, but in the small space, she had nowhere to go and they grabbed her arms with rough familiarity. "Stop it!"

"Shut up, woman." The captain ordered. "Or I will have them gag you. It is your choice."

"I'll have the law on you!" Shari screamed.

"Idiot!" The captain shouted back. "Is it not obvious that here, I am the law?" He looked at the men. "Take her down to the tendering shell."

Shari realized — in a state of shock — that she was no longer in control of her own destiny. The two men lifted her up between them, their expressionless faces not even registering her as they stared past her and shoved her out the door. She didn't even think of struggling, feeling the strength in the hands that gripped her, and for the first time, a whitewash of fear came over her.

Oh my god. "All I did was use the damn phone!" She suddenly called back over her shoulder. "I'll pay for it! Jesus!"

The captain had already disappeared, leaving the communications engineer to watch them go, a big grin on his face. He lifted his hand and waved at her, then slowly let his fingers close until only one was uplifted.

"Goddamn it!" Shari disappeared down the stairs between her captors, heading downward.

"Stupid bitch." The engineer commented, with a shake of his head.

"Loud as well." The captain reappeared. "It is good you came to get me, Igor. Now we will rid ourselves of this noisy piece of garbage, eh?"

"Eh." The engineer nodded.

"WHAT IN THE hell was that?" Sir Milton stared at the phone in outrage, tossing it onto the small table. "Patricia, what nonsense is this? Nothing on that line but a bunch of gibberish."

"Sorry, sir. It was a lady." The woman hurried over and replaced the phone. "Something about a business matter. She wouldn't leave a name."

"Pah. Someone trying to sue me for paternity again, more likely. Don't trust women further than you can throw them, Patricia."

"Of course not, sir." The aide gave him a brief smile. "Would you like some tea? I have some ready for you."

"Damn straight I do, and who's that out there?" The older man barked. "I see a shadow! Hello!"

"Oh, sir. It's just someone wanting a bit of your time, I told him he had to wait f — oh, sir, please, do wait outside..."

Sir Milton slapped his hand on the table. "Quiet, girl." He ordered, peering through the shadows. "Ah!" He straightened a little in surprise as the newcomer became visible. "Bloody hell, it's you!"

"It is." The visitor clasped his hands behind his back, and ducked his head as Patricia hurried past. "I know that you did not expect me," he said. "But I have something you will be interested in, that I promise."

Patricia paused at the doorway. "I'm terribly sorry sir," she said. "Do you know this person? He didn't say so, or I would have brought him in before now. "

Sir Milton snorted. "Know him? Bugger's my godson. Sit down you damn idiot and if she brings you tea, you drink it, hear me? No bloody arguments."

The visitor circled the small table and took a seat, folding his hands over one knee and issuing a polite smile. "Tea would be good, yes."

"Tea, Patricia. Tea." Sir Milton made a motion with one hand. "Now, what's this all about? Haven't seen you in a dog's age and here you are just like a bad pence turning up in my pocket again."

"You will not think so when I am done speaking."

"You say."

"I do say."

"I SAID, LET me go you apes!" Shari knew it was probably futile, but she struggled anyway, figuring that if she threw them all down the goddamn stairs at least she'd have the pleasure of landing on the fuckers. Her arms ached where the men gripped her, and as she fought against them the pain went from an ache to an outright searing. "Goddamn it!"

Stolidly, the two men dragged her down the last flight of steps and into the dark, cold loading area she'd first come down to. All the sea doors were closed tightly, but the creaking of the metal around them and the motion attested to the rising seas just beyond the steel walls.

"Uh." One man indicated a door at the far side of the hold and they dragged her over to it. Pushing it open.

Inside, it smelled strongly of diesel, rust, and the sea. "Stop!" Shari yelled desperately. "Help! Help!"

The second man pulled the door closed behind them and they started down a last flight of metal stairs, their boots and her curses echoing in the stairwell.

After the last step was a platform, facing yet another hatch, this one dripping with more grease and covered in more rust than even the ones up on the deck above. A series of letters and numbers were painted on the inside of the hatch. The first man used his free hand to lift up the receiver of a pristine, incongruous beige phone mounted firmly on the wall. He dialed a number. "Open 12." He muttered briefly after it was answered, then hung up.

Shari paused to catch her breath, her throat aching from the screams. It was quiet for a moment, then a loud boom almost scared her senseless, and she jerked back as the hydraulic lifting mechanism began to open the hatch.

It groaned in protest, and after it slid upward about a foot, the scent of the sea washed in strongly along with a bit of the ocean itself as a wave came up over the edge of the door. "Oh my god." Shari stared at it, the liquid pooling down in a grate and disappearing.

The wind blasted in a moment later as the door continued to rise, whipping them with sea water. Shari found herself being held tight, as she stared out the hatch at a very dark, very rolling sea.

There was nothing past the dim light the ship threw off. Just a faint suggestion of white ruffling, and a hint of what might have been cloud shadows to differentiate between the sky and the water.

The two men gazed impassively out at it, obviously unimpressed. "Gonna see fish." One commented jerking Shari's arm. "Betta keep y'mouth shut."

Shari felt her throat close, and for once she took someone's advice without commenting on it. They weren't really going to throw her out, were they?

A door opened to her right, and she looked quickly, to see a small, oval door folding in toward her, as the captain stepped over the sill and joined them. He turned and closed the portal after him, dogging the locks shut on what was obviously a watertight entryway. "Gentlemen." He greeted the two sailors, who both nodded respectfully but kept hold of Shari.

The captain went to the open hatch, stepping lightly on the edge and leaning out into the salt spray. He appeared to enjoy it, turning his head from side to side and then shaking it to rid it of its moisture. He stepped back and glanced at Shari. "A fine night to be on the sea, as you shall find out shortly."

"You can't put me out there." Shari kept her voice even, with a great deal of effort.

"Of course I can." The captain replied with a smile. "I am the master of the ship. These men will do whatever I ask of them, and we are in international waters."

Shari just looked at him.

"You are a stowaway. You have no papers. You have no identification." The man went on. "I have no obligation to carry you in my vessel, save that obligation that one has to any decent creature out here. However, you are no decent creature, and so, I will have you off my ship."

"There are laws." Shari managed to get out.

"Yes, there are." The captain agreed. "But you will be in no position to argue them." He stepped to one side. "Bring her here." He sniffed reflectively. "You might want to kick your shoes off."

Frozen in disbelief, Shari could only stare at him as she was dragged forward to the opening, a scream erupting only when she was shoved roughly out the hatch into the dark sea beyond.

"I'M SURE YOU won't mind if I just check up on your brilliant maneuvering, right?" Meyer held the phone up to his ear, as Pony Tail hurried to attach a small microphone to it. "Getting this?" He asked over his shoulder.

"Got it, sir." The man behind the sound console replied. "Got it all."

Dar had never considered herself to possess any acting skills whatsoever, and she knew the only thing keeping her from blowing everything was that she was too shocked to react. She let the knowledge of what Meyer was doing slip past her, and cocked her head, studying the mechanism of the camera instead.

There was nothing she could do. She leaned her elbow on the arm of the chair and propped her head up on her fist, resisting the urge to whistle aimlessly. She didn't dare so much as look at Kerry, and she could only imagine what facial expression her partner had.

Benign interest would have described it. Kerry leaned back in her chair and rested her elbows on the arms, appearing as relaxed as one could in front of two cameras. She'd had more practice than Dar had, and one of the first things she'd learned as a young girl was how to not let the press know when they'd gotten to her.

They were about to be busted on camera. Kerry reconciled herself to that, and didn't regret, even so, the course Dar had taken to get them where they were. If this was how it ended, then it was, and the worst thing that could possibly come out of this was...

"Hello, yes. I need to speak immediately with Sir Melton Gilberthwaite." Meyer said. "It's Jason Meyer. Urgent. Put him on the phone."

Pretentious jackass. Kerry wrinkled her nose. "I'm pretty sure Sir Melton doesn't appreciate being summoned, Mr. Meyer."

Meyer looked at her, but didn't reply.

Dar tipped her head back and studied the overhead lights. They hung from a bare, metal bar grid suspended from the ceiling, and it occurred to her that the stage, like the entire project, was just one big facade in the service of someone else's view of reality.

"I don't care. Put him on the phone." Meyer insisted. "I told you, this is urgent. I'm filming, and I need to speak with him at once."

Maybe they would get lucky. Dar pondered. Maybe Sir Melton would tell Meyer to kiss his ass.

"Thank you. Sir Melton? This is Jason Meyer."

Ah well. Dar tilted her head back to level and regarded Meyer. It had been a good old college try, right? Least she went out with a boom, instead of a whimper.

"That's right. Glad you remember me. Listen, I was just speaking with someone who says they're a new business partner of yours, and I just wa...excuse me?"

Dar's ear twitched.

"No, no, um, no it's ILS, and th—" Meyer listened, his face turning pale even as Dar watched. "Well, I'm very sorry, but—well, no, you see—oh, uh—I'm glad you've made a deal bu—sir? Sir? Hello?"

Kerry sensed a mole whacking in the process of occurring. Her hand twitched, as though reaching for a mallet. "Something wrong, Mr. Meyer?" She asked politely. "Would you like some water? You look a little funny."

Meyer folded his phone up and stared at it, then he let it drop to his knee and looked over at them. "Well, Ms. Roberts." He glanced at Kerry. "Ms. Stuart." He added, after a pause. "Congratulations."

"Thank you." Dar replied graciously.

"Your reputation is assuredly deserved. Since this challenge had ended up a no win situation, the best you should have been able to come out with is a reasonable loss, and yet, you come out with a win." Meyer was now looking at them with wry, bittersweet admiration. "How did you do that?"

And, Dar realized, he'd gotten his ending, despite her and everything else. Oh well. She was in no position to whine about it. "We're the best." She produced what she hoped was a sexy, confident smile. "What else do you need to know?"

Apparently it was enough—more than enough. "Cut." Meyer lifted his hand, and let it drop. "Boy, that's going to be an editing nightmare," he said. "But you gave me what I wanted, Ms. Roberts." He added. "Nice little bit of suspense at the end and everything, and a surprise. Studio'll love it."

Dar got up and brushed herself off. "Glad everyone walks away happy." She muttered. "Ker?"

"Right behind you." Kerry edged around the two men who had come forward to start taking away the set pieces. "Excuse us."

They walked together to the door and went through it, closing it behind them before they stopped and looked at each other. "How *did* we do that?" Kerry uttered, under her breath, giving the rest of the group a little smile as they got up and headed over.

Dar blinked wide, blue eyes at her, then jerked a little as her PDA went off. She studied the message, then smiled, and tucked it back away. "Well, we are the best." She told her partner. "And sometimes, we're just the luckiest." She put an arm around Kerry's shoulders and relaxed. "It's over, people."

"How'd you do?" Michelle asked.

"Bout like you'd expect." Kerry smiled charmingly at her. "Tell you what, let's go to dinner. We'll tell you all about it."

"Why," Michelle gave her a wary look, "do I get the feeling you're going to enjoy that a lot more than I am?"

"We're buying." Dar added. "C'mon." They led the way toward the outer door, where a small group of people had just entered and were looking around. They all wore leather jackets and gloomy expressions except for the woman in the center, who was dressed like a native and who had apparently been there before. "Excuse us."

"Sorry." The woman drew her group aside. "We're just doing a video here now."

"Good luck." Kerry smiled as she pushed the door open. "Make sure they give you chairs."

"Um thanks. I will." The woman gave them a very strange look, as the door closed and they were outside again in the warm humid air.

It was over. Dar felt about ten pounds lighter. It was over, and they'd won. Lucky or not, it didn't matter.

Oh, yeah.

SHARI FLAILED HER arms as she toppled out over the edge of the doorway, seeing a flash of white that abruptly turned into something big and hard and painful just before she should have felt the water's icy sting instead. "Yahhh!" She yelped in disoriented pain. "Ah! Ah!"

Confused, she rolled over, finding herself lying on a rough, sandpaper feeling surface, hurting like hell. Standing over her was a small, blonde woman she half recognized, who was snickering at her in a very unkind way. "Wh..." She struggled up onto one elbow and stared back at the ship, where the captain was in the opening waving at her. "What the f..."

"My American friends say this..." The captain yelled. "Psyche." He ducked inside after one last wave and the door ground its way tiredly shut.

The blonde woman snickered again. "He does have the damndest sense of humor." She turned her head. "We out of here, sailor boy?"

"Yeap."

Shari felt her throat go dry again, and she shaded her eyes as she looked up at the top level of the boat. A shadowy figure was up there, driving, and she knew suddenly who it was.

Oh shit. Now she wished she was back on the goddamned cruise ship headed for Hell again. She was screwed. She was totally, completely screwed. "Fuck."

"Occasionally." The woman sat down in a deck chair and tucked one leg up under her. "You might want to give it a try sometime."

Shari stared at her.

"Just think. It's how Dar got here." Ceci continued. "How bad could it be, really, hm?"

It was all just too much. Shari put her head back on the deck and just stared up at the clouds, not even caring where they were going or why.

THE MOON HAD come out from behind the summer clouds at last, here in the wee early hours of the morning. Kerry gazed up at it lovingly, letting its silver light soak into her eyes as the hot water of the Jacuzzi soaked into her bare body.

A soft clink nearby made her roll her head to one side, spotting Dar emerging from the condo carrying a champagne bottle and two glasses in one hand and a basket of strawberries in the other.

She was also naked, and as far as sensory pleasures went, Kerry figured she was pretty much on terminal overload at the moment. "Hey, sweetheart." She greeted Dar warmly.

"Hm?" Dar stepped into the hot tub and settled next to her, putting her treats down on the verge. "What can I do for you, beautiful?" She inquired, facing Kerry and giving her a rakish grin. "Now that we've gotten to the end of the project from Hell?"

It was so nice to see Dar in a truly good mood. Kerry smiled back at her, lifting one hand from the water and laying it across her partner's cheek without saying a word.

Dar seemed to understand. She reached back and picked up the glasses with one hand, pouring bubbly into them and then passing one to Kerry. They clinked their rims together and took mutual sips. "To winning," she said, with a wry twinkle in her eyes. "Even when it surprises us."

"To us." Kerry answered. "Because winning is pointless and empty unless you have someone to share it with."

"Mm." Dar squirmed closer until they were pressed against each other. She tipped her head back against the padded bumper and gazed up at the stars. "What an end to this day."

"Uh huh." Kerry sipped slowly at her champagne, enjoying the tickle of the bubbles going down that matched the tickle of the bubbles from the water jets around her. "I'm unbelievably glad it's over with, but I have to be honest and tell you I never expected it to come together the way it did."

Dar set her glass down and chuckled. "Anyone who could ever have expected this obviously spends a lot of time consuming illicit pharmaceuticals." She observed. "And since the wildest thing I've ever seen you swallow was orange flavored children's Tylenol, I'm not surprised you were surprised."

Kerry's face relaxed into a broad grin. "Aint' that the truth." She admitted. "As far as vices go, I'm pretty lightweight."

Dar selected a powdered sugar dusted berry and offered it to her.

"Do I count?"

"As a vice?" Kerry's eyes twinkled as she chewed her berry. "Oooo yeah, I think you do."

"Heh heh heh." Dar tossed a berry into the air and caught it in her teeth. "Good." She leaned over and waited for Kerry to bite the half sticking out of her mouth, then they both bit down at once and ended up pretty much in a lip lock.

Strawberry flavored, at that. "Mm." Dar straightened up and waggled her eyebrows. "Much more fun than drugs."

"Cheaper, too." Kerry agreed.

"Hey." Dar spread her arms out and indicated their surroundings. "This ain't the YMCA, Yankee. You insinuating I'm cheap?"

"No." Kerry placed a gentle kiss on her partner's shoulder. "You're priceless." She gazed up at Dar with utter seriousness. "Not to mention definitely one of a kind."

Dar blushed, and blinked a little, at the switch in attitude. "Um."

"And you're all mine." Kerry whispered, giving the shoulder near her lips a small bite, just to break the mood again. "Love you."

Wide, blue eyes gazed back at her.

Kerry winked and smiled.

After a second, Dar grinned back and slid down a bit into the water, giving the impression of a tail wiggling puppy totally at odds with her stature. "You're awesome."

"Am I?"

"Yeah. You really are." Dar put her arm across Kerry's shoulders, and hugged her. Then she picked up her glass and touched it against Kerry's again.

"Mm." Kerry stretched her legs out into the flow and leaned her head against Dar's shoulder. "You know, I thought those guys were going to be more pissed off than they were," she said. "Even Michelle was just sort of resigned about it."

Dar took a swallow of her champagne and licked her lips thoughtfully. "Want to offer her a job?"

"Gurk." Kerry almost ended up snorting her bubbly.

"Hey, they were trying to offer us jobs the last month." Dar said, reasonably. "She's not bad, and I'd rather have her on our team than heading up another attempt at screwing us over."

"That was Shari."

"The brains behind that was Michelle, and she's in a place where she wants to win for a change." Dar disagreed.

Kerry considered that while she drained her glass. She gently rolled the edge of the flute against her lower lip for a moment, and then shrugged. "Okay," she said. "At least then, if you and I decide to take off and go our own way, there'll be someone there who can make me feel like I'm not leaving the company totally tanked. "

Dar regarded her in some surprise. "Wasn't thinking of that

really...but you have a point."

Kerry nodded, holding her glass out. "Fill her up, Dixie. I'm in the mood to get a little silly tonight."

Dar obliged. "Feels good not to have to worry about this damn project, doesn't it?'

"You bet." Kerry leaned her head back and closed her eyes. "Feels very, very good." She murmured. "Very, very nice not to feel stressed to the point my guts ache."

Dar gazed off at the horizon, sipping the rest of her champagne as she watched the stars twinkle overhead. "It's going to be nice working from the cabin next week" She commented casually.

"Oh yeah."

"Maybe I can figure out a way to make that a more frequent arrangement."

Kerry opened her eyes and lifted her glass, taking a sip from it. "Maybe you can." She agreed quietly. "You hear from the folks yet?"

Dar nodded. "They're due into South Pointe in about an hour."

Kerry waited, but nothing more seemed to be forthcoming. "And?"

"Said they'd talk to me about it after they got back."

"Ah." Kerry drained her glass again and set it down. "Hope your mother kicked her ass to kingdom come."

"Huh?" Dar's cell phone rang, and she lifted it off the verge and opened it. "Ah." She held it to her ear. "Morning, Hans."

"Are you not sleeping?" Hans answered. "I will call later, if that is not the case."

Dar chuckled. "Kerry and I are in the hot tub. Don't bother calling later. What's up?"

"Ahem." The German cleared his throat. "You will need to come here so that this wonderful deal of ours can be signed. Perhaps after next week."

"Sure." Dar agreed. "Thanks for telling me you were part of the family over there, by the way."

Hans chuckled now. "We do not show all our cards, even to our friends," he said. "We were very fortunate that I moved when I did, you must realize. He was committed to say yes to whatever persons figured out the deal and asked him first."

"Really?" Dar glanced at Kerry, who had squirmed up to listen. "Risky, especially since he doesn't like Americans that much." She considered switching to English, then figured she'd just fill in the blonde woman afterward.

"He is not a stupid man. He knows who put the machines inside those ships. I have to say, however, that he was not so disappointed to find who my partner in this was."

"Ah."

"He seems to think that I have stepped up in the world, in fact."

Dar laughed. "Well, he hasn't met me yet." She remarked. "But I'm glad it worked out. Remind me to tell you what I went through tonight over this when we get together to sign it."

"I will do so. But before that can occur, there must be something straightened between us." Hans' voice became more serious. "There is something that before I did not tell you."

Dar's eyebrow quirked. "Yeah?"

"It is a matter of a piece of technology," Hans said. "A piece of cellular technology that you perhaps found inside of your office, at one time."

It was easily the last thing she expected to hear. "He's asking me about the gadget Mark found in the conference room." She murmured to Kerry. "I think he knows something about it."

"Really?" Kerry inched closer. "How?"

"What about it?" Dar responded in German. "How did you hear about that?"

Hans cleared his throat. "I caused it to be put there."

Dar's jaw dropped. "You did?" She managed to get out in something other than a squeak.

"What?" Kerry nearly crawled up Dar's body.

"I did." Hans confirmed. "It was not simple, you understand, to acquire the thing, and I am saying it was brilliant, even for myself, to arrange to be put there."

Several things jumped to Dar's lips, and she stifled them. "Why?" She kept her voice even.

"Ah heh." Hans seemed a little embarrassed. "To satisfy the little kicking that you gave to me, yes?" He admitted. "I could not let that go unanswered."

Dar put her glass down and raised her hand to cover her eyes instead. "Son of a bitch."

"What?" Kerry hissed. "What in the heck's going ofuf – mmph." She got the message, and subsided, her lips tingling from the kiss. Dar's free hand dropped under the water and she felt the pressure of it against her hip, her body responding to the touch immediately.

"It was clever, yes?" Hans said. "An intriguing machine, to be sure."

"Except I found it," Dar gathered her wits, "before it could do anything, so your little trick didn't quite work." Absently, she traced a line up Kerry's side and across her ribs.

"Ah, no."

"And the guys who own the thing are signing a development deal with us."

"Is that not always the case with you?" Hans sounded wryly humorous. "I am convinced if you fell into a puddle of mud you would get some free facials from it," he said. "But at any difference, if it does matter to you I am sorry if that caused you any difficulties."

Dar exhaled. "Hans, trust me when I tell you of all the crap I've had to deal with in the last month, that was the least of it. Glad you told me."

"I feel much better now. I will go have a beer." Hans replied.

"For breakfast?"

"It is better for you than is coffee. I will be in touch in some days to make plans. Good night."

Dar closed the phone and set it down. She looked at Kerry, who was crouched over her, chin resting on Dar's breastbone. "One more mystery solved." She informed her. "Seems like..."

Kerry's hands slid down Dar's body. "Know what?" She lifted her head up a little and kissed her partner. "I've got another mystery I'd rather talk about right now."

"Oh. Don't you want to hear — mph." Dar felt the bubbling water between them disappear, replaced by Kerry's body pressing against hers. "Guess not." Kerry's thigh slipped between hers and she felt Kerry's arm circle around her, pulling her even closer.

"No." Kerry kissed her again. "Tomorrow." She felt Dar's arms close around her. The pressure made her hiccup a little, and she accepted a touch of dizziness as the champagne worked into her bloodstream. "Or maybe the next day." She added, hearing Dar's soft chuckle in her ear. "What I want right now is you."

"Got me." Dar whispered. "C'mere."

Oh yeah. Kerry went willingly, losing all sense of her surroundings as Dar's touch became intimate, and the pressure of the water jets blasted against her suddenly very sensitive skin. Lovely way to end the day.

Lovely.

THE LIGHTS OF the city came into view on the horizon, twinkling gently and throwing a soft glow onto the overhead clouds. Ceci lifted her wine glass and sipped from it, enjoying the breeze the boat's speed was affording her at the moment.

It would slack down soon, when Andy entered the shipping channel but the up side to that was that they'd pull into their home marina soon after and rid themselves of their unwelcome guest. They'd hardly spoken a word to each other since leaving the cruise ship behind, and Ceci had refused to offer her even so much as a glass of water on top of it.

Dar had asked them to retrieve the wench, she hadn't said they needed to offer her hospitality, and Ceci was damned if she was going to attempt to be nice after all the crap the woman had pulled on her daughters.

Who-a. Ceci's eyeballs widened, and she hastily took a gulp of wine. Let's not take this whole maternal thing too far, hm?

"How much longer do we have to go?" Shari asked, in a subdued voice.

Ceci craned her neck and viewed the horizon. "About an hour." She decided. "Depends on whether or not my husband is in the mood for playing chicken with those freighters over there."

Shari looked up at the flying bridge, then returned her attention to the water. "Why did you bother doing that?" She asked suddenly. "Going all the way out there?'

"Dar asked us to." Ceci replied simply.

"Why?" Shari asked. "What the hell was she after this time?"

Ceci had pondered that very question herself, but didn't see any need to expose that fact. "You'll have to ask her that." She replied. "Of course, there's always the possibility she did it because it was a decent thing for her to do."

Shari snorted.

"In which case, you've got her father to thank for that trait, cause it certainly didn't come from me." Ceci smiled humorlessly. "I'd have let you go right to the bottom, which I think was a hundred fathoms there."

Shari looked at her in surprise.

"I am not idiot tolerant." Ceci explained. "And someone who keeps banging their head against a concrete sidewalk is a total idiot in my book."

Shari looked away. "I don't expect you to understand."

Ceci laughed. "See? You are an idiot," she said. "I raised her." She added, in an amused tone. "Of course I understand. You're the one who doesn't."

Shari looked toward the shore, as though wishing it would come closer faster.

"Listen." Ceci leaned on one chair arm. "I'll give you some free advice, and maybe it'll be worth the time it'll take for me to say it. You can't win."

Shari looked sharply at her. "Bull."

Ceci shook her head seriously. "You can't, because the harder you push, the harder she pushes back, and if you keep pushing, trust me kid, you're the one who is going to end up being knocked over." She held up a finger as Shari started to speak. "She gets that from him." A thumb pointed up toward the bridge. "There just is no losing in either of them."

Shari looked off into the distance and didn't answer.

Ah well. Ceci got up and stretched, setting down her cup and going over to the ladder to climb up it. She joined Andrew at the helm and sat down next to him, leaving the sulky obnoxi-tude down below. "Almost there? I want to jet clean the back deck."

"Heh." Andrew chuckled softly. "Ah do not get why Dar done that."

Ceci shrugged lightly. "Just wanted to do the right thing, maybe? She does that sometimes, you know."

Her husband looked at her, his pale blue eyes glinting softly in the reflection from the instruments. "Ain't that the truth," he said. "Howsomever, I could throw this here boat into a 360 and I figure we'd lose that trash off the back deck right quick."

Ceci put her arm around him. "No twirling, sailor boy. Just put this thing in the garage. It's getting late," she said. "Let's discharge our cargo and see if any of the neighbors are up for a nightcap."

"Sounds all right t'me." Andrew agreed. "Sooner's better, though." He grinned a little, and gunned the big engines. "I don't' figure to wait for them slow boats."

"Uh oh." Ceci took a firmer hold. "Glad I battened down the hatches inside."

"You want to give a warn to that there woman?" Andy asked.

"Nope."

"Heh."

Chapter Sixteen

KERRY PUSHED LAZILY against the post the hammock was anchored to, her eyes closed as she listened to the conference call going on in her ear bud. It was the weekly general administration meeting, which she usually chaired since operations tended to be in the center of whatever was going on.

Today though, she was merely listening as Jose rambled on about sales projections and Eleanor kept throwing in her two cents worth.

"Hey, Kerry?" Duks broke into the buzz. "Are you still there?"

"I'm here." Kerry replied, rocking herself in a gentle rhythm.

"Your entire department is empty, you do know that right?" Jose said. "If something stops working I don't know what in the hell we're going to do."

"I know," Kerry said. "We gave everyone the week off who worked the project."

"Including yourselves." Eleanor sniped mildly.

"Yup."

"I have heard through the grapevine," Duks regained the conversational ball, "that there is a large contract to come out of that calamity."

Silence. Kerry smiled into the warm salt air. "Of course," she said. "What'd you think Dar was doing it for, exercise?"

Everyone chuckled after a moment's awkward silence. "So we got one over on Telegenics, huh?" Jose said. "That is a pleasant change."

"Oh, I think Dar locked that one up for you too." Kerry reached over and retrieved her mug, sucking a mouthful of fragrant iced tea through a straw. "I don't think they'll be bothering us much anymore."

Silence again. "Did you guys go amok with a Gatling gun or something?" Eleanor asked.

"Long story." Kerry replied. "But you might want to prepare your people out there, Jose. Dar's going to move back into new business acquisitions."

"Eh?"

Kerry could well imagine the looks of consternation going around the table. She sucked another mouthful of tea contentedly, and was glad she wasn't there. "I'm going to be working on restructuring the back end of things. We need some changes."

"Uh."

The porch floorboards creaked, and Kerry felt warm fingers take hold of her bare toes, tweaking them.

"All right, ah, that's a little sudden, isn't it?" Eleanor hazarded. "But, then again, it's your department."

"Yup." Kerry agreed. "It is. Anything else, guys? I have another meeting to go to." She opened one eye and studied the mischievous expression on Dar's face. "And I think I'm late for it."

The sound of shifting furniture came through the line. "No, I think that's it." Jose said. "So, you are really going to just call in for this whole week? Must be very nice."

Kerry reached out and hooked a finger into the ragged pocket on Dar's shorts. "Don't like it? Find another set of ops management." She told Jose bluntly.

Dar leaned over and pressed her head against Kerry's so she could hear the bud also.

"Hey! I wasn't saying anything!" Jose protested. "Take it easy already. Jesu."

"I'm sure we'll adjust." Mariana broke in. "After all, we do all of our international calls remotely. This isn't anything different."

Kerry tweaked Dar's earlobe. "Exactly," she said. "You'll just have to cope with it because we have a life to live and that's just how it's going to be." She pressed her hand against Dar's stomach, suspended over her when she thought she heard purring and felt the vibration that confirmed it.

"Um, okay," Eleanor said. "More info than we needed, but whatever floats your boat, mmhm? Long as you keep producing, that is." She added. "But that's the same rule for all of us, isn't it?"

"Eh." Jose grunted. "C'mon, let's go do lunch," he said. "We're done here."

"Bye, Kerry." Eleanor added. "Thanks for the good news about the project."

"Bye." Kerry clicked the phone off and turned her attention fully to her partner. "Hi."

"They sound miffed." Dar carefully tumbled her way into the double size hammock, ending up next to Kerry. "Were they?"'

"I don't care." Kerry exhaled. "I think I realized something, Dar, over the past few weeks," she said. "Remember the argument we had at Disney?"

"We had an argument?"

"In the bus."

Dar went over her memories of the recent past. "That wasn't an argument."

Kerry offered her a sip of ice tea. "It was, because I was putting work ahead of us, and you damn well should have called me on it."

"Ker."

"We've only got one life." Kerry turned her head and regarded her partner. "We have to live every minute of it."

"Ah." Dar curled her fingers around Kerry's and squeezed them. "Might not be the best thing for our careers."

"Don't give a damn."

Dar leaned over and kissed her. "Then it probably won't matter." She answered. "But I don't care if it does either because I've learned something over the past few weeks too."

"Have you?" Kerry murmured.

"Yes." Dar touched her nose to Kerry's. "There is no other shoe." She tilted her head and kissed Kerry again. "And I want to live every second of this life all the way with you."

It was a truly sweet moment for both of them, and they paused to enjoy it, indulging in a long kiss as the tide rolled in against the rocks and sand nearby.

In the distance, a ship's bell rang.

"Ah, sounds like the fish boat's in." Kerry smiled and held up her cell phone, offering Dar an ear bud. "Want to sit in on my projections meeting?"

"Sure." Dar snuggled closer, fitting the bud into place. "Come with me to England next week?"

"Oh, you bet your buns I will." Kerry chuckled, as she dialed the phone.

"Sounds like we've got a plan"

"Sounds like we do."

OTHER MELISSA GOOD TITLES

Tropical Storm

From bestselling author Melissa Good comes a tale of heartache, longing, family strife, lust for love, and redemption. *Tropical Storm* took the lesbian reading world by storm when it was first written...now read this exciting revised "author's cut" edition.

Dar Roberts, corporate raider for a multi-national tech company is cold, practical, and merciless. She does her job with a razor-sharp accuracy. Friends are a luxury she cannot allow herself, and love is something she knows she'll never attain.

Kerry Stuart left Michigan for Florida in an attempt to get away from her domineering politician father and the constraints of the overly conservative life her family forced upon her. After college she worked her way into supervision at a small tech company, only to have it taken over by Dar Roberts' organization. Her association with Dar begins in disbelief, hatred, and disappointment, but when Dar unexpectedly hires Kerry as her work assistant, the dynamics of their relationship change. Over time, a bond begins to form.

But can Dar overcome years of habit and conditioning to open herself up to the uncertainty of love? And will Kerry escape from the clutches of her powerful father in order to live a better life?

ISBN 978-1-932300-60-4

Hurricane Watch

In this sequel to "Tropical Storm," Dar and Kerry are back and making their relationship permanent. But an ambitious new colleague threatens to divide them --- and out them. He wants Dar's head and her job, and he's willing to use Kerry to do it. Can their home life survive the office power play?

Dar and Kerry are redefining themselves and their priorities to build a life and a family together. But with the scheming colleagues and old flames trying to drive them apart and bring them down, the two women must overcome fear, prejudice, and their own pasts to protect the company and each other. Does their relationship have enough trust to survive the storm?

Enter the lives of two captivating characters and their world that Melissa Good's thousands of fans already know and love. Your heart will be touched by the poignant realism of the story. Your senses and emotions will be electrified by the intensity of their problems. You will care about these characters before you get very far into the story.

ISBN 978-1-935053-00

Thicker Than Water

This fifth entry in the continuing saga of Dar Roberts and Kerry Stuart starts off with Kerry involved in mentoring a church group of girls. Kerry is forced to acknowledge her own feelings toward and experiences with her own parents as she and Dar assist a teenager from the group who gets jailed because her parents tossed her out onto the streets when they found out she is gay. While trying to help the teenagers adjust to real world situations, Kerry gets a call concerning her father's health. Kerry flies to her family's side as her father dies, putting the family in crisis. Caught up in an international problem, Dar abandons the issue to go to Michigan, determined to support Kerry in the face of grief and hatred. Dar and Kerry face down Kerry's extended family with a little help from their own, and return home, where they decide to leave work and the world behind for a while for some time to themselves.

ISBN 978-1-932300-24-6

Terrors of the High Seas

After the stress of a long Navy project and Kerry's father's death, Dar and Kerry decide to take their first long vacation together. A cruise in the eastern Caribbean is just the nice, peaceful time they need — until they get involved in a family feud, an old murder, and come face to face with pirates as their vacation turns into a race to find the key to a decades old puzzle.

ISBN 978-1-932300-45-1

Tropical Convergence

There's trouble on the horizon for ILS when a rival challenges them head on, and their best weapons, Dar and Kerry, are distracted by life instead of focusing on the business. Add to that an old flame, and an aggressive entreprenaur throwing down the gauntlet and Dar at least is ready to throw in the towel. Is Kerry ready to follow suit, or will she decide to step out from behind Dar's shadow and step up to the challenges they both face?

ISBN 978-1-935053-18-7

Eye of the Storm

Eye of the Storm picks up the story of Dar Roberts and Kerry Stuart a few months after Hurricane Watch ends. At first it looks like they are settling into their lives together but, as readers of this series have learned, life is never simple around Dar and Kerry. Surrounded by endless corporate intrigue, Dar experiences personal discoveries that force her to deal with issues that she had buried long ago and Kerry finally faces the consequences of her own actions. As always, they help each other through these personal challenges that, in the end, strengthen them as individuals and as a couple.

ISBN 978-1-932300-13-0

Red Sky At Morning

A connection others don't understand...

A love that won't be denied...

Danger they can sense but cannot see...

Dar Roberts was always ruthless and single-minded...until she met Kerry Stuart.

Kerry was oppressed by her family's wealth and politics. But Dar saved her from that.

Now new dangers confront them from all sides. While traveling to Chicago, Kerry's plane is struck by lightning. Dar, in New York for a stockholders' meeting, senses Kerry is in trouble. They simultaneously experience feelings that are new, sensations that both are reluctant to admit when they are finally back together. Back in Miami, a cover-up of the worst kind, problems with the military, and unexpected betrayals will cause more danger. Can Kerry help as Dar has to examine her life and loyalties and call into question all she's believed in since childhood? Will their relationship deepen through it all? Or will it be destroyed?

ISBN 978-1-932300-80-2

Storm Surge

It's fall. Dar and Kerry are traveling—Dar overseas to clinch a deal with their new ship owner partners in England, and Kerry on a reluctant visit home for her high school reunion. In the midst of corporate deals and personal conflict, their world goes unexpectedly out of control when an early morning spurt of unusual alarms turns out to be the beginning of a shocking nightmare neither expected. Can they win the race against time to save their company and themselves?

Book One: ISBN 978-1-935053-28-6
Book Two: ISBN 978-1-935053-39-2

Stormy Waters

As Kerry begins work on the cruise ship project, Dar is attempting to produce a program to stop the hackers she has been chasing through cyberspace. When it appears that one of their cruise ship project rivals is behind the attempts to gain access to their system, things get more stressful than ever. Add in an unrelenting reporter who stalks them for her own agenda, an employee who is being paid to steal data for a competitor, and Army intelligence becoming involved and Dar and Kerry feel more off balance than ever. As the situation heats up, they consider again whether they want to stay with ILS or strike out on their own, but they know they must first finish the ship project.

ISBN 978-1-619293-082-2

Partners: Book One

After a massive volcanic eruption puts earth into nuclear winter, the planet is cloaked in clouds and no sun penetrates. Seas cover most of the land areas except high elevations which exist as islands where the remaining humans have learned to make do with much less. People survive on what they can take from the sea and with foodstuffs supplemented from an orbiting set of space stations.

Jess Drake is an agent for Interforce, a small and exclusive special forces organization that still possesses access to technology. Her job is to protect and serve the citizens of the American continent who are in conflict with those left on the European continent. The struggle for resources is brutal, and when a rogue agent nearly destroys everything, Interforce decides to trust no one. They send Jess a biologically-created agent who has been artificially devised and given knowledge using specialized brain programming techniques.

Instead of the mindless automaton one might expect, Biological Alternative NM-Dev-1 proves to be human and attractive. Against all odds, Jess and the new agent are swept into a relationship neither expected. Can they survive in these strange circumstances? And will they even be able to stay alive in this bleak new world?

ISBN 978-1-619293-118-1

OTHER YELLOW ROSE PUBLICATIONS

Brenda Adcock	Soiled Dove	978-1-935053-35-4
Brenda Adcock	The Sea Hawk	978-1-935053-10-1
Brenda Adcock	The Other Mrs. Champion	978-1-935053-46-0
Brenda Adcock	Picking Up the Pieces	978-1-61929-120-1
Janet Albert	Twenty-four Days	978-1-935053-16-3
Janet Albert	A Table for Two	978-1-935053-27-9
Janet Albert	Casa Parisi	978-1-61929-015-0
Georgia Beers	Thy Neighbor's Wife	1-932300-15-5
Georgia Beers	Turning the Page	978-1-932300-71-0
Carrie Brennan	Curve	978-1-932300-41-3
Carrie Carr	Destiny's Bridge	1-932300-11-2
Carrie Carr	Faith's Crossing	1-932300-12-0
Carrie Carr	Hope's Path	1-932300-40-6
Carrie Carr	Love's Journey	978-1-932300-65-9
Carrie Carr	Strength of the Heart	978-1-932300-81-9
Carrie Carr	The Way Things Should Be	978-1-932300-39-0
Carrie Carr	To Hold Forever	978-1-932300-21-5
Carrie Carr	Trust Our Tomorrows	978-1-61929-011-2
Carrie Carr	Piperton	978-1-935053-20-0
Carrie Carr	Something to Be Thankful For	1-932300-04-X
Carrie Carr	Diving Into the Turn	978-1-932300-54-3
Carrie Carr	Heart's Resolve	978-1-61929-051-8
Sky Croft	Amazonia	978-1-61929-066-2
Sky Croft	Mountain Rescue: The Ascent	978-1-61929-098-3
Cronin and Foster	Blue Collar Lesbian Erotica	978-1-935053-01-9
Cronin and Foster	Women in Uniform	978-1-935053-31-6
Pat Cronin	Souls' Rescue	978-1-935053-30-9
Verda Foster	The Gift	978-1-61929-029-7
Verda Foster	The Chosen	978-1-61929-027-3
Anna Furtado	The Heart's Desire	1-932300-32-5
Anna Furtado	The Heart's Strength	978-1-932300-93-2
Anna Furtado	The Heart's Longing	978-1-935053-26-2
Melissa Good	Eye of the Storm	1-932300-13-9
Melissa Good	Hurricane Watch	978-1-935053-00-2
Melissa Good	Moving Target	978-1-61929-150-8
Melissa Good	Red Sky At Morning	978-1-932300-80-2
Melissa Good	Storm Surge: Book One	978-1-935053-28-6
Melissa Good	Storm Surge: Book Two	978-1-935053-39-2
Melissa Good	Stormy Waters	978-1-61929-082-2
Melissa Good	Thicker Than Water	1-932300-24-4
Melissa Good	Terrors of the High Seas	1-932300-45-7
Melissa Good	Tropical Storm	978-1-932300-60-4
Melissa Good	Tropical Convergence	978-1-935053-18-7
Regina A. Hanel	Love Another Day	978-1-935053-44-6
Jeanine Hoffman	Lights & Sirens	978-1-61929-114-0
Jeanine Hoffman	Strength in Numbers	978-1-61929-108-9
Maya Indigal	Until Soon	978-1-932300-31-4
Jennifer Jackson	It's Elementary	978-1-61929-084-6
Lori L. Lake	Different Dress	1-932300-08-2
Lori L. Lake	Ricochet In Time	1-932300-17-1

About the Author

Melissa Good is a full time network engineer and part time writer who lives in Pembroke Pines, Florida with a handful of lizards and a dog. When not traveling for work, or participating in the usual chores she ejects several sets of clamoring voices onto a variety of keyboards and tries to entertain others with them to the best of her ability. You can find other info at www.merwolf.com.

CPSIA information can be obtained
at www.ICGtesting.com
Printed in the USA
BVHW030958120323
660252BV00004B/124

9 781619 291508